the rope of man

WITI IHIMAERA

REED

REED PUBLISHING (NZ) LTD
TE KARUHI TĀ TĀPUI O REED (AOTEAROA)

Established in 1907, Reed is New Zealand's largest
book publisher, with over 600 titles in print.

www.reed.co.nz

Published by Reed Books, a division of Reed Publishing (NZ) Ltd, 39 Rawene Rd,
Birkenhead, Auckland. Associated companies, branches and representatives
throughout the world.

Published by Reed Books

National Library of New Zealand Cataloguing-in-Publication Data
Ihimaera, Witi Tame, 1944-
The rope of man / Witi Ihimaera.
Contents: Tangi-The return.
ISBN 0-7900-0894-7
1. Title.
NZ823.2-dc 22

ISBN-10: 0 7900 0894 7
ISBN-13: 978 0 7900 0894 3

First published 2005
Reprinted 2006

The author and the publisher wish to gratefully acknowledge the following writers whose
work is reproduced here. (p 181) RAK Mason, 'Sonnet of Brotherhood' (in *Collected
Poems*, Victoria University Press, 1990: first published by the author in *The Beggar*,
Christchurch, 1924). (p 217) Denis Glover Estate and Pia Glover, copyright holder, 'Home
Thoughts' (in *Six Easy Ways*, Caxton Press, Christchurch, 1936). (p 323) the estate of
Allen Curnow, 'The Skeleton of the Great Moa in the Canterbury Museum, Christchurch'
(in *Sailing or Drowning*, Progressive Publishing Society, Wellington, 1943).

Design: Cheryl Rowe

Printed in New Zealand

For Te Haa & Turitumanareti

author note

Te torino haere whakamua, whakamuri

When my first novel, *Tangi*, was published in 1973, I planned a sequel which would follow its hero, Tama Mahana, after his return from his tribal village, Waituhi, to Wellington. However, life intervened, marriage, a family and a career in international diplomacy — and I also decided to place a ten-year embargo on writing. By the time the embargo was over, other literary projects like *The Matriarch* (1986) crowded out that original plan.

The Rope of Man comprises a new version of *Tangi* and, finally, a sequel — *The Return*, 2005 — written thirty-two years later. With its publication, the Ihimaera 30th Anniversary Collection comes full circle. The collection includes new versions of my first three books, *Pounamu Pounamu* (1972; 2002), *Tangi* (1973; 2005 as *The Rope of Man*) and *Whanau* (1974; 2004 as *Whanau II*; 2005 in the UK edition as *Band of Angels*). As part of the collection, I also added an international edition of *The Whale Rider* (1987/2002) and compiled a short story collection, *Ihimaera: His Best Stories* (2003). All the books in the collection celebrate a literary career that I never expected to have and provide my opportunity to convey to you my heartfelt thanks for the privilege of your company over the last thirty years.

At the same time as the spiral is going forward,
it is returning

tangi
1973

He aha te mea nui o te ao? Maku e kii atu:
He tangata, he tangata, aa, he tangata.
Listen to the song of the flax:
What is the greatest treasure of the world?
It is men, women, children
Aa, all humankind.

part one

1

This is where it ends and begins. Here on the railway station, Gisborne, waiting to board the train to Wellington. Here begins the first step into the future, the first step from the past.

The platform is crowded with people. They stand in small groups farewelling one another. A well-dressed woman smooths her two-piece suit and pats at her hair. A young teenager kisses his mother, then looks around hoping nobody has seen. Sitting on his small suitcase, an orphan boy reads a child's book, tracing the lines with a finger and silently mouthing the words. A little girl holds on to her father's hand; hold tight darling, don't let him go. Rows of cars line the barrier to the station. A green stationwagon pulls to a halt, and a father opens the back to get his son's suitcase. Together they rush to the booking office, disappearing among the crowd.

People cluster along the train, milling thickly round the steps to each carriage. Railway porters load suitcases into the luggage compartment. Already passengers are climbing onto the train. The well dressed woman has stepped aboard and is winding down a window so that she can talk to her friends on the platform. Soon I, Tama Mahana, will also get on board. I am 20, and I have a job to go back to in Wellington. I will sit at the window, looking out on the platform. It will be crowded with people shouting farewell. The train whistle will blow. The bell on the platform will ring. The train will move away, along the railway tracks as they cross the road leading from Gisborne to Waikanae Beach. Red lights will flicker on and off at the crossing. The traffic will stop, letting the train pass.

I will journey away from Gisborne, but I will leave my heart here, to be reclaimed when I return. This is where it belongs and this is where my life begins.

This day, too, is beginning. The sky is crystal clear, the morning brisk with the wind and the air still crisp with frost. Rising above the city, Kaiti Hill incises a sharp edge into the sky. It sparkles with a serenity not yet destroyed by the brooding city below. Gisborne is slowly awakening. Traffic bumps across the railway lines at the crossing, rushing toward the city. A cyclist weaves amid the speeding cars. Along the pavement, office girls hasten to work. For them, today is like any other day. Nothing will upset the tempo of their hours.

For me, however, this day is not like any other day. This day, beginning on a railway platform, is the first.

2

Wellington, and I am at work. It is Tuesday and still morning, a day like any other day. The phone rings, clamouring for my attention.

'Tama?' Stephanie, one of our phone operators, asks. 'You've got a person-to-person call. Mrs Ripeka Kingi on the line from Waituhi. I'll put her through.'

I am a reporter at *The Evening Post* and I'm in the middle of doing a story about the prime minister's Polynesian immigration policies. I haven't heard from my sister, Ripeka, or any of my family for such a long time. They live in Waituhi, where our farm is, just outside Gisborne on the East Coast. Sometimes I suspect they have forgotten all about me here in Wellington.

'Tama?' Ripeka is hesitant. But her voice is enough to bring memories of Waituhi that make me yearn to be out in the open air doing something physical and ordinary rather than this story for the evening edition.

'Hello, Ripeka.' I can see our chief reporter, Ted Smith, frowning. He must know this is a private telephone call but, tough, I'll get back to my story as soon as I can. 'It's so good to hear from you, sis. How are things at home? All right?' But she does not answer. The telephone is silent.

'Aue, Tama,' she says. That's when I know that something bad has happened. Immediately I think of my mother. She's been sick all winter, coughing her lungs out.

'What is it, Ripeka?'

My sister's voice breaks and it sounds like she is crying. I don't really want to know her news. Mum has always been a heavy smoker. I warned her to stop. I gave her the statistics for smokers, and how Maori women were at the top of the list — I should know, I did a front-page story for the paper — but maybe the damage has already been done. I should have tried harder. I should have forced her to throw her cigarettes away. 'Ripeka, what's wrong?'

My sister is silent for a moment. Then her voice lifts in a rush of disbelief and an incredible sense of loss. 'Dad's dead, Tama.'

I look out the window of the office, across the harbour. A cold front is approaching from the south. The clouds are towering as if to split through the sky. We've been expecting it all day.

Did I hear her right? Dad? Not Mum? But Dad was supposed to live forever. I have the absurd desire to laugh out loud. It's so ridiculous. It couldn't possibly be true. Our father, gone? It only seems like yesterday that he and I were working at the farm at Waituhi. We were repairing the fences, digging in new fenceposts where the cattle had trampled through. Dad looked at the sky, where clouds similar to these ones were mounting, and then into my eyes. 'We better get on home, son. The wind's coming up. I think we might be in for a storm.'

'Yes, Tama, Dad died last night.'

No, I must have misheard her. But her voice is clear. Her words are clear. Dad? Dead?

The first rain stipples the windows of the office. I touch the glass with my fingers. The weather in Wellington always surprises me, the way the southerly can come rolling over the city and across the harbour. Before you know it, it's all around you.

This time, the storm has come invoked by my sister's words. I want to take her arm, twist it and demand of her, 'Take your words back, Ripeka, take them back.' Even when we were children she would pretend that something had happened when it hadn't.

'Tama, can you come home, please? As soon as you can.'

3

the loudspeaker system crackles with an announcement.

'The Wellington express will be leaving Gisborne in five minutes. Five minutes please for passengers travelling to Wellington.'

Two years ago, when I was offered the job at *The Evening Post* and moved to the capital, Dad said, 'Well, being a reporter will beat digging in fenceposts, eh, son?' I left from the same place on the platform where I am standing now, with the same battered suitcase in my hands. Today only my mother, sisters and brother are here, and this is the way it's going to be for the rest of our lives. Nor can I pretend that Dad has just gone back to the car, as he did on that day when I left to take up my new career as a reporter. When he returned he had a present for me. 'Here,' he said, his eyes twinkling with humour. In his hands was a hammer and a piece of four by two with a nail in it. 'Whenever you think that job's getting difficult, bang on this and take a reality check.' He shook my hand. 'I'm proud of you, son.'

'Are you sure you've got everything?' Mum asks. 'We didn't leave anything behind, did we?'

We can wait, look, watch and hope that Dad may still arrive, the crowd eddying around him as he comes walking through it, but that's not going to happen. I never did tell him what I did with his piece of four by two. I hung it on the wall in the reporters' room. Every time anybody got pissed off at Ted Smith, they took a swing at it.

Mum, Ripeka and my other siblings have come to see me off. Ripeka is a year younger than I am. She is 'a child bride', as she likes to call herself to cover up her clumsiness in getting pregnant to Victor just out of high school. Mere is the sister after her. She's eighteen and I thought she had enough common sense to promise her boyfriends everything but not give it to them; but her husband Koro managed to see past her defences and now she has a baby too. Wiki is at high school, petulant, pretty, and moaning about sitting exams, so she couldn't come. Ten years separate her from Marama who, according to Mum, was an afterthought. Hone is the youngest, the child made to keep Marama company.

Marama and Hone are frightened. Any separation now, any saying goodbye, brings for them the possibility that the person being farewelled may never return. I smile encouragingly at them, 'I'll be back soon.'

'How soon is soon?' Marama asks. Her question makes me wonder how anybody can give any guarantees. For a child, soon can mean anything. A day. A week. A month. When you tell a child you'll be back soon, they start waiting at the window for your return, keeping their vigil, looking down the road for you to appear.

'It's not as if Tama's leaving for good,' Ripeka says, exasperated. Although she and Victor have their own child, she's always favoured Marama and Hone and gets jealous when they show affection for others.

'He's just going back to Wellington to resign from his job and pack his clothes,' Mere adds, 'and then he'll be returning.' She says the words loudly; the way she looks at me makes me realise that she doesn't quite believe it.

'You'll be all right,' I say to everyone. 'We'll all be all right.' But in my heart of hearts I know that that will not be true.

'And when you come back,' Hone says, 'you're going to look after us, eh.'

I look into Hone's eyes. How am I going to get through all this? How will I manage to look after the family? On this, the first day, I am selfish enough to be afraid that I might not be able to do it and angry at having the responsibility.

I suspect my mother knows how I am feeling. 'Do what you have to do, son,' she says. 'When you have done that, ka hoki mai ano.' She makes me feel ashamed at my thoughts. I realise that I have to be stronger, to create a sense of certainty for the little ones. I have to find ways of soothing them, of finding the right words. But words are so meaningless at moments of separation. They are only stitches across the wounds of the heart. Better to touch each other, to reaffirm by embracing, by the feel of skin on skin, that we believe in each other and that we are here. In life. Still in the world.

I turn to Marama and Hone. 'Both of you will have to be the bosses while I'm away. I don't want you two to fight. You've got to be good kids. You have to help Mum. That means you must be very obedient and always do what she says. If she wants you to chop some wood for the fire, Hone, you'll have to try very hard to do it for her. If she's sad, you cheer her up, eh? You sing her a little song and make her happy.'

'I know lots of songs,' Hone says, brightening. He begins to sing the current favourite from his primary school class. 'Oma rapiti, oma rapiti, oma, oma, oma.' It's a song about a rabbit and a farmer who is trying to stop it from eating his carrots.

'I'm sick of that song,' Mum says.

Mere agrees with her. 'All day and all night,' she grumbles, 'that rabbit — hop, hop, hopping about the carrot patch. The sooner the farmer shoots him the better.'

This family is my world. When they are sad, I am sad. When they are happy, I am happy. The other people on the railway platform belong to another world, other lives. We are strangers to each other, holding only one bond in common: that we travel together.

Once the world went on forever. Dad's tangi, his funeral, has ended that. He has been laid to earth in the graveyard near Rongopai, and I will never see him again.

4

aphone call from home, and two words have destroyed the calm of my world. 'Dad's dead.'

'Mum rang me at five this morning,' Ripeka says. 'You know how early she gets up. Victor answered the phone. I was still asleep. Victor put on the light and woke me. "Your Mum wants to talk to you," he said. When Mum told me I didn't want to believe her. Not Daddy . . .'

Dad said to me once, 'Whenever you need me, just call, son.' I call for him now to come and rescue me. I am sinking, drowning on a midnight sea. The waves are tall, wild and, by the moon's wan light, white-tipped with foam. The waves rise over me and, suddenly, my mouth is filled with water. A current pulls me under.

I struggle upward, wanting my sister to stop telling me Dad has died. She was always like this. Telling me things I didn't really want to know. But even as the demand rises on my lips I know that there are some things that can never be returned to their proper places.

'Victor and I went straight out to Waituhi,' Ripeka continues. 'I'm ringing from there. Mum was still beside Dad in their big double bed. She was just lying there as if she was waiting for him to wake up. Do you know what she was doing as she was waiting? She was talking to him and, while she spoke to him, she was knitting a jersey for him that he will never wear.'

Where are you, Dad? Alone on that midnight sea, I call to him. The sea is pounding louder and louder. The current is taking me towards a dark whirlpool.

Already the centrifugal forces are pulling me in. It is a wide supernatural sea, filled with the detritus of life, flowing with ragged kelp.

'Mum looked up when Victor and I came in,' Ripeka says. 'We embraced. Then she smiled at me. She brushed Dad's forehead and kissed him. She said to me, "To papa, to papa . . . kua mate to papa."'

My sister's voice breaks. In my mind a window glimmers. The curtains billow from it that I may look in. I see my parents' bedroom, soft and dim with morning light. Mum and Dad are lying together in the big bed which my sisters and I would crawl into when winter was cold: Mum, Dad and us children, all huddled beneath the patchwork blankets. Mum is propped up among the pillows, knitting a jersey. She nudges Dad. 'Time to get up,' she says. 'Rongo! Get up!' He moans and pulls the blankets around him. I am on the other side of the bed and I pull them back. Mum pokes Dad with a knitting needle. 'E koe, you mangere thing! Now get up!'

'Aue! What do you want to do that for?' Dad asks. He puts his feet onto the floor, 'Brrr! Makariri!' He tries to get back into bed but Mum pushes him away with her feet.

'Now you're up,' Mum says, 'light the stove, eh? Put the kettle on. I'll make the kai soon.'

Dad groans, 'Why don't you do it?' He grins ruefully at her. He kisses her. 'None of that, Rongo,' Mum whispers. 'The kids, they might see.' He smooches her again and then looks straight at me. 'Yeah, like this no-good, lazy, pretending-to-be-asleep son of ours, eh Tama!'

'But how, Ripeka?' I ask. 'How could this happen?'

'I don't know, Tama. He was old. He's been sick for a long time. He just died in his sleep, while Mum was sleeping. When she woke up this morning she shook him and told him to get up. But he was cold. Then she knew. Even so, she told me she wanted to have some more time alone with him before we phoned everybody. She wouldn't let me call anyone till nine and, ever since, it's been pretty busy. Uncle Pita came straight over. He's been making the arrangements for the tangi. Dad's old friends have been dropping in to see him. He was supposed to pick up the shearing gang this morning for Maera Station. The phone's been going all the time for Dad. "Where's Rongo?" people ask. They're shocked when we tell them.

They don't believe he's dead.'

I can't believe it either. I don't want to believe it. The storm clouds scud across Wellington. The southerly pall over the city is complete. I am drowning, drowning.

'Dad's lying in the front room at the moment until the marae is ready at Rongopai. Victor has rung the funeral director from Gisborne and we're expecting him any moment now. Uncle Pita has taken his boys down to Rongopai to open the meeting house and set up a tent next to it. The Matua and Nani Tama have been and gone. Nani Miro did her prayers for Dad before they left. She's organising the women, and Nani Tama and Uncle Pita are organising the men. The fires have been lit in the cookhouse at Rongopai and up at Takitimu Hall to feed all the people who will come. I can see the smoke from the window, curling across the hills. You know, that smoke signal is the best way of letting people know that something has happened. Trust us to copy from the Red Indians. Now, the bell is tolling at Rongopai. Ka tangi te pere. Everybody knows that someone is dead.'

Rongopai is my marae. It is the ancestral house of the Whanau a Kai, the physical symbol of our kinship. All tribal ceremonials of birth, marriage and death are performed there. My father once said to me, 'No matter where you go in the world, your meeting house will always be there for you to return to. No matter what kind of life you live, your right is to be able to call Rongopai your home.' Beside Rongopai is a small bell which, in the old days, was rung to bring the people to silence and prayer before church services on the marae.

As Ripeka talks on, Rongopai begins to shimmer. Wisps of smoke drift across it. The meeting house of my ancestors, of my people, holding up the sky. And now the bell is tolling for my father.

'Ripeka, how are Marama and Hone? Are they all right?'

'They don't understand, Tama. They wanted to see Dad so Mum took them in to him and told them he was gone. Hone asked, "Really gone, Mum?" And Mum said, "Yes." Marama started shaking Dad and crying, "Wake up, Daddy, wake up." Auntie Teria has taken them around to her place to play with Daisy and Mutunga.' My sister begins to sob again, and my world resounds with her grief. 'Some of the other Waituhi women are here with Mum. Aunt Ruth, Maka tiko bum, Aunt Sarah, Mattie Jones, Hine Ropiho, the usual crowd. They sit with her, wailing softly. But she's so calm, Tama. So calm.'

'Let me speak to her, Ripeka.'

'Here she is,' Ripeka answers. There are obsidian splinters at my heart, poised above the greenstone landscape of my mind.

'Tama? Hello, son.'

The splinters rain down, the painted panels of Rongopai crumble, the beams of that ancient roof fall.

For a moment I cannot answer. My words are crippled, without wings or speech. 'Are you all right, Mum?'

'Yes, don't you worry about me. He was a good husband, your father. He was a good man. Now that he's gone, I'm so lonely, son. I want him to come back. Come back Rongo. Rongo, Rongo, Rongo . . .' My mother cries Dad's name over and over again. Then, 'Tama, you come home soon, eh?'

5

the flower wreaths have wilted above the soft earth. Like a host of butterflies, the petals have scattered in the wind. Here I stand on the Gisborne railway platform, isolated in my sadness. So many people are here this bright morning, a whole world with me, waiting to travel away on a train to Wellington.

But I should be giving comfort to my mother, sisters and brother. I shake myself out of my memories and wink at Marama and Hone. 'Do you kids want an icecream?' Their eyes light up when I give them some money and they are off, chasing each other, flitting and circling through the crowd.

'You're just like your father,' Mum says. 'He was always bribing you kids, buying you lollies and icecreams. He wanted you to have the best of everything. He was able to do that for you older ones but who will be the parent for Marama and Hone?'

I put my arms around her. Elsewhere, I see an old woman cradling a child on her lap, singing the child to sleep. Two lovers hold hands against any invasion of their world. 'If you loved me, you wouldn't be leaving me,' the boy says. His girlfriend looks up into his face, 'But I do love you, Rob.' Puzzled, he asks, 'Then why are you going?' She is evasive, unsure how to respond. 'We'll see each other. You can come down to Wellington sometime or else I'll come back here now and then.' The boy is brusque. 'Sometimes I wonder whether you really love me at all.'

Above the railway platform a large ornate clock snaps the time forward. Five minutes to eight. Five minutes before the train is due to leave. Five, ive, ve, e.

Dad, if I could I would grasp those ticking hands and force them back through all those yesterdays gone, just to be with you again.

'All aboard please,' the stationmaster calls. 'All aboard for the train to Wellington.'

The noise level rises on the railway station and I am buffeted by waves of people as they prepare for the departure. The announcement intersects all those lives revolving, those destinies evolving. Chapters begun, chapters ending, chapters continuing. Conversations caught in mid-flight: 'Thanks for having me, Uncle.' 'That's okay, Kim. Come again soon.' 'You will look after yourself, won't you dear?' 'Yes, Mum.' 'You'll write?' 'Of course, Mum. Don't worry.' 'Oh, Rob, please don't go on about it.' 'If you loved me, you wouldn't be going away.'

'You better get on the train,' Mum says, 'otherwise it will leave without you.' We link hands and walk towards the steps to my carriage. My sisters follow. They are my world now.

'Ae, I better go,' I answer. I look at Mum with aroha. The railway platform becomes blurred with shadows. My mother's face gleams alone like a glowing star.

Suddenly, the train whistle shrieks. And the clock ticks, the clock ticks, pushing all of us forward, always forward; I cannot stop it. The people on the railway platform put their hands over their ears, waiting for the train's whistle to end. Far off, I see Marama and Hone panicking, running through the crowd towards me. Who will be their parent? I guess it will have to be me now. I'll have to bring them up as best I can, answer their questions, provide for them, make them happy, teach them who they are and try to instill all the best values of Maoritanga. They must be made strong. They need to know that no matter where they wander in the poisonous garden of the world they will always belong. To Waituhi. To the whanau. To us. To me.

No, little ones, I'll not leave without saying goodbye. Not ever.

When they reach me I gather them in my arms. I am more than my father's son. I have become the head of the family now. We belong to each other, a family joined in a new and different way by Dad's death.

'Okay, Mum, time for me to go. I'll call you when I arrive in Wellington. Victor, don't forget the cattle should be moved to the hill paddock where there's more feed. Please don't cry, Mum.'

My mother's tears bring memories of the tangi, reminding me of a graveyard where the earth still lies warm above my father. I look at Mum. One last embrace.

Our love is expressed in the soft, moist pressing of cheeks against each other.

'Tama, come back soon.'

The porter pauses to tell us, 'All aboard. Move away from the train, please.'

I step aboard. All around me, other goodbyes are being said. All along the train, windows are wound down and hands flutter from them. My family crowds round the steps of the carriage. My mother's hand tightens on mine. Steam hisses from beneath the train. The couplings grow taut, strain, jerk tight, and the train begins to move. My mother's eyes glisten. Once, Dad was her guiding star. But he has drifted beneath the reddening horizon. Now, she gleams with her own light.

'Come back soon, son.' Her grip tightens. She won't let go. The train moves down the platform and still our hands are linked. But as it moves faster, our fingers are forced apart. Slowly they untwine, drifting, drifting away; and the separation is agony. Yet Mum still follows along the platform. She pushes through the other people, her face distraught.

'Tama . . .' She begins to run. Her long scarf falls from her hair. People watch her, curious.

The train gathers speed and draws away. I lean further from the steps to keep my mother in sight. I see Ripeka and Mere trying to comfort her. Marama and Hone cling to her skirt.

Mum covers her face with her hands.

6

'**W**e're truly sorry, Tama.'

My friends at work cluster at my desk. I look at them, dazed. Stephanie must have told them about Dad. How else would the news have got around? The world is dimming, but, even so, there are recognisable strangers. Why are they sorry, why sad? Does the world end for them too?

'Tama, old chap,' Ted Smith begins, 'I've just heard your news.'

My body feels numb, so numb. The midnight sea is cold, so cold. I am afraid to be alone and adrift on the waves, the cascading sea, amid the falling rain. Drifting amid the swirling, freezing tide, upon the dark, dark sea. The waves are mounting high and, suddenly, I am pulled down by a dark undertow. I struggle upward, take my first tortured gasp of air and cry out:

'Dad, don't go.'

'Oh, Ted . . .' I remember the story on the prime minister for the evening edition. 'I'll get right on it.'

'No, no,' he answers. 'Somebody else can do that. Come on, boy, come and sit down.' He puts his arm firmly around my shoulders and leads me out of the reporters' room. The news is spreading quickly, and I can see Stephanie knocking on the chief editor, Mr Ralston's, door. So what else should I have expected? Why should I be so surprised? After all, I'm in the newspaper business. We deal with news of death, sickness, accident, famine and war, and getting it out to the world by three in the afternoon.

Even so I am taken aback, almost embarrassed, as I see my colleagues talking quietly about me. 'His father's dead, Tama's father,' they say behind their cupped hands. 'Tama's father.' Why is the news of death always whispered? 'He'll be going home now. To Gisborne. To a Maori place just out of the city.'

And now Ray Hargraves, our parliamentary reporter, enters the room. 'Who's dead?' he asks. When he is told, he takes a step back.

Yes, Ray, you do right to hesitate and step out of the line of fire. Death has become my companion.

But Ray is fearless. He comes across to me. 'Tama, mate, is it true about your Dad?' I'd forgotten Ray had met Dad when he stopped over in Wellington after attending to some business in the South Island. Although Dad was a teetotaller, Ray insisted on taking him to the pub — where Dad got drunk. 'You never drink beer,' I said to him when he got back to the flat, 'ever.' He roared with laughter and wagged a finger at me, 'There's lots you don't know about me, son.'

My head spins. Death has happened too quickly and I am not prepared for it. I want to stay the darkness and halt its progress. Don't let the news be published so soon that Dad is dead. Stop the printing presses. Let my friend, Ray, take him back to the pub again. Delay the vans waiting at the docks for today's early edition. Let everything go back to the way it was with my father still here, keeping the sky above, the earth below, so that I can stay in a world filled with forever sun.

Ted and Ray usher me into Mr Ralston's office. The boss is sympathetic and already has matters under control. He has instructed Stephanie to make a plane booking for this afternoon. 'Okay, Tama, let's take you home to pack a suitcase. We'll pick up some cash for you from accounts on the way out. I'll get you to the airport as fast as I can.'

I am treading water. I'm drifting on a tide, way out in the middle of the sea.

'Off we go then, lad,' Mr Ralston continues. He pushes me firmly towards the door. Stephanie gives me a quick peck on the cheek as I exit the office.

'Thanks, Mr Ralston,' I answer. 'Thanks.'

All around are mountainous waves. Overhead is a wide, empty, sky. Below is a dark ocean filled with hidden terrors. If I don't watch out, I could easily succumb to my imagination and scream with fear.

'Dad, you said you'd always be here. If ever I was lost on the sea at midnight, you said you would be here for me. But you lied to me. You lied. Where are you, you bastard?'

Then I hear a splashing sound. By the moon's light, I see a dark shape cutting across the whirlpool. At first I think it's a shark and my blood freezes. It is a swimmer, trailing phosphorescence in his wake. He is strong, courageous and, as he comes, he waves, 'Is that you, Tama? Hang on, son, hang on.' I laugh with joy. I knew all along that Ripeka was just kidding me.

Dad bodysurfs toward me with a whoop and a holler.

'I didn't know you could do that!' I laugh.

He winks, embraces me in his protective arms and kisses my forehead. 'I'm full of surprises, son.' He slips behind, holding my head above the water, cradling me against his body. But instead of feeling happy, all I can feel is a deep, ineffable sadness.

'Oh, Dad,' I begin, 'when I was home last, you wanted me to stay. You asked me not to go back to Wellington. Why didn't I understand?'

Strongly, my father kicks with his legs, pulling me away from the maw of the whirlpool. 'You have your own life, Tama. You mustn't blame yourself.' He drags me across the currents. The waves are angry and roar their disapproval. They cascade around us, pushing us under. But always, Dad pulls us back up and into the clear dark air. Even so, I can hear him struggling, his chest heaving with exhaustion. And his kiss is so cold. I know, right at the moment when he pulls me beyond the whirlpool's reach, that he has come not to rescue me but to say goodbye.

'Why didn't I stay, Dad?' My tears begin to flow, bitter, the salt of them like the salt of the sea. 'Why didn't I see that you needed me?'

'Son, you know I have always loved you. You are my oldest. Look after your mother and your brother and sisters.'

The stars come out. My father and I are floating on a luminescent skein of silver dreams. A shooting star blazes a terrible glorious beauty across the night. 'Time for me to go, son.'

One moment he is there, the next moment he is gone, swimming back toward the whirlpool, and all that is left is a sea of stars.

part two

7

The great Rope of Man, Te Taura Tangata, stretches from the beginning of the universe to the universe's end. The rope comes roaring from out of Te Kore, the Void, through Te Po, the Night, and the first time we see it is when light flashes on it at the First Dawning. As it comes, the gods of the Maori weave their kaleidoscopic power into it. When they create man and woman, the rope sparkles and gleams with breathless excitement.

Ever-changing, the rope is a magnificent icon spiralling from one aeon to the next, charting the history of humankind. At the beginning of its life, it was strong, tightly bound by Maori strands. Some Maori believe that with the coming of the Pakeha it became frayed, and almost snapped during the Land Wars. Perhaps there were only a few strands holding it together. But the songs of the people can still be sung through one or two strands as they are through many.

When we see the rope again, after the wars, it is a different rope. It is different because the Pakeha became added to it, the strands of Pakeha culture entwining with ours, adding different textures and colours. It's also fiercely twisted and soldered together by many different histories, as Maori and Pakeha began not only to live together but to fall in love, marry and have children with each other. Some people think that diminished our strength. Others think it strengthened us.

The rope continues its journey, spinning, singing, weaving, sparkling, chanting its way through time. It charts the changing nature of the human odyssey. All our successes and failures as a people are woven into it, all our lapses from divinity and our triumphs over our inhumanity.

The energy of the rope is awesome and awe-inspiring. As it continues into the future, parts of it split off through space, crackling and thundering, heading for other suns, ever, ever spinning, ever, ever singing, ever, ever glowing, onward and onward, ever, ever, forever.

The houses are little flags fluttering past. Some are drab, others gaily painted, a jumbled mass of roofs extending across the plain to the mountains. Sometimes I glimpse traffic at a railway crossing. Then, as the train leaves Gisborne behind, the sky stretches ahead to the horizon.

'The Sky Father is above,' Dad would say on those sunlit mornings when we were beginning our work, 'the Earth Mother is below.' He would take off his hat and salute the day with a greeting which was also a prayer. 'Ko Ranginui kei runga, ko Papatuanuku kei raro, tena korua.'

Earth and Sky were the First Parents. They were born at the very beginning of time, when space was still being formed from out of the primal abyss. First there was blackness, then there was light and then, spiralling out of the light, Ranginui and Papatuanuku in close and passionate embrace. They were unwilling to let go of each other a moment, and their children lived in whatever spaces could be found in armpits, thighs, and cracks between the two bodies whenever their parents moved. The children were the first gods. Among them were Tangaroa, god of the sea, Tane, god of the land, Tawhirimatea, god of the winds, Tumatauenga, god of war, Ruaumoko, god of earthquakes and Rongo, god of crops and cultivations. My father was named after Rongo and, like his namesake, was a farmer, a good keeper of his animals and cultivator of the soil. It was Tane, Rongo's brother, who conspired to separate Rangi and Papa so that the light, which was outside the embrace of the parents, could be let in. As well, Tane wanted room to grow. Some of his brothers supported him. Others didn't. There was a war between them all but, finally, Tane had his way. He placed his hands on his mother and his feet against his father and kicked them apart. Tane became the god of Man. Because of him humankind is able to stand in the light on the bright strand between.

One of these days, perhaps, I will welcome the separation. Right now, however, if I could stand at the pillars of the sky, I would try to bring Earth and Sky back together, join the seams, and return life to the way it once had been.

The door to the railway carriage opens. Amid the sudden sound of clacking wheels the conductor calls, 'All tickets, please, all tickets.' I pull out my wallet and pass the ticket to him. He looks at it, frowns, but clips it. His is such a simple action but all actions these days, no matter how simple, take on symbolic meaning. The conductor is like the ferryman come to ferry me back into the land of the living. As he passes, I catch a glimpse of my reflection in the window.

Yes, that's me, Tama Mahana, son of Rongo and Huia Mahana. Some people have told me I am handsome, not in the same way as my father, but good-looking enough. I take my looks from my mother's people of Ngati Porou. I remind Mum of her brother, Rangiora, who was killed during World War Two at Takrouna, Tunisia in 1943. Like him I am slim, slightly awkward in a suit, tall enough, with a habit of self-deprecation. I have Maori features, strong, dark, and eyes that somebody once described as quizzical, as if I was always trying to figure out what life was all about. Along with these features, I also have what is known as a lopsided smile and a way of looking down which some people equate with diffidence and shyness. But it's really my way of catching my breath, of giving myself the time to think before I face the reality I am confronted with. My lopsided smile has a lot to do with being a shearer's son, with living most of my life among itinerant rural workers who were never quite sure what the next day would bring. The shearing life is like the gypsy life and, when you live like that, moving from one shearing or contracting job to the next — cutting scrub, picking tomatoes, fencing, mustering and breaking in horses — you learn to make the most of your pauses and to mark each step before you take the next with a measure of respect.

My personal style has therefore been marked as much by the hesitancies, the pauses, as by the confidence with which I take the next stride. My friends are always waiting for me to catch up: 'Jeez, Tama, get a move on.' But never underestimate a person who stops often to think before he takes the next step. The sense of touching the earth, the surety of having both feet on the ground, is what gives him the power by which he can spring forward in ways that often surprise and confound.

All those years moving from job to job with Dad and Mum are to blame for my disposition. Even before they met, married and became parents they had already been on the move — Mum as a kitchenhand for various employers around Poverty Bay and Dad as a member of the Mahana Four shearing gang; it's a wonder they were ever in one place long enough to be able to meet and court each other. The way Dad tells it, he first saw Mum at a Maori hockey tournament held at Waituhi. She was an East Coast girl from Ruatoria, the captain of her hockey team. Dad had his eye on her all that week and just loved her forthright — some would call it bossy — captaining. From her position as halfback she yelled her comments across the field. 'You call yourself a hockey player, Henrietta? Get after that ball and be quick about it. And you, Wiki Hiroki, what are you standing around for? The goal posts are the only ones supposed to stand still! Hey, Arihia, this isn't a beauty contest so never mind about your hair and just chase that ball, eh!'

On warm nights when he was in a mischievous mood, Dad loved to embellish the story of how he wooed and won our mother. 'As soon as I saw her,' he would tell us, 'I knew she was the girl for me.'

'Well,' Mum would respond, 'I certainly didn't know he was the boy for me. I already had a boyfriend and, anyhow, I had been warned about your father's tribe. You know the old saying, "Don't ever go out with boys from Te Whanau a Kai. They have a hundred lovers and they are not faithful."'

'Her boyfriend wasn't much competition,' Dad would scoff. 'As soon as he saw me he knew his goose was cooked. As for your mother, I used strategy to win her. Winning a woman, kids, is like playing a game of football. I had to go wide out, around the scrum, and come up on her blindside when she wasn't looking. I tackled her, brought her to the ground and got through her defences before she could fend me off.'

'Don't listen to a word your father says,' Mum would respond. 'He was only after one thing. But before he could kick for touch, I needed a certain little gold ring on the fourth finger of my left hand, eh, dear!'

Before he knew it, Dad was married to Mum and, although he used to moan about 'East Coast girls being so fertile', he welcomed fatherhood. 'He blames me,' Mum used to giggle, 'but he forgets that a Mahana boy only had to look at a girl for her to get pregnant.' Not that their first parental experiences were happy; my brother, Rawiri, fell victim to diphtheria and died in infancy. I came along second and was the only son among all the daughters until they had Hone. Even so, I have never felt as if I am the oldest. It's a ranking that I suspect I have had to grow into, being not quite my natural position.

My first childhood memories are all to do with belonging to a family and proclaiming our kinship relationships with the land and the people of the land, not just assuming them. They are memories of belonging to a people who had migrated over 1200 years ago from Hawaiki — reputed to be eastward, across the sea where the sun rises — to this land. Dad loved telling me the legendary stories of their migration. 'They came on seven canoes,' he said with fierce pride. 'Takitimu, Tainui, Te Arawa, Mataatua, Kurahaupo, Tokomaru, Aotea.'

'But my people,' Mum would intervene, 'didn't want to bother with all that rowing. So my ancestor hitched a ride on a whale.' She was referring to the ancestor of all Ngati Porou, the whale rider, Paikea. Mum was very proud to be descended from him.

'How our ancestors got here is beside the point,' Dad would reply. 'Just remember, son, that you are descended from great sea voyagers.' He would press the palms of his hands against my heart. 'To manawa, o ratou manawa. It is their blood which beats in your heart.'

One magical afternoon Dad and I were walking along Wainui Beach. We came across a fisherman pulling in the white-winged floats which had taken his fishing hooks to sea. Dad knelt beside me, pointed toward the floats, and made the migration come alive. 'Look, Tama! See the canoes coming? See? Across the great ocean of Kiwa from Hawaiki nui, Hawaiki roa, Hawaiki pamamao. See how they ride the waves to this shore! And there, Tama, comes the Takitimu! Look how it comes!'

On settling, the canoe voyagers became known as the Maori, the original inhabitants of Aotearoa. They established tribal confederations throughout the discovered land. Some of these settlers ran the prows of their canoes to ground at a place called Turanga, where Gisborne now stands. Over time, four main tribes evolved: Rongowhakaata, Te Aitanga a Mahaki, Ngai Tamanuhiri and Te Whanau a Kai. It was this last tribe who struck inland towards the mountains. They found a valley which they called the Waituhi. It had a river known as the Waipaoa, running through it. They built a palisaded pa at one end of the valley to protect themselves, proclaimed a sacred mountain at the other and, much later, built a meeting house, Rongopai, to keep up the sky. There they maintained the myths, legends and culture of their ancestors and built strong economies from the bounty of the land, forests, rivers and sea.

'Your valley is a place to love,' Dad would say. 'Wherever you go, it is a place to return to. How fortunate is any man or woman to have a valley in their lives, a people to love and live for — and, if necessary, to die for.'

The Waituhi Valley was Dad's papakainga. It belonged to his people, Te Whanau a Kai. They lived tribally, communally, maintaining political alliances with other neighbouring iwi. Then one day, seven hundred or so years after they had settled in Aotearoa, there came news of a huge white-winged bird which had alighted on the sea, and the god birds that had come with it. Aotearoa was discovered by the European explorers in their great seafaring voyages of conquest and discovery; we were claimed by Great Britain and renamed New Zealand. A treaty was signed at Waitangi in 1840 but the two peoples could not accommodate each other. Escalating tensions over land which Maori owned and Pakeha wanted culminated in a period known as the Land Wars. At the end of it, the hold of the Maori on the land was broken — even in the Waituhi Valley. Everywhere, the land crumbled like pieces of a broken biscuit.

But I never knew any of this history when I was growing up. The great Mahana family who created my cradle wove it with strength, love and faith but took upon themselves the responsibility of prosecuting the great burden of the Treaty. Our valley had a history of women leaders, and among our greatest patriots were Riripeti, whom some call the Matriarch, and Miro Mananui, whom we know as the Matua. 'When you get older,' Nani Miro used to say to us younger ones, 'then you get wiser and, maybe, then we pass the responsibility of the Treaty to you.'

Isn't this what all parents do? So no matter the impoverished circumstances of our existence as a result of land confiscations, the kuia and kaumatua of the iwi ensured that my passage through life — and that of all the younger generation, like my cousins Tamatea, Simeon and Andrew Whatu — was achieved with as much grace as they could give us.

This is why I don't begrudge the makeshift stops along the way — draughty shearing huts, shepherds' quarters and one-room scrubcutters' shacks — or hazy glimpses of Mum struggling to cook kai at an open fire. I don't feel hard done by, in spite of that succession of long nights filled with the small, flickering light of a solitary candle, huddling with my brothers and sisters in a wooden bunk on a straw mattress. I have no regrets or judgements about life and about our lot. Perhaps it's because there was always a certain fatalism anyway about our situation as the last of the Ringatu. As followers of Te Kooti Arikirangi, who had led us during the wars, we would always wander as the morehu, the lost people, until fortune's wheel returned us to our promised land.

What I remember most is not the harshness of our lives but the radiance that Mum and Dad always tried to bring to it. Good humour and love characterised their approach. Leavened within this approach was the deep trust in their God to provide, so long as we lived within the moral compass prescribed by our biblical teachings.

Our tribal and religious relationships gave us a huge amount of kin. My sisters and I thought we were related to every Maori we met. We'd be walking along the road with Dad and meet one of them and have to press noses or shake hands. 'Who was that lady?' Ripeka would ask.

'That's your Auntie Molly,' he would answer.

'But wasn't that Auntie Molly we met last week?'

'Oh, that Auntie Molly was a cook for our shearing gang,' he would reply, 'and this Auntie Molly is a kitchenhand for another shearing gang. Don't ever get them mixed up or else they will get very cross.'

No wonder we were often confused about our relationships. There were so many names and faces to remember. Nani Katarina was the one with the moko. Uncle Charlie Whatu had a big puku. Cousin Sam Walker was the cheeky one with the sexy wink. Nani Tama always had a tokotoko, a walking stick. Uncle Hepa Walker worked in the City Council. Auntie Ruth was different from our other Auntie Ruth on Mum's side because she had no teeth. So many of them, and all our relatives.

'Your Auntie Sarah,' Dad would tell us, 'she was married to my cousin, Jack. She's really his relative down the line because her father was your Nan's uncle. His name was Morrie, and he was married to Mereira on your mother's side.' We tended to get confused when Dad was explaining how we were related. Even Nani Miro, who could recite all the whakapapa or genealogy of our family off by heart, couldn't make us understand.

'I'll wait until you're older,' she finally said. 'Then you won't be so, well, slow.'

My parents had a working partnership. During the shearing season they worked for Bulibasha. When the season was over, they took husband and wife contracts either scrubcutting, bushfelling, shepherding, breaking in horses or picking fruit. I have a photograph, an old sepia print that Dad was very proud of, showing him and Mum with slashers in their hands. Wrapped on Mum's back was a child with a monkey face that Ripeka and I would each insist was the other — and which our parents would intimate was me or her depending on how good or bad we were. Mum and Dad sometimes paired up with Uncle Joshua and Auntie Huria, who were also always looking for work. Their contracts were for a month, six weeks or, if they were lucky, for two or three months during the hard winter season when jobs were hard to come by. Often, they had to accept contracts way up the back of beyond where nobody else would go except those with a family to feed. Mum still declares that those times way out where nobody else was — where the bush was always raucous at night and wekas sang their harsh melodies and where, during the day, there was no sound except for the rushing wind and you were always aware of the sun on your back — were the happiest she had ever spent. 'For one thing,' she would say, 'I had your father to myself, even if he only had one thing on his mind.'

I'm not sure how Mum and Dad felt whenever they came to the end of a contract. Probably relief, mixed with apprehension that they would have to throw their bread on the waters and wait to see where they would next be delivered up to. After Dad had finished a contract at one farm, we would pack our belongings and move to the next job. We always arrived at a new place in the late afternoon or early evening to the same old story: a whare that was dirty, its walls smeared with black smoke, the table and cupboards still strewn with the mess left by the previous hands, and the floor littered with smashed crockery or broken chairs. Sometimes a window would be cracked or a door just managing to stay closed on its one rusty hinge. We would stand in the doorway, surveying the whare in silence, until the light cast by a match burnt out. There were so many desolate beginnings. Whenever we finished at one place and were on our way to another, I would close my eyes and cross my fingers and pray, 'Let the next place be a nice place, please let it be clean and tidy.' It never was.

It's no wonder that I developed my lopsided grin, halting steps, and my habit of crossing my fingers. Even now, sitting in the train travelling to Wellington, my fingers are crossed in that same childish way. This train trip is like one of those many journeys I remember. I have the same feeling as I had then, after we'd arrived at a new home; that I am back at the beginning, starting all over again. Except that the conductor has come, clipped my ticket and urged me onward.

'Tama, take your sisters and help your Dad bring our things from the truck,' Mum would instruct us.

Ripeka, Mere, Wiki and I would run back to the truck. Often that meant going for miles because some of the places we worked at were a long way from the road or nearest track. Sometimes Dad had to leave the truck on the other side of a river and we'd have to wade through the water to get to our new home. We were never afraid of the dark because we were often left alone when Mum and Dad were working late. No matter how dark it was or how far we had to go to reach the truck, all we did was keep our eyes fixed on the headlights shining far away. Anyway, Dad was with us, so nothing could happen to us and not even kehua, ghosts, could frighten us.

'What shall I take, Dad?' Ripeka would ask him.

'What shall I carry?' I would ask.

He'd be standing in the light of the truck and he'd look at us and think for a moment. 'Ripeka, you take those blankets. You, Tama, take that big box. I'll bring this suitcase and this other box. Okay? Are you both feeling strong? It'll take a few trips. We'll have to come back for this other stuff.'

'We can manage, Dad.'

'Show me your muscles then! Your muscles first, Tama. Big, eh? Now yours, Ripeka. Only small so far, Ripeka.'

'My muscles, they're just as big as Tama's,' Ripeka would pout. 'You feel again, Dad, I can beat him any day.'

Dad would have to say that she was as strong as I was, even though she wasn't. Then we'd start back together, pushing through the scrub towards the whare. Sometimes we'd have to put our loads down and stretch, and Dad's eyes would twinkle. 'Are you kids feeling tired, eh?'

'No, we're just stopping so you can rest, Dad.'

We'd set off again. After we'd dropped off the first load we'd return to the truck to get the next few pieces of our belongings. We never had much: some crockery, blankets, two dogs, a few pots, a saddle, a big suitcase of clothes, lots of nappies, perhaps some leftover kai, a bottle of tomato sauce, a rooster and some hens.

The memories eddy softly like a warm wind. The countryside has opened up. On one side of the train is the sea. On the other are the hills that enclose Poverty Bay. Ahead rise the Wharerata ranges. The main highway out of Gisborne winds its way upward across the ranges.

When I was a boy I used to marvel that our truck could make that climb. The road wasn't sealed then and our truck was old. Although we didn't have that many belongings, it would groan and shudder so much we'd have to get out and push.

Wherever we went, we took our household with us. It's difficult not to be sentimental about the way we must have looked to others on the road. It's like watching an old black and white movie filmed when the world was a different place. We were a family trying to escape the harsh circumstances of our lives. Our parents were never too proud to be poor or continually on the road, sitting in the front of the truck with baby Wiki sleeping between them. We older children would be in the back with the dogs and the hens, rooster and chickens.

'No time to rest,' Mum would say to us. 'When you've finished bringing everything from the truck, then you can take a breather.' Sometimes Dad wouldn't listen to her so she'd get in a temper and hit him with her broom. 'Hurry up, Rongo! Plenty of time for sitting down later.'

We left the hens until last. Dad would put a fowl under one arm and a pullet under the other. I would take two of the other hens and Ripeka would carry some of the chickens. Our fowls were very tame, unless they were clucky. Then they were just like Mum when she was angry, and pecked at us all the time. As for the chickens, when we were travelling from one place to the next on our truck, they slept with us in our blankets.

I cherish the memories of those first nights at a new home. Good Boy and Lady, our two sheepdogs, guarded the front door. Mere and Wiki slept with Mum and Dad, and Ripeka and I bunked in together; if the whare was big enough, I had my own bed. The hens and chickens settled close to the kitchen hearth where it was warm.

But there was so much to do before we went to bed. We'd all have a cup of tea. Dad would try to sneak off.

'No you don't, Rongo,' Mum would say. 'We've still got to clean the whare yet.' She would thrust a scrubbing brush into his hands before he could get away.

'I have to fix my saddle,' Dad would grumble. 'I have to make a coop for these hens. They're getting too accustomed to sleeping inside; before you know it, they'll be talking in Maori. If you think I'm going to sleep in the same room as fowls you've got another think coming, woman.'

Mum never listened. 'Plenty of time for your saddle tomorrow. Now start cleaning!'

Scrub, scrub, scrub. The sound of the train clacking along the rails towards the ranges echoes the sound of Mum and Dad as they cleaned the whare. The first job was to sweep the ceilings free of dust and cobwebs. While this was being done, Mum lit the copper so that all the bedding, curtains, anything made of fabric could be boiled clean to rid them of vermin. Next, Dad would splash the walls with antiseptic and do the same with the mattresses. As for my sisters and me, we swept the floor. Most times we were very glad if our new place had dirt for a floor. Even then, Mum made us sweep and sweep it until she was satisfied it was clean.

If the floor was wooden, we scrubbed it. Ripeka and I sloshed the water on the floor, Mum and Dad scrubbed, and we doubled back and mopped after them. Every now and then we'd have to stop the chickens from running over the wet floor. Sometimes Mere would try to splash the water in the bucket. She loved water. All surfaces were cleaned; the rule was, 'If it doesn't move, scrub it.' The walls and floors, oven, tables, kitchen cabinets, beds, wardrobes, bath and basin all got the treatment until they gleamed with antiseptic and soapy water.

While we waited for everything to dry, Dad would be chopping firewood, inspecting for leaks just in case it rained and filling in holes in the walls. The worst job was to take a look at the outhouse and, if it was full, dig another one.

Only when everything was to Mum's satisfaction would she let us rest. 'Now we can go to bed,' she would say. Ripeka and I would get our pyjamas and warm them by the fire before putting them on. Dad would start pulling off his boots. 'Not you, Rongo,' Mum would tell him. 'Still plenty for you to do.'

'Have a heart, Huia,' Dad would moan. 'Leave it for tomorrow.'

'No. Tonight, husband.'

Dad would have to do what he was told: fix that chair, move the table, unpack the bags, put a board across that broken window, bring the pots over to this corner and, 'Rongo!' Mum would shriek, 'kill that weta!' Mum was a hard taskmaster but, after everything was completed for the night, she melted like butter.

'I'm sorry I'm so awful to you, husband. We couldn't lay down our heads and go to sleep in filth, could we? We're not animals, Rongo. We deserve respect.'

'There, there, Huia. You're a good wife.' Dad would lead Mum to bed and comfort her, and she would make warm noises as soft as those of a cooing dove. But it never lasted. The next morning:

'Get up, Rongo! Rongo? Did you hear me? Taking advantage of me like that last night, I should be onto your tricks by now. Come on, move yourself.'

Dad would moan and I'd hear him walking about the whare and lighting the fire. 'What a woman,' he would say. 'Still as bossy as ever.'

Mum and Dad were always like that. They growled at each other one minute and loved each other the next. Their behaviour often puzzled me, and once I asked Dad about it. He just shrugged his shoulders. 'That's love,' he said. 'One day you'll understand.'

Even the last time I saw Dad, he and Mum hadn't changed. I'd laughed at him, 'That's love?'

'Ae, Tama,' he'd sighed. 'Ae . . .'

This is where the memories begin to hurt. There was always a reason for our parents cleaning every whare, every shearer's shack so thoroughly — it was for love of us kids. Some of those places were dangerous. They were unsafe and unsanitary. Straw and feather mattresses filled with ticks, fleas and bacteria. Mosquito larvae swimming in water tanks or in the ponds where we were supposed to get our drinking water. Flies swarming over meat left rotting in the larders. I still remember times when Dad would try the water himself first — if he didn't get sick, only then would he allow Mum and us children to drink it. On another occasion, he was woken by Wiki wailing in her cot and found three large rats nibbling at her. They had already drawn blood and I remember his white-faced alarm as he and Mum bundled Wiki in their arms and raced her down to the nearest doctor.

'Look after your sisters,' Dad said as they left.

For the rest of the night, Ripeka, Mere and I huddled close together, shining a torch into the darkness, holding sticks in our hands just in case other rats were waiting to attack us.

And always, on the first morning, we would go up to the big house to say hello to the farm owner and his wife. Wherever we went there was always a big house to be made obeisance to, and a boss and his missus to thank. Mum would put on her nice blue polka dot dress and Dad would put on a jacket. I'd have to wear a white shirt and my sisters looked so cute in their yellow frocks. Off we'd go, up to the back door, to introduce ourselves.

'This is my wife, Huia,' Dad would say.

Mum would shake hands with the farm owner and his wife, if she was there. 'Pleased to meet you,' she would say, addressing herself to Mrs Boss. 'If there's any cleaning work you want done, or any cooking, don't hesitate to ask.' Mum was always poised, reciting the words off by heart.

'These are my children,' Dad would continue, introducing us. 'They won't get in the way.'

It was our turn to shake hands. We were often ill at ease doing this, afraid we would do something wrong.

Sometimes we'd be asked in for a cup of tea. 'No, thank you,' Mum would answer. 'Perhaps another time.'

The lady of the house would agree. 'Yes, that's a good idea. You must have a lot of settling in to do.' Then she would ask, 'Is the whare all right? Are you comfortable? It's in a bit of a mess, isn't it. Ah well, if you ever need anything, just sing out and we'll see what we can do.'

'No, we'll be fine,' Mum would answer. 'Don't you worry about us.' Mum always said that even if things were really bad. She didn't like being a bother. She was forever telling us not to be nuisances either. We were there to work, not to bother the people we were working for. 'We'll go now,' Mum would say when she thought we'd stayed long enough. We'd shake hands again and walk back to the whare.

When we thought we were far enough away, Ripeka and I would chat excitedly to each other. 'What a neat house. All those flowers. Did you see that beaut car? And what about those nice chairs and that stove and carpet and . . . Boy, wish we had a house like that.' We would exchange our views all the way back to the whare. We never thought we might be hurting Mum. But once, she told us to stop it.

'We won't always be on the outside looking in,' she began. 'One day we'll have a house like that. You kids will have the best of everything. But we have to work for it, kids. Nothing of worth comes to anybody on a silver plate. That's why your dad works so hard; that's why we move around. We won't always be working for other people. You wait and see, Tama. You just watch, Ripeka. One day.'

Dad took her words badly. He seemed to think they reflected on his own inability to make something of himself. I'll never forget what she said to him.

'We are doing this together, husband. You may think you blindsided me when we were courting but the truth is that I fell gladly into your arms when you tackled me. I knew that wherever you went, I would follow. Where you put your head down, I would pillow you. When I married you, I knew that together we would make fine children. You took me to your valley and I loved your people and they became my people. And I loved your God and he became my God.'

Mum and Dad, they kept their promise to us in the end. Eventually we grew up, as Mum had said we would, with the best of everything.

8

'**i**'m coming home, Dad. Wait for me, e pa.'

I remember again that day walking along Wainui Beach with my father. We saw the fisherman pulling in his white-winged floats. Dad was telling me about seven canoes. But only seven canoes, Dad? There is a legend which tells of an eighth waka. Its name was Karamurauriki and it brought Aitua to Aotearoa. The bowpiece and sternpiece were fastened and decked with streamers of white albatross feathers. The bailer was Tataeore.

Karamurauriki: the canoe of Death.

It has taken Dad away from me.

The southerly has broken above Wellington, lashing the city with rain.

I look out the window of Mr Ralston's car. He is driving me back to my flat in Island Bay. The rain has slowed the traffic at Courtenay Place, but once past the Basin Reserve the traffic flow improves and we are soon making good time past the hospital and the sprawl of Newtown suburb. We take a right turn at the lights and head up towards Berhampore. Other traffic glides up with us, draws abreast, then overtakes in a sudden blast of noise receding.

'Left here, Tama?' Mr Ralston asks.

I nod, and the car makes the turn, dipping down between two crowded ridges. The sky constricts, becomes a smaller patch of blue as the houses rise up to spike the skyline. As the car turns I see people stepping off a trolley bus. They gather at the corner, waiting to pay their respects, as if they know that I am passing by. 'Baldwin Street's coming up,' I tell Mr Ralston.

The car slows down. Mr Ralston indicates, and a red light flickers on the dashboard, on, off, on, off; dead, alive, dead, alive, dead. Ahead, the street winds up a steep hill cut off by the sky. Telephone poles bend past. A young girl is walking down to the bus stop.

'It's number forty-one, Mr Ralston. The house with the flight of steps.'

The steps ascend between a thin stand of trees, disappear into the shadow of a small alleyway, then reappear, leading up to an old house, crushed with other houses on the side of the hill. My flatmates, Jasper and William, will be at work. They are two wild Scottish guys who wanted a third flatmate who could cook; in my case, as a Maori, I got extra brownie points because a piupiu — the Maori man's flax skirt — was almost the same as a Highland kilt.

The car draws to a stop. 'Do you want to come up, Mr Ralston?'

'No, I'll wait here. Don't take too long, old chap. I have to get you checked in at the airport in half an hour. We don't want you to miss your flight, do we?'

Miss the flight? It's tempting. Do I really want to go? Do I want to face the reality of the funeral? Maybe I can stay in Wellington and pretend that nothing has happened . . . that time is only passing where I am and not where Dad is. There, nobody has changed, nothing has changed, nothing. Dad is still there, Mum is still there, nobody has died.

But no. Ripeka has phoned. The words have been said, the death proclaimed.

'I won't be long, Mr Ralston.' The door of the car slams shut behind me. The sound echoes along the street. The cold slices into my skin. A vicious gust of rain has me reeling across the pavement under the rippling branches of the trees. They shiver and whisper to one another, and their shadows reach across the pavement to clutch at me with flickering fingers. Between the shadows the steps rise up into the deep darkness of the alleyway. I pull my coat around me and begin to climb.

The first step . . . and many more to follow. Behind me I hear Mr Ralston turning the car to point back down the street. The engine stops and there is silence. I am thinking ahead to what I should pack: the black suit. Better take the grey one too, I might need it. Two white shirts. A couple of ties. Underwear. Pair of shoes. Toilet gear. Electric shaver — a birthday present from Dad. I must remember to ring my girlfriend, Sandra, when I get to the airport. And write a note to Jasper and William to let them know.

All of a sudden a shadow flits ahead of me, a little bird, a fantail. He chirrups a cheeky bird call, 'Come Tama! Quickly Tama!' His fanned tail bobs and flashes ribbons of fire. I remember that when the demigod Maui tried to conquer Hinenuitepo, the Great Mother of the Night, and bring immortality to all humankind, his companion was the fantail. Maui passed through the gateway into Rarohenga where his intention was to creep up on Hinenuitepo while she lay sleeping in her meeting house, Wharaurangi. There, he planned to enter her body as she slept, and cut her heart out. In defeating her, he would save the passage of men and women from life to death, from the Kingdom of the Light to her Dominion of the Night. But the fantail laughed, Hinenuitepo awoke and, instead, it was Maui who was defeated when she crushed him between her thighs.

I mate mai te rangi
i a Maui i komia
e Hinenuitepo,
waiho ki te ao, na i —

Death came to the mighty
when Maui was crushed
by Hinenuitepo,
and so it remained in the world —

Alas, fantail, the way of life and death has already been ordained. Neither you nor I can change it.

I continue up the steps into the shadow of the alleyway. The darkness closes; only dull light shining through the pickets of the tall, wooden fence between the flat and the house next to it. The darkness makes me remember when Riripeti died, and the pearls in her hair were forever dimmed. When she was buried, she lay beneath the earth where there was no light. I was confused, just a child at the time, and filled with fear. I imagined myself under the earth, the darkness perfumed with the sweet smell of funeral ointments. For a long time afterward, my dreams were ugly and deformed by a small boy's terror of the dark. I would thrust my arms upward and outward searching for quilted walls that were never there.

The fantail sings disconsolately as I climb the steps. Suddenly a gust of wind flips it away in a turbulent stream and it tumbles across the trees into oblivion.

The shock of the news about Dad is getting to me. The steps seem to extend upward through the clouds into a turbulent sky. The ground falls away, leaving only a precarious ladder in the air. I am dangling from it. I hold on tight, sweat popping on my forehead. If I was to fall, nobody would catch me.

I shake my head and regain my orientation. There, in front of me, is the alleyway that opens into the backyard of the flat. It is cluttered with wood, tin and beer bottles from our party last weekend. The windows are shut and the blinds are drawn. The key is hidden under a brick. With a scratch and a grating sound, the door to the house is unlocked. I open the door and slam it quickly behind me. I feel safe, as if I have been playing hopscotch and made my way home without stepping on a crack.

The house is cold, the passageway silent and dark. I walk quickly to my bedroom.

Open the windows and part the curtains, for darkness is fearsome and other dreams may come. Let the light fill every corner of this room and chase the darkness away.

The delayed reaction hits me and I am frozen, unable to move. I turn to Dad for his help.

Do you remember, Dad, shortly after Riripeti's funeral, you took me into town and it was so crowded? I was only a little boy then, about five, I suppose. 'You wait here,' you said. You disappeared with the crowd and left me standing on the pavement. I waited and waited, Dad. But you didn't come back. Where did you go to?

'Are you lost, little boy?' a lady asked.

'No,' I answered. 'My father's just gone away for a while. He's coming back to get me, though. He told me to wait here.'

The lady left me. I wanted to shout, 'Come back!' I was frightened. All those people jostled and pushed against me. They couldn't see me; I was so small. I felt as if I was in a land full of giants. In the end, I decided I would find you. I wandered along the streets and everybody was laughing and having a good time. Where were you, Dad? I looked carefully at everybody but I couldn't see you anywhere. I pulled at a man's coat to make him turn around. But he wasn't you, either. I went into the shops, pushing between people's legs; I tried to look in all the dark places, but I wouldn't go there because I was scared. I went into a hotel and I said to the man, 'Have you seen my father?'

'Go away, kid,' the man growled. 'You're not allowed in here.'

I ran out. I sat down on the kerb. I looked at everybody passing but I couldn't see you. I tried to be brave. Then, there you were, across the road. You were looking for me just as I was looking for you. And I shouted, 'Dad, Dad —'

I wrench the curtains open. My breath is coming in ragged gasps. My heart is beating hard. The light shines dully in the room. It is a small room, furnished with a single bed and a chest of drawers. In one corner is a large wardrobe, inset with a long, glistening mirror. On one wall is a painting given me by Sandra. Mum made the quilt on this bed. There, on the bedside table, is a photograph of myself with Dad. Outside the window, Island Bay is grey and windy. The roofs of the houses fall away from the side of the hill, tiers of multicoloured tin tumbling down to the sea. Cars glide along the Esplanade. The waves are choppy and flecked with foam. A ferry is approaching the heads, seeking safe haven and the calmer water within. Its bow thrusts through the waves, sending cascades of spray into the air. Beyond the heads, the hills are dark and bleak. Above them, a brown haze seeps into the sky. I pick up the photograph of my father. The fantail has returned to sing at the window.

We found each other. You lifted me up, Dad. When you hugged me, 'Hello son,' you were laughing. I think you were surprised when I hit you. Hard.

'Don't go away like that, Dad. Don't you leave me again.'

You promised you wouldn't.

9

The train rushes across the landscape, over the plain that rolls away toward the Wharerata ranges. A farm passes by, then a small ribbon of houses along the main highway. For a moment the train blurs past a small railway siding, Bartlett's township, and breaks across the highway between the clanging bells of a railway crossing. At the crossing an old truck waits for the train to pass. There, on the back, children stand and wave. I lift my hand to wave back to them. They are suddenly gone. The Whareratas begin to crowd the sky with rugged peaks.

The first few days at a new home were always the busiest. Dad would start his job straight away. If it was scrubcutting he'd sharpen his machetes, kiss Mum and us too, and then be off.

According to Mum, when I was born, she would accompany Dad with me slung on her back. However, when Ripeka, Mere and Wiki came along, that complicated matters. 'How was I to carry the four of you?' she would ask us. So Dad would go alone, waking before dawn. Somewhere in my drifting dreams I'd hear the soft stamping of his feet, the clink and rustle of strange sounds, Mum whispering to him as she put on her dressing gown and got out of bed. A match would flare, casting a sudden light in the morning darkness. A flame would begin to flicker from a candle or lamp in the room. Dad would light the fire and Mum would hang a billy of water on one of the wire hooks above the burning wood. Smoke would billow into the room when the wind gusted down the sheet-iron chimney. Mum would prepare Dad his breakfast: oats with water, maybe some stew made of potatoes, puha and pork bones, accompanied by damper bread and tea. There'd be the sounds as Dad had his kai and then the soft scraping of his chair when he finished. Wiki would cry from her cradle. Dad would whisper to her for a moment. Then softly he would kiss her, Mere, Ripeka and me.

'Goodbye, Daddy,' Ripeka would say sleepily.

'I'll come and help you when I get back from school,' I would add.

'Look after your mother and sisters, son.'

The door would creak. Mum would curl her arms round Dad's neck. For a moment there'd be silence. Then the door would shut and far away in my dreams I'd hear Good Boy and Lady barking as Dad untied them.

I look out the window of the train. We are heading into the ranges.

The place where mountain ridges meet rushing clouds appears seamless. I can almost convince myself that Earth and Sky have, indeed, found their long embrace again, but I know they haven't. The old Maori myths say that when the god brothers separated the two parents, they placed four upright poles between them so that they could not reach each other again. Even so, Ranginui's endeavours were so persistent that, in the end, Tane agreed that his limbs should be severed. When that was done, having lost his hold, the Sky Father sprang up to where he lies now between earth and the stars. As surety, one of the god brothers, Paia, braced him there, carrying the weight of the father on his shoulders.

But the god brothers fell out with each other. Some disagreed with the continuation by Tane of his plans, especially when he decided to turn the Earth Mother on her front so that she would provide less temptation to her husband. On one side was the faction led by Tane, Tu, Rongo and Paia. On the other side were the dissenters led by Tawhirimatea, god of winds, Tangaroa, god of the ocean and Ruaumoko, god of earthquakes. Even today, whenever Tangaroa rages against the land or Tawhirimatea lashes us with his hurricanes or Ruaumoko makes the earth rumble and quake, we still feel their continuing disquiet at the Separation. It was so tumultuous that Uru, god of the night sky, became distressed enough to flood his domain with his tears. Known as purapurawhetu, they became the seeds for what we know today as Te Ika o te Rangi, the Milky Way, the broad beautiful band of stars that crowns the night.

Eventually, Tane fashioned a woman out of red clay. She became the First Mother of humankind, and we became Tane's legal heirs to the world. This was his redemption.

When my father first told me the story of the Separation my first thought was, Why would a son do such a thing? Why would he want to separate his parents in such a way?

I must have been about ten at the time. Dad and Mum were on a fencing contract at a farm near the Waioeka Gorge. The quarters where we were staying were on one side of a steep ravine crossed by a swingbridge. Mum was at home with my sisters and Dad had roped fenceposts to two packhorses, taking them across the ravine to the job on the other side. There was one more fenceline to do and the contract would be completed.

'You and your questions, son,' Dad laughed. 'It's just a story. Tane had no option. If he wanted to stand up, to grow, to get some space and not be cramped any longer, this was the only way he could do it. Hence the saying, "Tama tu tama ora, tama noho tama mate. If you stand you live, if you lie down you die." Tane wanted to be free. And after all, don't forget he was a god and had a date with destiny. His great purpose was to create the world and a people to live in it. This is why one should give thanks to Ranginui and Papatuanuku on one hand, and to Tane on the other. In the first case, we thank the parents for nurturing us and caring for us. In the second, we thank Tane for giving us the freedom for the son to take his own destiny in his hands and strike out in whatever direction he wants to. The two are not mutually exclusive. The one depends on the other. And,' he winked slyly, 'one should never question the motives of the gods, especially since they might be listening.'

We came to the swingbridge. There it was, swaying dangerously in the wind coming up the valley. That morning it had poured down and the rain, dripping from the wire frame, transformed the bridge into a shivering jewelled cobweb spun in the air. With every gust of wind the bridge would yaw, the wires twanging with the strain, and raindrops would scatter from the bridge like diamonds.

Dad stopped the packhorses and pondered what to do. 'I think we better go down to the river rather than use the swingbridge today,' he said.

'It will be faster if we use the bridge,' I answered.

'Yes,' he said, 'but you're with me,' as if that explained everything. Before I could protest he kicked his horse and we continued further down the track to the river. Even so, after we had forded the river, I took it up with him.

'The bridge would have been quicker,' I said.

'When you're a man,' he answered, 'and have the capability of getting yourself out of trouble, then you can cross whatever bridge you want to. You'll be old enough to make your own decisions, stupid or not, and if you do get into trouble you won't be able to blame anybody else except yourself. But you're still a boy and I am your father and this is my watch, son.'

This is my watch.

I never realised until much later how precarious our lives were. Children were vulnerable to all kinds of illnesses in those days; my mother had already lost her firstborn son, my brother Rawiri, and did not want to lose another child to diphtheria, pneumonia, tetanus, blood poisoning, polio or whatever else was waiting to claim us. She was always dosing us up on malt, codliver oil, olive oil or other medicines so that we would not get sick. At the slightest rise in temperature she would inspect our bodies to see if we had any flea, spider or mosquito bites. If that didn't work, she would question us, 'What have you eaten? Did you drink the water in the river? You didn't eat any mushrooms did you?' At the smallest cough, she would bundle us up in blankets. Unlike many of our relatives who were afraid of doctors and hospitals, we were lucky that our parents were not.

Accidental death was also a high risk in those days. I had a number of cousins who died from accidents while farming, or travelling from one job to the next. If you were careless on the farm or made the wrong decision you could pay the price: an arm sliced off while you were sawing wood on a timber contract, a leg crushed when a horse slipped and fell on you during mustering. And the possibility of a road crash was always waiting when you travelled in dangerous vehicles driven too fast and without lights. Once, on our own travels, we were overtaken by a car out of control on a steep descent. When we rounded the next bend, there it was, slammed against a tree; the car's brakes had failed. There were six people in the car and two more on the road, all broken and bloodied. Dad went to help. When he came back, he said to us, 'Don't come any closer. One of those people is dead. The other has bad injuries.' He told Mum to drive back up the road and seek help.

Life was like that swingbridge. At any point in crossing it, we might fall into the ravine below. Or we might meet somebody who would want to throw us down into it. Physical and sexual abuse seemed to come with rural living, especially to those who, like us, lived on the borderline. Alcohol fuelled arguments between friends. Before you knew it, people were fighting. Jealousies and old enmities would be raised and, next minute, somebody had a knife in their back or else had been shot when they opened the door to a stranger. Mum and Dad did not drink, but we saw the impact on our relatives who did. We used to laugh at uncles and aunties as they fell out of hotels at six o'clock clutching their flagons of grog. We would watch them dancing and falling down drunk in the middle of a song at the weekend-long parties they had. We always backed off when they became vicious and wanted to beat us up. Unemployment only made the situation worse. 'When a man who's on the booze isn't working,' Mum used to say, 'he takes it out on the person next to him, even if it's his wife or children.' She was always giving advice to her own battered friends. 'Leave him. Get out of the house before it's too late.'

Mum and Dad made us feel safe. My sisters, brother and I grew up with a father in the house and a mother in the house. They were hardworking parents, and we were fortunate that our father came from such a strong and determined clan. The Mahana family gained its strength from adversity, from maintaining its loyalty during the Land Wars to the rebel leader, Te Kooti Arikirangi, in his fight against the Pakeha settlers. However, the family, like the rest of the iwi, was punished for its opposition by having 56,000 acres of tribal land confiscated — the very land that provided our economic livelihood. Te Kooti's warrior ways were taken up by Dad's mother, my grandmother, Riripeti Mahana, from whom I am descended. Riripeti tried her best to get the land back. She and her husband, Grandfather Ihaka, had fourteen children. Dad and Uncle Pita were the youngest. Before she died, Riripeti anointed a successor, my cousin, Tamatea, overseas right now; it was his father, Riripeti's eldest son, Te Ariki, who headed the clan. When Riripeti died, the dream of the land's restitution died with her. If it wasn't for Miro Mananui or old man Bulibasha, who established the Mahana shearing gangs, the iwi's economic livelihood would have disappeared altogether. Dad's older brothers and sisters remained in Waituhi, on the little parcels of land left to the family, but the younger ones, like Dad, inevitably began to fend for themselves.

It took guts to strike out from home and forage for work wherever it could be obtained in the nearby lands of the Pakeha. It took fortitude and a certain kind of strength to keep going from one job to the next with only small gains to show for it. There were battles that were won and battles that were lost, failures and disappointments that had to be got over, tears of anger at a cancelled contract, as well as elation at a long job completed. There was also a certain measure of fatalism, of acceptance, in being an itinerant worker. 'Ah well, another day tomorrow,' Dad would say if rain delayed his work. Sometimes there were things you had no control over.

Above all, it took a great deal of watchfulness and care to be able to negotiate and traverse a landscape that was often dangerous. Beyond the safety of tribal boundaries we were at risk of anything and anyone coming out of anywhere and placing our family in peril. But my parents only had one choice — and that was no choice but to make the best of our perilous passage through an unsafe world. They had children to feed and provide for. While they were at it, they did their best to protect us.

No matter how vigilant Dad was, however, not even he could keep irrational violence from the door.

The sound of the train shunts my memories onward. The hills rear up; the train curves through a cleft in upthrusting peaks. The sunlight falls across the country, lighting up the greenstone years of a boy with his father.

The greenstone years.

That's what I call them, those years of wandering from the time I was born until I was fourteen. They are luminous like pounamu, the precious Maori jade, and flecked with roimata toroa, the tears of the albatross. I prize those years just as greenstone is valued. They comprise over half my life, so is it any wonder that I am still in thrall to their rare quality? Yet, although it was only a few years ago, it always seems to be a short time in my memory. Indeed, sometimes I think it was only yesterday that I was a young boy who, finally, was old enough to go out and help Dad at his work.

I took my schooling wherever we were staying, at small rural or native schools taught by solo teachers in backblock places with pupils whom I only got to know slightly because we were always on the move. I guess this is why the world beyond Mum and Dad and the family seemed so unreal, a place to pass through, and why the only centre was where the family was. Where Mum was. Where Dad was. Where my sisters were. Because of this, I measured my days at school with impatience, constantly watching the clock and waiting to get back home to them.

There was one farming job Dad hired on for that I especially remember. It was a fencing contract in the backblocks behind Matawai, but it also involved some work mustering wild horses and breaking them in. I'd taken a particular shine to a newly bridled piebald, which I named Blue, even though he was white and brown.

When I arrived home from school, I threw my satchel on my bed. 'Where's Dad working today, Mum?' I asked. Mum was nursing one of my sisters. I was already moving around the kitchen, packing a saddlebag with cordial and bread.

'On the other side of the big mountain,' she answered. 'It's still light and there's a few hours of good work left. But night's coming on and I don't want him riding the mountain track in the dark.' My mother and I had become allies, joined in the job of getting Dad to stop work for the day. If we didn't, he'd work all night.

I went down to the horse paddock. 'How are you, Blue?' I asked as I put the reins and saddle on the piebald and threw the saddlebag across his back. Then off we went, over the warm land, around the big mountain, to where Dad was working. I was eager to reach the place where he was. 'Dad? Where are you?' I yelled. The valleys echoed my call to him, a song of the faraway hills. After a while, from somewhere came the sounds of Good Boy and Lady, alerted by my yelling, and then Dad's whistled reply. I never quite mastered his art of whistling: three fingers in his mouth, a tensing of his cheeks, and then that ear-piercing blast, loud enough to bring the walls of Jericho down.

'School over already?' Dad asked. 'Or did you play truant again! You know, if your mother catches you, you'll be for the high jump. She wants you to get a good education, though God knows how you're going to do that the way we move around. So, tell me, what great new wisdom did the Pakeha teach you today, son?'

As we worked — piling the scrub for burning or dragging battens down to the fenceline or mustering cattle into makeshift cattleyards or pulling tree stumps out — we talked about what I had learnt at school. Our conversation spun off into love, life and the whole damn universe. It was father and son talk about what life was all about and what was important about it; at the same time he also cautioned me that you could not always escape the whims of the world. He offered advice on the times to fight them and the times to accept.

One day, however, Dad completely put me off my stroke. He liked to come up on people's blindside while they weren't looking and surprise them with some statement or other. He was digging in a post and said, 'You know, son, if I hadn't met your mother I would have met somebody else and married her.' At the time I didn't understand what he was trying to say, because I knew he loved Mum. I actually hated him for a long time because in negating her he was denying me; telling me that being born to him was a whim. But I now know that he was trying to teach me about, yes, irrationality, and that life doesn't always unfold as simply as one might expect.

The best times with Dad were often when we never spoke at all. Instead, there was the quiet understanding that comes with working together on a task, unified in a single purpose: to get the work done before it became too dark. Finally, as the sunlight rippled across the paddocks and the evening breeze cooled our sweat, he'd put down his tools. 'Huh? Do you want to be here all night?' His laughter would chuckle through the air. Actually, I wouldn't have minded.

One evening, on our way home, we reined our horses at the top of the big mountain where we could look down on the whare. The stars were out and, down in the valley, our house was shining with lights. It was like a beacon in the night, guiding us home. Everything was quiet and drowsy. As we approached the cottage, Mum came to the door, silhouetted there, waiting in the lamplight. Dad gave a huge grin.

'So you decided to come home, did you?' Mum called.

Don't get me wrong. Those greenstone years were not lonely years and, apart from the times we went back to the raucous Mahana iwi at Waituhi, there were other travellers who intersected our lives. When I grew older Mum was surprised that I even remembered them.

'Ae, Mum, I remember Bulla. He was a rabbiter Dad met when he was out fencing. Bulla had kai with us. We had some mussels, and there was a small crab in one. Bulla said, "Mmm, good," and he swallowed it whole. Yes, I recall the Heperi family too. Mr Heperi was a roadman fixing up bridges and patching up potholes, and he and Mrs Heperi used to come and play cards when we were staying at Mr Jobson's farm. Georgina? She had a big puku because she was having a baby. We met her in Gisborne one night and you and she had a good cry because she didn't have a husband. You told her to come out shearing with us and she did. No, I don't remember what shed it was but I remember Georgina though. She was good to me and she played marbles with me sometimes. I remember all those people, Mum. Yes, even Boy Boy and Miriama and Sambo and . . .'

My mother looked at me askance. 'Hmmn,' she said, 'no wonder you're a reporter. You've been spying on us all our lives, haven't you, just waiting for the day when you can put us in a newspaper.'

We never did get to know the other travellers for long. The day would come when we had to move again. But I've always remembered them with gratitude: like Mrs Karaka and all her kids who walked for miles just to say goodbye. The truck had been loaded with our belongings and we were ready to go. Mrs Karaka yelled out to us, 'Hey, Rongo, Huia.' There she was, wading across the river, holding the smaller kids above the water. Behind her came her other children: Ani, George, Danny, Ron and Roimata. Ron was giving Ani a piggyback. Roimata was almost drowning because she was carrying a big sack above her head so it wouldn't get wet.

We rushed down to the river and helped them up the bank. We had a difficult time with Mrs Karaka because she was, well, not exactly slim. Dad grabbed one hand, Mum grabbed the other, and Ripeka and I pulled at her puku. Her kids pushed her up from the back. ' One, two, three and heave,' Dad yelled. She burst out of the water like a big fish and flopped, gasping, on the grass.

'We've come to say haere ra,' she said. She opened up the sack which Roimata had been carrying. 'This is for you,' she said. Inside was some Maori bread and scones, still warm from the oven.

'You shouldn't have,' Mum said. 'All of this trouble just for us. And to come all this way . . .'

Mrs Karaka laughed and hugged Mum. 'Takes more than a river to stop me, Huia,' she said. 'And who knows when the next time will be that we see each other again, eh?'

But not all our visitors were so benign. After we finished the Matawai job, Dad was lucky enough to get a scrubcutting contract on a remote coastal farm just beyond Ruatoria. Something happened while we were at that job. Dad never knew about it.

'It's way up the Coast,' Dad told me, 'among your mother's relatives. There's a block of land that Jack Mills has, and it's got thistles, gorse and blackberries all over it. We'll be there, maybe eight weeks. I'll have to ride in every day to the job, but the whare is close to the road and there's a schoolbus that can take you and your sisters to school.' His eyes twinkled. 'It will be good for you to get to know those cannibals from the Coast.'

The best surprise awaited our arrival. This time, the whare was the kind of place I had always crossed my fingers about: a nice place in a valley near the sea. The previous occupants had left it in good condition and there was wood in the woodbox. All the same, we cleaned and scrubbed it — but instead of washing in the bathtub, Dad said, 'Why waste the whole sea outside?' With that, he led us yelling and screaming down to the beach. It was a mix of sand and pebbles with a reef stretching from a crumbling cliff out into the bay. The surf came crashing over the reef. Mum took one look at it and shivered. 'This place looks dangerous,' she said. 'Too many cross-tides and undercurrents.' Even so, it was always a thrill for us kids to go down there on those days when Mum would take us shellfishing after school. Like all young boys I was at that point in my life where I liked to test my mother's boundaries. I knew she couldn't swim and that she hated my going to a particular spot where, on stormy days, the waves came rushing through the reef into a blowhole. 'Don't go too far out, Tama. Tama? Come back in.' I would laugh and laugh and, as the spray spumed about me, do a boyish haka filled with bravado.

'Don't do that,' Mum said to me one day. 'You might make Tangaroa angry.' She may have been right. Perhaps, in my innocence, I was the one who invoked the events that occurred.

We were happy on that contract. Every morning, Dad would leave for the block of land to be cleared: two hours there and two back. As for my sisters and me, we had breakfast with Mum and caught the rattling schoolbus to the nearest district school, ten miles away. During the early part of the contract, Mum sometimes went with Dad. But, after a while, it just wasn't worth it: by the time she got there, she'd only be able to spend a couple of hours before having to come back to meet us on our return from school.

I loved that school. I was beginning to enjoy having school friends and playing football during lunchtime. The sports master, Mr Granger, told Dad I was developing into a very good winger and that he hoped I would stay on for a game with a neighbouring school in the spring. I was also learning about the wide world outside the compass of our lives. Although I had begun to read books, I had never realised the enormity of the world until our teacher, Miss Wilson, brought a globe to the class, spun it a few times, and showed us where New Zealand was — way at the bottom of the globe — and Waituhi, let alone Ruatoria, weren't even on it. After that nobody could stop me. On a visit to Gisborne I pestered Dad about buying me an encyclopedia from a church charity shop; Mum actually did it behind his back. I became ravenous to learn about all the countries on the globe and soon bored everybody at home and school by knowing all the capitals of the states of America, Italy, Germany, France and Russia. The irony was that I was never interested in learning about the country that lay closest to my understanding: New Zealand. And, as far as the teacher was concerned, Maori didn't have a history really.

Enthusiasm for learning got me some of the way but basically, at school, I was a slogger. Mine was not a quick mind and I found it difficult to keep up. Constantly being on the move meant that I'd missed out on a lot of elementary reading, writing and comprehension. As a consequence I was kept back in the same class for a year and, by the time I was at Ruatoria, I was still running at the back of the pack.

'Never mind, son,' Dad told me. 'Some people run a fast race, some people run a slow one. In the end you'll get there.' But even he complained, later, that the tortoise hadn't taken so long as I did to get through my schooling.

While we were up the Coast, construction work began on the road into the valley. Every morning and afternoon, the schoolbus would pass the road gang where they were installing a new culvert; winter was coming and the old culvert had a habit of flooding. The men would smile, sometimes wave and, as we passed, take a smoko break. From the back window of the bus I would watch them leaning on their shovels and talking to one another. Four of them I took particular note of: a red-haired big beefy man and three of his younger mates. The big beefy man wore a white singlet and he was the leader. Whenever he caught sight of any of the girls on the bus he would hold his crotch, bunch his fist and make a gesture

— there was no doubt what it meant. His three mates would laugh and laugh.

After a month on the job, Dad realised he was wasting too much time travelling every day to do his work. 'It might be better,' he told Mum, 'if I camp overnight and come back home to you and the kids every second day.' Although Mum didn't like the idea, she agreed. She didn't let on that the red-haired man had already paid her a visit when she was alone in the whare. He asked for a drink of water. While he was there he made advances to her. She told him to get out and never come back.

Mum thought she could handle the red-haired man, but she didn't realise that the next time he came he would bring his mates. Those four men in the road gang must have been keeping an eye on Dad's movements. Women were always vulnerable in those days. There were men of a predatory nature who made a game of staking out the land, watching for their best opportunity and, when a woman was defenceless and had nobody to protect her, moving in like a pack of wolves.

I returned from school one day and as soon as I walked through the door of the house and saw the men there — two were holding my mother — I knew something was wrong.

'What are you doing here?' I asked the red-haired man.

'Is this the man of the house?' he mocked. 'Hello, little man. Your mum invited us over for a couple of drinks and a bit of fun, didn't you, darling?'

The men were drunk. Mum tried to stop one of them as he lunged towards Wiki and grabbed her. 'Lookee here,' he laughed. 'Now I've got two little girlies.'

Mum cried out, 'No.' She gave me a look of panic. 'Tama, take your sisters to the beach. Now. And don't look back, son, don't come back. Wait until I come and get you. Now *go*.' She glared commandingly at the red-haired man.

'All right, Mummy darling,' he nodded. 'Your kiddies can go but you'll stay and we'll party, right?'

I was trembling with fear. I took Wiki in my arms and we all ran down to the beach. There was a cave in the cliffs. 'You girls stay here,' I told them. 'I'm going back for Mum.' I picked up a piece of wood and raced back. I could hear my mother's cries. As I ran through the door she was fighting the men, trying to get away from them. When she saw me coming she yelled out, 'Tama, no.' Maybe it was to stop me from seeing what they were doing to her. One of the men punched me in the stomach and, when I went down, kicked me in the head. The red-haired man picked me up and threw me against the wall of the shack. I blacked out.

When I came to, Mum was lying on the floor, unconscious. The men had gone. I cleaned her up and waited. When she recovered, there was a look of enormous grief on her face. She stroked my hair. 'My brave, brave boy,' she said.

'I'd better go and get the others,' I answered. 'I won't be long.'

Mum restrained me a moment.

'When your father comes back tomorrow, don't tell him about any of this,' she said. 'He is not to know. Ever. You hear me, Tama? Don't ever, ever tell him.'

I never did.

10

below in the street, Mr Ralston waits in his car. There's a plane to catch at the airport. Get the suitcase. Open it. Now pack. Keep moving. Concentrate. Don't stop because, if I stop, I mightn't be able to start again. Got everything? Now shut the suitcase.

But not quick enough. Suddenly, the world is aglow with the sunset. Grief sneaks up on me, gotcha, and my eyes prick with tears. The clouds seep with the fire of the falling sun. The flames spread higher through the clouds as if they are the branches of a burning tree.

At Te Reinga, the northernmost point of Aotearoa, there is a pohutukawa tree which grows on a promontory jutting into the sea. The promontory is called Rerenga Wairua. It is the place where all spirits gather when they die. Dad will be making his way there, with other Maori dead. On this, his last journey, he goes to wait for the sun to set. He will descend Aka ki Te Reinga, the Root to the Underworld, to a rocky platform on the edge of the sea. A deep hole will appear, fringed with floating seaweed. It is the way across the sea, the point of departure from the Overworld to the Underworld. Once the sun goes down, the spirits will leap into the hole, one after another, leaping, leaping, leaping. Dad will be among them. The waves will flow in. The seaweed will sweep over the hole. The platform where he was standing will be empty.

Already, the tree drips gold from the sun and the blossoms catch fire. Already the sea burns. Already Dad is looking back for me from Te Reinga. 'Don't go,

Dad,' I plead. 'Let the sea turn crimson, the pohutukawa tree blossom with flame, but don't make your last leap from earth yet. Not yet —'

The telephone rings in the hallway. The sound brings me back to reality. I walk quickly out of the bedroom to answer it.

'Is that you, Tama?' It's my girlfriend, Sandra. 'I've just rung your office and Ray told me you've had some bad news. Thank God I caught you at the flat. He told me you're on your way to the airport.'

'Yes,' I answer. 'I was going to call you from there. It's Dad. He died this morning.'

Dad really liked Sandra. He only met her once and kept kidding her about why she was wasting her time with somebody like me. 'You've obviously got intelligence,' he said, implying that she had made a very grave mistake in her choice of boyfriend.

'Oh no,' Sandra says. 'I'm so sorry, Tama. I thought it might be your mother. I know you've been worried about her. But it's your father? Honey, I know how much you loved your dad. How long will you be away?'

'A week or so,' I answer. 'The tangi will take three days and then there'll be a lot of other stuff to think about: the will, sorting out what Mum wants to do with the farm.' Does Mum want to keep the farm going or will she go and live with Ripeka? 'I'll call you when I know what's happening.'

'Do you want me to come to Gisborne for the funeral?' Sandra asks. 'I really liked your dad, Tama.'

'Do you want to? That would be just wonderful. I think I'll need you to be there with me.' At that moment, I love her more than I have ever loved her before. 'And will you let Jasper and William know?'

'I'll make bookings and come up to Gisborne as soon as I can,' Sandra says. 'Honey, be strong, won't you. Do give my love to your mother and my deepest respects to your family.'

I put the phone back down. Talking to Sandra has raised my spirits. How can anyone cope with any tragedy, any adversity, if you haven't got a shoulder to cry on?

Although my fears about facing Dad's death have returned, there's no more delaying. There is a plane to catch. I smooth my clothes. Close the windows. Go along the hallway and out the front door. Lock it.

Down on the road, Mr Ralston is waiting.

'All set, old chap?' Mr Ralston asks. 'Let's put your suitcase in the back. Sure you haven't forgotten anything? No? Off we go then.' He is avuncular, kind, keeping me moving. 'Let's see,' he says, looking at his watch, 'it's five o'clock now and you don't have to check in for your flight until half past. Good, we've just enough time to get you to your plane.'

Time . . . suddenly so important. A telephone call from home, just a few hours ago and here I am bringing my last moments with my father to a close. Tomorrow, the world is changed. If I had the power to do it, I would force those ticking hands back from the top of the clock, back to the faraway side of the hour.

We head seaward and turn left into the road that unwinds along the Parade. The wind has risen and the waves slap angrily against the sea wall. Kelp writhes beneath the surface. Sand churns muddy patterns among the waves as they break on the shore. A young boy plays with his small terrier on a stretch of sand. He throws a stick for his dog to fetch and shouts soundless commands to the wind. Further along, a man leans into the wind as he walks. He grips his coat tightly and holds onto his hat. In a calm patch of sea, a covey of seagulls waits out the rough weather.

Mr Ralston gives a slight cough. 'Was your father an old man, Tama?' he asks, making conversation.

'Fifty-five or fifty-six, I think.' Is that old? Mr Ralston must be approaching that age. But Maori don't live as long. Riripeti died in her fifties and so did many uncles and aunties of my whanau. Bearing lots of kids or smoking killed the women. Hard living, hard drinking and eating a dozen eggs a day for breakfast clogged the arteries and killed the men.

'And your mother, Tama? Is she taking it well?'

I nod and Mr Ralston offers a small gesture of sympathy. 'Thanks, Mr Ralston, I'm okay. It's a bit of a shock though. I never thought that Dad would . . . go.'

The car turns into Evans Bay and for a moment is buffeted by the wind. Small boats bob and sway in the marina. From out of nowhere, Mr Ralston starts talking about his own dad. 'You know,' he begins, 'I never knew my father. He and Mother met each other a few years before the First World War. He had come out from England to New Zealand. Mother was a farmer's daughter from Taranaki, and my father went up to New Plymouth to work on the railways. He was an engineer, a bridge builder. Anyhow, when the war began, he enlisted. But he and Mother decided to get married before he went. He died in France. He never knew about me —'

I look ahead. The road curves round the coastline into Lyall Bay. Beyond the Bay I can see the airport. A plane is taking off. It gathers speed, then lifts into the grey sky. There is a thunderous rumble as it disappears across Wellington, leaving a thin, wispy vapour trail.

'You're lucky to have known your father, Tama,' Mr Ralston continues. 'I have no memories of mine at all. What I have are photographs of him and Mother on their wedding day, some stories that Mother told me of his family in England, and the medals that he was awarded for his gallantry in action. When Mother married again, my stepfather, Robert, was everything a boy could wish for. Even so, there are times when I wish I could have known my real father.'

The car joins the stream of traffic moving toward Rongotai airport. Ahead is the terminal building, the parking lot, cars stopping and people trying to escape the storm and running inside. Soon I'll be flying to Gisborne. Ripeka has organised for Mere to meet me at Gisborne airport.

'Well, Tama,' Mr Ralston says, 'here we are. Do you want me to come in with you?'

'No,' I answer. 'I'll be okay. Thanks for bringing me here.' I get my suitcase from the back.

Mr Ralston grips my hand. He is trying to find some comforting words to say. In his editorials he is so direct and to the point; how ironic that in personal conversations he is so elliptical. 'The closest I ever got to my father,' he begins, 'was when I went to Staffordshire on a visit and I met Uncle Harry, his younger brother. He looked something like my father in photographs and when he greeted me, "Hello, lad," and shook my hand, I felt . . .' Mr Ralston's eyes are moist and his lips are trembling '. . . so close to my own father and, also, so far away. I realised how much I had missed him and how much would always be missing from my own life —'

Then he is gone. The car speeds away from the airport and joins the stream of traffic travelling back toward Wellington.

I turn and enter the terminal building. The doors close behind me. I am amid the echoing sounds of people conversing with one another, and the sharp clicking of people hurrying across the gleaming floor. A man brushes past me, dashing outside to hail a taxi. The wind disturbs a small shrub near the entrance. An air hostess flashes a quick smile from behind a counter. A thousand destinies are in motion. Mine is one of them.

For one brief moment the sun comes out, blazing through the dark evening clouds.

Oh, Sun, be my friend. If death must come, move quickly now. Let the three days of the tangi, the mourning time, pass by like a dream. Once you moved too fast across the sky and men were angry because you brought night too soon. You rose, raced fiercely across smaller hours, and plunged quickly into the sea. The demigod Maui changed all that. He waited for you to rise and ensnared you with a magic net. You battled against him and scattered the sky with flaming sparks. It was a long battle. Maui would not give in. Finally, you surrendered and promised you would move slowly and make the days longer. Only then did Maui release you.

Ae, Sun, I see the white whorls of light, the remnants of those taut thongs. I see your anguished form, still bent from that battle. But listen: your agony is my agony. Do not prolong it with such slow procession.

And all of a sudden I think of my mother and see her face. She too is staring at the sun but, unlike me, she would rather that it go slower and leave more time with Dad.

Hers has always been a handsome face. The features are sculpted of warm earth; the chiselled planes softened by wind, rain and sun. It is a face that has seen the passing of the seasons and understands that all things decay and fall of their own accord. A calm face, which understands the inevitable rhythms of life: that the sun rises and sets, night follows day, and that winter is always followed by spring.

The face belongs to a woman who has always cleaved to her husband. Once, she looked out the window and saw the hills streaming with rain. Her husband and son were still out there somewhere and she realised they must be running behind schedule; they hadn't come back to pick up the next lot of battens and take them across the river.

She attended to Ripeka, Mere and Wiki and then put on her gumboots and a raincoat. She went down to the shearing shed where the battens were stacked. She loaded them onto the packhorse, saddled another horse and rode down the track toward the river. The rain was bucketing down. Right at the moment she reached the river her husband and son arrived on the opposite side. Her husband realised what she intended to do — and that nothing would stop her.

'No, Huia, stay there. It's too dangerous.'

She had no intention of staying anywhere. She rode down to the river.

'Go back, Huia. Go back.' The river was swollen and thick with silt. It roared with the voice of thunder. Every now and then an uprooted tree would leap past upon the heaving water. 'Woman, are you deaf? Go back.'

Did she listen? No. Her husband's words went in one ear and out the other.

Her horse whinnied and backed away from the rushing water. She screamed at it, 'Hup! Hup!' She put her spurs into its side, urging it into the river. She pulled the packhorse after her. Her husband blanched, wondering if she was going to make it. Her son watched with pride, knowing that she would. But it was touch and go as the horse battled against the current. She held on tightly while the yellow water pounded down on her. The horse wanted to turn back. She pulled its head round again, towards the bank where her husband and son waited. The packhorse was faltering.

'Let the packhorse go,' her husband yelled.

Was she going to do that and waste all that energy and effort getting it across the river? What must her husband be thinking?

'Bloody stubborn woman.' He rushed down to the bank and waded towards her to help her. When he reached her, he lifted her from the horse. He embraced her in the rain. 'You shouldn't have done that,' he said.

No time to be sentimental. She was already handing him the reins to the packhorse. 'Don't stay out too late,' she said. Before he could stop her, she turned her horse back into the river. After all, she had to get back to her daughters at home.

My mother was the Earth. My father was the Sky. They were Ranginui and Papatuanuku, the first parents, who clasped each other so tightly that there was no day. Their children were born into darkness. They lived among the shadows of their mother's breasts and thighs and groped in blindness among the long black strands of her hair.

Until the time of separation and the dawning of the first day.

part three

11

the clouds catch fire from the sun. Below, the land is streaked with long shadows cast from the hills. Wellington already glitters with evening light. Above the clouds, it is still day. The sun is a glowing orb upon a sea of clouds. Everything is at peace here, above the world's storms. This quiet time is the sunset of my world. Soon, the dawning of my own day will burst with the wailing and grief of the tangi.

The sun disappears. The night comes, drenching the sky with darkness.

According to Maori mythology, the god Tane wished to have children to inherit the bright strand of earth which he had created when he separated Earth and Sky. His mother, Papatuanuku, told him to use the red earth which was to be found at her sexual cleft. Tane fashioned his woman and she is known as Hineahuone, the woman made from earth. Tane breathed life into her and took her virginity.

Hineahuone's purpose was to become the mother of progeny who were half godly and half earthly. The daughter that was born of her union with Tane was Hinetitama, child of the dawn. She was bright, lovely and innocent, and grew up not knowing that Tane was her father. Without this knowledge, she was not to blame when Tane took her to wife and mated with her. This was the First Incest. However, Hinetitama was of a curious nature and, when Tane wouldn't tell her who her father was, she asked the posts that had been used to construct the house she and Tane lived in. The posts answered her, 'Tane the husband is also Tane the father.' Shame overwhelmed her. She left Te Ao Marama, the world of light, and fled to Rarohenga. She reached the guardhouse of Poutererangi and sought entry from Te Kuwatawata, the guardian of the gateway. Taking one last look at the Overworld, she saw Tane following swiftly after her.

'Haere atu, Tane,' she farewelled him. 'Hapai a tatou tamariki i te ao. Goodbye, Tane. Raise our children in the light. I shall stay here, to gather them to me in death.'

From child of the dawn, she became Hinenuitepo, whom all men must follow into Rarohenga, the world after death.

I feel a soft hand touching me. The woman sitting next to me is afraid. Her name is Anne, she must be in her forties, and this is her first flight on a plane. 'Are you sure we'll be all right?' she asks again.

'Quite sure,' I answer. When I boarded, Anne was seated next to the window but asked if we could swap so that she could be in an aisle seat. Bravely she leans across me to take a look.

'Oh, dear,' she says, biting her lips. 'It feels strange to be so far off the ground.'

I try to change the conversation. 'Do you come from Gisborne, too?'

'Oh, dear no,' Anne answers, 'I'm a grandmother.' Realising that she doesn't make sense, she explains. 'My daughter got married a while ago to a doctor. He practises in Gisborne. They've just had a baby. It's my first grandchild. It's such a special occasion, that's why I'm flying there. And you? Do you come from Gisborne?'

'Gisborne's my family home,' I tell her. 'I'm going home to see . . . to see my father.'

Going home . . . as others of the Mahana clan will be doing tonight. Perhaps Dad has sent his wairua to them. They see him in the twilight, waving from a pohutukawa tree ablaze with sunset. Or they will see a sign: a morepork, or a moth flitting against a window. The Matua once told me, 'Why should people be so afraid of one of nature's harbingers? They are only messengers from one world to the other. Whenever you see them, acknowledge them and say, "Thank you for delivering your message." Don't go into hysterics like Maka tiko bum.'

Whatever way the message is delivered, the tribe will know that someone has died and they will make ready to answer the call. And so they will journey. The voice of the tangi has curled across the land. A member of the whanau has gone, and the breaking apart is so profound that the sudden emptiness is felt in every heart.

The plane passes through some turbulence. I am brought back to Anne's voice. 'So when my daughter, Georgia's her name, told me she was pregnant, I just couldn't believe it. Me, a grandmother? No!'

'You don't look old enough to be a grandmother.'

'Why, thank you!' Anne smiles, pleased. 'It's a boy, you know, the baby. Arthur they've called him. After my husband. I'm a widow. My husband died a few years ago. You get over it after a while. At first it's such a shock but . . .'

My memory goes back to my grandmother Riripeti's tangi. Part of my anxiety about Dad's death is because when the Matriarch died, I was not very good at accepting her death. I was too young to fully understand, and the emotion of the tangi was more than I could bear. Dad received a telephone call from his oldest brother, Te Ariki, who asked him to pick up Uncle Alexis, arriving that evening by train from Wellington. Uncle Alexis looked as if he had been crying for years. All the way to Waituhi we children sat in the back. Dad and Mum were in the front and, although Dad was driving, Uncle had his head on Dad's shoulder. They were all speaking in Maori so we couldn't understand what they were saying. Uncle was so grief-stricken that he made us sad, too.

When we arrived at Rongopai, Riripeti looked as magnificent and as charismatic in death as she had been in life. She wore pearls in her hair and she was lying there as if she was just asleep. She was surrounded by black-gowned kuia, and they were weeping and sobbing. When we came onto the marae, they started to wail.

I had never heard such a sound. I became very frightened. Tamati Kota, Riripeti's priest, called us on. But Uncle Alexis couldn't wait. He stumbled across the marae and flung himself across his mother, holding her and calling out her name. It all seemed so final. That's when I thought to myself, 'Don't die, Dad. don't ever die like Riripeti.'

It was only when Dad and I were standing before Riripeti that I realised the immensity of that moment. He gave a groan which seemed to come from out of the depths of Te Po, the Great Night.

'Mum . . .' He sank to his knees. In his deep groan was conveyed the immeasurable loss of losing a parent. My own understanding did not come until we were lowering Riripeti into the cool ground.

Anne takes some photographs out of her handbag. They are of her daughter, her daughter's partner and her new baby grandson. Across the aisle, another passenger engages Anne in conversation.

'A new grandchild, eh?' he asks. Delighted and proud, Anne leans across to involve him in her happy news. 'Why,' he says, 'the baby looks just like you!'

Their world is happy. How can that be so? My father is dead, yet they laugh and chatter.

'Goodbye, Riripeti.'

Grandmother's casket was lowering, my uncles straining at the ropes to ensure that it had a slow and controlled descent. As it thudded to rest, my uncles let go the ropes, which slackened and fell. It had been raining and the bottom of the grave was wet. Around the graveside, the mourners were stricken with grief.

'Aue, Matua. Haere ki te Po, haere, haere, haere.' The women were keening, that high, extraordinary sound of a hundred hearts breaking. My grandmother was going away, never to return. Her casket lay in the earth.

Tamati Kota ordered the gravediggers to begin shovelling the dirt in. The earth splashed in the puddles and thudded on the casket. Each thudding was like a dull bell tolling. My father joined his brothers in performing a ritual haka.

'Ka mate, ka mate! ka ora, ka ora!

It is death, it is death! It is life, it is life!'

The wailing soared, lifting above the hill, and aimed sharp blows at heaven. The sky opened and rain began to fall. The rain diverted me and I asked Dad, 'Why is it raining?'

Dad took the time to answer, 'It always rains when a chief dies, son.'

When I looked back at the grave, the burial was over. But for a long time after, I had to have the light on in my room during the night. Even then I would wake up, screaming, and thrust my arms into the air to make sure I hadn't been buried.

One night, a beautiful moth came into the room with markings like pearls across its wings. A messenger between our worlds, it started to whir around the room and then alighted on my shoulder, its wings glowing.

Go to sleep, grandchild. Be at peace now.

I turned down the lamp. The oil burnt low. I never needed the lamp again.

12

The Wharerata ranges fall away. The train speeds from their shadows and clacks along the widening river valley. A highway follows the river out of the hills and runs parallel with the railway. The valley widens and, with splayed fingers, takes one final grasp of the earth. The train roars past the fingertips into Nuhaka and steams slowly into the station.

'Can we get off here, guard?' a man asks.

'Sorry,' the guard answers. 'We're just picking up passengers. First refreshment stop will be at Wairoa.'

A soldier gets on the train and lifts his canvas bag onto a luggage rack; outside, a young pregnant woman waves to him. From the other end of the carriage, a Maori girl carrying a guitar gets on and finds her seat. She winds down the window and whispers affectionately to her grandmother on the platform. 'E kui, kaua koe e tangi.'

'I am crying for my granddaughter,' the old lady answers.

'Ahakoa e haere tawhiti ana ahau,' the girl answers, 'to manawa, e taku manawa, mo ake, mo ake. Although I'm going away, a long way, your heart is my heart, for always, for ever.'

The grandmother's lips quiver, and she brushes her tears with the edge of her scarf. She presses her face against the window and reaches up to caress the girl. A bell on the platform rings. Passengers rush back to the train, shoving past the old woman. 'Haere ra, Arihia. Ka hoki mai ano. Goodbye, Arihia. Come back to me soon.'

The train begins to move again. The carriage fills with the strains of the girl as she strums on her guitar and sings quietly to herself. The train rocks and sways, as if to the rhythm of her song. Out of Nuhaka the train speeds, past green paddocks and small wooden farmhouses. A milk truck trundles along the highway and the driver looks across at the thundering train. Then, there is the sea, sparkling with the bright sun. It is a long blue ribbon, tying the land to the sky. Sand dunes reach up, cutting the ribbon, until there is only earth and sky. At one section of the line, men are working. The train slows down as it passes them. A man leans on his shovel, wiping the sun's heat from his brow. Another lights a cigarette. Then they are gone.

The door to the carriage opens. The guard enters. 'Wairoa in two minutes.' He passes down the aisle.

At Wairoa, I mill with people at the railway cafeteria, shoving forward to the counter for a pie, a soft drink and a bar of chocolate. Other passengers stand beside the train, conversing and laughing. The young soldier puffs at his cigarette and watches the girls pass by. I lean against a railway hoarding, watching and thinking.

Following the contract job near Ruatoria my mother, whom I had always thought of as being so strong, became ill. I don't know what ailed her because from the outside she looked well, but inside something was broken. Dad couldn't look after her and us by himself so he packed us all up and moved us back to the Waituhi valley, to the bosom of the tribe. There he found us a place to live in a small cottage close to Miro Mananui's house and managed to get a job working for the Wi Pere Estate as a hired hand. As for us, we started school at nearby Patutahi Primary School and settled ourselves among our blood kin. Two months later Mum was still not well so Dad took her to Nani Miro to be healed.

The Matua scolded Dad. 'The only trouble with Huia,' she said, 'is that no sooner has she had one baby than she has another. She's had too many babies too soon and you, Rongo, you should know better.' However, it was clear to that clairvoyant old lady that Mum's illness was more deeply rooted. She suggested that Mum should have a break. 'Huia needs a really long rest,' she said. 'Four months, maybe five.'

We assumed that Mum would go to her folks on the East Coast for her rest but, instead, she decided to go to stay with her younger sister, Auntie Maggie, down in the South Island. 'Maggie always makes your mother laugh,' Dad said.

Mum wept when we saw her off on the bus. 'How will you get along without me?' she asked. She was extremely distressed.

'Don't worry about us,' Dad answered. 'You'll be back soon. Meantime, you must get better. And I'll have a surprise for you when you come home.'

My sisters and I loved surprises. But we hated having to wait to find out what they were. 'Tell us, tell us!' we pleaded. 'What's Mum's surprise?'

'You'll just have to wait and see,' Dad said.

Te Whanau a Kai panapana maro.
Te Whanau a Kai never retreat.

Waituhi . . . It was the place of the heart, a Maori village eighteen kilometres from Gisborne. There were no shops, no reason at all for Waituhi to be here except that this was the hearth of the Whanau a Kai. This was their home and here they lived. They were the tangata whenua and they had fought tooth and nail to hold on to their land.

To get to Waituhi, you headed inland, northwest from Gisborne city, taking your bearings from Maungatapere, a prominent flat-topped hill. Just past Matawhero you came to a red, one-way bridge spanning the river, famed because of the races to the bridge by two competing shearing gangs — the Mahana gangs from Waituhi and the Poata gangs from Manutuke. On the other side of the bridge you had three destinations to choose from: south to Manutuke, west to Ngatapa (if you followed this road you reached the mountain fortress where Maori rebels were executed by government troops in 1869), or northwest to Patutahi. You went to the Patutahi turnoff, took a right past the pub, primary school and war memorial — after the Land Wars all this land was confiscated from Te Whanau a Kai — and, once you were over a small bridge, you knew you were nearing Waituhi.

Every day, returning on the schoolbus from Patutahi, I always looked forward to the first glimpse of the village. Once the bus was over the bridge, there it was, the entrance: a powerful-looking hill, Pukepoto, an ancient Maori fort. Beyond Pukepoto, a sharp corner curved round the terraces of the ancient fort; below was the Dodds' colonial home.

Waituhi was my Eden. The fort protected it at one end, a sacred mountain at the other, and the Waipaoa River ran right through the middle of it. The houses were strung like beads along the road, named Lavenham Road by the Pakeha surveyors and contractors who constructed it along an old Maori track. Most of the houses were very old, with paint peeling from the boards and rusting corrugated roofs. Some were state houses, shining and new. A few were just tin shacks, lined with sheets of newspaper and pictures from magazines. Dilapidated caravans, like mechanical horses, were hitched to a couple of the houses. Dirt tracks led from the road and along them lived others of my family. More wooden houses dotted the paddocks like tiny ships bobbing on a sea of tall waving maize, or clustered about with fruit trees — loquat, apple, pear and lemon — and willows. On one side of Waituhi were the hills, pushing small spurs down towards the village. Cattle and sheep grazed on the slopes. On the other side, the flat land rolled away to the river. The river changed its course across this country many times. During the winter, it was swollen with silted water.

There were three main meeting houses in Waituhi: Pakowhai, Rongopai and Takitimu. Sometimes I would meet Dad after he had finished work on the Wi Pere Estate and we would walk back to our home past Pakowhai. If we met anybody we would stop and talk. Sometimes, somebody would wave to us from Takitimu and we'd wave back. If it was twilight, always somewhere we'd hear a guitar being strummed. Of the three marae, Rongopai held the place of honour. It was set near the side of a hill. Beside the meeting house was a tin cookhouse. Behind, there were fields, some covered with gorse. Everywhere were tall purple Scotch thistles, waving in the wind.

Rongopai was the heart of Eden, the centre of my universe. On our walks homeward through the village, Dad and I would often stop there and have a drink from the spring behind it. He would unlatch the gate and stand before the meeting house, silent a moment. I would see the roof, sloping upward to the painted koruru at the apex; the koruru held up the sky. I would see the paint peeling from the panels of the maihi, the boards extending like arms from the koruru, to welcome me. Inside the porch, I would glimpse swirling kowhaiwhai designs and other painted decorations. This was the meeting house of my tupuna, my ancestors. It was my meeting house too. When Dad opened the door I beheld the millennial dreams of the iwi.

Walking into Rongopai was like stepping into a bright, illuminated forest. It was like entering another world. There was no other illumination except the light which streamed through the open door. The floor was dirt. The panels took root in the soil: they were tall, elaborately painted in greens, blues and reds. Made of pukatea wood, they extended along both walls like trees. Vines twined and climbed around them, curling up to the roof. Between them, brilliant flowers blossomed in a profusion of extraordinary colours. As we opened the door further, crimson petals drank in the light. Fantastic birds flew through that timeless forest. They were joined by fabulous monsters of the deep ocean and creatures from myth and fantasy. And the ancestors were everywhere in that holistic world where the natural and supernatural conjoined.

I gasped every time I saw that illuminated interior. It always filled me with wonder. I would look up at the roof, my eyes following the glistening creatures as they slithered amid the stars of that woven sky. Everywhere painted people stood among the trees or climbed among the branches as they soared upward to the rafters. As I followed Dad into Rongopai, that world reached outward to enclose me.

Here was where my tupuna lived. Woven into the panels above the door were the eyes of the twins who had been murdered by Tupurupuru. Dad pointed them out to me, and then others from our tribal past. He showed me how the young men had changed tradition. On one panel was an ancestor who wore in his hair not the royal huia feather but a Scotch thistle. On another, a young woman stood timeless in a Pakeha gown, holding a rose to her lips. Strange animals appeared from amid the painted foliage. At a third panel, I knelt down to take a closer look at two men sparring in a boxing match. And there, on a fourth, horses gleamed as they lifted their hooves in a never-ending race. Right at the end of the building, figures reached out of the darkness to brandish taiaha and mere, spear and fighting club. There, standing by his parliamentary chair was my ancestor, Wi Pere Halbert, with his mother Riria Mauaranui sitting on his shoulder like a wise owl.

These were my people and this was my meeting house. They were tupuna and they were glad that I had come. I heard their laughter, glittering like a waterfall in my ears. As I listened, Dad told me the history of Rongopai and our village's place in the resistance history of Aotearoa.

'Son, our family have always been followers of Te Kooti Arikirangi. He was wrongfully imprisoned after the fall of Waerenga a Hika Pa in 1865. This happened during the Poverty Bay wars with the Pakeha. They sent Te Kooti and his followers to the Chatham Islands but he escaped and returned to us as a holy man in 1868. The Spirit of God had visited him and told him he had work to do, establishing the Lord's Maori church in Aotearoa. And so we became Ringatu, son, and it was my mother Riripeti who became the leader of the church in this Waituhi valley. We follow the Old Testament that God preached to Moses. But the Pakeha would not leave Te Kooti in peace and they pursued him throughout the land and there was much killing on both sides. Many Pakeha were killed at Matawhero when Te Kooti attacked the military garrison there on 9 November 1868; many Maori went to their deaths at the executions of the rebels on 4 January 1869. But Te Kooti survived, son, and this meeting house was built for him and completed in 1887.'

That was long ago, even before Dad's time. The work was carried out by young men who painted Rongopai with bright swirling colours. It was one of the very few painted meeting houses remaining and was still beautiful to look upon, despite the decay brought by wind, rain and sun. But when it was finished, the elders came and some say they were shocked at what they saw. The young men, in decorating the house, had departed from the traditional designs. They had blended both Maori and Pakeha art and scenes of life together. For the elders, this was not right. But perhaps even then, the young men had seen that the old life was ending. Perhaps the young men were foretelling the coming of a new Maori generation.

> *Kei muri i te awe kapara he tangata ke,*
> *mana te ao, he ma.*
> *Shadowed behind the tattooed face*
> *a stranger stands, he who will claim the earth,*
> *and he is without tattoo.*

My father wasn't often vocal about his politics, but there were times when his fires could be stoked. On one of our visits to Rongopai, he pressed me close. 'It is you, son, and your generation, who must work for the people, just as Riripeti did. You must help the iwi to get the whenua back, the land taken by the Pakeha soldiers in retribution for our resistance against them. All the expanse between here and Patutahi is ours.'

We stayed long and often at Rongopai, where I would pledge my allegiance again and again to the house and the tribe and the valley. I was always aware of the whakapapa, the genealogy, the line of ancestors from whom I was descended. For me they were not in the past. The past was always in front of us, a long line of ancestors to whom I was accountable and with whom I had an implicit contract. At the time I was only too willing to commit myself to the valley. Little did I realise that when my ambitions began to take me beyond the valley and out into the wide world, I would be placed on a collision course with my commitment to the valley and the people I loved.

I walked Lavenham Road many times during those months we lived in Waituhi, sometimes with Dad, sometimes with my best cousins Tamatea, Simeon, Michael and Haromi, and sometimes by myself. During that time, I made a kind of breakthrough, the type where a lightbulb goes on in your head. I was reading my encyclopedia and brushing up on the states of the USA when it dawned on me that I knew more about Wisconsin and Washington DC than I did about Waituhi. The thought floored me, and I went up to the ridge above Takitimu Hall where the village graveyard was, to think about it. I wandered through the cemetery, paid my respects to Riripeti and said hello to Rawiri, my dead brother. Somebody had left a shovel lying against the fence. I picked it up and began to clear away gorse that was creeping across some of the older graves. After a while, sweating, I took a breather and sat down.

I could see all Waituhi from the ridge. From that hill known as Tawhiti Kaahu, I could see the houses of the Matua and Nani Tama, Bulibasha and Grandmother Ramona, Uncle Pita, Aunt Teria and, behind Maka tiko bum's place, Sam Walker's shack. On the outskirts of the village was the old homestead where Riripeti had reigned and, not too far along from it, the small cottage where Dad had brought my sisters and me to live while Mum was away getting better. It was spring, and the fields were green with crops of kumara and sweetcorn. The orchards were orange and yellow, ripe with fruit.

What was life all about? That afternoon, I sat between the earth and the sky, the dead and the living, Waituhi and the world beyond, and the past, present and future. I came to realise that the world close to me was just as important as the world far away.

But it was not enough for me to know this. Others had to know it too.

The Maori girl with her guitar has started to sing. When I look at her, I see that she is unaware that her voice is carrying through the carriage. There is such unconscious beauty and innocence in her voice. Other passengers smile and sway with her song.

Me he manurere, aue,
Kua rere ki to moenga,
Ki te awhi to tinana,
Aue, aue, e te tau tahuri mai . . .

The song fills me with memories, warm and playful, of Waituhi my home. Some of the memories are wistful, magical and as fleeting as the wind. Of feeling the earth, our land, beneath my feet, the sun soaring over the hills, the wind blowing across fields and seeing sun-stars scattering light across the Waipaoa River.

I remember a gathering of the tribe for a Ringatu commemoration of Grandmother Riripeti's death. All the Ringatu faithful were there, the iwi and aunties, uncles, cousins and friends. Tamati Kota officiated at the church service. Afterwards there was a big feast presided over by Uncle Te Ariki, Riripeti's eldest. It was the largest Ringatu and tribal gathering I had ever seen, a tremendous demonstration of kotahitanga, unity and kinship.

A Maori hockey tournament at Waituhi, that I remember also. The teams came from all over Poverty Bay, parading with self-conscious pride around the muddy field. Pennants fluttered in the wind. Nani Miro told my beautiful cousin, Moana, to play for the Waituhi women's team because they were short a player. On she went, exchanging high-heels for hockey boots and tucking her designer-label dress into her pants. The women's games were always fierce and funny, particularly when we played Hukareka, our arch enemies. The play was the subject of lots of sideline barracking and cheering, and goals scored and not scored were argued over again and again. As for the men's games, I remember one in which I played against Dad. He kept on saying to me, 'Will you let your father get a goal, eh? I'm old. You be a good son!' When he actually did manage to get past me, I was pissed off. I got ribbed by Simeon, 'Hey, Tama, don't let your old man beat you!'

The close kinship of the shearing gang is among my memories. Old man Bulibasha had set up the Mahana family as a shearing dynasty with four shearing gangs on the go. That summer I joined Michael and Haromi as shed hands for Mahana No. 4, bossed by Uncle Hone. Actually, I hated those five o'clock starts, day after day through summer, but at least I worked in the shearing shed; much better to work there, as a roustabout, than as a kitchenhand in the cookhouse under the steely eye and hard-hitting hand of Auntie Molly. While I worked I often fantasised that I was on holiday in Fiji. The closest I ever got to a pineapple was juice out of a can at smoko time. However, when I accepted my fate, I could find epiphanic moments in shearing. The family working together. The drone of handpieces. The bustle of women on the board. The cry of Sheepo! Hot dust. Somewhere, the clanking of the press. My cousin, Mohi, the Stud Who Walks, used to brag as he sheared, 'I was born to this game!' Not me, though. I daydreamed about jobs that didn't start until eight o'clock and that were as far away from sheep dags as possible.

Kapa haka concerts at Takitimu Hall I remember, too. The thunderous applause and yells for a number well sung. Aunt Sarah singing for all she was worth. Haromi, my cousin, swinging as much as possible so that the boys could see her lovely legs. The swishing and crackling of the piupius. The quivering of hands moving in unison. The stamping feet of the men as the Mahana boys moved through the ranks, chanting the haka:

> *Ko Ruaumoko e ngunguru nei!*
> *Au! Au! Aue ha!*

I loved standing next to my father, uncles and cousins. I'd see Dad, sweating with the exertion of the haka and tease him, 'Come on, old man! Lift those feet! Not enough kaha! Put some more energy into it!'

The weekend dances at Patutahi, they were also fun. Simeon and I would stand near the door, eager hopefuls eyeing the girls as they walked past. 'Which one do you want, cuz?' he would ask. 'That one there, in the red dress,' I'd answer, but the truth was that any girl would have been okay. Sometimes we were lucky and would pick up a couple of girls and take them into the middle of the dance floor. Once we got there the object was to be cool, real laidback, man. The trouble was that sometimes we were so cool the girls would get bored and go off with other boys who were, well, hotter. I remember a party at Nani Tama's home. Mind you, he often had to wait until Nani Miro left the house for a couple of days on some tribal or land business or other before phoning everybody. 'The old lady's gone,' he'd say, 'let's get down and dirty.' For as long she was away, the beery songs echoed through the darkness. People going, people coming, people passing out. Nani Tama used to say to me, 'Come on, nephew, have a glass, I won't tell your father. Come on, it'll make you a man!' Once, I arrived home after the party, drunk. Dad was waiting for me. 'You can go and sleep with the dogs, tonight, son. I'm not having a drunk in the house.' Of course, when Nani Miro returned to Waituhi from her business, she always knew about the parties. 'I could smell the beer even before I hit Patutahi.'

Waituhi was the close kinship of the whanau. Sometimes we got too close. Ripeka often agreed with Haromi when she moaned that everybody knew each other's business, even before they did themselves. Waituhi was big family with big heart, laughing and squabbling, then laughing again. It was helping each other with money or in the fields. It was growing up with uncles, aunties and cousins as one family. Waituhi was about keeping open house, too. If anybody didn't have a home, you invited them in. Sam Walker came to stay with us for a month because his father, the uptight Hepa Walker, sir, had kicked him out. I went to stay at Uncle Pita's after a party one night, scared because Dad had locked the doors on me at midnight — and I hadn't made it home by curfew. The next day I sneaked home but Dad was waiting to wallop me.

Waituhi was the place of the heart. When you went out getting kina and paua at Makarori Beach, you stopped off at other houses to ask if anybody else wanted to go diving. When you returned home, you told everybody to come round and have a good kai. If somebody got married, nobody waited for an invitation; you just went to the wedding, because you were a member of the family. And if there was a tangi, you stopped whatever you were doing and went home to pay your respects, acknowledge your kinship and blood ties and help support the bereaved family. The tangi, it was the homecalling.

Home was Waituhi. It was all the family living together around Rongopai, the family meeting house. We lived belonging to each other, not apart from each other. We lived with our family present and our family dead who slept on the hill near Rongopai.

'This is where your bones are,' Dad would say. 'They lie deep in the land, they sleep lovingly in the memory.'

For us, yes, as long as we stayed in Waituhi. But for others?

My father had relatives who lived in Gisborne and, next door, there was a girl who would watch out for me whenever I visited. She'd be sitting on the fence, and she'd yell and scream, 'Maori boy! Maori boy!'

I've always been puzzled about her. That young Maori girl not knowing she was the same as me, pointing a finger at one of her own.

13

the air hostess walks down the aisle, pausing to bend and talk with passengers. 'Are you all right, sir? Would you like a magazine, madam? We have *Time*, *Newsweek, Australian Post, Pix* . . .'

Anne watches her with admiration. 'She's very efficient, isn't she? I can't believe she spends every day flying on a plane and, here I am, wanting to get my feet back on the ground.' She giggles — and the plane dips suddenly in an air pocket. 'Oh dear,' she gasps. She clutches the armrest. 'Did you feel that? Oh.'

The plane rocks again. The air hostess comes alongside. 'Just a bit of turbulence, madam,' she says reassuringly. 'Nothing to worry about. The weather over Gisborne isn't the best at the moment. A cold front has come up from the south. Strap yourself in — it could get bumpier.'

Anne and the air hostess laugh together. Anne begins to show her the photographs of her grandson, Arthur. I turn away. Outside, the sun has moved below the clouds like a glowing golden meniscus. The night is coming, stealing across the horizon, spellbinding.

I remember other magical nights, when the sky was so clear that you could see all the way to the end of the universe. They were the calm summer nights of that time in Waituhi, while Mum was away in the South Island. On some of those evenings, the sky above Waituhi was like a funnel and all the stars of the Milky Way would shower down upon us.

One night, Dad and I went eeling. We headed out behind Waituhi to Lake

Repongaere, which was well known for its tuna. In fact, it was a giant eel which made the lake. The warrior who hooked it would not let it go, and they battled each other for many days. The tuna thrashed around so hard that it created a huge hollow and, when the rain came down, the water filled the hole.

Dad and I had oil lamps and we wandered along the banks of the lake. We came to a bend where trees drifted their branches in the dark water. 'This is a good place,' Dad said. He placed a lamp over the edge and I could see the flame reflected in the water. The eels came, attracted to the light, to twist and slide — steely shapes beneath the water. 'Now,' Dad called. We thrust with spears at them.

Caught up in the excitement, I kept spearing the eels, one after the other, as if I was racing Dad. As they were lifted out of the lake, they flashed the moonlight from their wriggling backs, scattering the darkness with shafts of silver. With a laugh I saw that I had more eels at my feet than Dad had at his. I saw the surprise in his eyes and the way he looked at me, as if he'd never really seen me before.

'You're growing up, aren't you,' he said.

We stayed beside the lake for a long time. The lamps burnt out and there was no more oil. 'We'd better be getting back,' Dad said.

We packed up and, with the eels in sugarbags over our shoulders, headed back home from the lake. The stars were wheeling across the sky like fish trying to escape a net being thrown to catch them.

Dad paused halfway down the valley. 'Son,' he began, 'I should have seen it before, that one day, you'll be a man. Right now, if you have bad dreams, you need only open your eyes and they'll be gone. But when you're a man and facing life's nightmares, they'll still be there when you wake up. Sometimes, son, things happen in life that you can't control. This business with your mother, for instance, how were any of us to know it would be so serious? And even though I'm the head of the family, who knows when or if I might get sick or have an accident or not be around to look after you all?'

It was a long speech and Dad's words were trembling with anxiety. 'You're the oldest, Tama. If anything happens to me, you come home straight away. The oldest always looks after the younger ones of the family. I was taught that as a child; I teach you the same thing now. If I should die, come home to your mother and your sisters.'

It was the first time my father had ever mentioned the possibility of dying. 'Don't talk like that, Dad.'

'I have to go sometime, son. Everybody does. One of these days I will be caught, just like the eels we have caught tonight, on the hook of death. You just remember, that's all. If anything should happen to me, come back. That's the Maori way. My father said these words to me when I was your age. I say the same words to you now. Never forget.'

The wings of the plane dip. The engine takes on a different sound. 'We're beginning our descent to Gisborne airport,' the air hostess tells us. 'Please check that your seatbelts are fastened.'

The plane rocks violently. 'Oh, dear,' Anne gasps. 'How much longer before we're on the ground?'

Suddenly we are through the clouds. It's raining, and the window streaks with raindrops flicking away into the night. Far below is the sea, like a sheet of tin made silver by the moon, rippling with corrugations. Nestling in the bay is Gisborne, dripping with gleaming lights.

'I didn't think it would look so beautiful,' Anne says.

In the falling rain, the lights of the city look like a lot of small fires streaking the night. The lights leap up as if this is the entrance to Rarohenga, the domain of Hinenuitepo. Some people consider that when she transformed from Hinetitama, child of the dawn, she became a monstrous inversion of herself. Her eyes were said to be flecked with greenstone. Her hair was sea-kelp still moist from the sea. She was a fearsome apparition with a mouth like a barracouta. I like to think of her differently. Not as some Maori Medusa but, rather, as the Great Mother who gives birth to us and who, in death, takes us back to her breast at the end of our lives.

Ahead, the airport flames in the dark. Lining both sides of the runway are points of firelight flickering.

'Is anybody meeting you?' Anne asks. The hum of the plane whines lower and the earth rises.

'My sister, Mere.' The plane glides lower. The wheels have unfolded from the undercarriage. The landing lights flash on and off, on and off. A sharp shriek of tyres, a jolt, and the plane rolls quickly between the flickering lights, taxiing towards the terminal. The passengers peer out into the night at the people huddled in the blazing light, waiting. Where are you, Mere?

'Well, we're here,' Anne says with a sigh. 'On the ground. Thank you for being so kind and patient with me. Goodbye.' She joins the passengers as they file out of the plane. I watch them as they step quickly across the tarmac toward the terminal building. They are shadows, moving into the brightness of another world. I unbuckle my seatbelt and stand. My head whirls.

At the door, the air hostess smiles, 'Goodbye, sir.'

Mere, where are you? The wind is cold. My feet click slowly across the tarmac into the arc of lights. People are milling at the gateway, greeting, laughing, and embracing one another.

Where are you, sister? One step. And one step further now.

Then I see her, coming out of the darkness. She walks towards me, through the milling people, through the laughing crowd, towards the gate. Of all of us children, Mere was the one who loved and needed Dad the most. Now that he is gone, she must be really hurting. Realising this, I offer a plea to Hinenuitepo.

'Great Mother of the Night, I beg of you, give our father back. Across the night, these dark strands of your hair, I will journey to make my plea. Toward your domain in Rarohenga, unafraid. From your guardian of the Underworld, Te Kuwatawata, I will gain entrance through the gateway. I will come to your house, Wharaurangi. In the courtyard before your house, I will beg with you: Give our father back to the light. Give him back to my mother, his daughters and his young son. Me, the oldest, take me instead. Me, Great Mother. Take me.'

This is my journey into the Underworld. Far ahead I can see the points of flame glittering.

Mere rushes into my arms.

14

The train sways and clatters over a railway bridge. A startled kingfisher skims away, casting its outstretched wings across my mind. Across the land of Maui the train rushes, along a jagged fin of Te Ika a Maui. The sun leaps toward midday.

People are dozing in the heat. A child cries because he is thirsty. His mother strokes him tenderly, looking with glazed eyes out on the passing country. The schoolboy takes off his cap to brush at his forehead.

The train curves outward, following the railway track as it loops along the perimeter of the ranges. It passes through a deep ravine, along a steep embankment and through a series of tunnels. On the other side, the hills unfold, rugged and rising up to the sun, an almost limitless vista stretching into a distant sky. The train shudders at another bend and jerks up an incline. The window is drenched with blue, the colour of dreams, the colour of the sea. Below the train, the cliff face falls away onto a long winding beach. A promontory juts into the waves. White gannets wheel above it; white foam curls among the rocks below. Slowly the sea unfolds until there seems no land, only sea merging into sky, a strand of sparking blue. The rays of the sun are ropes of the net cast across the sun's face by Maui.

During the Hawke's Bay earthquake, the sea claimed all the land the train traverses. Ruaumoko awoke from the breast of Papatuanuku, and split the earth with his awakening yawn. With his fiery hands, he pushed up the land and toppled the city that stood above him.

Time has taken my father away. And this too is my life beginning again.

Napier. With a hiss of steam, the train arrives at the platform. Passengers alight, passengers depart. People rush on the platform. Bags are unloaded, luggage loaded. Passengers board the train. On the platform a group of teenagers take the chance to relax with a game of basketball. The young soldier joins in. Then the train whistle sounds and a voice over the loudspeaker announces the departure of the train.

I realise how long this journey to Wellington will be. It is just past midday; the train will not arrive until late at night. Across this land of Te Ika a Maui it will roar, through Waipukurau, Palmerston North and all the small towns that make up this country.

The train thunders through Napier. Houses have been built where the sea once was. A road runs where there was once no land. Crops now grow on the old seabed. Passengers look out the windows at the passing houses, which form small clusters along the railway track. The passengers settle themselves again into the journey. The carriage hums with their quiet conversations. A chance meeting, perhaps. Introductions exchanged. A life enriched with a new friend. Life, too, is people on a train. The train curves onward, ever onward.

When Mum came back from the South Island, it was clear that she was still not well. She had been phoning regularly and sending us letters from Auntie Maggie's on the West Coast. Whenever the post van came, my sisters and I would race each other to the letterbox to see if she had written. 'Dad! Dad! There's a letter for us from Mum!'

A letter from our mother seemed like a message from the other side of the world. We'd huddle around Dad as he read it to us. 'Dear children,' Mum would write in her careful hand. 'How are you all? Are you helping your father in his work and not being too much trouble for him? I hope so. I know you are all good children. As for me, your Auntie Maggie is helping me to get better and I can't wait to come home to you all. I miss you all very, very much. I think of you all every day and hope that God is looking after you. Love, Mum.'

Finally, a telegram arrived from Auntie Maggie: 'WILD HORSES HAVE NOT BEEN ABLE TO KEEP HUIA FROM COMING HOME TO YOU STOP SHE IS WELL ENOUGH AND LEFT THIS MORNING STOP SHE CROSSES ON THE COOK STRAIT FERRY TONIGHT AND SHOULD ARRIVE GISBORNE

TOMORROW BY RAILWAY SERVICES BUS FROM WELLINGTON IN THE AFTERNOON AT SIX STOP.'

We waited for Mum at the Gisborne bus terminal. The afternoon was waning. As the bus approached, I could see her face gleaming at the window like a glowing star. Fear was in her eyes and, when the bus came to a stop, she looked as if she didn't want to get off. But when the door opened, there she was, stepping down.

Dad had made us all dress in our Sunday best for the occasion. I was wearing my school shorts. Ripeka, Mere and Wiki were in identical pale yellow frocks and Dad had on an open-necked white shirt and a sports jacket. My sisters ran into our mother's arms, 'Mummy, Mummy, we've missed you.' Mum hugged them and gave a deep, hoarse moan. For a moment, Dad and I watched the reunion.

Then Mum looked up and saw me, astonished, and cried, 'This can't be my Tama. This handsome young man?' She sounded as if she hadn't seen me for years.

Dad came forward, hesitant, unsure, and said to her, 'It's so good to have you back, dear.' Until that time, Mum had not looked him in the face and, when she did, something like a plea for forgiveness flashed through her eyes. Dad embraced her, holding her so tight that I thought she would break in two.

'There, there, husband,' Mum said as she stroked his back. Her face stilled and became calm, as whatever apprehensions she had been harbouring drained from her.

'And now for your surprise,' Dad said.

Mum laughed, 'A welcome home present?' as Dad bundled us into the truck. 'I'd completely forgotten you had a surprise for me. What is it, Rongo?'

'You'll see when we get home,' he answered. However, Dad didn't mean home to Waituhi. Instead, after we'd picked up some groceries, he drove in the other direction, across the Kaiti Bridge, around Gisborne Harbour, past the freezing works, towards Kaiti Hill. For a moment we thought we were going to Poho o Rawiri meeting house for dinner, or maybe to the lookout on Kaiti Hill. From there you could see all the way to Young Nick's Head, named after the young lad who had been on Captain Cook's *Endeavour* when it sailed into the bay. No, we weren't going to either of those places. Dad turned into Crawford Road and stopped outside a small wooden bungalow.

We arrived just as it was getting dark. 'Here we are,' Dad said. With a twinkle in his eye, he got out of the truck. We followed him as he walked up a small path towards the house. He fumbled in his pockets, brought out a key, and unlocked the door. He swept Mum up in his arms and carried her across the threshhold. 'I've always wanted to do that,' he said.

This was his surprise for Mum, for all of us. He had bought the bungalow. 'Oh, Rongo,' Mum wept, 'why didn't you let me know?'

'And spoil your welcome home present?' Dad asked. 'I know it's what you've always wanted. A place of our own. No more gypsy life, going from place to place, living in shearers' quarters. Well, here it is. Tama can go to high school by bicycle and there's a primary school just down the road for the girls. You can have a vegetable garden at the back and there's some room for your hens. It's a bit of a walk to the dairy for groceries but . . .'

'I don't deserve this,' Mum said.

'You're wrong,' Dad answered. 'It's our just reward.'

Mum tried to smile, then nodded. She walked from room to room, dazed, switching on the lights until the house glowed. We followed behind, and we were very excited. We bounced on the beds, opened the cupboards and wardrobes and yelled each new discovery to one another.

'Not so much noise, children,' Mum said. 'We're living in the city now. The neighbours might complain.' She told Dad to get some wood for the kitchen range, opened the bag of groceries, and said she would make some kai because we hadn't had any tea.

I went with Dad to the woodshed and held a lamp while he chopped the wood. When we went back inside, I grinned my lopsided grin because Mum was scrubbing the kitchen floor, still in her hat and travelling clothes. 'Oh, no, Huia,' Dad moaned. 'Not tonight. I thought I would just show you the place and we could come back tomorrow.'

'Think again, husband,' she answered. 'You just get to cleaning while I make the tea. Kids, start making up the beds. I saw some sheets in one of the cupboards. We'll scrub the floors tonight and then tomorrow we'll see about getting some mops and we'll clean this house from top to bottom.'

It was just like the old times. But this time it was different, joyful and not heart-breaking. What was best was that Mum was home.

After tea, Mum made us stay up very late with all the work; it was worth it just to see how the floors shone. Wiki went to bed early because she was too young to stay up. But she couldn't go to sleep. Every now and then, she'd peep through the door at us. 'I want to help too,' she'd wail.

'No, you go to sleep,' Mum told her. 'Tomorrow, then you can help. Tomorrow.'

'What about leaving the scrubbing for tomorrow?' Dad grumbled.

Mum stood over him with her mop in hand. 'What did you say, Rongo Mahana? Eh?' She squeezed the water over his head.

We had fun that night. Mum gave the orders: 'Make the beds, wipe the ledges, sweep the floors . . .', and we obeyed them until it was finished. She showed us our rooms; one for Ripeka and Mere, and I had my own room. Wiki would sleep in Mum and Dad's room until she was older.

'Now,' Mum pronounced, 'we can go to bed. You children won't mind sleeping in your underwear, will you?' We kissed her and Dad goodnight. Quite suddenly, I was very tired, but I couldn't go to sleep because I was so happy. I lay in bed, watching the moon shining across the ceiling. In the kitchen, I could hear Mum and Dad talking about money. 'The mortgage has to be paid off before the house is really ours,' Dad said. 'The tin on the roof is old and will have to be replaced soon. And the piles are wooden and won't last long . . .'

'But do we have enough money to buy some material for curtains?' Mum asked. 'And a carpet for the front room? Oh, Rongo, our own place. Thank you, husband.'

Our own place. Not belonging to somebody else but to us. This was home, and this was my family and we were moving up in the world.

I lay there for a long time, looking at the walls of my bedroom. On one wall, I would start measuring how tall I was growing. The pencil marks would still be there in later years for me to see. On a desk in the corner, I would pile my schoolbooks and it would become a bigger pile over the years. In the wardrobe I would hang my clothes. In this bed, my body would change, through adolescence to manhood.

We were back to the beginning. But this was a different beginning. I wouldn't have to cross my fingers and make fierce wishes anymore. I lay awake and I was very happy. I heard Mum and Dad talking and laughing with one another and then the soft sounds as they got ready for bed.

'Go to sleep, Tama,' Dad growled through the wall.

This is our just reward.

The train curves round the side of a valley through the hills. The sky is wide and bright with the sun, the hills are like jagged fins thrusting proudly into the horizon.

A sudden shaft of sunlight dazzles my eyes. In the sky, a bird flies softly and calmly like a white feather drifting. Higher above it, another bird flies, a sparrow hawk. The hawk glides on the streams of air. Its wings hardly move and with outstretched pinions it follows the whim of the wind. It surveys the land through the slits of its eyes and sees a white feather flickering over green fields. The wings fold back. The hawk plummets. A scattered turbulence. It rises triumphant. Within its claws is a small white bird. I watch as it ascends the unfolding sky.

The calm swaying of the train as it traverses the mountains brings back the memories, like photographs thumbed through quickly.

The sun falls into the afternoon.

Looking back, it doesn't seem so long ago when we moved to that house in Crawford Road. Fortunately it was school holidays so Mum and Dad had plenty of time to concentrate on settling us in before school began.

The family were all still sleeping when I work up to my first morning in our new home. I dressed quickly and slipped out the front door. The morning was bright with sun and Kaiti Hill was diamond sharp, cutting a clean edge into the sky. I took a deep breath and began to run along the road that would take me up to the summit. I wanted to make sure of where I was, take some bearings on my new life and make sure this was really happening.

I was panting when I arrived at the lookout with its rusty cannon. There seemed so much sky, so much sea. The toetoe was rustling in the wind, its tall white plumes waving signs of welcome in the air. The flax was clicking and speaking its eternal lessons to any who could hear:

He aha te mea nui o te ao?
Maku e kii atu: He tangata, he tangata, aa, he tangata.
Listen to the song of the flax: What is the greatest treasure of the world?
It is men, women, children, aa, all humankind.

Down below me was Gisborne, curving around the bay. Its long main street, Gladstone Road, was intersected with other streets and already early morning traffic was flowing along the commerical centre between Kaiti Bridge and

Roebuck Road. Behind me was Kaiti suburb and Poho o Rawiri meeting house protecting my back.

Then, almost on the edge of space, I saw a portent — the tall spume rising from a whale's deep plunging. I started to laugh, out of pure joy. The world was just waiting for me and I could be a part of it. All I had to do was go out and claim it. Lying on the ground was a fallen cabbage tree; its head of broad leaves made an ideal sled. I straddled it and with a whoop, 'Yahoo!' leapt aboard and began a headlong, bouncing ride down the slope. A couple of times I was airborne, sailing through the air — but I was too blissed out to care. I careened, soared, flipped and crashed like a madman through the bushes. When I reached the bottom, I was amazed that I didn't have any broken bones. I felt invincible. I couldn't stop laughing and laughing.

I don't know how long I stayed at the lookout. When I finally went home, I got a clip over the ear from Mum. 'Where have you been?' she asked me crossly. 'Look at your clothes! You look as if you've been rolling around in cow dung.' Mum never swore; I never heard her say words like 'shit' or 'piss' or 'bugger' or anything. 'There's work to do!'

I suspect that setting up our new house kept our mother so busy that she couldn't dwell too much on what still seemed to be some inner pain or problem. When Nani Miro came to see us one day, and Dad remarked on it, I overheard Miro say to him, 'Huia is going through the change.' My father blanched because, like most men, the thought of women's problems always made him somewhat nervous and faint.

Well, whatever Mum was going through didn't stop her and Dad from becoming expectant parents again, much to our disgust. We were old enough to know about sex. To have parents who were still, well, doing *it*, and a mother who was still fertile, was mortifying.

'How could you!' Ripeka wailed at Mum. 'What will the kids at school say?'

'It's the best thing for Huia,' Miro Mananui told Dad, 'to have children.'

And so we got on with life.

I didn't realise it then, although I do now, that our moving to Gisborne was part of a well known demographic of the mid twentieth century. It was called the rural to urban migration and its main characteristic in New Zealand was all those Maori families who left their village homes and tribal land in search of employment and what they thought was a better life. Some settled only briefly in Gisborne before travelling further afield to the larger cities to the north and to the south — Wellington or Auckland. There, divorced from their rural economies, they tried to make the transition to urban worker.

Our transition to urban life did not get off to a good start. Dad got a new job at the freezing works. Uncle Joshua and Uncle Hone, who worked there, told him about an opening as a knifehand, slicing the skin off animal carcasses as they came down the chain. After his first day in the slaughter room, despite scrubbing himself in the showers, Dad came home reeking of blood and animal fat. What was worse was that he seemed affected by the work. It wasn't just a matter of slicing skin or, later, slitting the throats of sheep — he was doing it repetitively all day long, and watching the blood spurt from the open wounds. How long could he keep it up? Only the fact that my uncles and other friends worked by his side there sustained him. Mum, however, was horrified at Dad's dilemma. Dad had always had such a respect for animals, and commercial slaughtering was a shock to him.

'Oh, Rongo, why don't you find a job somewhere else? Go back to shepherding.'

'No,' Dad answered, 'Joshua tells me I'll get used to it, the money's good, and it's better for me to be close to my family than to be apart from you.' He was shivering, his eyes wild, as Mum tried to calm him.

Mum's own job wasn't much better. Although she was pregnant with Marama, she planned to work right up to the day the baby was due. On the advice of Aunt Sarah, she applied for a job at a canning factory. Her interview was dispiriting. 'We've only got jobs going in the early morning shift from four to eleven, take it or leave it.' The plus side was that the pay was good. 'I'll take it,' Mum said.

Every morning, before dawn, she joined other Maori workers as they walked through the streets to the factory. But when her pregnancy began to show, she was laid off.

As for me and my sisters, we had our own challenges to face when the holidays came to a close and we started school. First to be enrolled were my sisters, at the local primary school. Not until that moment did it dawn on us that we would be separated. We'd always been each other's best companions and friends and, when the time came for us to say goodbye to each other, the separation was difficult.

'It's only for the day,' I said. I can still remember the look of terror in their eyes as they contemplated the hours that we would be apart.

'Come on, son,' Dad said. 'Let's get you to high school. I don't want to be late for work.'

Dad was in his white freezing works overalls, apron and boots, the uniform of the men on the chain. When we walked along the hallway in the administration building, people gave us a wide berth as if we shouldn't really be there. A lanky, freckle-faced boy saw us and, when he found out what we wanted, said, 'Oh, you'll have to see Batman.' The boy's name was Michael Kavanagh and, later, he became my best friend. He took us to the headmaster's office.

'Do you have an appointment?' the headmaster's secretary asked. 'No? Well, you'll have to join the line with the others.'

We queued with the other parents waiting with their own sons. The boys were the usual suspects, the odds-and-sods boys who had been up to no good, juvenile delinquents, hooligans, reprobates, petty adolescent crims, bad boys with their shirt tails hanging out. Every now and then, a parent and son would be called in and, when they came out of the headmaster's office you could tell which boys had gotten away with their misdemeanours and been enrolled and who hadn't. Then it was my turn.

The headmaster was clearly harassed and he obviously thought I was another miscreant. He was dressed in a long black gown. One look at him and I realised that no matter that I had achieved good marks at former schools, and never mind the encyclopaedia Mum had bought for me to read, this was going to be a difficult interview. For one thing, Dad was not dressed properly. For another we had brought no previous school records. And I was already one year behind most of the other boys being enrolled.

After a minute or so, the headmaster cut my father short. 'I'm very sorry, Mr Mahana,' he said, 'but our school is already full and you might be better advised to try to enrol your son elsewhere.' With that, he picked some papers up from his desk and began to read them.

I had always, in the past, seen my father as a reasonable man who tried to get along with everybody. Whenever we had gone to meet the bosses in the big houses Dad had always appeared to be accommodating. Not today. He had no intention of budging from his seat.

'I realise, sir,' Dad began quietly, 'that you've had a really bad morning, but it could get a whole lot worse. That depends on you.' Dad never raised his voice in anger, but there was an authority about the force of his words that made the headmaster look up and at him. 'I apologise,' Dad went on, 'that I did not make an appointment to see you on my son, Tama's, behalf, and I further apologise that I am not properly dressed for this interview and that I probably stink from my job. I also accept that I have not brought Tama's academic records with me but will you accept my assurances, from one honest man to another, that my son is qualified for your school? I am already late for work and I'll probably have my pay docked, but my son's education is important to me and his mother. I pay my taxes and this is a public school and I am not leaving until Tama is enrolled.'

My father and the headmaster sat eyeballing each other. As for me, I was feeling really proud. This was the first time Dad had ever mentioned how important my education was to him and Mum, and I took this as permission to grow.

The minutes ticked by. The secretary came in to remind the headmaster of his next appointment with a city councillor. Still Dad did not budge, so the headmaster whispered to her. When she exited the room we heard her explaining to the official, 'I'm sorry, but the headmaster has been delayed. He is with a very stubborn father who wants to enrol his son and he won't take no for an answer.'

Finally, the headmaster relaxed. 'All right, Mr Mahana,' he said. He stood up and started hitting his hands with a cane for impact. 'Here's what I'll do. I will ask one of my senior teachers to take your son in a quick examination in English, history and mathematics. Pending receipt of his academic records which I will expect you to provide in due course, I will admit him. And you, Master Mahana,' the headmaster said, pointing his cane at me, 'if you do pass, which I very much doubt you will, I will have my eye on you every minute of every day you are at my school. If at any stage I see you not pulling your weight or getting in trouble, you'll be out of here so fast your feet won't touch the ground. Good day to you both.'

My impromptu examination was supervised by a small man named Mr Grundy. Dad waited in the corridor while I sat the examination. My results, particularly in mathematics, were mediocre but Mr Grundy's eyebrows arched when he read my essay which, on the spur of the moment, I had written on the subject: Everybody is Innocent Until they are Proved Guilty. Mr Grundy saw it for what it was, a defence against the headmaster's attitude. 'The Lord be praised,' he said, 'passion, a sense of justice and signs of a pulse.' He passed me on the basis of the essay.

The headmaster, however, was not pleased; but a deal was a deal and he signed my admission form. As we left his office, 'Get a haircut, Master Mahana,' he said.

Dad and I went back to the truck. Just before starting the motor he turned to me and said, 'You must do well at school, son. Your mother and I don't want you to grow up to be seasonal labourers like we are. We don't want you to have hard lives like we had. You show the headmaster what you're made of. Get a good certificate that will show you're the equal of anyone else. He doesn't realise that we are of the Maori race, a race with the indomitable courage of the undefeated.'

I was at Gisborne Boys High School for four years, until I was seventeen. They were years filled with uncertainty as I struggled to cope with all the new experiences coming my way. Many teachers drifted in and out of my life, forming parts of it, destroying others. I made good friends, some who remained friends like Michael, the freckle-faced lanky boy I had met on my first day at school, and others who now pass by without even the briefest nod of acknowledgement. My school years were a time of joy and puzzlement and sometimes, oh, so much confusion; of a world filled with so much to learn and understand or comprehend. Stubborn, I pushed out, bewildered, into that world, always questioning, searching; sometimes finding answers, sometimes not. A lot of times, I didn't understand at all but was able to fake it.

I was not a top student, but I was able to scrape through School Certificate with the bare minimum 200 marks and then to get University Entrance by sitting the examination. The headmaster indeed kept his eagle eye on me throughout my school days and I was caned four times by him during that period — two times justly, two times unjustly. When I graduated, he had the good grace to compliment me.

'What do you plan to do as a career?' he asked.

'I've got a job with *The Gisborne Herald* as a cadet reporter,' I said. 'I want to be a journalist.'

The headmaster smiled. 'You'll have lots to write about,' he answered. 'I well remember the day your father brought you to my school to enrol you. I never thought you would amount to anything, young Mahana. Do give my regards to your father.'

When I left to go to Wellington, two years later, to work at *The Evening Post*,

Dad told me he met the headmaster in the street and told him the news. The headmaster shook his hand.

'You are a credit to your son,' he said.

He's right. I am the man I am because of my father.

15

'Kia kaha, Mere,' I say to my sister. 'I'm here, hush now.'

Mere weeps on my shoulder. I could almost believe she is a little girl again bringing her sorrows to me. Behind her in the shadows, Koro waits, holding Kataraina, their baby. Kataraina is bundled in a blanket. Koro raises it to protect her from the cold wind.

I hold my sister a little while longer. Gently I break our embrace. She lifts her head. 'What will we do now, brother?' she asks. 'What will become of us?'

This was the little sister whom Ripeka and I had to leave in a different class while we went to school in Gisborne. Mere was accustomed to doing everything with us and did not like being left with strangers one bit. Not only that, but she got out of class earlier than we did. There she was in a long street with not a brown person in sight. On that first day while she waited, she sat on the fence watching the people and traffic stream past. A lady said, 'Hello!' but Mere was too confused and shy to answer her. On another day, she decided she wasn't going to her school, and she followed me as I was biking to high school. 'Stop following, Mere,' I yelled. 'No,' she said. 'Go to your own school,' I insisted. She wouldn't, so I jumped on my bike and pedalled fast so that she couldn't follow. But all that day I was worried that she might have run after me and become lost in Gisborne. I imagined her wandering the streets, crying, or worse, going down to the harbour and falling in. When I got home and found her sitting and waiting, I hugged her. 'I'm sorry, Mere,' I said. She looked at me as if what I had done was the end of the world.

Mere and I walk towards Koro. 'Tena koe, Koro,' I greet him. 'Kei te pehea koe? How are you?'

'Kei te pai,' he answers. 'Say hello to Uncle Tama, bub,' he says to Kataraina. She puts her hands around my neck, briefly, before turning back to her father. 'It's been a long day for her, Tama. Have you brought any luggage?'

'A suitcase,' Mere tells him, as if he's a chauffeur. 'Bring it to the car.'

I look resignedly at Koro and give him a wink. 'Don't blame me,' I tell him, 'I'm just the brother.' All my sisters have a bossy streak about them.

Koro grins, passes Kataraina to Mere, and does as he is told. I follow Mere as she walks toward the car, opens the back door and lays Kataraina down, carefully folding the blanket over the baby so she won't get cold. 'You, me and Koro can all sit in the front,' she says.

I put a hand on her stomach. 'Be a bit of a squeeze won't it?'

'Oh no,' Mere says. 'I'm not showing already, am I? Koro just can't keep his hands off my beautiful body. Don't you worry, brother, we'll fit.'

I shut the door. As we wait for Koro, Mere starts to weep again. I put my arms round her and she pokes me and prods me as if I was a pillow. She is trying to find the same configuration as Dad had whenever he cradled her. He was more ample than I am and had more give whenever you put your head against him. But I try my best, cradling her like he would have done.

'Aue, brother,' Mere weeps. 'Koro and I were out shearing at Mangatu when we got the news. Ripeka was trying to get us by telephone all morning. By mid afternoon she still hadn't reached us, so she rang Uncle Pita to come and tell us. Koro reckons I was hysterical. He says I screamed and when he tried to comfort me I started to hit him. Uncle told me to calm down as I might lose this baby I'm carrying. We went to Waituhi straight away. Didn't even bother to get changed out of our shearing clothes. All the formal stuff that happens when a person dies had been completed by the time we got there. I saw Ripeka and Marama at Mum and Dad's bedroom door and I said to them, "Where's Dad, I want to see Dad . . ." I pushed them away and ran into the bedroom and . . . Oh, Tama, he was just lying there. I cried out his name and held him to me.'

I hug my sister closer. In the back seat Kataraina stirs. Koro comes to the car with my suitcase. He puts it in the boot and steps into the car. He sees Mere weeping. 'It's been a rough day,' he says. He starts the car and switches on the lights. The night is filled with rain. The car draws away from the air terminal, the windscreen wipers flicking back and forth across the window. The world my father was in has gone full circle. Yet, some time, the world must turn again. Another hour must begin, the hands moving away from the hour gone. From the sadness of an old life, a new life must rise. Some day.

'The one who was most upset was Wiki,' Mere continues. 'She was away on a school trip and she arrived home half an hour after me. One of her teachers brought her and, at first, Wiki didn't want to get out of the car. So I went and got her. Mum knew how distraught she was and called, "Baby? Come to me, Wiki." Her face was white with shock, and she cried out, "No, Daddy, no."'

The lights of the air terminal recede. The car turns through Te Hapara. Mere becomes calm and together we watch the rain falling. Kataraina cries in her sleep. I look back at her to see that she's all right. The car turns onto the main road out of Gisborne.

'After a while, Mum calmed us all down,' Mere resumes. 'She looked Ripeka, Wiki and me straight in the eyes and said, "Good, all my daughters are here? All the noble daughters of Rongo, you are all here to do your duty to your father? Okay, let's begin."'

'Mum told Uncle Pita to take Hone with him and leave us. When they had gone she turned to us again. "This is what daughters do," she said. "You must help me prepare your dad for the funeral. This is your final act of love to your father. He would not want anybody else except us to handle him."'

'Oh, Tama, it was so wonderful,' Mere whispers, her voice lightening with awe. 'I didn't expect it to be. But Mum led the way, holding him so that we could undress him and I never expected him to be so . . . so beautiful. Mum stroked and massaged him so that his limbs would be supple and allow us to do our work. She told us to go and get a basin of warm water, towels and sponges, and we began to wash him. While we were doing this, Mum talked to us about him. How he courted her. How she resisted. How he won her over. Some of the memories were so tender, Tama. Then she spoke directly to Dad and told him how honoured she had been to be his wife and how much she would miss his passion when they were making love. "No more will I have your body to play with," she said, "and I will miss our mornings, husband." Some of her stories were so outrageous that we couldn't stop laughing. She nodded, approvingly, and said, "It's good to laugh, it's good to remember."'

'We dressed Dad in his best shirt, tie and suit and put brown shoes on his feet. I said to Mum, "What kind of fashion statement is that!" because he was wearing a black suit, and she said, "You know your father and, anyhow, nobody will know except us," and that made us laugh again. Then Ripeka and Mum had a squabble about where to part his hair and Mum insisted that he parted it on the left but Ripeka got her way and Mum said to her, "You girls, sometimes I think you knew more about your father than I did." When it was done, Mum stepped back and admired Dad. She said to him, "Look what your daughters have done for you, husband. How handsome and beautiful they have made you look for all the world to see."'

The car passes through Makaraka. The hotel is bright with lights and there is a burst of sudden laughter as we pass. Koro looks at Mere and reaches out to press her hand.

'Koro, you just watch the road,' Mere warns as the car swerves. Quickly, she presses his hand. 'I'm sorry, Koro . . . Don't you leave me, don't you leave me . . .'

'What's wrong with you?' Koro smiles. 'I'll never leave you! You've got all my money in your cheque book.'

I watch the darkness, and it unfolds like a dream before me. I could almost believe that this was our family's old truck, and Dad was driving, and those headlights shining are the lights seeking the way home to the farm. Dad and I are laughing and . . .

But Dad is dead. I look ahead, and there is only this night not any other evening. I see Matawhero blur past through the rain. Dad used to sell his stock at the sale yards there. All those days, they're gone now.

'Mum asked us to leave her with Dad for a while,' Mere continues. 'She wanted to be alone with him. By that time, Uncle Pita and Hone had returned. So had the Matua, Nani Tama, Aunt Sarah, Aunt Ruth, Auntie Maka and Mattie Jones. Nani Miro came over and hugged us. "Have you done as all daughters of man have done since the beginning of time? Have you rendered unto your father and have you done it well?" Mum appeared at the doorway and answered, "Yes, Matua, they have done their job well, as befitting the daughters of Eve." Then the Matua said, "Then let us take him to the people." We took him to Rongopai this afternoon.'

The headlights swing over empty fields and point into the country. The car swerves, and Kataraina wakes and begins to cry. She lifts her hands into the air, wanting to be picked up. I reach over to get her. 'There, there, Kara, come to uncle.' But she just looks at me as if I was a stranger and reaches out for her mother. 'She doesn't remember me.'

'You've been gone from home a long time, that's why,' Mere answers. She soothes Kataraina, making soft sucking noises. 'What's wrong, baby? See your uncle? He's come all the way from Wellington. A long, long way. He's home to look after us. No more cry now. Everything's all right.'

I notice a pile of clothes stacked in the back seat.

'We've been round home collecting some sleeping gear,' Mere explains. 'We've also got some of Dad's photos, the trophies he won at hockey, football and wrestling in the boot. Mum kept on saying to us, "See this one? He won that at Hamilton. This one he got at the tennis tournament at Poho o Rawiri . . ."'

The car crosses a large concrete bridge and, on the other side of it, roads fork in different directions. We take the road to Waituhi.

'How are the arrangements at Rongopai?' I ask.

'Everything's just about ready,' Mere answers. 'Nani Tama and Uncle Pita have organised the iwi and they have been working flat out all day. Uncle Pita's supervising the kai. I don't know what we would have done if he wasn't there. Sam Walker and some of the boys are in charge of getting the meat; the freezing works are donating some beef. Simeon and Andrew are off on a mission to Whangara to ask those people to provide some seafood. Uncle Hepa is erecting a marquee outside Takitimu Hall. Uncle Pita reckons a lot of people will be coming. Everybody's been pitching in.'

'Ae,' Koro answers. 'We just dropped everything. Old man Bulibasha sent some of the boys out pig-hunting to get some pigs for the hangi. There'll be a lot of people to feed over the three days. The Wi Pere Estate has donated some mutton. The Mahana shearing gangs have dubbed in big dollars to buy other provisions. Mattie Jones and Hine Ropiho have been getting the cookhouse ready. Aunt Sarah has been in her element, collecting mattresses and blankets for the visitors. Most will sleep at Rongopai. Others will be accommodated at Takitimu or Pakowhai. The meals will be served at Takitimu.'

'Luckily,' Mere sighs, 'the weather's been good for most of the day. It was hard enough getting the marquee up as it was. It'll be nice and dry in there tonight.

Uncle Charlie Whatu and our cousins dug the pits for the hangi. When everybody found out about Dad they all came to help. Lots of spuds to peel. Even Auntie Rose, you know how flash we used to think she was, she came down to the hall. She yelled out, "Where's a knife, somebody give me a knife, I'll show you fellas how to peel spuds." Maka tiko bum turned up too. You know what she's like — always making us laugh, swivelling her googly eyes left and right to make sure everybody was pulling their weight. All the time, the trucks were arriving and people were coming with more potatoes, pumpkins, mutton and . . .'

The iwi is relieving us of those duties, allowing us to get on with the business of grieving for Dad.

Waituhi is family. The whanau is my home. The love and affection they hold for each other are the ridgepoles of my heart. The sharing and enjoying of each other are the rafters. Within those walls and roof, my heart is shared with my whanau, so closely intertwined, that I burst with pride that I am a son of the iwi.

Taku manawa, o ratou manawa. My heart is also their heart. Their heart is mine. I am their father, son and friend. They, too, are my mothers, fathers, sons and friends.

If you want to know what my heart looks like, look to the whanau.

Look to Rongopai.

The car turns at the T-junction which leads to Patutahi. On the other side of it, some kilometres further on, is Waituhi. Already I see Dad, lying on the marae at Rongopai. In my mind's eye I see the meeting house, the place of love, ablaze with light. Mum is watching over Dad. Marama and Hone are with her. The black-gowned kuia are there too, ready to welcome the mourners whenever they come. Thinking of them reminds me of a painting I once saw of a medieval king being ferried on a funeral barge surrounded by such proud, mourning women as the kuia of my race. My father is mine own king, as great as any of legend, and he shall be taken to Hawaiki on a waka of burnished splendour across the sea of death.

'Aue. Aue . . .' This is the cry of sadness. 'Aue. Aue . . .' This is the keening of the women on the marae. 'Aue. Aue . . .' This is the call that has come to me, the call home to farewell my father. The call has gone out across this land. The tangi is the home-calling.

Patutahi glimmers and fades past. The car crosses a small bridge. The road stretches away in front of me, endless and unending, towards Waituhi, where Dad waits.

So many words were left unsaid between us. Did he know that I loved him?

There were so many things that we meant to do together. How can I do them without him?

The road curves round the hill we call Pukepoto, the entrance to Waituhi, cutting a protective serrated edge into the night sky. The lights of the village appear, streaming down the windscreen like falling stars. Mere clutches my hand. She looks up at me and the moon gleams in her eyes. Everything starts spinning past, the church at Pakowhai, the houses all blazing with lights to show me the way homeward. The people must know that I am coming because I can see them, heads bowed, paying homage to a returning son. Holding candles, they step aside to let the car pass. The headlights swing over them as they clutch at their coats against the wind.

Ahead, the night opens. In a widening cleft of dark, Rongopai appears. The marae has been strung with electric bulbs. The gateway is open. People are huddled in the rain. My courage fails me. 'Oh, Mere.'

I could die of the love I am feeling for Dad. My heart could stop with the pain of my sadness.

How will I be able to look upon him in death and survive?

I close my eyes, tightly, tightly closed. I cross my fingers. When I open my eyes, Dad will be there. He will say, 'I knew you would come home, son. I knew you'd come home to help me.' We will embrace one another. He will laugh and say, 'Come on then, now that you're home, there's plenty for you to do. No rest for my son.'

All this will happen when I open my eyes. When the car slows down, when it stops bumping and swaying through the gateway to Rongopai. I will open my eyes and see my father, and I will be with him again. We will embrace one another and I will tell him, 'Hello, Dad.'

The car has stopped. Now I will open my eyes.

So much light, so much blinding light.

'Tama,' Mere says. 'Our father —'

The women begin to wail, welcoming me. I lift my eyes and I see him, dark, within the radiant light.

Death cannot be denied.

So it really is true then.

16

You are alone.

Behind you all is darkness. In front of you the light blazes on the marae. See how the light arcs on the ground and diffuses into the night. Here you stand, still in the darkness. Perhaps you can turn away. No, it is too late. The black-gowned women of your iwi raise their arms, beckoning you forward. The sound of the wailing is like the wind calling.

Haere mai ki o tatou mate e.

Do you know what they say?

Come to our dead.

So take one step forward. There is no escaping the sorrow of the marae.

The cry echoes across the darkness. The kuia are opening their voices to you. They fill the night with their keening. The sound grows louder and in its spiralling flight it gathers other carolling voices. Higher and higher it spirals, louder and louder.

Your tears fall. The wailing has opened up your heart and you remember your father.

Come to our dead. Come. Come.

No, don't force the memories back. Let them come to you with the remembering of the good times you shared together. He was a good man. He lived only for you. Now he is gone. Remember him and weep. Don't hold back the memories. Let them flow as your tears flow. As you remember, call out to him. 'Dad? Dad.'

And one step further now.

Rongopai rises up before you.

The roof holds up the sky. The foundations stand firmly in the earth. All humanity is therefore able to stand in the strand of life between, sustained by the strength of your ancestral house. Remember that it will always transcend the ebb and flow of human folly.

Haere mai, haere mai. Step into the light. This is the longest journey of all. It is the loneliest of journeys. On both sides of the marae the mourners are watching you. You must not falter. You must be proud. Step boldly, step firmly.

Come to our dead. The kuia, the revered women of your tribe, assemble in the light. Their faces are veiled in shadows. Upon their heads they wear plaited wreaths of kawakawa leaves. They have threaded their gowns with sprigs of greenery. In their outstretched hands, they wave green leaves.

Haere mai ki o tatou mate e. Nani Miro has signed to Mattie Jones to make a personal karanga to you. You remember Mattie, don't you? She came to Waituhi a few years ago, covered in red earth, raw, bleeding, from east of Eden, out of the Land of Nod, to take her position as acolyte to the Matua. One day, like you, she will take a greater place of responsibility to the iwi.

The women move in time with the wailing. Their bodies sway, their hands quiver, and the green branches cast fleeting shadows. This is the aroarowhaki, strange and tremulous, the giving up of the body to grief.

What are the leaves we hold in our hands?

The faces of the kuia are filled with sorrow. For three days they will sing their welcomes across the marae. They will take turns being out in front — Nani Miro, Aunt Ruth, Aunt Sarah, Mattie Jones and others — and their karanga will soar like glistening spears. The karanga opens up the hearts of all those who come to mourn so that they are able to obtain the catharsis that comes with tears. Who better than the kuia to do this? After all, they are the women who have given birth to the tribe. They have suckled the children, taught them to walk, tried to give them all moral compass and to pass on the wisdom of the iwi. They have been there to pick you up when you have fallen and to dry your tears when you have experienced disappointment. They have seen the children grow into adulthood, marry, and in turn have children of their own. They have witnessed all the triumph and heartbreak of the tribe as it has negotiated this vale of tears.

Now, a good man, a good provider, has gone and must be farewelled.

The lines on the faces of the kuia will grow deep with fatigue and grief. Their eyes will be heavy-lidded with wanting to sleep. But, always, they watch over the tribe in life and death. They will take turns to rest, always leaving someone on watch, as eternal sentinel. No matter what time of day or night the mourners come, they must always be welcomed with the same dignity and passion and warmth accorded to all.

'Come. Look upon our son where he lies. Share your grief with us.'

One of the old women steps forward from the ranks of the kuia. It is the Matua, Miro Mananui herself, according you the privilege of the waiata tangi. Her voice quivers like the outstretched branches she holds in her hands, then soars above the wailing.

Haruru ana te Tira a Whiro
taia ake ahau e te mate
i muri nei ei.

Her voice sings above the marae, curling and fluttering like a wounded bird. As she sings, Aunt Ruth and other kuia come to join her. From the darkness more voices come like a rush of wings to join in her lament.

Death comes, but I am
not yet dead.
I breathe, I live.

The words express the sorrow of this gathering. Your father has not only left you; he has also left them. This is not just a personal loss. It is a loss to the tribe. This night is like the sea and they are gulls wheeling and crying above the waves, dazed and bewildered because your father has gone from everyone. Open your heart. Let your sorrow, too, wing upward to join with theirs.

Your father was their brother, son, and friend, not only your father. They were his family. Now that he is gone, they weep. Don't brush your own tears away. There is no shame in weeping. Let them fall, let them fall. 'Dad? Dad.'

One step. And one step further now.

Haere mai ki o tatou mate e.

In the karanga, the women are able to express everything that a man does when he makes a speech. It can be as short as the women wish it to be or as long as they wish. It can caress; it can kill. It can also heal. This lament, which the

Matua brings into the karanga, recalls memories of your father. It sings of happy days when you were a child and he was with you. You trusted in him. If you were afraid, you went to him and your fear went away because he was there.

Memories rise in the still air

like smoke from many fires.

He raised you well, your dad. He was always trying to teach you lessons about life and how to conduct good passage through it. Later, when you grew into the young, strong man that you are now, his lessons were more difficult to learn. Sometimes he taught you without giving any explanation as to why.

'Never forget your responsibilities to your tribe. Your iwi always comes first. What profits a man if he wins the world's accolades but loses the respect of his people? Always look after your mother, brother and sisters. When visitors come to your house, make sure they are fed first. When you go fishing in the sea or hunting in the forest, always return the first fish or first bird back to Tangaroa or Tane as your acknowledgement of their rules of conservation. Do not ask others to do something that you should do. A warrior never lets a boy go out in front. When it is time for you to keep the watch, keep it with vigilance.'

No matter that his strictures often seemed so old-fashioned, you tried to abide by them. Why? He was your father. You were his son. You wanted him to be proud of you. Although you didn't know it then, you wanted to be like him. But did you ever expect that you would, one day, have to take over from him? No. You had no fear because he looked after you. You were content. If there was a storm, you used to look out the window at the rushing clouds and the trees bending in the wind, and yet you would be calm because he was there. At night, if you were afraid, you needed only to call to him and he would come. He was always there when you needed him. Your life with him was a summer without end.

Kua makariri ke

te okiokinga puea kau?

Not any longer. Now your father is dead. From this moment, life has forever changed and winter has come. Although you are a man now you grieve like a child for him. You never thought that he could die. Sometimes, you were so interested in your own life you forgot about him. Perhaps you even thought you didn't need him. Now, you are alone. And you sorrow not only for him, but for yourself also. With his death, the world has changed for you.

Is this the same place,

this place of ashes?

No, don't stop. If you stop, even for a moment, the grief will possess you totally, and you might not complete this journey. You are your father's son. You are the oldest. You must have courage. If you stop, you will be like an empty canoe adrift on the sea. Take up the oar. Strike deep into the water.

Look around you and regain your bearings. This is Rongopai, your meeting house. This is the house of the Whanau a Kai and this is Waituhi their home. You have happy memories of this place.

Look again. There is your mother, waiting for you. She sits beside your father. With her are Ripeka and Wiki and the little ones, Marama and Hone. They wait for you. Your father waits for you. You mustn't falter now. Let your mother be your guiding star. Point your prow toward that star and let her know that you are here. Strike strongly, strike deep.

Suddenly, the darkness is behind you. Rongopai has reached out with arms of light to enfold you. Look how the light shines brilliantly from the porch, and is enclosed within the peak of the sloping roof. The roof seems to move, seems to topple, and in falling would crush you . . . No, it is only your senses reeling, your heart breaking. Remember what your father told you, remember? He told you many stories about this meeting house. Think back on them. He sat with you here, one day, and told you of Rongopai.

'Our meeting house, son, is not just a building of four walls and a roof. It is also the body of an ancestor. See the koruru, at the top of the entrance? That is the head. The arms are the maihi, the boards sloping down from the koruru to form the roof. See the ridgepole? It holds up the roof and is the backbone. There, inside the house, those panels are the ribs. And you are one of its children.'

The meeting house waits to embrace you. It opens its arms to you with aroha. It beckons you closer towards the brilliant flower wreaths banked high upon the porch. Among them are photographs of revered family members who have passed away before your dad. They, too, seem to hold green branches in their hands. They, too, wear chaplets of kawakawa leaves upon their heads. They, too, have come to mourn with the living for your father.

Pumau tonu atu

te rere o nga awa

te tonga o te ra

nga maunga tu noa.

All the world should end now that your father is dead, but it is only your world that ends. Elsewhere people are laughing and enjoying life. Why is this so? There should be no happiness now that he has gone.

Yet the stream still runs

and the sun rides over the sky

and the mountains

are always there.

Ah, *there's* the clue. Within the gnomic, runic nature of waiata there is always a lesson. It is a lesson that your Matua has given you, embedded within the melodic line of her song. Always remember that words are talismanic. In them is contained magic. In them is contained life. Hold fast to the lesson.

What is the lesson? That the world does not end. Night comes but, after night, comes the day. The procession of days, seasons and years continues. You still live, you still breathe. He is gone, you are still here, to remember him and sorrow for him and then? And then, son?

The wailing grows louder and more passionate. It soars from one sound to another, dignified and slow-moving, fading at the end of one phrase and then soaring higher and catching the next phrase with a sudden burst of anger. It is the shrill sound of grief, bringing with it ineffable loneliness. But do not falter, do not hesitate. Strike deep, strike strongly.

Wait. A voice rings across the marae above the wailing. 'Tena koe, mokopuna.'

It is your elder, Tamati Kota. Is he still alive? He is supported by his relative, Hine Ropiho. She looks after him in his ancient years. Holding him by the hand is young Pene, his mate on his walks around Waituhi. Tamati Kota is like an old whale stranded in an alien present. Surely, he must be the oldest living member of the tribe. He served Riripeti when she was alive and the great Mahana family after she died. Your father was one of her favourite sons, along with Te Ariki and Alexis; Tamati Kota took a special shine to your dad.

'Alas, mokopuna,' he calls. 'Why is it that I am still here and your father has gone? Aue, a wilful and stubborn heart still pumps the blood red rich through my veins.' The words are phrased with ancient dignity. They ring the air with sadness. 'I should be the one lying there, not your father. He was in his prime and a fine brother and son to all the iwi. He had within him the possibility, also, of fulfilling Riripeti's dreams. Now we must look again among us to find the brave-hearted one, the one marked with wisdom and strength, the brother and son to feed the family, aue, aue.'

The mourners nod at Tamati Kota's words. 'Ae, ae,' they say. There, brushing at her tears, is Auntie Annie Terekia. She is your father's cousin and she remembers how he looked after her when she was a young girl. Over there is Uncle Pita, the youngest of the brothers, recalling the times your father helped him and how good it was to be protected by him. His sister, Teria, she remembers how your father would come and see that she was all right and that she had enough money to feed her children after her husband died. They remember and are sad.

'Your father was not a selfish man,' Tamati Kota continues. 'He gave his heart to the iwi, as was the Maori way. He was the shelterer from storms, the giver of food, a kauri protecting the whanau from the wind and rain. That was why he was well loved, that is why his people mourn him.'

Tamati Kota rests and lowers his head. When he looks up, his body straightens. He turns to the meeting house where your father lies and extends his arms to him. 'We are sad that you leave us, son. We wait here, looking over you. And look how your own son comes to you.'

And one step further now.

The leaves are the signs of grief. They are kawakawa leaves.

See? Almost there. On either side of you the porch extends. Above you, the roof thrusts into the night sky. Around the electric lights moths have gathered. The light highlights the painted panels of the porch. Some of the panels have decayed with the seasons and the paint has blistered and flaked away. There, in one corner, is a silken spider's web, cast between an eave and a wall of the porch, beaded with rain.

Look downward from the apex. The photographs of your tupuna, your ancestors, are closer now. You know some of these tupuna well. That woman there with the pearls in her hair was Riripeti, the Matriarch. After she died and you visited Rongopai, you would stand before her photograph, lift the veil covering her face and trace the spirals of her moko with your fingers. There, beside her photograph, is another of an old kaumatua. He was Riripeti's father, Moanaroa. Pride of place has been given to the dignified photograph of her grandfather, Waituhi's most famous son, the parliamentarian Wi Pere Halbert. He wears a feather cloak, fastened about his neck, that has been handed down through your family for many generations.

Haruru ana
Te Tira a Whiro
Taia ake ahau e te mate
i muri nei ei.

The porch has been decorated with greenery. It shimmers with the wind, like a forest in a dark evening. Somewhere, you hear the disconsolate twittering of the piwakawaka as it flees further into the forest.

Haere mai. Haere mai.
Death comes, but I am
not yet dead.
I breathe, I live.

The porch is suddenly brilliant with a mass of flower wreaths. They are banked high on the floor. The petals shiver and drops of rain fall from them.

There, amid the wreaths, your father lies. Among a profusion of flowers he lies, among glistening white flowers. Brush away your tears. Look up. Be proud. Look upon your mother and your family where they wait for you, their oldest brother and son to come. They sit round your father's casket on a wide flax mat which has been laid on the floor of the porch.

Marama and Hone are crying. They are too young to understand about death. You didn't understand either, remember? When Riripeti died, you sat beside her casket looking out into the darkness. Grief was all around you, too large to comprehend. You knew only that Riripeti was going to be buried in the ground where it was cold. Remember your fear. Think how much greater it must be for Marama and Hone. After Riripeti died, your father was still with you. For these two children, there is no father now. For them, the light has been suddenly extinguished and this is no momentary eclipse. They do not understand the finality of that darkness. They look out into it and see you. You are the oldest brother, and they cry out to you. From out of this dark night, you must bring them light again.

Yet the stream still runs
and the sun rides over the sky
and the mountains
are always there.

Yes, that's it. The lesson again. Forget your own grief. You must look after your younger brother and sisters, your mother too. Dad is gone but the family remains.

Look now, upon your mother. Your father was her world. She weeps because he is gone. She kneels close to the casket, brushing your father's face with her hands. Her tight embrace with him has been broken, and she is Papatuanuku who reaches out to hold him again. This is the day of her separation.

Sorrow has made your mother transcendent. She is the Earth and she has eternity in her. Her hair is silver with the mists of the hills. The contours of her face are the sculpted landscapes of earth. Her moods are the seasons. This is her winter unending, the most bitter season of all. She has frost on her cheeks, ice glittering in her hair, and the cold wind blows snow across her body. She has known other winters but they have been followed by thaw and sparkling sun. No spring will follow this winter.

And one step further now.

Through the spray of my glistening

tears, I see you, my father.

And now you stand on the edge of the porch. The air is sweet with love and longing. In the night, a clap of thunder reverberates across the hills and rain begins to fall, softly, like a benediction.

Your sight blurs with tears. You see only an aureole of light, shimmering and glistening like a silver mist. Brush away your tears, brush away the wisps of the mist. There lies your father.

It's *okay*. Death has visited the iwi and taken your dad away. Acknowledge that and let the knowledge seep through your bones to the very core of your being. There is nothing you can do about it.

Take a deep breath now, and step over the threshold of understanding.

I weep, for the carved prow

sinks slowly beneath the sea.

Your sisters have indeed rendered unto your father with love. His face is calm. He lies as if he is only asleep. He looks calm and younger than his years. His face is smooth and glistening. His hair is threaded with grey strands. His hands are folded over his breast, across the white coverlet.

Stand for a while, loving him.

And the kawakawa leaves in my hands?

They are the signs of mourning.

'I'm glad you're home, son,' your mother says.

Kneel down beside her. With tenderness, she touches your face with her hands, tracing your forehead, your cheeks, your brow. She curls her hands under your chin to bring your lips together. Lips, and then noses to touch.

'Doesn't your father look so handsome?'

There is only the sound of the rain falling.

'Hello, Dad. I've come back. I'm here.'

Death comes, but I

am not yet dead.

I breathe

I live . . .

part four

■17

t he tangi marks the end of one life, the beginning of another. Before it stretch the greenstone years of a boy with his father. They were happy years, possessed with aroha, and that love created a world for me which I thought I would never want to leave. Yet, eventually, leave I did.

I'm not going to say that my schooling was easy; far from it. I soon realised that maintaining my own personal sovereignty as a Maori was something I had to fight for. I wasn't the only one: all my other male cousins, like Tamatea, Simeon and Andrew, had a hard time of it. In those days, schooling was streamed and, depending on your educational background, you were either placed in academic or commercial, which was the 'A' stream, or trade training or home sciences, which was the 'B' stream. The majority of Maori students were automatically placed in 3B, 4B and 5B — that is, if they hadn't already left school at fifteen. At Dad's insistence, and despite the headmaster's objections, I was placed in the 'A' stream. I was like an eel out of water, thrashing my way through 3A, 4A and 5A in maths, geometry and algebra with rock-bottom grades but making up in geography, history and English.

As well as the battles with education at school, there was also the matter of coping with the world of Gisborne society. On the surface, the town was the model of a bicultural society where Maori and Pakeha got on very well with each other; however, the same kind of 'streaming' was at work. Nobody commented on it — it was just the way the world was — but Pakeha were 'A' citizens and

Maori were 'B' citizens. Some of my elders, particularly if they had Anglican or Roman Catholic connections, like Hepa Walker, made it to the society pages, but there was not much crossing over.

I don't think anybody thought about it as racism as such. At the boyhood level I had good Pakeha mates with whom I played in the school rugby, hockey and tennis teams. When puberty kicked in, I was attracted to Pakeha girls and they to me, and nobody appeared to raise any objections to it. However, scratch the surface, and what you found was the potential for conflict, the inequality that was exposed during the 1970s when Maori began to notice their 'B' status. Riripeti would have told us that it had always been there from the beginning; migration simply brought to it a different, urban focus. There were Pakeha bosses and Maori workers. There were the Pakeha who had the privileges and the Maori who did not. There were the Pakeha parts of town and the Maori parts of town. Sometimes the barriers were permeable but most times they could not be negotiated. One day, my best friend, Michael, invited me to his fourteenth birthday. Came the day, his mother rang up and said he was sick. I'd already bought him a present so I went to give it to him. I knocked on the door. His mother answered it. Behind her, I could see Michael and other friends sitting down to the birthday feast. His mother at least had the decency to appear embarrassed.

'Would you like to come in?' she asked.

'Thank you, but no,' I answered.

Michael came to the door to see me. 'I told Mum I wanted you here,' he said. 'I've never ever thought of you as being a Maori, Tama. You're just my mate, eh.'

Then there was the matter of my dating Rebecca. She was my first sweetheart, a lovely, kind-hearted girl who was at Sacred Heart College. We started going out when we were fifth formers, and we were getting pretty serious. Her parents must have noticed how strongly the relationship was developing because, one night, when I went to pick her up to take her to a movie, her dad came to the door.

'Hello, Tama,' he said. 'I'm afraid I have to put a stop to your seeing our Becky, mate. We like you and while you two were having fun we didn't mind. But Becky has her future to think about.'

As soon as Mr Jackson said the words, I knew exactly what the problem was. Although he went on about how important it was for Rebecca to go to university,

I knew that there was no way in which I would ever be considered as any kind of fixture in her bright future.

Rebecca didn't have the same attitude. 'Can't they see you?' she asked on our last night together, her tears streaming, tracing her fingers tenderly across my face. 'You're just Tama. Your being Maori and my being Pakeha, what's that got to do with the way we feel about each other?'

Race politics was something that I never expected. Neither did Andrew, who wanted to be a lawyer, or Simeon and Haromi. We all shared the same experiences of prejudice and we became wary and distrustful. If it wasn't for my form teacher, Mr Grundy, I might have chucked it all in, joined other Maori friends and got flushed down the drain with the rest of the tuna in the 'B' stream. But Mr Grundy, who was an old closet Marxist, took a keen interest in my abilities in English and history. The history text we were reading privileged the British perspective of colonisation, and therefore every battle fought by British soldiers at Khartoum, Cairo, Delhi, Ottawa or in good old Aotearoa was either a marvellous victory or a marvellous defeat. When Mr Grundy taught us about 'The Maori Wars', in which Great Britain responded to the valiant settlers because of a native uprising, he was watching me closely to see my reaction. I was wondering, 'When do these people get off?' I remembered the globe without Waituhi on it, my encyclopedia (consigned to the rubbish bin long ago) with lists of capitals of the states of America, Great Britain and Europe — and now this textbook telling me how to view my own history? I walked out of the class. Of course, when I returned I got six of the best for truancy from Mr Grundy. After he administered the punishment, however, he both complimented and criticised me.

'I always felt that you showed signs of an individual mind,' he began, 'and at least you didn't just sit there while I dished up all that regurgitated rubbish. But never walk away, Master Mahana. Walking away is not an appropriate response. Fight back, young sir.'

It was old Grundy who helped to develop my sense of a social conscience. Although I sometimes failed him — 'Oh, Master Mahana,' he would sigh, 'don't tell me what you see. Tell me what you *see*' — by the time I reached the sixth form I was making more hits than misses in my attempts to interrogate the processes of history and literature and the difference between seeing and *seeing*. 'You have Maori eyes,

Master Mahana,' he would tell me. 'For God's sake, boy, bloody well use them.'

I wrote an essay for the school magazine competition. It was entitled, 'The Maori Wars? No, They Were the Pakeha Wars.' In the essay I asked why we were studying from textbooks published in Great Britain. I challenged why the Treaty of Waitangi was not even mentioned in any of them. I didn't win the competition but, after I left school and was desperate for a job, Mr Grundy would not let me go the way of my peers into oblivion. He asked me to tea at his home. When I arrived, there was another gentleman with him, Jock Burns, chief editor of our city newspaper.

'Mr Grundy has spoken very highly of you,' Mr Burns said. 'He believes you have a questing mind but, even better, an exceptional eye and an opinion. Have you thought of a career in journalism?'

I joined *The Gisborne Herald*. Mum and Dad were thrilled. But, for them, my career was to prove a double-edged sword. The fact was that not only was I growing up, I was also growing out. There comes a time when, no matter how much you are loved, you really want to be free. Working at the newspaper only exacerbated my burgeoning independence. I saw change, read about change and wrote about change every day when I went to work. I should have known that all this would bring me head to head with Dad.

That's the rub. Although Dad had earlier led me to believe I could grow, his permission had limits. I wasn't the first son to come to the realisation that the only person stopping me from becoming what I wanted was my dad.

When does it start, this battle between father and son?

I was still at home, boarding, when I began my working life. Mum was proud of the paycheck I was bringing to the household. My father was happy, also, but he still had his rules and I had to live by them. They were the usual rules that all teenagers since the days of Elvis have fought against: 'Don't smoke, don't hang out at the billiard saloon, don't move with the wrong crowd, don't have sex, don't stay out all night, just don't.'

Some people would say that our battles, when they began, were inevitable. They came with the territory. In the first instance, they came with puberty and adolescence. They came with sex, drugs and rock 'n' roll. They came with James Dean and *Rebel Without a Cause*, the film that set me alight with feelings of rebellion. They came with the day when I suddenly I realised that I was taller than my father, bigger than he was and arrogant enough to feel I was better than a man who worked on the chain in the freezing works.

One evening, I exploded. 'Why don't you ever say yes to me, Dad? Why do you always say no?'

'That's what fathers are supposed to do,' Dad answered. 'If I don't tell you when I think your behaviour is wrong, then you might believe I condone what you're doing — and I don't. Now, some of my prohibitions might sound harsh, and I'm the first to concede that I might make the wrong decisions for you. But you're still my son and you're still living under my roof. Is that clear enough?'

Yes sirree, it was all loud and clear. *You're still living under my roof.*

My sisters had their own complaints. Like me, they were also growing up and out, adding further strain to Mum and Dad's strictures. My previous close relationship with Ripeka changed as she developed from a girl into a young woman of sixteen; eventually she substituted me with Victor, her one and only serious boyfriend. Mere and Wiki also both became too cute and vivacious for their own good and were soon playing havoc with the teenage boys in the neighbourhood, much to Mum and Dad's disapproval. As for me, I had another girlfriend by then, Janice, a nurse, and we had begun sleeping together. All our relationships with each other — mine with my sisters, theirs with each other, ours with Mum and Dad — were marked by growing tensions and arguments as we developed other interests, loyalties and lives beyond the obligations to family. Mum and Dad's reaction, however, was not to loosen the belt but to tighten it, and commiserate with each other. 'Oh, who would want to be a parent?' I heard Dad moan through the wall between my bedroom and theirs. 'Never mind, dear,' Mum answered. 'Tell you what, when all this is over, let's run away from home.'

Let's face it: growing up is messy. The father I loved began to become too confining. It was still his watch but he wasn't aware that I was starting to look out for myself. Admittedly, he was excited by the way I was developing but, when I started to go what he called 'wide out' — as if I was one of his sheepdogs, like Good Boy, disobedient to his whistle — he became anxious. He feared that my trajectory was taking me beyond family expectations and tribal frameworks. He wasn't able to cut me loose, let alone cut me some slack. As well, there were more financial strains on the family. My younger brother, Hone, was born to keep Marama company; what with Dad being the sole breadwinner, we sure needed the extra money.

But once you get the taste of freedom, it becomes a drug. A couple of my friends, including Michael, decided to go flatting, and once I saw the freedom that came with living away from one's family, man oh man, I wanted it. For one thing, Michael's flat was the only place I could spend the night with Janice. One weekend, Dad came around. We'd had a party the night before and he was shocked at the mess, the women, the chaos, and told me I was to come home. I said no.

Our battles escalated. 'I don't recognise you, son,' Dad would say. 'You're growing into somebody I don't understand.'

He was having problems? What about *me?* Sometimes, when I looked in the mirror I couldn't recognise myself, either. It wasn't a matter of physical appearance — I became a young man who looked as if he could own the world — but more of what was happening inside. My soul hungered to escape, not just from Dad's prohibitions, but also from the overlay of his traditional Maori values. Immured in them — the role of the oldest, the obligations to marae and to kin — he began to view my growing independence as a moving away from my duties as a Maori and a son of the iwi.

'Dad, can you blame me?' I asked him. 'There's a great wind of change blowing through our country, through New Zealand as a whole, and I want to make it in the Pakeha world now.'

His response? 'Sometimes you have to stand against the wind.'

'If you do that, you can be uprooted, Dad, and blown away.'

'Then bend with it, son, and let the wind blow over you.'

I couldn't do that. I was affected by the new perspectives that life was bringing. I'm talking about a time when movies began with a clip of 'God Save the Queen' and people stood up while it played. During that same period people stopped standing up because Great Britain was cutting the apron strings with its colonies like New Zealand and Australia, and we were forced to look for other markets for our lamb and butter. With the cutting of the umbilical cord, a different kind of nationalism was abroad, a new optimism about the ways in which New Zealand was creating fresh relationships for itself in the world and the roles that young New Zealanders had in making it happen.

The umbilical cord was also being cut at the personal level. I liked this terrible thing, this independent person I was becoming, even if others didn't. I couldn't see anything wrong in wanting to be somebody and grabbing everything the world had to offer — even if I had to walk away from the Maori world to do it.

My clashes, not just with Dad but with my mother and sisters, began to go more and more into the danger zone. They called me 'whakahihi', getting too big for my boots, or having ideas above my station. Instead of enthusing with me whenever I returned from a day at *The Gisborne Herald*, filled to the brim with news of what was happening out there in the big wide international world, they would retreat to the safety of their own. If I talked about what was happening in the USA, about Martin Luther King or Malcolm X, or the great changes that were sweeping Africa in Kenya and Rhodesia, it was like talking to the air.

Was it any wonder, therefore, that I sought to share ideas with friends beyond my family — or that those friends were Pakeha? Instead of going home from the flat at weekends, like a dutiful son, I stayed with Janice and my mates, drinking, arguing, having fun, talking politics, economics, films and music, and playing rugby on Saturdays. The disapproval from Mum, Dad and my sisters, whenever I did manage to visit, became palpable; with them I was reduced to being a son again. The slightest change in my physical appearance would be marked by a comment like, 'You're looking like a Pakeha in that suit and tie.' Any verbal acuity I showed was put down with, 'You're talking all la de da like a Pakeha.' Whenever I took Janice, Michael or any of my other mates around to the house, Mum would say, 'What's wrong with Maori girls? And have you stopped seeing your Maori friends?' I now know that this conflict is inevitable between one generation and another, but it was still bruising.

One evening, I was supposed to go with Mum and Dad to a wedding on Mum's side of the family at Ruatoria. However, Jock Burns wanted me to stand by the teletype at *The Gisborne Herald* as news was coming in about Richard Nixon's inauguration as the thirty-seventh president of the United States. Even so, I dashed around home to explain to Mum and Dad. I thought they would understand.

'What's President Nixon got to do with us?' Dad asked. 'You are failing in your obligations to whanau. Where's your sense of aroha, whanaungatanga and manaakitanga?'

He made me so angry. I suddenly realised why Tane, god of Man, had separated his parents, Earth and Sky. It was so that he could stand in the bright strand between and *breathe*.

I took my first gasp of air, flexed my muscles and heaved. 'What would you know about what's important in the world?' I said to Dad. 'You're just a freezing worker who's so busy slitting sheep's throats you wouldn't recognise what's happening around you until it shat in your face.'

It was a terrible thing to say. Dad came roaring at me, fists raised and before we knew it we were fighting. Mum and my sisters began screaming. 'Tama,' Mum yelled, 'apologise to your father.'

Damned if I was going to let him keep on stopping me from what I wanted to do with my life. The decisions he was making for me were based on his life, his traditions, his values and his expectations. They were right for him and for the son he thought that I should be; but they were wrong for me, for the son I wanted to be.

We wove around each other, throwing punches, blocking, trying to get between each other's guard. I saw a look pass over my father's face — and he began to go on the defensive and not push his offensive. He began to retreat — but did I care? I should have known what he was thinking.

'I can't defeat my son. If I do that, what will that say to him about who is stronger?'

When Dad finally put down his guard and opened himself to the blow that knocked him to the ground, I should have known this was an act of love, an act of acceptance. My fist smashed through his defences and he went down.

My mother slapped me hard. My sisters began to rail against me. I lifted Dad from the floor and sobbed on his shoulders. 'Dad, you've brought me all this way through my life, and I thank you for it. But you're going to have to let me go, Dad, please. Where will I go and what will I become? I don't know. Will I make mistakes? Yes, a lot, probably. But I've got to figure out my own destiny and I'm sorry I have to say it, but don't keep standing in my way. Please, Dad, stand aside. Let me pass.'

A few weeks later, I saw a job being advertised at *The Evening Post* in Wellington. I didn't tell Dad about my application. He would only have said no. I was offered the job and I accepted it.

Mum was furious when I told her I was leaving home. 'Don't we have a say at all, son?'

As for Dad, he had just come back from another day at the office, slicing sheep's throats. He was looking haunted, weary, defeated. He said to Mum, 'Let him go to Wellington, Huia. It's better this way.'

I was eighteen when I left Gisborne and went to Wellington. Janice was a good sport about it; 'Go for it,' she said. My feelings, I suppose, were not too different from those of the young soldier who boarded the train at Wairoa. He sits opposite me, staring out the window as the train leaves Waipukurau. In his eyes I see the sadness and eagerness of all young men and women who have lived in small country towns and are travelling somewhere else.

What are the dreams of young soldier boys?

A year after I left Gisborne, Dad phoned to tell me that he and Mum were moving back to family land at Waituhi. A lot happened during that year. I had gone, my sister Ripeka married Victor and Mere became pregnant to Koro. So, that year there were two weddings and I went back to Gisborne for both of them. At Mere's nuptials Nani Miro made a droll remark about my bachelor status. 'You better watch out, boy,' she said, 'your gears might go rotten.'

After the wedding Dad explained why he had decided to return to the valley. 'The only ones at home now are me and your mother and the three younger ones,' he said, 'and the Matua has been after me to attend to our family responsibilities in Waituhi. There's a small farm with a cottage on it that she's giving us.'

I was really pleased for Dad. Working on the killing chain had taken a lot out of him, physically diminishing him. 'That's great news, Dad,' I said to him. 'Waituhi is where you belong.' I was also relieved for another reason. In the back of my mind I had always known that my parents had shifted us to Gisborne to ensure a better education for me and my sisters. Now the responsibility of carrying that knowledge and feeling obligated to it was gone.

Dad gave a small laugh. 'It's the best thing that your mum and I can do,' he began. 'You and your entire generation are going too wide out into the Pakeha world, especially you. Somebody has got to keep ahi kaa, keep the home fires going, so that you know how to find your way back again. We have to be your lifeline back to us.'

When Dad said that, I was reminded of a scene in *2001: A Space Odyssey*. A crewman on a spaceship had gone tumbling into space; it was only because he was attached by a line to the spaceship that he was able to be pulled back to it. I liked Dad's image of himself pulling me back across the dark void of the universe to Spaceship Waituhi. I had to admit to myself that, just in case anything happened to me, the thought of Dad reeling me back in, reeling me home, made me feel safe.

Waituhi was Dad; Dad was Waituhi. The least I could do was to take a week off, go back and help him and Mum move to the valley. Everybody helped — my sisters and brother and brothers-in-law — and we laughed and joked as we remembered those many other times we had shifted from one place to the next. But, somehow, this shift was different.

It was the last, and I think we all knew it.

Now that Dad has gone, who will pull me back to safety?

18

*W*ho *are these people coming out of the sun?*

The mourners are stirring again, unfolding, to peer into the sunlight. They look into the red haze of another day, another welcoming. A black veiled group is approaching Rongopai. More visitors have arrived. From out of the sun they are coming. The old women of the marae open their arms to welcome them.

'Welcome. Welcome. Welcome. Come to our dead.'

Is that the karanga again? Haere mai ki o tatou mate e, haere mai, haere mai.

The Matua has directed Mattie Jones to call the visitors onto the marae. Her call grows more intense, soaring louder and higher. The sound pierces the sun. It shatters into ribbons of light as the mourners step through the gateway. The visiting group comes forward to stand, heads bowed, in front of the porch of Rongopai. There, my father lies in state, in an open casket, surrounded by weeping women.

On the first day, it is the locals, the people of Te Whanau a Kai, who attend: kuia, koroua, whanaunga, tamariki, all those with whom I share a kin relationship. They come; they stay. They know what their role is. It is to help the whanau pani, the grieving family, by mourning with them and then taking the logistical burden of the tangi off their shoulders.

'Tama, we are so sorry about Rongo. He was a wonderful provider, not just for the family but for the iwi. How will we get on without him?'

Is this still the first day? Yes, it is still the first day.

Ours is a tribal response to death. When death comes, everybody feels it. The loss resonates through the tribal whakapapa, heartfelt, reminding all about bloodlines and how blood links family to family, generation to generation, all the way back to the beginning of the world. The iwi comes to pay tribute not only to the deceased but also to history and the place of all the tribe in it. They come onto the marae, walking in groups as small as three people to groups as large as thirty. They come led by their own family elder and senior women. They bring their children and grandchildren with them to witness the death, to say goodbye to Dad and to acknowledge their continuing loyalty and love to the grieving family. In some cases, this is the first time any of the tamariki have seen a person in death. Every attempt is made to make the encounter as affirming as possible for them.

The women are attired in black, the old men in suits and ties, the younger generation more casually dressed. Some of the young fathers carry their children in their arms, hugging them closely. Many of them do not speak Maori. They rely on their elder to speak for them, watching him and listening to him as, after the karanga, he speaks on their behalf.

The family groups are welcomed from the paepae, the place of chiefs, by one of our own elders. They are the traditional spokesmen of the iwi: Ringatu elders like Tamati Kota, who once served Riripeti; or Nani Tama, Miro Mananui's husband. They also include the senior men of the Mahana clan, like Uncle Pita, or local men like Hepa Walker and Charlie Whatu — kicking and protesting because he has never liked to be in front. The welcomes are formal and conducted with grave dignity.

'Welcome, ki a tatou te whanau. Welcome to Rongopai. Come, let us say farewell to our dead.'

After each group has been welcomed, both sides sing a waiata to complete the mihimihi. They sit beside my mother and comfort her and leave a koha, a gift of money or promise of support to see us through the expenses of the tangi.

But that is not all. The men come to me or Uncle Pita. 'We'll do our usual thing,' they say. Before you know it, some of them have joined the paepae, because the duties of welcoming visitors are arduous and better shared. Others go to help the men and boys putting down the hangi, out fishing or pig hunting, or up preparing the cemetery for the third day. As for the women, they take mattresses into Rongopai or Takitimu Hall and make up their beds before joining others doing the karanga or working in the kitchen.

During all this, my mother and sisters sit beside Dad. But they are not asleep. By the end of the tangi their eyes will be fevered with the days of sun and with watching, through the night, the flights of falling stars across the midnight universe.

I stand close by, and my mother catches my eye. 'I see the mourners, son. I see them coming.'

What night is this? Let this night be endless. Let the sun never rise.

When the darkness falls, it brings relief from the day. The night is clear and filled with a deep and utter stillness. The earth is replenishing the indefinable aroha between earth and man.

I walk through the evening to Takitimu Hall. Mum has told me to come to make sure the people who are sleeping here are comfortably settled. She also wants me to thank the ringawera, the 'hot hands' who are working in the kitchen. Dinner is over and they are clearing the tables.

The Matua, Nani Miro, comes to sit beside me. She wags a stern finger. 'Long time no see,' she says. 'If you don't watch out, we'll forget what you look like. How long has it been since you were home? And look at you! You're too skinny. Are you sick or are you in love?' She jostles me playfully and I smile at her. ' See?' she yells to the women in the kitchen. 'I told you I could make him smile!'

The women come out and sit with me: Aunt Ruth, Aunt Sarah, Haromi and some of the younger girls. 'You haven't made him laugh though,' Maka tiko bum says. 'I could do the thing with my eyes. Or shall I wiggle my bum?'

'Oh, puh-lease don't do that,' one of the other women says. 'If you wiggle your bum, a screw might come loose and it will fall off.'

They all start laughing and I can't help joining in.

'We made him laugh,' they yell triumphantly.

'We made our nephew laugh.'

Nani Miro hugs me. 'It's always the women who keep the people together,' she says. 'In sickness or health, laughter or tears, till death do us part. Never forget, nephew. And come back more often.'

Back at Rongopai, the children lie curled near Mum, sleeping with their heads in her lap, their hands tightly locked in hers. The electric light in the porch cuts the darkness with a gleaming arc. Within the light the mourners sit huddled in blankets.

A car swings round the road. For a moment its headlights dazzle me. It roars towards the meeting house and then, oops, the driver remembers the tangi is being held. He sheepishly turns off the engine and the car coasts past in silence. Then, with another roar and a couple of sharp reports like farts, the car zooms on again. 'Bimbo's feeding his car too much hay,' someone complains.

My mother is still awake. The wind blows beneath the eaves of the meeting house. She shivers.

'Mum, are you warm enough?'

She puts her hands across Dad's body and places her head close to his. 'Your father keeps me warm.' After a while, she adds, 'And you keep me warm, too, son. I'm glad you came back.'

The moon rises, casting a calm glow over the land. Wisps of smoke curl from the houses like fingers clutching at the moon. Afar off, the mountains are silhouetted against the blue drenched sky.

Sleep well, whanau, sleep well, until the sun shines again.

Around two o'clock in the morning, somebody starts to sing. They sing to keep company with my mother as she maintains her vigil beside Dad. It's Aunt Sarah; she always had a loud and awful voice. Luckily, someone with a sweeter voice is also keeping the watch.

'E pari ra, nga tai ki te akau, e hotu ra ko taku manawa

As the tide beats against the shore so beats my sorrowing heart —'

Other voices join in the song; I recognise Aunt Molly, Aunt Ruth and Aunt Teria. One by one, the mourners lift their heads to the light, looking toward the place where Dad lies. The trouble is that everybody is singing out of tune and their rhythms are all shot to pieces.

Agnes Whatu comes grumbling from inside the meeting house. 'How do you expect anybody to sleep with all this racket! And singing so badly, gee whiz, come on people! Shift over and give me the guitar.' That does it. More mourners come out to join us. They pull their gumboots over pyjamas and slip jerseys over their shoulders because the night is cold. They come from the cookhouse, from tending the hangi, to sit with the night watchers and share their blankets with them.

'Tena ra, tahuri mai, e te tau, te aroha.' The people come, the whanau sit and fill the night with their song.

'That's better,' Agnes Whatu says. 'Your singing was oh so tragic.'

'Tenei ra, ahau te tangi nei, mohou kua wehea nei.' They sing in unison, swaying and holding hands, looking at Dad. 'Haere ra, mahara mai, e te tau, kia mau ki au. Haere ra, ka tuturu ahau. Haere ra.'

The song comes to a close and, yay, everybody manages to end on the same note. Aunt Sarah yells, 'So how did you like our song, Rongo?'

Once they have started, the whanau can't be stopped. Song follows song and, very soon, people are doing kapa haka, standing up and doing the actions, the men trying to keep their pyjama bottoms from falling around their ankles.

'Oh no,' Aunt Sarah says as Uncle Jack shows everything. 'Stop flashing, Jack.'

As long as the people are joined together, there is no darkness. As long as there is such aroha as this, I will never be alone.

And now it is the second day. The tribes of Aotearoa are coming.

In the early morning, Uncle Pita takes me aside. 'Come with me,' he says. 'We have to set up another marquee beside Takitimu Hall. We're expecting a lot of people today and we might need an exra tent for the overflow.' He yells out to Dad, 'Hey, brother, why didn't you tell us you were so popular?'

I get into the truck. Uncle starts the engine and we leave Rongopai behind. The road unwinds before us. We do not speak for a while. We pass a field, half-ploughed.

'Actually,' Uncle Pita begins, 'there's something we have to talk about. You know, don't you, that your father was the one who looked after the Mahana land out here? He was the one who spoke on our behalf at the land meetings. Now that he's gone, who's going to do that? Are you coming home to take his place?'

'I've always been hopeless at tribal things,' I answer. 'Everybody knows that.'

'You'll just have to learn, like the rest of us,' Uncle Pita replies. We grow silent again. The truck slows down and bumps through a paddock to a shed where hay is kept. Uncle Pita switches off the engine. He turns to me. 'Tama, you have responsibilities. You do not shoulder them by yourself. You have always had the strength but never the test of that strength. Don't worry about the future. If you feel it's getting too much for you, you lean on me, eh? You lean on me.'

We walk up the hill to Takitimu Hall. By chance, Uncle Pita looks back the way we've come. Far off he sees a cloud of dust coming along Lavenham Road.

'What the heck is that?'

Back at Rongopai, I hear the rituals of welcome again.

Our people say that you can never take the measure of a man until it is shown to you at his death.

A large group, the biggest that has come to the tangi so far, is approaching. They are stirring the dust with their feet, the dust swirling like angels in the clear sky. Already, even though they are not in sight of the marae, their women are calling, karanga pealing through the air.

Immediately, the Matua is on the alert. 'E hika,' she says, 'we've been caught on the hop.' She calls for reinforcements of men and women to do the karanga and a haka powhiri. She yells to Nani Tama, 'Don't just sit there, Tama. Get your paepae ready.' The Matua is always bossy. To add insult to injury, she tells Nani Tama, 'You'll need five speakers. Put Tamati Kota on with you.'

Nani Tama and the other men sharing the paepae with him grumble to each other. 'Who does the Matua think she is, telling us what to do? Let her do her job and let us do ours.'

The travelling mourners appear at the bend of the road. They come to a halt, the dust swirling over them. They seem to have come out of some cyclonic eye of time, from the land of Sheba. Striking, proud, polished ebony by the sun, their impact is stunning.

'They are our own people of the Ringatu,' the Matua says. 'They have come from their land of exile at Ohiwa. Oh, welcome them, people, acclaim them, for they have not been seen in our own lands for many years!' She steps forward and her voice rings with pride, 'Haere mai, e nga manuhiri,' she calls. 'E nga morehu, haere mai, haere mai, haere mai.'

Tamati Kota is so overcome at the sight of the visitors that he jumps out in front of the men to do a haka of welcome. 'Ka mate, ka mate! Ka ora, ka ora!'

The people from Ohiwa make stately procession onto the marae. Tamati Kota is so fired up with passion that he takes the main speaking position on the paepae. He lets rip with an ancient tauparapara of spellbinding intellectual power, and hits his chest with his old fists. 'I can go to my own death gladly and with joy now that I have seen that you still survive your exile, you, of the Ringatu, whom the government pursued throughout our lands. Children of the

Israelites, welcome to Rongopai.'

Ah yes, the remembering of history is also what happens at the tangihanga. It is the occasion for linkages, long sundered by time, to be forged again. The whole history of our tribe, as followers of the Ringatu religion, has been one of resistance and the pursuit of Riripeti's dream of sovereignty. Some of these visitors were survivors of the flu epidemic of 1918. They were children at the time, and were saved by Riripeti, who built Te Waka o te Atua, the Ship of God, a tented hospital on the slopes behind Rongopai.

'When the wind came up the valley,' the visitors tell us later, 'its canvas tents flapped like beautiful white sails in the wind. The Matriarch was a great patriot. It is only right that we come to pay tribute to Riripeti at the tangihanga of her beloved son.'

On the marae, men, women and children who have not seen each other for years come together in joy and to shed tears not just for Dad but for their survival. During the afternoon, they introduce new family members, husbands, wives, and children born into a new generation.

'Yeah, my new son-in-law,' one of the elders from Ohiwa tells Uncle Pita. 'I caught him sneaking out of Bessie's window, and they got married just two months before she dropped her sweet little bundle of joy on us all, eh babe.'

Uncle Pita looks askance at his own son, my cousin Waka, now married to Ani, who is pregnant. 'Through the window, eh? Must run in the family,' he answers drily.

Meanwhile, Tamati Kota, Nani Miro and Nani Tama are in deep conversation with other Ohiwa elders. Large books carrying the whakapapa of the Ohiwa people have been brought to the tangihanga so that their genealogies and the whakapapa of the people of Te Whanau a Kai can be updated and amended.

'Wharaurangi is gone?' Nani Miro asks. 'But he had four sons, didn't he? Oh, five? What were their names? And did they have children? Who have their children married? Where have their lines gone in the weaving of te taura tangata?'

Her eyes are shining with joy. With this new information, the covenant of Israel can be kept.

A moment of aching, breathtaking beauty arrests the world. While the old ones discuss the whakapapa, an ancient kuia, who had met Te Kooti Arikirangi, stands to sing farewell to Dad, a mokopuna of Te Kooti.

'Haruru ana te Tira a Whiro taia ake ahau e te mate i muri nei e,' she sings.

She encompasses me in her song. 'From this day forward you will always be alone. Your father is gone now and the world is filled with darkness. He was a good man, the axis of your universe, the sun giving light to your day. Now clouds obscure the sun. All the world laments with you. And this place has become desolate with ashes and sorrow. You breathe, you live, you call, but there will be no answering reply. The tide ebbs silently away.'

The ancient one comes across to me, still singing, her hands outstretched. 'Whakarongo ki te tai e tangi haere ana, whakariri ana te rae ki Turanga. Listen, child, to the tides lamenting as they flow, surging sullenly by the headland at Turanga. I weep with you. Our anchor is gone and we are cast adrift together at the mercy of the sea.'

She performs movements to her lament. They are slow ritual movements, one gesture blending into another. She touches her breast with her palms and turns the palms toward the gathering. Her fingers quiver upon her eyes, then flicker down her body, enacting the falling of her tears. With a bold sweep, she touches her lips with her hands and lifts her hands, shivering the aroarowhaki toward the sky. She becomes a gannet circling and calling for a companion, sweeping low over the water to touch the tips of the waves with her wings. Soaring aloft, she flutes her sorrow across the desolate expanse. Far away she sees another bird. She wings after it, a solitary feather rising in pursuit in a soft grey sky. The wailing soars around her like spray spuming ever higher up the face of a cliff. And she soars through it, through the waves cascading and the spray falling.

'The clouds in the south I see before me as you wend your way over Maungapohatu. But I cannot follow you for you have already gone into the clouds.'

Later, after the people from Ohiwa have gone to eat and to unpack their gear, I see Ripeka and Mere are still crying. The Matua goes up to them and hugs them.

'Daughters, why are you still weeping? Haven't you been uplifted by the love of the people for your father? Were you not made proud and happy by the tributes paid by the morehu of Ohiwa? Take strength from them. Save some tears for tomorrow.'

'We can't stop,' Ripeka says. 'Nor is there any tomorrow now that Dad's dead.'

'Alas, tomorrow will certainly come,' Miro answers. 'Cry again then, girls. Weep then.'

The women are calling again. Is this still the second day? Who is coming?

The tribal visitors keep coming. They interrupt a conversation I'm having with Charlie Whatu, Sam Walker and some of the other so-called no-hopers of the village with their tats and prison records. The men expect me to take some measure of charge. Is this not the role of the son? To stand in the place of the father when he is gone?

Actually, Charlie Whatu has been quite sneaky in making me think I am making the decisions. 'The drinking water is running low,' he says. 'Do you think, Tama, that Sam and some of the other boys should go into town and get a small tanker?' Or, 'Mattie Jones tells me that some of the toilets are blocked over at Takitimu Hall. Who do you want to go over there and fix the situation?' Quickly I tell Charlie what I know he would have done anyway. 'You're the boss,' he says.

I walk back to the marae and see, with some relief, that the kuia and koroua on the paepae have the welcome to the new group of mourners well under control.

'It's another big group, nephew,' Uncle Pita tells me. 'They have come from just over the hill.'

When he says it like that, 'just over the hill,' I hear chuckles from the old men on the paepae, yeah, right. The Tuhoe people, the Children of the Mist, are our close kin, but it's mountains rather than a hill between us. They are gorgeous, glossy, handsome, dark-skinned people, and they will have come by walking down Rua's track from Maungapohatu. In the old days, up to the 1930s, Tuhoe horse teams some forty strong would be spread out over a mile as they trekked into our lands.

The mihimihi is in full swing. Nani Tama is alert to all the nuances of the speechmaking. He is from Tuhoe himself and, in the past, has often had to defend his marriage to Nani Miro; their wedding was a taumau contract between our tribes. It was a great scandal when it occurred because the Matua was twenty years older than Nani Tama and, well, she was not exactly a beauty. 'Just let any of them discuss her appearance or cast one off-colour reference to our marriage,' he tells me, 'and they'll get a taiaha up their bum.'

Today, however, the people from Tuhoe are on their best behaviour;

surprising because not only are they the most passionate and fiery people who walk the earth, but they also have an unrestrained wit. Their kaumatua, Hori Rua, wears a feather cloak and stands in the centre of the marae.

'Tihei mauri ora,' Hori begins. His eyes flash fire; his shark-tooth earpieces flash with danger. He speaks of the relationship between Tuhoe and Te Whanau a Kai. Wi Pere gave some land at Ngatapa to Tuhoe, and a reciprocal relationship based on aroha, whanaungatanga and manaakitanga has been maintained ever since. Hori recites the whakapapa, the descent lines, which join us. He is a terrific recitalist. Although the Matua is approving, Nani Tama is not convinced.

'The old windbag,' Nani Tama mutters. 'He's just showing off to Miro. He was always after her.'

Hori Rua begins to speak about Dad. 'I knew Rongo when he came over the hill to help us out with our shearing and mustering. He was like a son to me.' Slowly, he unclasps the feather cloak from his shoulders. He brings it across to the porch where Dad is lying, lifts the cloak high, then drapes it on Dad's casket. 'Haere ra, tama. Farewell, nephew. Go to Te Reinga, the world after this life. Go to Hawaiki. There your ancestors will greet you. Heart of the whanau, haere ra. Shelterer from the winds, farewell. Giver of shade, haere ra. Farewell to Tawhiti-pamamao. Haere ra, Rongo. Haere. Haere. Haere.'

The cloak spreads across the porch like blood-gorged wings, curling slowly up and out toward the sky.

Who are these people who come to see Dad? I do not know them. Who are they?

My brother, Hone, comes running through the sunlight. 'Mummy told me to come and get you,' he says. I have been talking with the Matua about her dreams to resuscitate the great Maori hockey tournaments on the East Coast. When I get back to the marae, Mum is relieved. She points to the new visitors, standing at the gateway.

'They are some of your father's Pakeha friends from the freezing works. Tell them they are welcome and that our family is pleased to see them.'

I cross the marae toward the visitors. Two couples stand there. The men are ill at ease. Their wives are hesitant. 'I am Tama Mahana and Rongo Mahana is my father. Thank you for coming.'

'We wish to pay our respects,' one of the men answers. 'I'm Conrad

Bridger and I was Rongo's supervisor. Your father worked for me on the chain. He was one of the finest workers I ever had. The other men looked up to him. He was in line for a promotion.'

Mr Bridger's friend, Alfred Johnson, representing the working men's union, shakes my hand. 'We brought a wreath with us and a cheque to help with the funeral expenses. Rongo was a good bloke.'

'Thank you. Please join us.'

The wreath shimmers in the hot sunlight. The flowers glow with the colour of burning coals, with the crimson flickering of petals. Wild bees come to drink of the honey of the wreath.

Meanwhile, Nani Miro has joined Mum beside Dad on the porch. She looks at Marama and Hone, concerned. 'Go and play, you two. You've been good children sitting here with your mother, but join the other kids now.'

'Will Daddy mind?' Hone asks.

'No,' Mum says. 'Your Nani Miro is right. Go and play. Over there, on the edge of the marae, and let your father see you enjoying yourselves.'

'Okay,' Hone nods. He looks at Dad. 'But how can Daddy see when his eyes are closed?'

Even so, he and Marama run into the sunlight. A dog begins to bark. It is Good Boy, hurtling onto the marae to chase Marama. She yells with delight and plays hide and seek among the mourners.

'Hey, you kids,' Maka tiko bum says, 'don't you come and hide behind me. That dog's already bitten me once.'

My cousin, Haromi, sighs languidly. 'Now there's a thought,' she says. 'Hey, Good Boy, take another bite of Maka's big juicy bum.'

Hine Ropiho makes big eyes at Haromi. 'Oh no, don't get the poor dog to do that. He'll get poisoned.'

The assembly laughs. Other children appear. The afternoon sings with laughter. Good Boy barks and chases them, and the children scream and scatter in the sun. Hone turns toward the meeting house. His eyes are bright. His voice sparkles. 'Are you watching, Daddy? Are you watching?'

E kore au e ngaro,
He kakano i ruiruia mai i Raiatea.

Hone, you are of the seed of man that was brought from the ancient homeland of Raiatea to Aotearoa by canoe voyagers. You have their heritage in your veins. Every generation has the duty of ensuring that the next generation prosper. You will be nurtured.

Who is coming? Is that the women calling? No, it is only the wind. Let it be just the wind.

A bus, packed with people, stops just outside Rongopai. Passengers step down from it. The haze shimmers over them. Mattie Jones calls them onto the marae. Mum looks across at their kaumatua, shades her eyes from the sun, and looks again. She gives a cry of emotion.

'See, Rongo?' Mum weeps. 'My own father comes; Dad, my sisters and my people of Ngati Porou are here to mourn with us.'

They are a magnificent sight, the people from the East Coast. Vigorous in the karanga and haka, they pull the sky down in their grief. Grandfather Moana approaches the porch. Between the vanguard of welcoming women he comes. He spreads his arms and tells the assembly about Dad, and how Dad had taken away one of his daughters.

'When Rongo came to ask for Huia's hand in marriage, I didn't want to let her go to him. I was very angry that he stole her away from me. For a long time I couldn't speak to either of them. Then one day Huia came back to visit me, and I could tell that she was happy. My heart melted toward this man. We began to know each other.' Grandfather Moana turns to me, my sisters and my little brother. 'I have travelled a long way to honour your father. He looked after your mother, cared for her and cleaved only unto her. And together your mother and father made fine and handsome children. What father-in-law can ask for more than to have grandchildren who will carry on the line? I tell you, his children, that his love for you all was boundless. He gave you love when you needed it and help when you asked for it. He did all things with aroha. I come to say to him: Go now, e Rongo, travel from this place, haere ra, e tama. Your journey to the other world is before you.'

The speech ends. Grandfather Moana comes forward, kneels beside Mum and presses noses with her.

'It's good to see you, Dad,' Mum says.

What day is this? So much light, so much sun.

Is that the karanga again? Which day is this? Has the sun risen once, twice, or is this its third rising?

The sky is a huge glistening eye, limitless and without depth. The sun is the eye's roving iris, swinging from one corner to the other. Its gaze is baleful and without compassion. It beats down heavily upon the marae where the throng of mourners gather. So many of them are here. Some sit on the long benches that ring the space around Rongopai. Others kneel on the wilting grass. Children play beyond the marae. An old kuia is asleep in the sun. A young woman rocks her child in her protecting arms. A boy is wandering back to the marquee where there is shade from the sun.

My mother reaches out to touch Ripeka's hand. 'Ripeka, you must be hungry. Go and eat, daughter. Mere, isn't it time to feed Kataraina? Go, all of you. Wiki, go. Take Marama and Hone with you. Go to Takitimu Hall and eat. Afterwards, play with the children. They must learn to laugh again.'

Mum tries to leaven her scolding with levity. 'Our children are still the same, Rongo,' she says to Dad. 'We've never had any privacy with them around, have we!'

I sign to Ripeka, Mere and Wiki to do as Mum has asked.

'You'll be okay, Mum?' Mere asks.

'Of course I will,' Mum replies. 'Now all of you, leave.'

Mere departs the porch. She washes her face and hands. The cool water is such a blessed relief. She picks up Kataraina, and unbuttons her blouse so that Kataraina can suckle at her breast. In the midst of death, Mere is the perfect image of life.

The rest of us walk over to the truck where Victor is waiting. 'We have to talk about where Mum should stay after all this is over,' Ripeka says. 'Victor and I have been thinking that we should come back here and stay with her. She'll need to have somebody around. The farm will be lonely now. Mum might have growled at Dad a lot, but she needed him. She thinks she's strong, but she isn't; she's just stubborn.'

'That sounds like a great idea,' I tell her.

'I'm not asking you,' Ripeka answers. 'I'm telling you what we're doing.' She hits me hard. 'You're never coming home, are you.'

Alway the sun spinning, spinning, spinning across the sky.

Which night is this? Is it the second night?

No, let it be the first night. If it's the second, then tomorrow will be the third day and soon afterward Dad will be buried in the family graveyard. I can't cope with the thought of burying him in the ground.

I sit with the men as they have a late-night beer. 'A lot of people came today,' Uncle Pita says. 'Looks like the boys will have to go pig-hunting again.' It was Uncle Pita's suggestion that I make sure we have some kegs handy for the workers at the end of the day.

'How about tonight?' Sam Walker asks. 'A good moon tonight.'

'That would be a way of keeping you from sneaking into the meeting house to sleep next to some unsuspecting girl,' Uncle Pita laughs. 'One thing about the tangi,' he says as he rolls himself a cigarette. 'It sure brings everybody together. Take my house: I've got my brothers back there with their kids, and my own kids too. There's hardly any room to move. But I'm enjoying it all.'

'We won't forget your father in a hurry,' Charlie Whatu continues. 'He kept himself in good shape, that cuz of mine. I can still see him now, running down that sideline in the game against East Coast a few years ago. It was my pass to him that saved our bacon that day.'

'Ah well, Tama,' Sam Walker says, 'you'll take your Dad's place on the wing, eh?'

Uncle Pita gets up and stretches. 'Let's hit the sack, boys. Another day tomorrow.'

Another day tomorrow; another life tomorrow.

Around midnight there is a punch-up in the meeting house between Hori Rua, the Tuhoe kaumatua, and Nani Tama. The fight has been simmering ever since the Tuhoe people arrived. While they are undressing for bed, Hori makes a reference to Nani Tama's manhood. No matter how hard Nani Tama tried, the Matua had moved beyond her child-bearing years and remained childless. 'Your sperm didn't do their job because they were fired from a very short cannon,' the Tuhoe elder scoffs. 'Whereas, if they had come from mine —'

Nani Tama is so apoplectic that he almost swallows his front teeth. He runs across everybody, raises a fist, lands one, and Hori is seeing stars.

Later, in the early morning, while the moon shines full across the land, the songs begin again. They are the songs and chants of the Ringatu people, bringing

God's presence to the tangi. After the songs come the stories, sung, chanted and spoken through the stomach of the night. They are stories of Te Kooti Arikirangi and the Prophet's escape from the Chatham Islands. They are tales of valour, telling of the morehu as they were pursued throughout the length and breadth of the land, even unto Puketapu Mountain. They are stories of the fall of Waerenga a Hika pa and the siege at Ngatapa.

No, the past is never behind us. It is always before us.

Is this the third day? What day is this? When will the tangi be at an end?

When will there be an end to the long procession of mourners? They come, they still arrive. To weep over Dad where he lies, and then to weep with us, his family, where we watch over him. They bend toward us, to express their love and grief in the pressing of noses in the hongi.

They still come, still bend. They whisper of their love for Dad and for us, his family. As they do so, I realise that something wonderful is beginning to happen. We, the whanau pani, become buoyed by the love, lifted in the spirit, in such an extraordinary and loving way that it's like being held up in a cocoon of light. It's an indescribable feeling of weightlessness.

As the mourners bend toward us they leave behind a token of their aroha: a greenstone pendant to place with Dad in his grave, or a koha of money to help us and tide the family over our time of distress, or a flower wreath to make beautiful Dad's place of rest.

Every time they do this I feel myself lifting, lifting.

All of a sudden, Nani Miro looks at me. Although I am lifted in my spirit, she wants me to go into freefall. She gives me a grin, wags a finger and begins a comedic dance. Some of the other women watch her as she dips and sways like a coquette.

'E kii, Miro,' Maka tiko bum yells. 'Go, girl.'

'Tahi nei taru kino,' the Matua sings, swinging her hips and ogling me. 'Oh when I look at you, don't turn your face away. In your heart, darling, you know you love me. Welcome, oh welcome to you, my darling. Welcome, oh welcome, welcome to me.'

She plants a big juicy kiss from her big juicy lips on my face.

'And don't you forget it,' she says.

More people are coming. Out of the sun they are coming. Is it the afternoon already?

Another group of Pakeha approach the gateway. My heart melts when I see them. At long last, Sandra has arrived.

'Those Maori need a suntan,' Auntie Ruth quips. 'Friends of yours, Tama? Go and bring them on, nephew.'

I walk to the gateway to greet the group: Ted Smith and Ray Hargraves from *The Evening Post* have come with Sandra and my flatmate, Jasper. I hug Sandra and kiss her. She has dressed with care, covering her hair with a scarf.

'Hello, honey,' I say to her, my voice choking. 'I really appreciate your coming.'

'Oh Tama,' she answers. 'Are you managing okay?'

'We drove straight from the airport,' Ted says. 'George Ralston would have come, too, but somebody has to stay behind and get the paper out.'

'Cheers, mate,' Jasper says. 'What's up?' He's never been on a marae before and he's jittery and nervous.

I lead the group onto the marae. I can see Nani Miro, Maka tiko bum and Aunt Ruth nudgng each other. 'That must be Tama's girlfriend,' they whisper. When we stand before Dad, I address my thoughts to him.

'Dad, I know you only met Sandra once. I only wish you had got to know her better. You'd have really liked her, Dad, she's just gorgeous. You've met Ray Hargraves before; I've never quite forgiven you for going out that night on the town with him and getting drunk. How come you and I never had a drink together, Dad? Ted Smith is representing the office, Dad, and my flatmate Jasper is here too.'

Sandra has never seen a dead person in an open coffin. She handles the encounter with grace and tenderness. She spends some time sitting beside the casket, talking to Mum and my sisters. When she takes her scarf off, everybody gasps at her blonde hair.

'And here was I,' the Matua sighs to me, 'thinking I was your sweetheart, you heartbreaker you.'

Meanwhile, Auntie Maka has to get her two cents' worth in. 'Gee, she's pretty. You must have told her lots of lies about yourself.'

'Are you staying on the marae?' Mum asks Sandra.

Sandra looks at me, and I nod. Sam Walker says, 'There's room beside me, darling.' Everyone laughs.

Mum looks at me thoughtfully. 'No, she can sleep beside me. That way she'll be safe from everybody.'

Later, I take Sandra for a walk in the dark. 'When will your father be buried?' she asks.

I hug her closely. 'Tomorrow.'

Tomorrow?

And tomorrow has come and, no matter that the whanau has buoyed me with their love, I must rely on my own resources of strength to get me through this, the last day of the tangi.

Across the blazing sunlight, I see my Uncle Pita walking towards me. 'Come, Tama. You have your job to do.'

My mother senses Uncle Pita's presence, looks at him and his truck, and covers her face with her hands. 'No, no, no.' She strokes Dad's forehead, speaking his name over and over again. The other women on the porch begin to weep with her.

Uncle Pita and I drive to Tawhiti Kaahu, where the graveyard is. The bus into Gisborne speeds past. There are no passengers, nor will there be any until the tangi is ended. The hill grows larger, like a pyramid in the sky. The truck stops at the gate.

The day is hot, the wind is warm. 'Bring the shovels, nephew.'

I follow Uncle Pita through the sun and wind and green grass waving. The hill. The path. I remember following after Riripeti when she died. My father was one of the pallbearers and he slipped on the pathway. Aunty Sarah wept all the way up the hill.

My feet are leaden, my heart is breaking. The hillside sparkles with long glistening spider's threads, gossamer strands strung from blade to blade. As we pass by, spiders leap in salutation into the sun. Uncle Pita is walking through wild buttercups, crushing yellow flowers with his footsteps. He stoops to wash his hands at the gate to the graveyard.

'Haramai, nephew.'

The graveyard is looking beautiful. I soon see why. Standing, waiting for me and Uncle Pita, are men of my whanau: Nani Tama, Hepa Walker,

Sam Walker, Charlie Whatu, Uncle Joshua, Uncle Pani, my two cousins Simeon and Andrew, my cousin Michael and my brothers-in-law Victor and Koro. They have been working for the past two days to prepare the graveyard for Dad, beautifying everyone else's resting places as they do it. As I approach, they stop their work and watch me, respectful.

My eyes blur with tears. 'Tena koutou,' I say to the men. 'Thank you for joining me on this day.'

Nani Tama signs that he will say a karakia for us. 'Kororia ki To Ingoa Tapu,' he prays. Once the prayer is over, Uncle Pita looks at me. 'Kia kaha, Tama. You make the first cut. We will help you with the rest. Let us dig true and deep and make a fitting resting place for your father.'

My tears scald my cheeks. It feels like somebody has thrown acid in my face. I trace out the length of my father and the width of my father. Only a son knows this, only a son should do the measurements. Once it is done, Nani Tama asks me the question:

'This, then, has it been done correctly?'

I nod. 'Yes, it has been done correctly and is befitting for a man honoured among the whanau.'

The digging begins. The digging is hard. We are all soon sweating like blazes. We reach the clay. Something about the change of colour makes my head spin. In this clay, Dad will lie. Here, in this yellow earth. He will be gone forever.

This is what a good son does. Just as a good daughter washes her father at death so does the dutiful son prepare the place where his father will be laid in earth.

'Okay,' Uncle Pita says when the task is done. 'Let's go and get him.'

My father and I have been floating on a dark sea at midnight. All around are mountainous waves. Above, a wide empty sky. Dad has saved me from the maw of a whirlpool, but he has not been able to save himself. I watch him as he is dragged away from me.

'No,' I yell. 'No. I will not let this happen.'

I turn back from safety and swim towards him. The waves are angry and roar their disapproval. They cascade around me, trying to stop me from crossing the conflicting currents.

The gods are kind. They allow me to reach him for one last embrace.

The stars come out. My father and I are floating on a luminescent skein of silver dreams. A shooting star blazes a terrible glorious beauty across the night.

'Time for me to go, son.'

One moment he is there, the next moment he is gone, sucked away by the whirlpool. The sea becomes calm. The waves diminish. I am floating, floating, and all that is left is a sea of stars.

19

The train moves slowly into Palmerston North. For half an hour it stands at the station, then away from the brightly lit city it thunders, toward the towering mountains. Clouds are lowering upon them swirling down with drifting grace, shedding eternal tears. The earth is a desolate sea, howling in darkness.

Far, far on the other side of the mountains, lies Wellington.

Memories rise in the still air like smoke from many fires. Is this the same place, this place of ashes? Yet the stream still runs and the sun rides over the sky. The mountains are always there. A bitter wind blows dust and ashes from the south. I can no longer see the stream, the sun, the mountains.

I am ready now. I have brushed my hair and put on my jacket, and I am composed.

On the marae at Rongopai, people are weeping. Women are softly wailing. All around me are the sights and sounds of people grieving. As soon as I stand to speak, the mourners fall silent.

'Kua tae mai te wa,' I begin, 'the time has come to take our father to the graveyard.' I thank everyone for coming. On behalf of my mother, sisters and brother, I thank them for comforting us and giving of their strength during the time of the tangi. I tell them how proud I am of my blood links with all of them. What are we if we are not a whanau? Where would we be, if we did not have a meeting house to belong to? I have tried to be strong and to make it through my short korero.

I hope I have done my father proud.

The Matua and Nani Tama, assisted by Mattie Jones, lead the Ringatu church service, the karakia and himene to the dead. The Ringatu faithful intone the prayers, 'Kororia ki To Ingoa Tapu.' The bell begins tolling, tolling, tolling across the Waituhi valley. Mourners form a line across the marae so that they can have one last look at Dad and whisper a loving message of farewell to him before he is closed away from us.

Tamati Kota is the first to kiss Dad before the casket is closed. Who would have known that such an old man, after all these years of his life, could still have so many tears left in him? Mourners from the various tribes follow, old people, koroua, kuia, whanau and tamariki. Each in turn takes off shoes and crawls onto the porch, to lie beside him and whisper farewell.

'We must make haste, people,' Nani Tama says, but each mourner must be given the time for this poroporoaki, this personal farewell to Dad.

The iwi from Waituhi and the Mahana family follow. Hepa Walker salutes, as is fitting an old Maori Battalion leader, and his son, Sam, lets out an agonised cry of grief. I hadn't realised that Sam and Dad had been so close; but Mum has told me that over the last few years, when Dad needed help with cutting scrub or fencing, it was Sam who would say, 'Need a hand, Rongo?' It was Sam who joined him in the work without being asked. Sam became the son I never was.

Following Sam, old man Bulibasha, my uncles Hone and Joshua and their wives, and all my revered aunties, Ruth, Sarah, Hiria, Molly, Maka and others have traced Dad's profile with tenderness. So many, many mourners, among them my sweetheart Sandra, Jasper, Ray, Ted, and other Pakeha, coming to stand with bowed heads, honouring Dad.

It is the turn of my sisters. Ripeka, Mere, Wiki and Marama rise to the task, transfigured by the process of the tangihanga. I follow them with Hone. I stroke Dad's hair and let my tears fall on him.

'E pa, you should not have let me love you so much. You should not have been so much a maker of my world. At your going, my world goes too. It is like the going down of the sun. And when the sun rises again, it rises upon ashes and wisps of smoke curling from a hundred fires. In whatever life I find for myself, I must be a man now. Pray for me, Dad, as I try to find a way to walk upright and proudly, in the bright strand between.'

Now it is Mum's turn. There is a role for daughters, there is a role for sons, there is also a role for wives. It is the most difficult role of all. My mother has had to bear the grief of others before her own. She has had to hold so many mourners during the tangi and give them succour. She has had to put all others first and place herself last.

But, oh, how very sweet it is to be the last one of all to see her husband's beloved face.

'Goodbye, Rongo. I have always loved you.'

Always the bell tolling, tolling, tolling.

Now, the whispered farewells are ended.

The Matua calls Uncle Pita forward. He tells Sam Walker and Uncle Joshua to bring the lid to be placed over Dad. The mourners open a way for us. The women are gaunt, the men are grave. The children look at us, suddenly afraid. *Tama, you'll have to come home. Dad's dead.* The sun shines on the lid. It gleams on the silver inset upon which are inscribed the words: Rongo Mahana Born 1916 Died 1973. Part of the casket is covered with a feather cloak, rippling across the porch with the bronze fire of a moth's wings. At his feet, the flower wreaths are a blaze of dazzling colours. The photographs of Dad, displayed on the porch, flash in the falling sunlight.

Nani Miro and Mattie Jones remove the cloak. Uncle Pita bends over my mother where she kneels, her arms spread across the polished wood. *Mum was just lying there as if she was waiting for Dad to wake up.* He speaks to Mum. For a moment, she is unwilling to let go. She shakes her head and clutches more tightly at Dad. Uncle Pita speaks to her again and holds her shoulders. My sisters come to prise her away. Her fingers fall away as she breaks her clasp. She gives a deep groan, 'Uh,' for this is the final physical contact she will have with Dad.

A storm arises among the mourners. Women gather round my mother, weeping with her. *Come home, son.* Marama and Hone are afraid. Mum looks at them, dazed, and gathers them into her arms. The children calm her. She reaches for her black scarf and puts it over her hair. Wiki and Mere help her to stand. She sways, almost falls. *Come home, Tama.* But her face is calm now. She stands. I screw the lid on the casket.

'Feet first,' the Matua reminds us as the pallbearers come forward. 'He must leave this world feet first.'

I stand with my uncles Pita, Joshua and Hone, and my cousins Andrew and

Simeon. We wait while the hearse reverses slowly through the crowd toward the porch. The hearse stops, the door swings open. Carefully we lift Dad into it. *I must go home, Mr Ralston.* He is so heavy, so heavy. Although it is only a few steps to the hearse, it seems a long journey. Flower wreaths are placed in with him. The doors close behind him. People gather at the glistening windows, and palms press silently on the glass.

'Haramai, Mum,' Ripeka says. 'You're riding with Dad and we'll be with you.' My mother gets into the hearse with Ripeka, Mere, Marama and Hone. At the last moment she looks for me, alarmed. 'You'll follow, son?'

I nod my head, and she is reassured. Another car draws up near the porch. It is the Matua's flash Lagonda; Nani Miro is inside with Tamati Kota, and Nani Tama is driving. 'Come along, mokopuna,' Nani Miro says.

From the Lagonda, I see Uncle Pita bringing his truck to the front. Victor and Koro are putting the rest of the flower wreaths and the photographs of Dad on the back. Elsewhere, other mourners are hastening to their vehicles, a motley lot of cars and trucks of all makes and models. It doesn't matter — the dust of Waituhi will treat them exactly the same. Headlights are being switched on, in the age-old sign that a funeral cortege is in procession.

Many of the mourners elect to walk. Already they are streaming toward the hill where the graveyard is, calling to Tawhiti Kaahu, calling to the hill, that Dad is coming.

The Lagonda begins to move. It follows the hearse as it slowly moves through the mourners to the gate. The mourners make way. Behind us, other cars begin to follow.

Glimpsed for a moment is the grief-stricken face of my sister, Mere.

Nani Tama drives out of Rongopai's gateway. He turns onto the road, following the hearse. *No, Mr Ralston, he was not an old man.* Far ahead, the road streams with people walking to the graveyard. People cluster round the hearse. Auntie Ruth is among them. Her lips are moving as she speaks to Dad.

'It's good for your father to know,' Nani Miro tells me, 'that he is still accompanied in life and that so many people wish him well as he now returns to God.'

I look away from the road, away from the hill. I see the farm that Dad worked in Waituhi. I imagine myself there, in the cottage, watching from a window. I see people walking along Lavenham Road. They raise swirls of dust. A long line of cars shines among them, more swinging into view. The cars come from Rongopai, heading for Tawhiti Kaahu. People are clustering at the bottom, resting, before streaming up the hill toward the graveyard.

The road unfolds through the green fields. This is my home, this is my whanau. This is Waituhi. *Do you want me to come to Gisborne for the funeral? Sandra asks.* How fortunate I am to have a valley to come from with a fortress at one end, a sacred mountain at the other, and a river running through it.

Suddenly the light begins to fade. A shadow advances across the landscape. It ripples across the houses. The wind and clouds are gathering at the hill. The coldness strikes with a sudden blast of wind.

'Huh?' Nani Miro asks. 'Where did that come from?'

The sun starts to go out. *Goodness, Anne asks, how long before we get back on the ground?* The sky comes to embrace the earth. Tawhiti Kaahu is rising higher. The wind increases, and as mourners climb the hill toward the graveyard, they clasp their coats around them.

The Lagonda slows down. The crowd thickens at the windows. In front, the hearse comes to a halt. The doors swing open. For a moment, the world is a blur of rushing shadows. Uncle Pita, together with the other pallbearers, takes Dad from the hearse.

I step from the Lagonda, walk to the hearse and open the door for Mum. Ripeka and Wiki are beside her as she gathers the children. Mere joins them. *Don't weep, my sister. I am here now.* Together we walk through the bustling crowd to where the pallbearers are waiting.

I take my place with the pallbearers. Dad is so heavy. His body moves inside the casket as we carry him through the crowd. 'Don't forget,' other men and boys say to us as we carry Dad, 'we're here to take over when you need us.' So many young men and boys, all wishing to carry my father to his rest. How can I ever thank them?

My heart is breaking. My tears are falling. A storm is gathering across the hill. *Dad waits for you at Rongopai, Tama.* The sky is thick with dark clouds, surging and lowering. The day becomes ashen. The air shifts, swells and subsides. The mourners must struggle against the wind as they climb the hill. The wind and clouds are coming to the tangihanga.

Beyond the hill, the sun is shafting sunlight upon another world.

Uncle Pita signals a change of pallbearers. 'Do you want a break?' he asks me. All of us are panting, the hill is so steep, and it is difficult to keep step as we climb. The break brings sweat popping on my forehead.

'No,' I tell him. 'This is my father. He'll expect me to carry him most of the way.'

'Okay,' Uncle Pita says, 'but all of you, be generous, give Rongo up to other men so that they may have the privilege of carrying him.'

During the break, Mum comes to rest her head against the casket. Behind, more mourners are streaming up the hill. *Dad waits, Tama.* Above, mourners are waiting at the graveyard where headstones and crosses prick at the ashen sky. *Tama, he waits.*

'Okay, boys,' Uncle Pita instructs. 'Lift. Ready? On we go.'

And the rain begins to fall. 'Gee, thank you so much, Rongo,' Aunt Ruth growls him. 'I knew I should have worn my gumboots instead of my flash high-heeled shoes.'

The rain splashes on my mother's face. It splashes on my father's casket, glistening, covering it with diamonds. He is so heavy, my father. But one step. Then another.

And one step further now.

Through the rain, carrying Dad. Up the hill, through the press of mourners. So heavy he is; he is so heavy. As I am carrying him, my feet slip. We have another break, and another group of pallbearers take the casket onward. Among them is Sam Walker, and he is desperate to carry Dad. When I left for Wellington, Sam was the one who helped Dad on the farm. I look at my mother and she nods.

'Sam,' I call to him. 'Will you take my place so that I can join Mum?'

Sam's face looks ready to break apart with tears. He has always had strong shoulders and great goodness. 'Okay, uncle,' he says to Dad, 'I'm here. Don't make my job hard for me now. And no complaining, eh?'

The path becomes muddy and trickles with rivulets of rain. On the path lies a fallen chaplet of kawakawa leaves. The mourners gather round the gateway to the graveyard. *Haere mai ki o tatou mate e.* They open up before us, waving sprigs of greenery in their hands. They glisten in the rain. Their hair is matted and they lift their faces to the darkening sky. *Haere mai, haere mai.* The women sway and keen a lament. They raise their arms toward my father.

Uncle Pita gives me his strength. *You must make your father proud, mokopuna.* And one step further now, through the gateway into the graveyard.

Here, in this place, lie my whanau, my family dead. Here among the flowering gorse they lie, beneath simple headstones. Dad comes to sleep among them.

Strange, the wind has ceased a moment. Strange, the clouds are still. Nothing moves in this world except the mourners following through the graveyard after father. *There is no sound. The tide ebbs silently away.* But a further step forward now. Past the headstones to the place where Dad will rest. Until the pallbearers are standing with the coffin at the newly dug ground, this ground dug by strong, loving, hands.

The casket is laid on the ground. *Death comes but I am not yet dead.* Sam steps back, letting me take my place again. 'You didn't mind, did you Dad? You know I love you, but I know you loved Sam also.' The mourners press close to the casket. To one side, Mum is standing with Ripeka, Mere, Marama and Hone. Grandfather Moana is with them too.

The Matua steps forward and addresses the mourners. She says a final karakia for Dad. 'Go to Paerau, go to the eyes of heaven, stand on the threshold of Matariki, the Pleiades. To Antares, farewell. Go to our ancestors, join them.'

My mother links hands with my sisters, brother and me: Ripeka, the strong one, Mere, the calm one, Wiki and Marama and Hone. *Kua mate taku papa. We breathe, we live.* We don't want to let each other go. Not now. Not ever.

'Okay, boys,' Uncle Pita says. He motions us to lower Dad into the ground.

I take hold of the cord. Nani Tama reads from the Bible, a hand raised in the air. *Dad, don't leave me.* Slowly, slowly the casket descends. The cord slackens.

The rain drives without pity across the hill. The women clutch their scarves and the men bow their heads against the wind. Petals fly loose from the flower wreaths. The leaves of the kawakawa chaplets swirl away in the wind. The black skirts of the women flap in the storm. Clay trickles upon the casket. *I bend toward him and my shadow falls across him.*

E pa, farewell, e pa.

In the driving rain, Mum steps forward. She bends to the earth, gathers some clay, and casts it into the grave. Gravediggers begin to shovel earth over him. *The dirt falls*, the rain falls. *The rain falls*, the dirt falls.

Earth reaches for Sky and Sky bends to Earth. One last passionate clasp in rain and wind and wind and rain. One last embrace of joy and love and thankfulness. One last clinging of body to body, of Earth to Sky. One last meeting of lips to lips and tears to tears.

Then the slow drawing away, the slow tearing away, the slow wrenching away in the final, sorrowful separation.

Haere ra, e pa.

Goodbye, Dad.

20

i haven't told you everything.

Seven months before he died, Dad came to see me in Wellington. I had already been away from Gisborne over a year. My Matua, Nani Miro, was right to reprove me when she said, 'If you don't watch out, we'll forget what you look like.'

Since arriving in the capital, life had captured me in its grasp. I was enjoying the city, meeting new friends, I had a gorgeous girlfriend and I was keen on making a go as a journalist. My career at *The Evening Post* was going so well that I got a rise and Mr Ralston had assigned me as the paper's Maori Affairs reporter. Ted Smith had actually suggested I also have a byline on the feature articles I was writing about Waitangi, land and other Maori issues.

'Better your name than mine,' Ted said when I thanked him. 'Your name will give the articles more authenticity and if you get it wrong, well, it'll be you with tutae all over your face. Just remember one thing, boy. Be partisan but never forget that in the end, truth has no colour, race or gender.'

I received a telephone call from Dad. He was calling from Nelson in the South Island.

'What are you doing down there?' I asked. The only relative we had in that part of the country was Mum's sister, Auntie Maggie, but she wasn't there any longer, having joined the Maori diaspora in Sydney, Australia.

'There's some business I've had to attend to,' Dad said.

'What business?' I asked.

'Family business,' he answered. 'But I can't talk about that now. My plane's leaving in ten minutes. I'm coming through Wellington to make the connection to Gisborne. I have an hour on the ground. Can you come out to the airport and see me?'

'Of course, Dad,' I answered. Damn, I was supposed to have dinner with Sandra. I rang to tell her I would be late getting to her place and then dashed out to the airport on my motorbike. The weather was pretty miserable, with rain pelting down.

When I arrived at the airport, Dad was waiting at the terminal entrance in the rain. 'What are you doing out here?' I asked. I was alarmed when I saw him. He was gaunt, and he didn't look well. Working all that time on the killing chain had taken a lot out of him.

'This place is too big and you mightn't have found me,' he answered.

Yeah, right. Wellington airport was small but all my whanau have complained about getting lost in it. Their ancestors travelled all the way from Raiatea to Aotearoa, navigating by stars, and they couldn't find their way from the gate to the taxi rank.

I chained my motorbike to a sturdy steel post; the only way anybody would be able to steal it would be to use a towaway truck to pull up the post. I took Dad to the airport cafeteria where I ordered him some fish and chips.

Even before we had sat down for our feed, Dad came straight to the point. 'I need you, son. I want you to come home and help me run the farm at Waituhi. I'm not as young as I used to be, and these days the work is tough on the old body. I've also been talking to your Uncle Pita about our family resuming its leadership position again.' Dad went on and on, detailing his discussions with the Matua, and what he wanted to do. He became animated and excited as he outlined his vision.

All the time Dad was talking, I kept thinking to myself. 'Why now, Dad? Why ask me now?' Surely he should have known that I loved my career, I loved my life, I was on my way somewhere — even if I didn't know yet where that 'somewhere' was. Sure, it might be a Pakeha 'somewhere' rather than a Maori 'somewhere' but wherever it was, I wasn't about to make a detour back to Waituhi. For a while, when Dad was most animated, I got really angry with him. But what was the use of arguing with him? He would never understand me and my own dreams, never.

In the end, when Dad asked me again to come home, I took the easy way out. 'Can I have some time to think about it?'

For a moment, there was silence. 'Can't you make your decision now, son?' he asked. When I didn't answer, the light went out of his eyes and he was diplomatic. 'Okay, son, you take some time to think it over. Some of your young cousins are happy to help me meantime with my sheep and cattle. Young Sam Walker likes to talk as we dig in fenceposts, but he doesn't do it the way I like it done. And he's not you, son.'

We finished our fish and chips. Somebody spilled the tomato sauce, it was probably me, because I was getting upset at not being able to say yes to my dad. We made small talk. I asked him what his family business had been about in the South Island.

'I went down there to find somebody,' he said.

'Were you successful?' I asked. I already suspected why he'd been down there and told him so.

'If you know so much,' he answered, 'and if I can't finish the job, you might have to.'

The flight to Gisborne was called. It was a relief to both of us. Even so, when we said goodbye, he gave me the fiercest hug.

'Don't forget, if ever anything happens to me, you must look after the family, Tama. You must come home. Your mother will need you. Your brother and sisters will need you too. You are the oldest. The oldest always looks after the younger ones of the family. I was taught that when I was a child. I teach you the same thing now. Never forget.'

I put my hands up, 'Okay, okay, Dad, you're the sheriff.'

He laughed at my response. I accompanied him to the gate. We hugged again and he went through. Suddenly he turned and gave me such a look, as if his heart would burst.

'Have I ever told you how proud I am of you, son?' he asked.

I bring all the guilt about saying no to my grief about Dad's death.

I should have said yes to him.

I should never have left home.

Never.

21

the train curves into the dark bleakness ahead, breaking through the rain. The carriage rocks and sways like a canoe adrift. The mountains are the ridged backbone of a giant fish. The landscape is flooded with the turmoiled waves of its huge tail flukes descending. A sheet of rain dashes against the window. The raindrops scatter through my reflection.

The train stops briefly at Levin. We are nearing Wellington. It's seven o'clock in the evening. In a short while my journey will be over. I am Tama Mahana, and my father is dead. This is the end of my journey but it is also my journey beginning. There is a world outside the world of the tangihanga. My journey is taking me out of the upheaval of death and back into life where people are still following the accustomed patterns of their lives.

The hands of the clock stand at the beginning of another hour.

The Maori people say that after the world had been made by the gods, there arose the demigod Maui. Among his many feats he tamed the sun, brought fire to the world and, with a magic hook, pulled to the surface of the ocean the Great Fish of Maui. On breaking through the sea, the fish changed into land — and it was to this land that the ancestors of the Maori came.

The one task Maui could not complete was to conquer Death. His great triumph, however, was to usher in the Time of Man, the reign of mortals on the earth. Each generation of men, women and children continue the great journey of humankind. Each death does not diminish the breath of life and memory that is passed on from one generation to the next.

As long as the memory *holds*, my father will always belong to the grace, forgiveness and strength of our history. He will always be part of te taura tangata.

After Dad's burial, the world began to renew itself.

The next day, I took Sandra and the others to catch their plane back to Wellington. 'Take as much time as you need before you return,' Ted said.

Sandra's eyes sparkled with indignity, 'What, Ted Smith, are you saying!' she laughed. 'You be back by next weekend, Tama Mahana.'

When I got back to Waituhi from the airport, people were already packing up at Rongopai, Pakowhai and Takitimu Hall to return to their homes. In Maoridom, however, you don't just leave; you must be farewelled, and that is an entirely different matter. Nobody should really leave a funeral until after the poroporoaki, the concluding ceremony. If you do, you miss out on the great secret of the tangihanga.

The secret is contained in the persistence of the phrases recited during the poroporoaki:

'Apiti hono, tatai hono, te hunga mate o te wa, haere, haere, haere. Apiti hono, tatai hono, te hunga ora katoa, tena koutou, tena koutou, tena koutou katoa. And so, let the dead go to the dead, farewell, farewell, farewell. And now let us turn back to the living, the living return to living, greetings, greetings, greetings.'

The words bring the living back to living. They tell us that now the mourning is over we must return to the present and the future. They give us the permission to live again, to believe in the generosity of God, and to laugh and indulge in all our wayward and passionate humanity.

The first of the tribes to leave were the Ringatu people from Ohiwa. They had another hui to go to, and they were champing at the bit. They observed the protocols impeccably, giving fabulous farewell speeches, eating enough kai to keep them from going hungry on the road, singing and dancing up a storm and making a great fuss over the ringawera and all the people who had cooked for them and looked after them.

Not to be outdone, the Tuhoe people gave even more fabulous speeches, ate so much kai that they would have to diet for the rest of the year, and when they sang and danced, they shook the earth. Not only that, but they raised the levity by telling as many filthy jokes as they could get away with. Nani Tama had another dust-up with Hori Rua, who was still trying to bring scorn on Nani Tama's manhood.

'I may have erred,' he conceded, 'on the size of my rival's equipment but maturity has not brought artistry to his deployment of it. Perhaps he needs oysters, lots and lots of oysters to ensure staying power.'

Nani Tama clocked him one, bringing him down for the count.

Group by group, ope by ope, the poroporoaki proceeded. Laughter pealed out, tears flowed, promises of seeing each other soon were made, noses were pressed in the hongi, more jokes were told. Again the Matua was in her element as group after group made appropriate obeisance to her as the queen of Waituhi.

I gave my personal thanks at each farewelling. In response, people said, 'Tama, if you need us, just call and we will come.' Or, 'Look after your mother, Tama. Kia kaha, boy.' Or, 'Why don't you send Marama and Hone to us for a holiday? It's about time we had our mokopuna come to stay a while with us.' And, at each touching of cheek to cheek, the old ones told me: 'The time for grieving is over. You must go on living now.'

Always, that repeated phrase, 'Apiti hono, tatai hono, te hunga mate o te wa, haere, haere, haere. Apiti hono, tatai hono, te hunga ora katoa, tena koutou, tena koutou, tena koutou katoa.' Each time the phrase was uttered, it was an invocation:

Life, come again.

Finally, all the visitors, the waewae tapu, returned to their own lands to the north, south, east and west. The time came for the local people of Waituhi to also return to their own lives. Uncle Pita and the Matua organised the final kai, a boil-up at Takitimu Hall. Food has always been used as an element to bring life back to normal. Outside, the hangi gushed steam through the darkness. The smells lingered as the men took food from the earth oven and brought it into the hall. Tamati Kota sat with the Matua. Mattie Jones, Aunt Ruth, Aunt Teria and Maka tiko bum made the tables ready for the kai. Ripeka, Mere and Wiki helped in the kitchen. My mother sat with Aunt Sarah and Haromi and some of the younger girls, where Aunt Sarah was reading their palms and giving advice on love and marriage.

The locals overflowed from the hall, outside onto the grounds. Charlie Whatu was, as usual, boasting about his football exploits to his son, Andrew and my cousins Simeon and Michael. Sam Walker presided over one group of drinkers. Marama and Hone played with other children.

The kai was ready. 'Come and get it,' Aunt Sarah yodelled. Her voice was so loud, every cow in Waituhi must have heard her and, thinking it was time for milking, headed for the cowshed.

We ate, we sang, we told jokes and we sang more of the joyful songs of our people. When it was getting very late, the tables were cleared and put away. The cooks came from the kitchen. More speeches were given. Finally, it was my turn yet again.

I can't remember what I said but, whatever it was, it was sure *long*. When your heart is engaged your brain switches off. Time takes a deep breath and allows you to touch the very centre of your heart and unlock it so that you can share your feelings, without constraint, with others. My heart was overflowing and the voices of my ancestors were within me, speaking their eternal truths about loyalty, honour, maintaining one's commitment to family. I spoke of mountains that could never be moved, of rivers that would always flow, and a people who had, in my father's words, 'the indomitable spirit of the undefeated'.

'Thank you, Uncle Pita. On behalf of the family, thank you, Matua. Thank you, Nani Tama. Koroua, Tamati Kota, live forever. All my aunties, Sarah, Ruth, Maka, and all my kuia, thank you. Hey, Mattie, Sam. Andrew, Simeon, Uncle Hone, Uncle Joshua, everyone, from the bottom of my heart, thank you.'

'No need for thanks, nephew,' Uncle Pita said. 'We are whanau. This is what we do.' For him, it was all as simple as that.

'He wai,' Auntie Ruth said. 'Here's your song to bless your words.' She strummed on the guitar. 'Tahi nei taru kino . . . Oh how it grieves me to look inside your heart and think of parting, which brings such sorrow. There'll be a welcome when you return, you know our heart is yours.'

We sang of Maori aroha. 'Your heart is my heart. When you are sad, I am sad. When you are happy, I am happy. When you need love, I will give you love. Your tears are my tears. Your laughter is my laughter.'

Life was so fragile, so we sang our lungs out because this might be the last farewell for some of us. We swayed together and we sang of our love for our whanau. We said to each other, 'No matter how far away from Waituhi we will always remain family. No matter where we go, we will always leave our hearts here. Always remember us. Always remember.'

Always remember, always remember.

The train speeds across the night, closer to Wellington. I catch a sudden glimpse of traffic trickling along a wet shining highway. The fluorescent lights of a roadside cafeteria snap on and off with a bold orange glow.

The conductor comes walking through the carriage. 'Fifteen minutes to the captial. Wellington in quarter of an hour, folks.'

I lean back and look out the window as the train approaches the capital. The carriage is filled with the noises of travellers as they prepare for arrival. A woman wakes her small son who has been sleeping in her arms. An old man stretches and yawns. Three young men put away their playing cards. The Maori girl looks at her reflection in the window, combs her hair, and slings her guitar across her shoulders. The young soldier checks his army kit.

The train rushes through a tunnel and Wellington Harbour appears. The sea is calm with a metallic sheen. The interisland ferry is steaming out toward the heads. The ferry's glittering lights are reflected in the water. The train follows the railway track as it curves round the harbour. Wellington is ahead, stack upon stack of glowing lights rising on the hills.

And suddenly the train enters Wellington Railway Station. The engine whines down into silence. The passengers are excited, 'We're here!', 'Have you got our bag, darling?', 'Can you see Patrick? He said he'd meet us! There he is!' I remain in my seat, watching the passengers from the window as they step down from the train and are greeted. For a moment, I am so afraid, so frightened.

'What comes now?' I ask myself. I take a deep breath, stand and reach for my coat. My feet are wobbly and I feel just like a baby taking his first steps. I walk along the carriage and jump down to the platform.

'Tama? Tama!' Sandra is waiting at the end of the platform. Her face gleams like a glowing star. Will she come back to Waituhi with me? I walk towards her.

See, Dad? No more tears.

After the tangihanga the world began to renew itself. The tempo of village life returned to normal. Uncle Pita and I, helped by Charlie Whatu, Sam Walker and my cousin Andrew, pulled down the marquee and returned the hay and bedding.

Mattie Jones supervised the huge dish-washing session at Takitimu Hall. Mum, my sisters and brother scrubbed the floors. The leftover food was divided equally among everyone. I shouted Sam and the boys some beer. Sam lived just behind Maka tiko bum's house, and she did not thank me.

'What did you do that for?' she scolded. 'Now I won't get any sleep for weeks.'

A week after the tangihanga I wandered onto Rongopai marae. The roof still held up the sky. Only a few flower petals and drying leaves remained to remind me that here my father had lain.

I walked along Lavenham Road. Some of my uncles and aunties waved to me as I passed their houses. The bus into Gisborne idled past, filled with local people going into the city. I went up Tawhiti Kaahu to see my father where he lay in the graveyard. From his grave, I could see right across Waituhi to the surrounding hills. The village, the meeting house, my family, here we were, ready to go on.

I whispered the last thank you of all.

'Thank you, Dad.'

Later, while I was sitting with Mum, Uncle Pita came to visit us. He gave me the gifts of money which the mourners had left for our family. My mother wept at their generosity. I embraced Uncle Pita and closed a gap in the world.

That evening, I couldn't sleep. I went out onto the verandah and looked at the stars. The night sky over Waituhi was always so bright with stars, as if Waituhi was one of those special places that attracted them to cluster above. The stars were pouring into the valley.

I was still on the verandah just before dawn. I heard the twang of the door as it opened and saw that Mum had come to sit with me. She was wearing a dressing gown and had brought me a blanket. She kissed me on the forehead. 'You could catch a cold sitting out here all night,' she said. She draped the blanket around my shoulders. 'When do you have to go back to Wellington?' she asked.

'I should go soon,' I answered. The sun was rising, the stars wheeling away with the darkness.

'We'll be all right, son,' she said. 'Don't you worry. We'll be all right.'

The next morning, I watched my mother as she made breakfast. She looked at me, as if there was something she wanted to prove to me. 'Okay,' she said when the dishes had been done. Some inner purpose had taken her over. The next time I saw her she was wearing a straw hat and was dressed in old work clothes. She walked down to the shed where Dad kept his tractor.

'What the heck is your mother up to?' Ripeka sighed. Mystified, she, Mere and Wiki took their cup of tea and toast out on the verandah to watch. Marama and Hone ran after Mum.

Next moment, an almighty roar arose from inside the shed. The tractor, Mum driving, appeared and — well, Mum has never been the best driver in the world. She steered the tractor here, she steered it there, she steered it everywhere, down to the paddock that Dad had left unfinished.

'She'll kill herself,' Ripeka yelled. She started down the verandah towards the paddock.

'No, leave Mum alone.' I said. 'She doesn't want our help.' I watched as she hooked on the plough and began to pull it through the field. I was very proud of her when she had finished making a pass with the plough down the field. By the time Marama and Hone reached her, she had jumped down from the tractor to take a critical look at her work. She couldn't stop laughing and laughing.

Her furrows were as crooked as a dog's hind leg.

She looked across at me, the sun shining full on her face, and yelled, 'I'll get it right next time, son.'

epilogue

mourners are making their way down the hill from the family graveyard where we have laid our father to rest. They are streaming away through the sunset.

Together, we have stood beside his grave. We have listened as Tamati Kota blessed the ground into which our father was lowered. We have urged the diggers to work quicker with the chanting of a haka. We have told them to put their strength to the spade, so that our father is more quickly embraced by Papatuanuku, the Earth. Weeping, we have lain the flower wreaths upon him. Together, we have listened to the Matua intone an ancient lament.

It has rained. We have all waited through the rain and the burst of sun beside the grave of our father. We have not wanted to leave him. Now, the sunset has come. When it first drifted through the clouds, we began to sing hymns. Softly. Quietly. Trying to find peace with ourselves. Trying to calm our sorrow for our father.

Now, we are leaving him. My mother's arm rests on mine. My sisters and the little ones follow closely with her. People stream before us; people follow after us. I guide my mother to the bottom of the hill.

Suddenly, Mum lets go of my arm. She turns to face Tawhiti Kaahu, the hill where our father lies. The setting sun shines full upon her. Many emotions flicker over her face. The tears spill quickly. Then, from a well of strength within her, she calms her sorrow. She flicks her tears away. With pride, she looks upon the hill. Slowly, she lifts her arm to our father.

'Haere ra, Rongo. Haere! Haere! Haere!' Her voice is strong and ringing. It is fierce with pride and breaks the silence of the departing mourners. 'Farewell, husband. Farewell, farewell, farewell!'

All faces turn to look back at the hill. Many hands lift in the air and many voices join my mother's voice. 'Haere ra, Rongo. Haere! Haere! Haere!'

It is a cry of aroha, swelling louder and gathering in strength. It is an acclamation for our father, for his life as a man from his iwi.

It is the final farewell, echoed by earth and sky.

It is a roar of pride, before the slow descending of the sun.

the return
2005

E kore au e ngaro he kakano i ruiruia mai i Raiatea
You are a seed that was planted in Raiatea
and you will never be lost

part one

1

London.

John, our studio manager, was in the middle of asking a question when the phone rang: 'If you were running in a race and you passed the person who was coming second, what position would you have moved to?'

Kim, who always thinks she knows the answer to everything, said, 'First. You'd be winning.' John laughed and shook his head and Kim, who doesn't like being wrong insisted, 'Of course you'd be coming first.'

My PA, Harriet, answered the phone. We had just wrapped up my weekly hour-long Sunday evening television programme, *Spaceship Earth*. I hoped the telephone call wasn't from our executive producer, Paul, ringing to say that one of our segments would have to go because something new had blown up in Iraq, or President Bush had called a press conference at the White House that made one of our items obsolete. Harriet looked up at me and mouthed the words, 'It's a personal call for you from a Mrs Walker.'

I stepped past John and Kim. 'You'd be coming second,' I said.

Kim, cross at the answer, pinched John on the arm. 'You and your trick questions.'

I took the phone from Harriet. I didn't give my personal office number to anybody except my girlfriend Gabriella, son Nathan, daughter Holly and my family on the other side of the world, in New Zealand. The call was from my sister, Ripeka, in Waituhi. 'What's the time over there at the centre of the world?' Ripeka asked. She couldn't keep the sarcasm out of her voice. 'Can you get on a plane as soon as you can?'

I knew immediately what Ripeka was calling about. Our mother, Huia, had been admitted to a hospital two weeks ago. 'Is Mum all right?'

'Yes,' Ripeka answered. 'But who knows how long she's got?' Mum had been in and out of Gisborne Hospital for the past five months as the doctors tried to stop her cancer from spreading. 'She asked me to ring you straight away to come home. "Say to your brother," she told me, "it's time to tell the family."'

'Okay,' I answered. 'I'll try to get home soon.'

I asked Harriet to make a booking on the next flight from Heathrow.

'I can get you in business on the Air New Zealand flight tonight via Los Angeles,' Harriet said, 'and I'll try for an upgrade to first. Do you want to do it? You'd need to check in by 10.30.'

I looked at my watch: 4 pm. I had six hours up my sleeve. No problem. 'Would you call Gabriella for me?' I asked. 'Could you tell her to meet me at the apartment at six for dinner?'

'How long will you be away, Tom?' Paul asked. He needed to know if I would be in London to tape next week's show. The telecast was really important: *Spaceship Earth* was celebrating its tenth anniversary and plans were well underway to make sure it was a big on-screen party event.

'I don't know, Paul,' I answered. 'Who's our affiliate company in New Zealand? Television Three?'

Paul knew immediately what I was thinking, blanched, and shook his head. 'Call them and tell them I'll want a studio,' I insisted. 'I'll present the anniversary programme from there.' I watched Paul waver. I knew I had put him in an awkward position; he had to weigh the concerns of the programme against my pulling power as anchorman. But I also knew that whenever we did outside broadcasts our audience figures always peaked. When 9/11 happened in 2001, I fronted the programme from New York and our ratings went through the roof. When the tsunami broke on Boxing Day 2004, I flew to Banda Aceh, presented from a helicopter flying over the province and again the ratings soared.

'What about Tony Blair?' Paul asked. 'We were planning to have him on the programme, live, as part of the birthday event.'

'I'll think of something else,' I answered.

Paul paused, but he had already crunched the figures. 'God, Tom, why do you always have to be such a buccaneer?' He gave a sigh and turned to the crew.

'Okay, people, looks like we'll be doing the programme next week from the bottom of the world. You, Kim, obviously will have to go. John, are you available to manage the floor?' Paul saw Otis, our technical producer, coming through the door with a grim look on his face. 'I wasn't forgetting you, Otis. Of course you're coming with us, too.'

A ripple of excitement ran through the studio. Otis beamed; his was a stressful job and we wouldn't have been able to do it without him. Already I knew he was mentally organising a side trip to the set of *King Kong*. The rest of the technical staff began to clap at the boldness of the decision. The only person who wasn't happy was Harriet; she came running after me with a grim look on her face. 'I can cancel most of your engagements, but what are you going to do about your *Face to Face* interview? Bob Blakeney has been chasing you for six months and you've already said yes. You'll definitely have to be back for that.'

Face to Face? Of course. Bob Blakeney, once a close friend, fellow anchorman and presenter over at the BBC, wanted to interview me about the role of the television media in reporting on world events. Two weeks from now. 'Tell Bob not to worry,' I answered. 'I'll be back for his show.'

I left the set quickly, before Paul could change his mind. Ali, my driver, was waiting with the car at the kerb. 'Where to, sir?' he asked.

'Take me home.'

I lived in a new luxury highrise apartment building on the Thames, along with millionaire bankers, corporate lawyers, Arab oil magnates and other A-listers on the London Stock Exchange. People thought I couldn't afford it; they didn't know what Lord Sanderson, who owned World Wide News, paid me. WWN was the only international rival to CNN and the BBC in Great Britain, and *Spaceship Earth* was the highest rating news digest in Europe and Australasia; Dan Rather (although I heard he was retiring), Tom Brokaw, Peter Jennings and Ted Koppel still ruled the roost in the Americas.

The apartment was my one great act of vanity and ego. But the public expected television celebrities to live in a place like that — and the view was to die for. After having lived in London for over twenty years, I had earned it. From my waterfront windows I overlooked the Thames. The Houses of Parliament were opposite. Upriver was Westminster Bridge, the London Eye and the London Aquarium. In the distance were the towers, spires, government and commercial edifices and parks of one of the most triumphant and beautiful cities in the world. The only problem with the view was the tourists. They were like ants clambering over everything.

I let myself in to my apartment, took a shower and began to pack. I phoned my daughter, Holly, in Los Angeles, hoping that she might be able to meet me during my stopover, but all I got was her answering machine: 'Hi, this is Holly here. I can't come to the phone right now. Leave a message. Love youuuuuu.'

Halfway through the packing, the doorman called to tell me that Gabriella had arrived. 'Send her up,' I told him. I was wearing a towel and waiting for her at the door when the lift opened.

'Isn't loitering with intent a criminal offence?' Gabriella asked as I kissed her.

'Guilty as charged,' I laughed. 'Aren't you going to arrest me?'

Gabriella and I had been lovers for three years. We met at the premiere of *Vanilla Sky*, a movie starring Tom Cruise, when it opened in London. I interviewed Tom for *Spaceship Earth* and bumped into Gabriella, who was working as a publicist for the studio. From the South of France, Gabriella sparkled with wit and sexiness. We'd sparred, probed, defended, gone on the offensive and, by mutual agreement, settled into a relationship in which we saw one another once or twice a week. She had just come out of a long-term relationship and didn't want to commit. After two failed marriages I wasn't exactly enamoured with the idea of a third one. Gabriella and I both recognised in the other the need for independence; we were happy not to put any pressure on ourselves, for the moment anyway.

I took Gabriella to dinner at a small restaurant I knew in Charing Cross Road. It was 7 pm, and we had a couple of hours before she took me out to Heathrow. Franco, a friend of mine, owned the restaurant; he showed us to our favourite table at the window.

'You're busy tonight,' I said to Franco as we passed through the bar. Oh no, just my luck. The *Spaceship Earth* programme I had taped that afternoon was showing on an overhead television screen.

'Yes,' Franco answered. 'I have a few groups in this evening.' The crowd tonight was youthful, exuberant, and there was a particularly animated group sitting at the far end. They looked as if they were exchanging presents. As

Gabriella and I sat down, one of the young men in the group saw me and gave a start as he recognised me. He looked at the television screen and then at me again. I made a rueful gesture: Yes, it was possible, in the wonderful world of communications, to be in two places at once. The young man gave a huge grin of agreement.

Gabriella and I consulted the menu. Franco took our order. 'We're in a bit of a hurry, Franco, how is the kitchen tonight?'

'I'll try my best, Tom,' Franco responded in alarm, 'but the chef is already running half an hour late on orders.'

'Okay, that can't be helped,' I nodded. I ordered a bottle of a good red. 'It's all your fault,' I said to Gabriella. 'If you hadn't taken advantage of me in the corridor of my apartment building, we would have got here ages ago.'

Gabriella gave a small squeal of outrage and broke into a stream of French. When she realised I was teasing her she gave a delicious giggle. The wine arrived. I tasted it and nodded my approval. I made a toast, 'To us.'

'How long will you be gone this time?' Gabriella asked. We both travelled a lot, and often had to work very hard to get some time together. She had just been to Iceland to work on a French–German co-production and I had been in Sri Lanka covering the tsunami; I'd managed a quick few days in New Zealand to see Mum on the way back. She'd had some bad news: she had been diagnosed with leukaemia. Immediately, she went into hospital for more radiation treatment. Since then, she'd been in and out of hospital as the doctors vainly tried to delay the relentless progress of the cancer cells through her blood.

'Maybe a week,' I answered. 'Two at the most.' Even if Mum was still fighting off her cancer, I would have to come back to London. 'Aren't you going to Cannes this year for the film festival? Perhaps on my way back I could meet up with you there.'

At that moment, I heard a polite cough. Looking up, I saw the young man who had recognised me when Gabriella and I had come into the restaurant. 'Excuse me, sir,' he began, 'but are you Tom Mahana? Seeing you on the TV screen and in the restaurant, both at the same time, is somewhat disorienting.'

I picked up on the young man's New Zealand accent immediately. 'Ah, the power of television programming,' I laughed. 'Yes, I'm Tom.'

'Thank God for that,' the young man continued, relieved. 'I thought I was seeing double and I haven't drunk all that much yet.' He took a deep breath.

'Look, my name is David Carruthers, I feel like a perfect idiot but a friend of mine, Caroline, is having her birthday party tonight and, well, I just happen to have her gift with me and it's your book. Could you sign it for me?' He was holding a copy of *Only the Highest Mountain*, about my life and times as an international war correspondent and television anchorman.

'Do you have a pen?' I asked him. I was tempted to sign the book by doodling across my photograph on the back flap and adding glasses, a moustache and a beard. After all, if you can't draw over your own book, what else can you tag? However, a stern look from Gabriella made me sign my signature instead. 'Here you go,' I said.

However, David Carruthers appeared to be stuck to the floor, shifting from one foot to the next as if trying to shake chewing gum from his shoes. His group of friends were making gestures to him. He took another deep breath. 'Sir,' he said, 'we're just a bunch of young Kiwis but we're having a few drinks and we would be honoured if you would join us.'

Gabriella took sympathy on him. She smiled at me, 'Why not, Tom. After all, dinner is delayed?'

I nodded at David. 'I'm happy to join you all,' I answered.

He went into shock. 'Hey, guys,' he yelled to his mates. 'The Dude just said yes!'

2

Just a bunch of young Kiwis.

Actually, I enjoyed meeting the young New Zealanders. So did Gabriella; as she drove me to Heathrow, she couldn't stop talking about them.

'Are all New Zealanders like that?' she asked. 'Such a delightful group of young men and women. So much enthusiasm, so much excitement and brilliance and talent.'

David Carruthers was a lawyer; his girlfriend, Rosemary, was an accountant, and their friend Caroline, the one having the birthday, worked for a publishing company. Caroline's boyfriend, Darren, was another lawyer. He and David had rung around other friends in London, all recent arrivals, to make up a birthday party to celebrate Caroline's twenty-second birthday.

'Yes,' I answered Gabriella. 'They were special, weren't they. There's a huge diaspora of bright young New Zealanders, with skills that allow them to adapt and integrate with any international community. I meet them all over the planet, but London is a special destination. I've heard there's over 75,000 of them here. It's where they come to do their OE.'

'OE?' Gabriella asked. 'What is that?'

'It's our overseas experience,' I laughed, 'and it's pretty mandatory. It's like the gap year here. For us, it's a degree in overseas travel and work experience that we like to award ourselves before we go back to New Zealand to settle down, get married and have children. Of course, today, some of the reasons for travelling overseas have changed; for instance, there's huge student debt and some of our brightest young graduates come overseas to help pay it off. What's interesting, though, is that you might stay overseas for one, two, three years or longer, but the unspoken assumption is that you will go back.'

'Why do they come to London?' Gabriella asked.

'It's historical,' I answered. 'New Zealand has a special relationship with England because of our Commonwealth links. The Queen of England is also Queen of New Zealand. God help us, when Charlie and Camilla ascend to the throne, I think there might be a revolt down in Aotearoa which will see them given the heave-ho. Anyway, the point is that, for New Zealanders, England is a natural destination. We could go — and do — to Australia, but that's just across the ditch. Asia is becoming popular and so is the USA. We live so far down at the bottom of the world that the only place to travel is up.'

'What I like best,' Gabriella observed, 'is how much you Kiwis all enjoy each other's company. Your intimacy is so instant, oui?'

I couldn't help smiling in agreement. As soon as Gabriella and I joined David Carruthers' friends there had been a huge roof-rattling cheer for his bringing home the prize. We were immediately surrounded by young men asking us, 'What'll you have, Tom, mate? Let's have a pew for The Dude and his beautiful lady. Gabriella is it? Here you go, love, you'll be a bit close up and personal with our mate Gareth's hairy chest, but we sprayed it with some garden spray so it's not poisonous. Hey, garçon, how about a couple more bottles of your best red? Got anything from the Hawke's Bay or Nelson?'

Only New Zealanders would ever get away with calling a Spaniard like Marco *garçon*, but he entered into the spirit of things. Very soon, Gabriella and I were talking to the young New Zealanders as if we had known them all our lives. We were intimate strangers, all bound together by race, nationality and those two peculiar tensions that had always forced all New Zealanders to get on together: location and isolation.

'There's a poet who defined why it is that we immediately become friends,' I told Gabriella. 'His name was Ron Mason and he thought that New Zealanders were like garrisons pent up in a little fort. It was us, back to back, against the rest of the world. He wrote, "Such men as these not quarrel and divide but friend and foe are friends in their hard sort . . . here in this far-pitched perilous hostile place, this solitary hard-assaulted spot, fixed at the friendless outer edge of space."' I gave a surprised laugh. Who would have thought that I'd remember so much of Mason's poem from my days in Mr Grundy's class at Gisborne Boys High School?

'Ah,' Gabriella answered. 'That must be why you're also good at what you do when you come to the centre of the world. Are not such people who have fought back to back with each other also the very best people to follow in politics, economics, finance, even television companies? I think I have just discovered your secret, Tom.'

I took an immediate liking to David and Rosemary. Their friends called them Gandalf and Mrs Gandalf because they had been in London the longest and thus were considered the Wise Ones. New Zealanders had a habit of quickly giving each other nicknames; I'd been called The Dude ever since Sting said, 'Hey, Tom, you're some dude,' on an interview for *Spaceship Earth*. The group had all been doing well in London and laughed about the New Zealand mafia in broadcasting, banking, business, law, medical practice and the arts. Gareth was a top pathologist at London City Hospital. Caroline's job with her publishing company was taking her into international book marketing. I was impressed and loved the enthusiasm with which they spoke about their lives in London. Even so, their conversation was filled with a kind of yearning.

Gabriella picked up on it. 'No matter what you New Zealanders start talking about,' she said, 'you all end up conversing about your own country. The longing is so palpable. When you talk, you have what we would call mal du pays. But it's more than homesickness. It's love of country.'

'The Maori call that aroha ki te iwi.' I answered. 'It's having a country to live for and to die for. The French are the same, surely.'

'Yes,' Gabriella agreed, 'but you New Zealanders wear your hearts on your sleeves. You people cry over your country even in pubs and bars.'

She was right. As we drank with the roistering, rowdy, laughing crowd, the conversation had turned to Jonah Lomu, the All Blacks, Marmite, *Whale Rider* ('Hey, Moby Chick! Go, Pai! Go, girl!'), Carlos Spencer's form and the Auckland Blues ('Oh, matey, a grown man would weep, pretty dire!'), *Shortland Street*, chocolate fish, whether New Zealand would mount a decent challenge to the America's Cup ('Scrag the doubter! Shame! Shame! Shame!'), Molenberg bread, Michael King's history of New Zealand ('How many copies did you get for Christmas? I got three!'), and, finally, Peter Jackson and *Lord of the Rings: The Two Towers*. 'I defy any of you,' David Carruthers roared, 'to admit you did not cry when the bonfires were being lit on the tops of the Southern Alps. Peter Jackson rules!' Ah yes, I well remember sitting in a dark London movie theatre with Gabriella, overwhelmed by the spectacle of those torches of liberty flaming into infinity, affirming that freedom was highly prized in that hard-assaulted spot of ours far to the south. 'Oh,' Caroline cried, 'we're talking about New Zealand again. Why do we *do* it!'

All this, plus that eternal question: When *were* we all going home? 'David wants to stay here,' Rosemary told me, 'but I want to go back to New Zealand. It's time to get married and have children.' At that, everybody roared with laughter and David put up his hands and said, 'Oh no, no, no, beam me up, Scotty.' Despite David's denial, there was no doubt that, while many of the group were loving London, they were torn between staying and returning. When I mentioned that I was flying home that very night, Caroline got all misty-eyed. 'Do you think you will see my folks?' she asked, because every New Zealander thinks they know everybody else. 'Mum and Dad want me to go back home for good,' she explained, 'but I really don't know how I can do that. There's a part of me that wants to and a part of me that doesn't. I'm loving it over here, truly I am, but I do feel the distance keenly and yearn for the time when I am able to return. A trip now and then usually keeps the ache under control but, this year, for various reasons, I had to cancel those plans.'

At that point, Marco interrupted our conversation with the news that our dinner was being served. In farewell, David said, 'On behalf of everybody, sir, I want to say how proud we are, that you're a New Zealander. Thanks for drinking with us tonight.' Caroline's birthday cake arrived and, to cheer her up, all those gorgeous young men and women with the whole world in front of them sang a rousing Happy Birthday. 'If I didn't have friends from home with me in London,' Caroline said, 'I don't know what I would have done tonight.' She had tears on her cheeks as she blew out the candles.

Later, as Gabriella turned into Terminal Three, she had a questioning look on her face. 'But you never went back, did you Tom?' she asked. 'After you had your OE, you stayed.'

I nodded, 'Yes, I stayed.' Gabriella has a clever habit of lifting the skin on sentimentality and exploring the ambiguous reality beneath. I tried to get around her question by charm.

'My homing device malfunctioned,' I said.

What with the drinks with David Carruthers and his friends, plus the late arrival of our dinner, I was the last passenger to check in with Air New Zealand. But my whole career as an international television correspondent and anchorman had always operated on tight deadlines and catching flights at the last minute — so what was new?

At the Air New Zealand counter, I was pleased that Harriet had indeed managed to get me an upgrade. Once upon a time, travelling first class was so un-Kiwi, as if it was our born duty to sit at the back of the plane; but we were corporate travellers now, from the land of entrepreneurs.

In the lounge, I poured myself a gin and tonic and checked my emails from the business suite. Paul had already got the wheels rolling for the next broadcast of *Spaceship Earth* from the studios of Television Three, our WWN affiliate in Auckland.

'I'll be following you out to New Zealand with Kim in nine days' time,' Paul wrote. 'Meantime, I've been giving some thought to the theme we might use to link all the special segments we are covering in the programme. How about succession? We could look at the dilemma facing the Roman Catholic Church, now that Pope John Paul has been buried. Succession is also a great theme for our segment on the historical settlement that India and China may be reaching over the Himalayan border; shall we try to get the Dalai Lama? What about looking at the demise of the National Party in South Africa (they were the architects of apartheid) from the same perspective? Do you want Nelson Mandela to talk about South Africa today?' Paul had also written notes on other possible options for the programme. One alternative was to interview President Sharon on the steps agreed upon between Israel and Palestine to return to the roadmap for peace in the Middle East. Another was to do an update, on the occasion of the second anniversary of the fall of Saddam's regime, on how the new Iraqi government was handling the situation in Iraq.

I sipped at my drink and began to take notes on Paul's suggestions. The format of *Spaceship Earth* was pretty tight and the secret of a successful show was in the timing of the segments, building them through the hour and shaping them towards maximum visual and emotional impact. I sat at a 'captain's' console in a studio which was designed to look like the interior of a spaceship orbiting the earth. Kim, my 'co-pilot', sat at a second console; she anchored one or two of the segments during the hour. Our theme music, from *Star Trek*, reinforced the impression of reporting from space.

The set was a huge curved Vidiwall of one giant plasma screen. The screen was divided into six chroma-key windows — or portals, as we called them. At the beginning of the show the portals would slide open, revealing the stars above and the glowing green of earth below; it was always an arresting and breathtaking moment.

From my spaceship 'circling the earth' Kim and I would report on the international events that week, talking directly to our WWN reporters and stringers all over the world on one of the portals. As we were doing so, the live links and video (VT) items which had been pre-shot and edited to go with each story were mixed into the interview — either on the same portal or on others. The live links were relayed into our London studio either by microwave relays or an uplink from WWN's own satellite operating above the Indian Ocean. 'Hello, is that you, Sakiri? Tell us what can you report on from Banda Aceh today? How are our people managing, three months out from the tsunami? Will there be no respite for the people of your region?' Our viewers loved being taken by our reporters behind the news to scenes that were human rather than dramatic and made their impact not from montages of death, destruction and pestilence but from images of resilience, survival and the human capacity to fight back. 'Is that you, Umbelo? It looks like President Robert Mugabe is back in power again in Zimbabwe. God, what a mess that must be. We saw him sitting next to Prince Charles at the Pope's funeral. What hope is there for democracy for your people?' Indeed, our reporters and stringers became more than faces, not just reporters going about their business; some of them had become popular personalities in their own right.

It was Otis, our technical producer, who made it all work. 'I'd be better off being a juggler in a circus,' he sometimes grumbled. 'At least they get the opportunity to take a bow.' Otis was referring to the fact that he did his work unseen in a studio control room far from the madding crowd. There, he kept up the communications links with all his fellow producers in every location where a live relay was coming from. There was always a danger of losing them, especially if the link could only be made by satellite phone or, in extreme situations, via laptop or cellphone. Otis had to queue each link, achieve smooth transition, oversee the quality of the incoming feeds and make sure they were on the portals when Paul called 'Nairobi, Portal 2, take Nairobi.' I always gave Otis a special present at Christmas, usually some expensive piece of science fiction or fantasy memorabilia Harriet had found for me on eBay.

Sometimes we had studio guests who would be 'beamed aboard' *Spaceship Earth*. Other times we had a live audience, in which case Kim and I were radio-miked so that we could move around the studio.

All this work — but it was worth it, because *Spaceship Earth* had, from the very beginning, gone into orbit with viewers. What really sold the show, according to our audience surveys, was the sense of passion I brought to helming the programme as its captain and frontsman. Most television anchormen tended to be non-partisan; I was completely the opposite. If I didn't like it, I said it. I wasn't afraid to call a spade a spade or a dictator a dictator. The ratings soared when my errant passions took my interviews into places that probed beneath polite discourse and went straight for the jugular. Whenever I had one-on-one discussions with leaders like Tony Blair or Gerhard Schröder, nobody knew what to expect — even myself. That sense of uncertainty, of 'What will the Dude say tonight!' brought a level of energy and suspense to the interviews that kept the show fresh and popular. President Bush had so far given the programme a wide berth. His advisers did not like the potential for clashes that unscripted conversation might bring.

At the end of the evening, I turned to the camera and said, 'This is Tom Mahana, and this has been our report on the human race from *Spaceship Earth* this week.'

In my earpiece I would hear Paul giving his instructions from the control room. 'Fade up music and fade up all portals from black. Ten seconds to credits. Roll credits, standby to fade to black, fade music. It's a wrap.'

We signed out, reprised the theme tune, and the video portals closed. All that was left was a sea of stars.

I finished my notes, relying on my dramatic instincts to grade the proposed segments through a series of rising climaxes, and emailed them to Paul. I decided to try Holly in Los Angeles again. This time I got through, but when she answered her cellphone, she sent up a long huge wail, 'Daddy, I'm in a cab on Wall Street.'

'What are you doing in New York?' I asked, irritated. Holly was the younger of my two children. She was twenty-four, the sensible one, working for an international banking company with headquarters in Switzerland. I had been hoping to see her.

'I'm sorry, Dad,' Holly wailed again. 'My board has an urgent meeting with Donald Trump about the expansion of his hotel chain.'

'Can't be helped,' I answered. 'So is your brother anywhere in a civilised part of the planet?'

'Nathan's somewhere down in Antarctica,' Holly said. 'He sent me a text message to say he'll be back soon. Love you, Daddy! Gotta go.'

What was the use of having children if they were never around to visit? Nathan was a member of Greenpeace. Ever since he was a boy he was always trying to save whales. 'Must be my ancestry,' he used to sigh, referring to his Maori ancestor, Paikea. As a young man of twenty-eight, Nathan was daring and unafraid, an ecological buccaneer zipping about on a Zodiac, trying to stop Japanese whaling fleets from the hunt. I got the surprise of my life during one of my shows when, all of a sudden, there he was in a news report on a new protocol signed by the International Whaling Commission. He turned to the camera and gave a devastating wink, 'Hi, Dad.' During the wrap-up, Kim said, 'Tom, that boy looked familiar. Wasn't that Nathan? Like father like son.' I got a few letters from viewers of the female kind — not for me but for Nathan. That wink of his was *hot*.

The flight was called and I made my way to the gate. The purser showed me to my seat. 'Mr Mahana, a pleasure to have you aboard, sir.' Very soon the plane taxied onto the runway and, with a roar, took off over London. Heading home. Heading south.

After takeoff I took a sleeping pill. As I drifted off to sleep. I thought of Gabriella and, in particular, what she had said to me as we were saying our goodbyes at the kerb.

'Hélas,' she said as we kissed. 'Etre néo-zélandais, c'est un dilemme exquis.'

Alas, being a New Zealander is such an exquisite dilemma.

3

There's a moment I've always loved on the flight down to the bottom of the world. The moment makes the mind-numbing, body-tiring twenty-six-hour trip from London via Los Angeles worth it. To witness it, you have to be sitting in a window seat on the lefthand side of the plane, facing east. You must ask the purser to wake you at the right time. Most of the other people on the flight will be asleep; only a few hardy ones and those who have insomnia will still be up watching movies or playing video games.

'Mr Mahana?' the purser said. 'It's your wake-up call.'

I grunted, stretched, yawned and put up the window blind. Above was a gorgeous night sky: the stars like the eyes of heaven wheeling above, and was that the Southern Cross? Below, a dark sea of clouds spread out to the horizon. Unbuckling my seatbelt, I went to freshen up. Whoever was the architect of toilets on planes must have hated the human race: not only did you have the indignity of squeezing yourself in but the lighting was designed to make you look as terrible and ugly as possible.

My image stared back at me from the mirror. 'Yes, that's you all right,' I said. People told me that I had still 'kept my face'. Sure, the contours were not as sculpted, the hair had peaked at the temples where it was grey, and I had laugh lines around my eyes — but what could you expect when you were fifty-two? I had managed to keep, well, slim-ish, and I still retained my Maori features, though my usual tan had turned to paste with all my years in the northern hemisphere. Any awkwardness I once had in suits had been overcome by the maturation process as I got used to living in my skin. What really mattered was that the energy, the vitality, the creative approach to life still animated this body, gave intelligence to its movements, and an overriding sense of purpose which allowed me to keep springing ahead of my peers. And, of course, I still had my lopsided grin.

I splashed water onto my face and took another look. When I was younger, people mistook my boyish expression for diffidence and shyness. It wasn't that at all; rather, it was my way of catching my breath, giving myself the time to think before I faced the reality I was confronted with. It was a hangover of having been a shearer's son who had lived all his boyhood as an itinerant rural gypsy, moving with Mum and Dad and the family from one contracting job to the next. In those days my personal style had been marked as much by the hesitancies, the pauses, as by the confidence with which I took the next stride. Today, the hesitation had gone, and diffidence and shyness were not characteristics I felt were appropriate in a mature man who was in his best years and at the top of his game. These days, my lopsided grin was often deployed in a more knowing, charming way.

I went back to my seat, ordered up a cup of tea and biscuits, and sat quietly watching out the window. Very soon, the moment arrived. The stars, acknowledging defeat, began to wheel away from the horizon. A thin red line appeared, as if the finger of God had decided it was time to peel away the dark. The finger lifted the flap of night and the sun came blazing through. The dawn arose, the light flooding the world with the promise of a new day. As I had always done in all my trips backwards and forwards between the world's hemispheres, I gave a karakia to Mother Earth, Father Sky, and the god Tane for giving the gift of life to Man:

Whakataka te hau ki te uru, whakataka te hau ki te tonga,
Kia makinakina ki uta, kia mataratara ki tai,
He tio, he huka, he hauhunga,
Tihei mauri ora —

As I said my prayer, I thought of the great South Pacific Ocean that lay beneath the clouds, an ocean conquered by our sea-voyaging forebears. Only a Kiwi knows how huge that ocean is and, therefore, only a Kiwi knows of the courage of our ancestors in travelling across it. Our Maori ancestors travelled in their ocean-going waka, setting out from Raiatea, a small island near Borabora, Tahiti; they navigated by stars and by following the long-tailed cuckoo or the godwits as they made their annual migrations from the Arctic Circle to Aotearoa. Our Pakeha ancestors also made epic journeys in small sailing ships from England, Ireland, Wales and Scotland; some died on the way, others were born aboard those vessels. They found haven in New Zealand, taking their first shaky steps when they made landfall. The immensity of their courage beggars description. All they had when they set forth into unknown seas were hopes and dreams. They couldn't go any further south; the next stop was Antarctica. Without them, we are nothing.

A stream of light twinkled in the distance. I thought of the country that lay ahead. Lying in the molten sea was New Zealand, rising from the dark of night and streaming with clouds. Already the sun would be glinting on Mt Hikurangi, on the East Coast, the first place in the world to greet the morning sun. The Maori called the country Aotearoa and mythologised its islands as a canoe, an anchor and a fish hooked out of the sea. The Pakeha called it New Zealand, an anglicised version of the original Dutch name of Nieuw Zeeland, given by Abel Tasman, who foolishly did not claim it. Ah, how New Zealanders liked to reduce their mythology! Esther Glen, an early writer, thought we looked like a country whose edges had been nibbled around by mice. When I was growing up, people affectionately thought of themselves as some Antipodean elephant's graveyard where baby Austins, old steam engines and planes with propellers came to die. Today, add anything to that list without a microchip in it.

Our penchant for deflation, however, could not undercut the gift from the sea that our country of Aotearoa New Zealand has been to us. Although we talked freely among ourselves of our pride in being Kiwi, natural reticence and modesty prevented us from extolling our country to others. We were much happier when outsiders, like Mark Twain, praised us and defined the nature of the gift. 'The people are Scotch,' he said, referring to the citizens of Dunedin. 'They stopped here on their way to Heaven, thinking they had arrived.'

As I uttered my karakia of thanksgiving, all these thoughts went through my mind.

May the calm be widespread,
May the ocean gleam like greenstone,
And may the shimmer of sunlight ever dance
Across your pathway.

Heaven? Yeah, right.

It was bedlam when the plane landed at Auckland International Airport. Three other flights had arrived at the same time from China, South America and the Cook Islands. The customs hall was bottlenecked with passengers migrating, holidaying passengers returning, all trying to squeeze through three lanes of officialdom to freedom. Among them was a school group of uniformed Pakeha and Maori boys, proudly wearing Texan ten-gallon hats; their leader, a tall curly-haired blond boy with a South African accent, was holding aloft a gold shield. New Zealanders were a piratical lot. Vikings of the South Pacific, we made frequent excursions to raid and pillage the northern world for its treasures before retreating with our booty back to our island fortress. We also absconded with anything foolish northerners didn't nail down — and we lugged it all back in the bellies of our groaning, overloaded planes.

On this trip home, however, alas, I let the side down. I had no prizes or trophies to declare. 'Just passing through, Mr Mahana?' the customs officer quipped. I had no problem getting past New Zealand Customs, surely the most vigilant border service in the world. We're the last Eden so we have good reason to be protective.

I walked into the terminal. Excited parents were holding aloft a banner that read:

WELCOME HOME, GISBORNE BOYS HIGH, VICTORS OF THE WORLD.

When the school group appeared — the boys had been at an international school swimming tournament in Houston, Texas — there was a huge roar. The curly-haired blond boy was hoisted up on the shoulders of his mates. The shield he was holding glowed like burnished gold.

Right in the middle of the joyous melee, I heard a voice calling to me, 'Tom! Hey, Tom!'

Oh no. I'd hoped to sneak into New Zealand incognito but, somewhere along the way, I had been sprung. Through the crowd came John Campbell, Television Three's anchorman. He was accompanied by his beautiful and brilliant producer, Carol Hirschfeld, and they had a camera crew with them. John had heard about

Spaceship Earth's forthcoming broadcast from the Television Three studios and had come racing from an interview with the *Tampa* refugees, rescued from a sinking ship in the Indian Ocean in 2002; twenty-seven Afghani families had now become New Zealand citizens. He was one of the most ebullient and excitable newscasters I had ever known. He surely must have held the record for talking in long stretches without taking a breath.

'Hey, Tom, good to see you, how long are you home for, what great news that you're doing *Spaceship Earth* from our studios next week, you're looking great, Tom, how long has it been since you were last back in Aotearoa, you don't mind if we do just a tiny wee interview with you, do you, listen, it will be absolutely painless I promise you, but you're big news, you know, as the judge said to the bishop in bed, you won't even feel it, I knew you wouldn't mind, okay boys let's get rolling and, one, two, and —' a big gasp, and we were into the interview '— the dude is back! Just arrived in New Zealand this minute, this morning, straight off the plane from London, is Tom Mahana, anchorman of *Spaceship Earth*. Tom, welcome home, it's good to see you, mate, I hear a little rumour that you'll be celebrating your tenth anniversary of *Spaceship Earth* in New Zealand, isn't that just an honour, folks? So tell us, who's going to be on the programme and will there be a live audience, Tom, I've got to have a ticket, mate —'

The interview was upbeat and funny, and John made it even funnier by pretending to get me into a headlock until I agreed, 'Okay, okay, we'll have a live audience and I'll get you a ticket.'

John turned to the crowd and said, 'Did you hear that, folks, I'm going to be on *Spaceship Earth*! Shit a brick and bugger me.' The crowd cheered and, before I knew it, the school group got into the act. The curly-haired blond boy called to his classmates, 'Hey, guys, it's Tom Mahana, one of the old boys of our school.' Spontaneously, he gave the command, 'Kia mau.'

Kia mau? From a blond South African boy?

Next minute, the crowd cleared a space as the boys shucked off their blazers, threw their ten-gallon hats into the air, unbuttoned their shirts, rolled up their sleeves and hunkered down into a raucous, ringing, impromptu haka. 'Ka mate, ka mate! Ka ora, ka ora! Ka mate, ka mate! Ka ora, ka ora! Tenei te tangata puhuruhuru nana nei i tiki mai, whakawhiti te ra.' The ground shook, the earth roared.

I felt a lump come to my throat. What New Zealander can remain unmoved by the haka? It sends shivers down the spine. And led by a blond boy with a South African accent?

A memory flashed through my mind of one of my great Maori elders, John Rangihau, and an unforgettable afternoon I spent with him when I interviewed him for *The Evening Post* many years ago.

'Have you ever heard of Te Taura Tangata?' John asked. 'The Rope of Man? It is a rope that stretches from out of Te Kore, the Void at the beginning of the universe, and extends all the way through time to the end of the universe. At the beginning of its life, the rope was strong, tightly bound by Maori strands. Some Maori believe that with the coming of the Pakeha it became frayed and almost snapped during the New Zealand Wars. Only a few strands held it together.' John's eyes twinkled with good humour and wisdom. 'But, you know, the songs of the people can still be sung through one or two strands as they are through many, and that's what happened with the rope. It renewed itself, thickened, matted with strong twisting fibres and was as strong as it had been originally. But it was a *different* rope. It was different because the Pakeha became added to the rope, the strands of Pakeha culture entwining with ours, the blood of the Pakeha joining ours and going into the rope with our blood. Some people might think that that diminished our strength. I like to think the opposite. The Pakeha has become included with us in singing not our songs but *our* songs, and that rope, well, it's still roaring along carrying us all towards infinity.'

'Aue upane! Aue kaupane! Aue upane, kaupane, whiti te ra.' Boys were leaping, muscles bulging, splitting the air with their youth and vigour.

I arrived in Gisborne later that afternoon with the high school team in tow.

The blond South African boy had been sitting across the aisle from me. His name was Henrik Kruger and his parents had migrated to New Zealand to escape the repressive National Party and its support of apartheid.

'Your parents will be pleased to know,' I told him, 'that we're doing a segment on the next *Spaceship Earth* on the party's extinction. I hope we meet again.'

My sister, Ripeka, was waiting for me when I stepped off the plane at Gisborne airport. Instead of being happy about seeing me, she scolded, 'And who forgot to tell us what day and time he was getting in? Don't worry, we saw the smoke signals and heard the tomtom drums sending messages that you were on your way.'

Even as she was speaking I saw, on the television monitor, pictures of my arrival in Auckland.

part two

4

ipeka's vigorous life on the family farm at Waituhi over the past thirty years had kept her healthy and strong. Her complexion was polished by the sun and she was weathering really well. When we were younger, people saw the family resemblance between us but, over the years, her genetic inheritance had pushed her towards my father's side: muscular, stocky, an energetic disposition and strong lustrous hair. 'You can have some of mine when you go bald,' Ripeka loved telling me, 'and you won't have to dye it.'

Not only that, but Ripeka had stayed in Waituhi all her life while I had lived most of my life overseas. The difference in lifestyles was bound to give us different finishes, hers unvarnished and mine semi-glossed. I took after my mother's side so far as looks were concerned, being tall, angular and having what people liked to tell me were 'the lines of a racehorse'. I wished it had been the other way around; a son never liked to be told he looked like his mother and, as a young man growing up, I always wanted to take after Dad.

'How's Sam and the kids?' I asked Ripeka. We were heading away from Gisborne airport. My sister had always had a heavy foot and floored the accelerator, taking the speed up to the max.

'They're fine,' Ripeka answered. 'Sam's harvesting the grapes right now. As for the kids, Victor Junior is working in Gisborne City, Whetu is completing her university degree and Albie is somewhere in Australia doing God knows what.'

My sister's first husband, Victor, died twenty years ago in a car accident; he was at a railway crossing when a freight train crashed into the car. Luckily, none of their three kids had been in the car with him. At the time, Ripeka and Victor had been helping Mum with the winery, and Ripeka missed having a man around. After five years of widowhood, she took an interest in Sam Walker. Sam had become the foreman for Mahana Wines, and his on-again off-again relationship with Mattie Jones had fizzled. Single and available again, Sam was a stud and always too sexy for his own good. We shouldn't have been surprised when Ripeka married him. She was always clever at figuring out all the angles and must have realised her kids needed another father and marrying Sam was the best way of keeping her foreman forever. Indeed, once any of my sisters got anybody in their sights, that person didn't stand a chance.

Sam, however, took a lot of persuading. He had loved my father and worked for him in the old days. Sam knew that Dad, had he been alive, would have opposed the marriage. He told me on their wedding day that he'd been expecting Dad's ghost to turn up and boot him up the bum. My sister now had two children by Sam.

Ripeka reached the main road out of Gisborne but, instead of turning out to the country, she headed into the city. 'I'm taking you to see your mother,' she explained. 'She's still in the hospital, but today's the day she is being discharged, whoop de do and lucky us. While you're with her, I have some chores to do in Gisborne, some stuff to get for her room. You don't mind my leaving you with her for a couple of hours, do you? I was sure you and her would want to spend some time alone with each other.'

There was something mean and barbed about the way Ripeka was talking. She had always been cross with me for one reason or another. True, Mum indulged me in ways that she didn't her daughters; she let me get away with murder, but had a sterner relationship with Ripeka, Mere, Wiki and Marama. On top of that, I was the successful one whereas my sisters were, well, just the siblings of a famous brother.

I offered Ripeka an olive branch. 'Thank you, sister, for being the one who has looked after Mum.'

Did she take it? Nope. 'What else could I do?' she answered. 'You were never around. The rest of the family had their own lives and I was left holding the baby. You all know I've loved Mum more than any of you did. God, how many blood transfusions have I given her since she was diagnosed with leukaemia? I feel like a human pincushion.' Ripeka was voicing all the hurts of the daughter who stayed at home while the other siblings disappeared into the wild blue yonder, not to mention a prodigal son indulging himself in Babylon. 'There's another thing,' Ripeka continued. 'After I phoned you in London, Mum told me to ring Mere, Wiki, Marama and Hone to come home too. I asked her why she wanted everybody here. Does she want to talk about her will before she dies?'

'No,' I answered. 'You and Sam will inherit the farm. Mere, Wiki, Marama and Hone will receive cash settlements equivalent to the value of the farm.' I had long made it clear to Mum that I did not expect to benefit from her and Dad's estate. My sisters and brother didn't know that I would top up the cash settlements to ensure equity of inheritance.

'If it's not the will, what's the secret?' Ripeka growled.

'Let's wait until everybody's arrived,' I answered.

'I knew it,' Ripeka said. 'I suspected something was up between you and your mother. You didn't even hesitate about coming on the next flight. What's it all about, brother?'

'Mum will tell you,' I said.

Fortunately for me, we arrived at the hospital before Ripeka could interrogate me further. I gave her a kiss as she dropped me off at the entrance. She was very cross and hurt as she drove off, revving the motor and roaring at high speed around the corner. The secret that I had with my mother was poisoning the air as surely as her cancer.

I walked into the hospital. 'Could you tell me,' I asked the receptionist, 'what room Mrs Mahana is in?'

'Oh my goodness,' she answered. 'You haven't come for Huia already, have you? She's sedated right now and she won't be discharged until later this afternoon. I did speak to Mrs Walker about this. I told her we wouldn't be releasing your mother until three.'

'That's understood,' I answered. 'Ripeka's coming at the appointed time but I'm Mrs Mahana's son, and I've just travelled all the way from London. Would you mind if I sat with Mum until she wakes up?'

'Well,' the duty nurse said, uncertain. 'All right. As long as you give me your autograph.'

It's time, son, to tell everyone what happened.

My mother was lying in a room with three other dying women. Movable dividers separated them. As I passed by, I could hear them all sighing, a strange chorale that sounded almost ecstatic, like desire.

The women were silver-haired, their skins glistening too, as if spiders had spun gleaming filaments around them, cocooning them in the fine, filigreed silver of shimmering webs. A smell of antiseptic mixed with some cloying perfume hung so heavy in the air that I could almost taste it. The overall whiteness of the room was broken only by the splash of red or purple or yellow from vases of flowers, funerary floral urns for the dying.

Even from afar I could see Mum. She was lying at the far end of the room, sleeping, propped up in a bed facing an open verandah. As I drew nearer, I was grateful that her cancer had not robbed her of her appearance. Of course I could see that she was ill, gasping slightly for breath but, somehow, she had transcended Death. The closer He came, the more beautiful she looked. Even so, He was at hand's distance and would take her soon.

I took a chair beside her bed. Her vulnerability made me sob. She must have heard me because she frowned and tried to wake up from her sedated sleep. *Is that you, son? Don't cry. I'm coming.*

'We've come a long way together, haven't we, Mum?' I said to her.

Thirty-two years had passed since I wrote about my father's death, and here I was, waiting upon my mother's death. During that time Mum had never remarried, preferring to remain a widow. Almost eighty now, she had surprised us and probably shocked herself by surviving Dad for so long. She'd never left Gisborne, preferring to live and work on the family farm at Waituhi; joined by Ripeka, she had successfully turned it into a small boutique winery.

How does a woman survive the love of her life? I guess she goes on, minute by minute, day by day, week by week, month by month, year by year until, with a great sense of wonder, she realises — as my mother did — that all those years have passed. Even so, there were moments when she would rail against the unfairness of having a husband taken away from her when she was still young.

'I was so angry when your father died,' she once told me in a moment of truth. 'I was in my mid forties and your father and I were supposed to grow old together. When he went, I felt as if he had abandoned me, left me, and there wasn't even a note on the dresser to say how sorry he was. You know what particularly hurts? All my memories of him are of a young smiling husband. Look at me, son, I'm the one who's grown old. Today, with all my wrinkles, grey hair and sagging body, I look like his grandmother. If he came into the room and saw me as I am now, I would be so ashamed.'

My mother had no option. She had to carry on with a kind of stoicism that was heroic in its patience. After all, when Dad died, she still had young ones — Wiki, Marama and Hone — to get through school. There were compensations: she took immense pleasure in all her children and grandchildren, and she was proud of how successful the winery was. Living in Waituhi, also, was not without its moments of fun and joy. She loved going down to Rongopai for the housie nights and line dancing. As the years went by she developed some of the inevitable ills of old age — cataracts, rheumatic joints, loss of hearing — and she wasn't too happy about getting a replacement hip. 'Can't you just let me rust?' The news of her cancer did not make her feel tragic. Instead, 'Well, I never thought I would last as long as I have,' she said. 'Now I can join your father. Death at last? Thank God.'

Death at last. The midnight tide which had taken my father was rising again. Already, the waves were surging around Mum, sucking her out onto the silver skein of the sea. She was going away across a sea of stars.

I put out my hand and tenderly stroked her face. Yes, even in her comatose state she must have known that I was sitting beside her because she murmured again and, this time, her jaws tensed with the effort of waking up. *I must wake up. My son is crying. I must go to him. Son, I'm coming.*

I remembered once having the tables turned on me in one of my interviews for *Spaceship Earth*. I was discussing the nature of love with the eminent psychologist, Dr Alan Adamson, and he said, 'There's a question that can test who we love most, but be careful — the question also tests our own selfishness about love. The question is, "If you were alone on a dark sea at midnight, and there was only one person whom you could call to come and rescue you, who would it be?"'

Immediately I thought of my mother — not my father — and that surprised me. What also surprised me was that the question was not as easy as it looked. For instance, I could have responded that I would call my son Nathan or my daughter Holly or even Gabriella to rescue me. But who would want to put the people you loved so much at risk? I thought of God, a lifesaver, even Paikea himself coming in mythic splendour on his whale, but the answer kept on returning to Mum.

I realised that she would come without even needing to be asked. In her was the maternal instinct which would force her to respond without thought of danger to herself.

Sitting with her, I imagined her coming now, sick, dying, trying to dogpaddle towards me. *Don't cry, son. I'm coming.*

'Oh God, Mum,' I sighed, 'you can't even swim.'

I must have been by Mum's side for a good half hour before a doctor arrived. I didn't recognise him at first. Even when he greeted me, 'Hello Tama,' his American accent put me off the scent. It took me a while to look through the doctor's older self to realise it was Michael Kavanagh, my best friend and old mate from high school. His complexion was ruddy and he was obviously living the good life. Men tend to age more radically than women and Michael, who had been a bit of a hunk, was now a bit of a chunk. He'd always been taller than I was but his height could not obscure the fact that he'd put on a lot of weight. His girth was pushing at his belt and he looked like a piece of prime beef from the best butcher shop.

'I didn't know you were Mum's physician,' I said to Michael. I suddenly remembered how cavalier, spontaneous and, well, reckless he had sometimes been at high school; whenever we played football he had a habit of dropping the ball. 'Had I known you were looking after Mum, I would have asked for somebody else!'

Michael laughed and took me to one side. 'Look, you and I have always been able to speak plainly to one another,' he began. 'You know your mother has cancer and that it's terminal, don't you?

'Yes,' I answered. 'How much time has she got?'

'Anything from three weeks to three months, who knows? She's stabilised at the moment but, when the pain comes, well, Ripeka knows what to do.'

The thought of my mother in pain shook me, but Ripeka and all my sisters were good and strong women.

'Thanks, mate,' I said. A huge wave of emotion came over me, a delayed reaction to Mum's dying.

Kei whea iara te toka whaiapu, te homai nei kia ripiripia ki te kiri moko e mau atu nei? Where is the jagged rock with which I might lacerate this body I possess, where, where? Aue! Aue, a, e rua iara aku ringaringa ki te whakakopa mai i taku manawa, e kakapa ana mehe rau kahakaha. Alas, both my hands are needed to clutch and hold my heart within, as it wildly flutters like the kahakaha leaf.

My mother was the Earth. My father was the Sky. They were Ranginui and Papatuanuku, the first parents, who clasped each other so tightly that there was no day. Their children were born into darkness. They lived among the shadows of their mother's breasts and thighs and groped in blindness among the long black strands of her hair.

Until the time of separation and the dawning of the first day.

Upset and reeling, I just had to get out of the hospital. I pushed past Michael and walked out of the room. I asked the receptionist to call me a taxi. Five minutes later the cab appeared at the front entrance.

'When my sister, Mrs Walker, arrives,' I said to the receptionist, 'could you tell her to come to Kaiti Hill? I'll be waiting there for her.'

As if Mum's dying wasn't enough, she and I would have to tell the family the *truth*.

5

All my life I have liked to take my bearings from the top of Kaiti Hill. No matter the season, the hill was eternal. In summer it was diamond sharp, cutting a clean edge into the sky. In winter, it brooded with low-lying clouds. Autumn brought flame to the willows and burnished reds to the firs and pine trees. In spring, the hill was bright with the sun.

From the lookout, you could see to the horizon. Although the vista had changed somewhat — under Meng Foon, a Chinese–Maori mayor, Gisborne city was looking ultramodern and fantastic — there was still so much sky, so much sea and, sometimes, it was still possible to see at the edge of space the tall spume rising from a whale's deep plunging. As for the city itself, there might be new commercial buildings, more traffic lights, and The Warehouse like a big red inkblot soaking up customers — but the toetoe still waved in the wind, their white plumes inscribing signs of welcome in the air. Gladstone Road was still the wide main drag that it always had been, though somewhat prettified by palms and Victorian streetlamps. The chimes from the same old clocktower still reached the top of the hill; the only time they had ever stopped was when tremors from far-off Napier during the 1931 earthquake put the clock off its stroke. The harbour remained a hive of marine industry with fisheries packing plants and dry dock facilities. New hotels and upmarket eateries were doing great business on the quay — but the flax still clicked and spoke its eternal lessons to any who would hear.

Yes, everywhere were signs of vigour. After some years in the doldrums,

Gisborne was part of the forward engine of the national economy. Some things had gone, like the railway station, which had been the main passenger and transportation hub of the region. Today, the derelict buildings were the only evidence that once so many histories had revolved here. *All aboard please, the stationmaster calls. Immediately the noise level rises and I am buffeted by the conversations of passengers as they prepare for the departure of the train. You will look after yourself, won't you dear? I'll write to you, I promise. You will come back, won't you? Won't you?* Air travel had replaced rail. Taking off from Gisborne airport was the flight to the capital city. I watched the plane as it rose above the encircling bay.

I turned from looking across the city. Behind me was Kaiti suburb and Poho o Rawiri meeting house protecting my back. There, within arm's reach, was Crawford Road where my parents, sisters and brother had lived. The difficulties, disappointments and hard times do not have the power to overshadow the happiness of those years growing up in 1960s Kaiti. The freezing works where Dad was employed no longer existed, a casualty of changing times and changing economies — sheep and cattle were trucked to killing facilities at more profitable ports like Tauranga and Napier. Even the small factory that my mother worked in had gone. By that time, I was contributing to the family income with a job as a paper boy, delivering newspapers after school. Ripeka worked a few hours each weekend at Jobson's kennels. Mere used to help too by looking after Wiki, so Mum was able to take on cleaning jobs. My friends and I ruled the suburb's streets. We had running war games as we established our turfs across the unsuspecting back sections of the neighbourhood. Every Saturday I went to the two o'clock pictures at the Majestic, or to the Macrae Baths with Michael and other good mates from school. We raced rival gangs by bike down the road that wound down from the lookout point. Michael and I loved to do night patrols on lovers in their cars at the top of Kaiti Hill, jumping up and down on their fenders and watching boys with their arses hanging out of their pants clambering out and trying to catch us. Of course, when we started to double date and younger kids did that to us, we were not very happy ourselves.

Most of all, my memories were of surviving school. I was good at sports and played school rugby and indoor basketball; I was left wing for the First Fifteen and, like all young boys, dreamed of becoming an All Black. I made the athletics team and was third runner in the relay. Good at sports, yes, but not so good at my studies — I was still trying to figure out where being Maori fitted into the scheme of things. One morning, in science class, I doodled an unconscious formula:

$$\text{Maui} + \text{Mauri} = \text{Maori}$$

From the questing spirit of our ancestor Maui would come the mauri, the life force which would compel me to achieve a place in the world as a Maori.

Even with a clever formula to sustain me, however, my school studies and I had quite a tussle. For one thing, as I progressed upward, the classes got whiter and whiter. Want to find the nigger in the haystack? Easy. Some of my Maori mates at school didn't care about advancing; instead they banded together and began the process of flunking out. That was the way Mere chose. She was at high school, in the top form. Maata, a girl from Manutuke, was the only other Maori in the class. When Maata left, Mere felt isolated. Without telling Mum and Dad she enrolled in a lower class. By the time she was fifteen, she was already halfway out the back door.

As for me, I took wobbly steps forward into the Pakeha world and somehow managed to straddle most of it. Some things had to go: like my language, my whanau and tribal relationships, my culture. It didn't seem as if you could have one with the other.

A breeze came up the slopes of Kaiti Hill and my reverie was disturbed by the clicking and swaying of the flax spears. *So Tama Mahana, what happened then? What lesson was given to you?*

The lesson? Nobody makes it through the world without a lot of help. At the point when we have needed them the most, there is always somebody with all their generosity — call them guides, mentors, advisers, guardian angels — to help us.

I finally graduated from Gisborne Boys High with the hope that I might get a white-collar job at the city council. The council was offering five internships in the city planning office, harbour board, land valuation, city transport and waste disposal, but they all went to Pakeha boys. Optimistic, I turned to Radio 2ZG — but another Maori boy, Derek Fox, got ahead of me and the station was only taking one Maori that year, yeah. Third time lucky, I applied for teacher training at Ardmore College. Mum fancied the idea of having a brainy son who she could show off to her friends, but I failed to make the intake that year for having 'ideas above my station'. Fair enough, I thought, I'd try to join the army, one of the largest employers of Maori, and maybe they could batter me into submission. I kept my spirits up, but I was extremely worried. Despite staying at school, would I end up like all my cousins who had left school early in labouring jobs, after all? Was this the lot of Maori, no matter their qualifications?

My first mentor just happened to be in my path as I was on my way to my army interview.

'So, Master Mahana,' Mr Grundy said, as I was crossing the Peel Street bridge, 'when are you going on to highest education at university? Have you applied yet for a scholarship from the Maori Education Foundation or other Maori agencies?'

'Sir, going to university just isn't on the cards for me,' I told him. 'First of all, I don't think I am clever enough —' Only Pakeha from families with higher education in their cultural assumptions went to university '— and second, Mum and Dad couldn't afford it. Even if they could and I was able to grab a scholarship, I'm eighteen, sir, and I can't spend three or four years doing further study when I could be working.' Why dream about something that was clearly out of our reach?

I asked old Grundy to excuse me as I was already late for the interview. When I told him of my career intention he tried to talk me out of it. 'Oh, Master Mahana,' he clucked, 'I haven't been teaching you these last four years without a wish to see something from my investment.'

I became extremely angry. It was obvious that Mr Grundy would never understand the predicament of coming from a working-class Maori family, or lower-class Pakeha family for that matter, whose aspirations were limited by their cultural and economic conditioning. But old Grundy wasn't going to let me go so easily into the dark.

'All right, young man,' he sighed. 'I can understand your financial dilemma, and one has to work within one's reality. So it's a job you need, is it?'

I went on to my interview. While I was waiting to hear if I would be recruited, Mr Grundy talked about me with Jock Burns, chief editor of our city newspaper, *The Gisborne Herald*. He showed Mr Burns an essay I had written for the school magazine competition. It was entitled, 'The Maori Wars? No, They Were the Pakeha Wars'. The result was that I was interviewed by him at afternoon tea at Mr Grundy's house.

'Mr Grundy has spoken very highly of you,' Mr Burns said. 'He believes you have a questing mind but, even better, an exceptional eye and an opinion. I've read your essay and I think you have the makings of a good reporter. Have you thought of a career in journalism?'

Something leapt out of my heart and said *Yes*. Mr Burns smiled at my enthusiasm, shook my hand, and said, 'I'm prepared to give you a chance, young man. I'll place you on trial for three months and, if you're good enough, you can apply for a permanent position. Welcome.'

Just as well. The army, as it turned out, didn't want me either.

Yes indeed, you don't make it by yourself — and my next mentors were waiting for me on my first day as a cadet reporter at *The Gisborne Herald*.

Their names were Morag and Fiona, and they were the two old Scottish ladies who were in charge of the reading room. In those days, the chief editor and reporters wrote their stories on half-pages. Senior staff edited the stories, which then went to the printing room, where they were printed on long rolls or galleys. Both half-pages and galleys were delivered to the reading room where proofreaders checked for spelling, grammatical and other errors. Nothing was approved for print, including all the copy from the advertising section — houses for sale, situations vacant, notices of births, deaths and marriages — until they cleared the reading room.

Actually, Morag and Fiona would be hurt by the word 'old' but anybody over forty was well, not young, to an eighteen-year-old. When they saw me standing at the door they exchanged glances across their glasses — they wore the kind with loops attached so that the glasses could rest on their bosoms when not being used.

'What canna Jor-ck be thunkin'?' Fiona said. 'This will nay do.'

'Great,' I thought dismally. 'Fired on the first day and I haven't even touched a typewriter.'

I watched as Morag stormed in to see Jock Burns. She began remonstrating with him and pointing at me. Mr Burns sank further and further into his chair; it was obvious who ruled the roost. After a while, he interrupted Morag's monologue, heaved a sigh, nodded and made a phone call. Satisfied, she returned. 'Come with me, laddie,' she said. She turned to Fiona, 'Kindly hold the forrrt Muss Morrr-ison until I rrreturr-n.'

Morag was on my side after all. As I followed her out onto Gladstone Road, she gave me her first lesson. 'To be a jurrr-nalist, you must drrrress appro-priately and maintain a prr-oper station appro-priate to your calling. How canna ye be representin' your honorr-able profession dressed lak thut, lad?' She explained that a shirt and tie without a jacket would not do and that Mr Burns had given me an advance so that I could buy two sports coats, a couple of white shirts, another tie (I was wearing one with hula girls on it) and some good-quality pleated trousers. We had a stand-off about the length of my hair, which I won; but otherwise, so began my grooming.

That was just the beginning. Morag's glasses trembled on her bosom when she discovered I lacked a primary skill for any journalist: the art of typing. 'Tama! Did ye nay thunk, laddie, aboot having to use the sacred type-wrrriter? Don't be a two-fingerr typist like Jor-ck! Use all yourrr fingers and tuckle the typing keys!'

Morag duly enrolled me, with yet another advance from Mr Burns, in evening typing classes. Bang went my dreams of owning a motorbike by Christmas. The way my career was going, I would be like Ben Hur, chained to the oars of a Roman galley for years before I got paid.

The typing lessons weren't too bad because there were nocturnal benefits: my hormones were jumping, and I was one of only two boys in a whole class of girls who, although wanting to be secretaries so that they could marry the boss, could be persuaded to assuage the hyperactivity of my adrenal cortex with a walk on the wild side. However, Miss Pringle, our typing instructor, knew a gunslinger when she saw one.

I did not fail her. Man oh man I was fast, but the trouble was that we were not allowed to look at the keys as we typed. Three lessons later I was still typing THE CQT SHAT ON TJE MAT or TJE VAT SPAT ON TGW MAT or THV RAT SAT ON VHE CAT, which was, at least, creative.

'The object, Mr Mahana,' Miss Pringle would purr, 'is not to be the fastest gun in the West but the most correct.' She would beat out the time like a conductor and we would have to type in unison with her metronomic voice. When we arrived at the end of the each line of type, we all had to return the typewriter's carriage back to begin the next line — on Miss Pringle's beat. 'The quick brown fox jumped over the lazy dog CARRIAGE RETURN A stitch in time saves nine CARRIAGE RETURN It is better to have loved than not be loved at all

CARRIAGE RETURN Mr Mahana, please do not get ahead of the class!'

Miss Pringle loved harmony. She loved the sound of all those typewriter carriages pinging away in unison. Alas, my CARRIAGE RETURN was always pinging away out of sync. Before you knew it, confused pingings would begin to ricochet around the class like a virus bringing Miss Pringle's lovely vision of typing heaven crashing into chaos.

Meanwhile, back at the office, Morag and Fiona were trying to teach me how to *write*. Here was I, thinking I knew what writing was — but not according to the Morag and Fiona School of Journalism. 'Wrrite with the prr-oper wurrds in the prr-oper places at all times with arc-urr-acy and, Tama, nay splut your in-funitives.'

Their method was to teach on the job, correcting the copy against the galley proofs. For three painstaking months, I took turns reading to either Fiona or Morag, learning about what was correct and what was incorrect. It was our responsibility to ensure that the spelling was, as they would say in their Scottish brogue, 'worrrd purr-fect!' and that there were 'nay in-arrrr-curacies whayt-so-averrr!' All this was punctuated by frequent interruptions as Morag stormed in to see Jock Burns about something he had written.

'Ye canna say tha' Mister Burr-ns,' she would protest, jabbing at the offending paragraph in his carefully crafted editorials. 'For one thing it is not proper-ly exprrr-essed and, for anuth-err it is in-corrr-ect!'

Apart from reading for spelling and bad constructions, reading the galleys was an art form that required precise enunciation and exaggerated facial expression so that one person could 'see' the words the other was saying. I called it 'making faces,' and it went something like this:

'CAP When CAP Miss CAP Katherine with an E nay Y add E CAP Stephenson nay V add PH was brought before CAP Judge CAP Wilson repeat Wilson with an S nay Wilton comma, she pleaded not guilty STOP.'

We did this all *day*. When I first began reading, Morag and Fiona were both at their wits' end because, as they would moan, 'Tama, lad, your enuncia-shon is turr-ible!' Gee, *they* could talk. After a while I got good at making faces, but was it any wonder that my friends were sometimes amused when I would greet them after leaving the office with, 'How are ye, Hohepa, shall we gae to a fillum?' or, in a pub with friends, I would shout to the barman, 'CAP Two jugs of beer, comma, thanks laddie, comma, nay froth, for my friend CAP Jon nay H?'

There was nothing like reading other people's work with such specificity to teach you the Hallowed Art of Writing Journalism; SpellCheck on the computer nowadays just isn't the same. I learnt from Morag simplicity of utterance. Fiona taught me that it is 'preferrr-able' to write with one subject per sentence. Even now I can still hear their voices. 'A prop-errr sentence has a verb. Avoid adverbs. Always seek for clarrr-ity. Check the names of the people mentioned in the article. Check all historrr-ical inforr-mation. Do not assume. Do not be lazy. Do not falsify details. When you are checking burr-ths and deaths make sure you have the right father for the right baby and that it is Mrs Pamela Browne and not Mrs Pamela Brown nay e who is the duh-ceased. Be particularly careful about headlines and captions. A spelling error in a headline is unforr-givuh-ble.'

Indeed, when the occasional error went through, Morag would meekly go to apologise to Jock Burns, much to his delight, as there were few occasions when she was penitent.

'Also, Tama, nay double entendres or unintentionally funny errors like "Seen with his new organ, Reverend Clark said that it was bigger and better than ever," or "Pictured left at the Country Women's annual baking competition is Mrs Johnson with her prizewinning bums." Above all, nay splut in-funitives!'

Fiona and Morag hunted split infinitives down mercilessly. Whenever they found one, they would issue a Gaelic battlecry and pierce it, 'Dead, dead, away wi ye!'

I count my excellence as a journalist to Morag and Fiona. Those two wonderful ladies were not to know that teaching me how to dress, type and 'make faces' — shouting backwards and forwards from galley to copy — would provide the basis for anchoring on television: I developed a distinctive personal style and great diction and vocal production. Nor would Morag and Fiona have guessed that analysing writing was perfect training for an interviewer in keeping himself and his subject to the point.

Finally, my three months in the reading room were over. At Morag's recommendation, Mr Burns promoted me to junior reporter. I felt more honoured that I had passed Morag and Fiona's muster. 'Get away with ye, lad,' they said when I gave them roses and a big book of cryptic crosswords. 'No amount of flatter-y will stop us from crr-iticising your work tho' you're a guntle-man for all tha'.' But they accepted the roses with delight and began doing the crosswords during lunch.

Was I assigned to reporting duties? Was I any nearer to buying a motorbike? Nope. There was still so much training to get through.

Jock Burns assigned me to the graveyard shift. At five every morning I would ring the police station, hospital, airport, railway station, meteorological office, and harbourmaster to find out whether there had been any accidents or emergencies reported during the evening. I was so enthusiastic, hoping for something spectacular to happen, that some of my regular informants would take the mickey out of me. 'Ah yes, Tama, well, a low-flying unidentified flying seagull crashed at Gisborne airport this morning,' or 'Forest fires are raging on the East Coast after a meteor aimed at earth by the evil emperor Ming of Mars made a direct hit on Ruatoria.' By 6 am I was in the office checking the teleprinter for the NZPA and AAP-Reuter news reports that came into *The Gisborne Herald*. I had them stacked on the desks of the appropriate reporters by 7 am. Among the reporters, my idol was Gary Gorton, the sports reporter, who covered local sports events, and was always hopping on his bicycle to go and watch the soccer and hockey, and received free tickets to all the representative rugby games at Rugby Park. How I wished to do that! All I got, if I was lucky, was the occasional job reporting on the monthly meeting of the Gisborne Farmers' Wives Association or the mayoress cutting the ribbon at the opening of a charity bazaar. In despair, I once wrote a rather mean caption to a photograph, to wit:

'Old-age pensioner, Mr John Wilson, shows off the fashion for the elderly by wearing his favourite striped pyjamas. He is seen thanking the valiant fire officers of the Gisborne Fire Brigade for saving his pet cat, Maybelline.'

Morag caught the snide tone of the caption and, in front of everybody in the office, berated me for it. 'Arrogance becomes no man, Tama Mahana,' she began. 'I will not allow it in ye or anybody else. Pride cometh before a fall but 'tis better not to fall. Honour the person you are writing about. Be generous spirited because people will rrecog-nise it in ye and returr-n it to ye. Dinna put yourself above other purr-sons. Respect, Mr Mahana, show respect. Don't you be putting the powerless down, laddie. Stand up for them, the elderly, women, the coloured, the children of this world. Be their spokesman, laddie, because they have nae many who speak for them.'

Morag disciplined me lovingly. I took that lesson to heart. She taught me about advocacy; in this world, one should be spokesman for those who have nobody to stand up for them. For as long as I was with *The Gisborne Herald* and, subsequently, when I left for Wellington — and an international career in journalism and television — I tried my best not to be too proud.

I stood on Kaiti Hill in the sunlight, the memories coming thick and fast. I heard the horn of an approaching vehicle and a voice calling, 'Hey, Tama.' I was surprised to see Michael Kavanagh waving to me. He was behind the wheel of a four-wheel-drive, driving as badly as I remembered and running over the kerb before he braked.

'I'm definitely pulling Mum from your care,' I laughed as he got out. 'What are you doing here?'

'I know you're expecting your sister,' he answered, 'but she and my nurses have given me the boot. They told me they had a job to do, you know, women's work, getting your mother ready to be discharged, and I was in the way. I ask you, how did we let women do this to us? Look who's running the country! We've got a woman as prime minister, female governor-general, a woman as government whip, a female chief judge, and the top corporation in the country, Telecom, is run by a woman. All these women, including your sisters and my nurses, ordering us around. Ah well, I needed a break and your sister told me to do something useful and come and pick you up. So here I am, despatched to get you.'

Not long after I joined *The Gisborne Herald*, Michael and I had flatted together. We shared some boyhood memories of Kaiti Hill. 'I haven't been up here for ages,' he said. 'The last time was when we brought our girlfriends up here; but don't tell my wife! I think you were going out with Rebecca Simpson at the time. And didn't you have something going with a nurse? Janice or Gillian somebody? How long has it been since you and I last saw each other?'

'You were the one who left Gisborne before I did,' I answered. 'What happened to *you*? After you left I had to get a new flatmate.' I was often blamed, wrongly, by friends who believed that it was my fault we hadn't kept in touch.

'Oh, that's right,' Michael conceded. 'You were trying to be a reporter and I think I had bummed out at school, right? Do you remember my dad? He was a doctor and he got fed up with me in the end because I seemed to lack ambition. He offered to pay me to go to medical school at Otago and, well, it was a way of going somewhere he couldn't see what I was doing.'

'You went overseas too, didn't you?' I asked.

'I surprised myself by enjoying medicine,' Michael nodded. 'After I finished my degree in genetic research, I went to Johns Hopkins University in Baltimore. Did you know my wife, Cathy, was an American? I transferred to Sloan Kettering where I got into Aids research and, you know, I had a great career going for me, travelling to Paris and Atlanta and to Africa when the Aids crisis began to sweep that continent. Cathy and I had three boisterous boys and I was on a roll but, two years ago, I just couldn't hack it any longer. Since returning to good old New Zealand I've realised how much America took out of me in terms of stress and, what with the current political situation, I couldn't accept the Bush administration. America is no longer the land of the free. The human rights breaches since the Iraq war made me feel personally violated. I landed back here a bit wounded, on a wing and a prayer. Working in public medicine might look like a bit of a come-down but, hey, I'm not complaining. It was the best thing I ever did, coming home — just like the godwits, I guess.'

Godwits were Arctic waders that migrated south to Aotearoa to get away from the Arctic winter. They normally wintered over at Rangaunu Harbour, at the neck of Aupouri Peninsula, or at Parengarenga Harbour. Around 10,000 godwits made that extraordinary annual trip the breadth of the world. Their route was southwest down from the northern hemisphere and into the western Pacific. They flew in a compact flock, a snowstorm of feathers, twisting and turning in unison; some never made it, falling, exhausted, into the sea. I liked the idea of Michael arriving, like the godwits, on a wing and a prayer, to find safe haven in New Zealand. I was glad he hadn't fallen into the sea.

Michael and I took a walk down the hill and sat looking over the harbour and out to sea.

'Can you remember old Grundy?' Michael asked.

Ah yes, my high school teacher. *The Lord be praised, Mr Grundy said. Passion, a sense of justice and signs of a pulse.*

'You knew he died last year at the ripe old age of ninety-six, didn't you?' Michael continued. 'I was his doctor and, when he saw me with a scalpel in my hands, he said to me, "Oh dear, Dr Kavanagh, now I wish I had given you more As in your essays." At school I tried so hard for him but, somehow, you always did better. I can remember how much I personally objected when you got an A+ for an essay in which you had got everything wrong! But what was Grundy's explanation?'

'I completely disagree with you, Master Mahana,' I remembered, imitating Mr Grundy's lofty tones, 'but your essay does, by being so convincingly argued, what an essay whose argument I might agree with, does not.'

Michael laughed along with me. 'I got to know old Grundy really well. He always called me Doctor. He was good enough to congratulate me for my achievements but, really, you were always his favourite student. Were you the anonymous donor who paid for his private room?'

'He never found out, did he?' I asked, alarmed. 'He was such a private man, I could never have let him spend his last days in a public ward.'

'We talked about you a lot,' Michael continued. 'He was really proud of you, Tama. One night, around six o'clock news time, he looked at his watch and asked me to put the television on. There you were, getting a decoration from the queen for services to international journalism. "Ah, what it is to bask in reflected glory," old Grundy said. "Who would have thought that one of my pupils would be like Sir Edmund Hillary, standing at the top of the highest mountain in the world, not so that we can see him standing there but showing us where it is." Although he was an old royalist, Grundy told me how, in 1953, he privately hoped the new Queen Elizabeth would forgive him for being more thrilled about Hillary's conquest of Mt Everest than about her coronation. I had the same feeling when Charles married Diana and Kiri Te Kanawa was singing *Let the bright seraphim* in that ridiculous hat.'

'I remember it well,' I laughed. At the time of Prince Charles' wedding, I was at the protest in Molesworth Street facing baton charges from the police over the Springbok tour. As a baton crashed on my helmet, I saw on a TV set in a shop window a broadcast of the wedding and Kiri carolling away invoking angels to come down and bless the union.

'I have another bee in my bonnet about you,' Michael chuckled again.

I thought of Ripeka. 'Join the queue,' I invited him.

'There was another lesson with old Grundy,' he said. 'To tell you the truth, it's bothered me all my life. During the history period, the class was laboriously copying out appropriate paragraphs from our history text on the *History of the British Isles* when old Grundy made us shut our books, put away our pens and asked us to ponder our own New Zealand history.'

'Think, boys, *think*,' I remembered, imitating Mr Grundy's voice again. 'Do you think the study of the British Isles is appropriate for boys who live in the colonies? What do you know of your own country, eh boys, eh? Oh, Captain

Cook, yes yes, Abel Tasman, yes yes, Hongi Hika, Te Rauparaha, the chopping of the flagpole at Kororareka, yes yes, but is that enough, boys, is it enough?'

Michael grinned with delight and took over imitating our old teacher. 'Until it is created, a country doesn't exist, boys! And how is a country created? It has to be named, claimed, possessed. It has to be written into existence, sung about, spoken into existence. People have to fight for this land, boys, be born in it and be buried in its soil and be cried over. They have to develop their own identity.' Michael turned to me, 'And then old Grundy asked us all a question —'

'I remember,' I answered. '"Prove to me that you are a New Zealander!"'

The volume, anger and pleading in Mr Grundy's voice shocked us. '"What credentials can you offer to prove to me that you belong to this bloody country!"'

'For God's sake,' Michael said, exasperated, 'what did he expect us to tell him? I think somebody offered, "Well, we're not British and we're not Australian." Somebody else said "I was born here." Old Grundy asked us, "Is that all? Is that enough?"' Michael's voice rose as he remembered what happened in class that day long ago. 'We were just too young. We didn't know enough of our history or geography. But did old Grundy accept that? "Boys your age went to fight the Gallipoli campaign," he railed. "They went because they loved this country and were prepared to die for it. But why, boys, why? It wasn't just because they had an *idea* of New Zealand. It was also because, because —" His arms were flailing the air and he was waiting for us to answer him and, all of a sudden, you started to chant from the back of the room —'

All I did was to recite my whakapapa, my genealogy, all the people who had gone before me and who had died before me and had given me turangawaewae and ahi kaa: a place to stand and a fire to keep burning in the belly of the land. And Mr Grundy had *beamed*. Even so, after I had finished and silence had fallen, he still challenged all of us.

'By virtue of his Maori ancestry,' Mr Grundy said, 'Master Mahana, as an indigenous citizen, is ahead of the rest of us in being able to claim the rights of a Maori New Zealander. But his founding document, the Treaty of Waitangi, is also ours. That document gives the rest of us rights, also, boys, and you, Master Mahana, don't you ever be complacent enough to forget it. Boys, you must study your own history and, in particular, you must create as personal a history as Master Mahana has with this soil. The next time I ask you this question I expect you all to tell me who you are.'

'Then,' Michael said, 'old Grundy turned to me, I don't know whether by chance or design, and he asked me, "Who are you, Master Kavanagh? No, not who are you; who *are* you?"'

'Ah,' I smiled, 'that was Mr Grundy's favourite question.'

'As I said before,' Michael continued, 'I've been haunted by that history lesson, and old Grundy's personal question to me, all my life.' Michael looked up at the sun. His eyes watered and he put a hand across his face. 'Fortunately, before he died I was able to tell him who I was, why I was a New Zealander, and to give him a particular piece of proof. I always carry a copy of it around with me —'

Michael fumbled in his vest pocket for his wallet and extracted a piece of paper. 'This belonged to my great-great-great-grandmother. She was one of the first settlers to come out to New Zealand in the early 1800s. Her name was Esme Eleanor Elizabeth Warner and this is a copy of her bill of passage. Her husband Peter Adam Drummond died on the voyage and so did one of her two children. But Esme and her other child, Andrew, came to land at Port Nicholson and she married a young man, William James Parker, who told her he was coming to the Poverty Bay to buy farmland.'

Michael's eyes were moist. 'Well, when I showed old Grundy, he was so very proud. He managed to sit up and jab a finger at my forehead. "Ah, Dr Kavanagh, it is so gratifying for a teacher to know that for one of his pupils something got through."'

I started to laugh because Michael looked so mournful. He stared at me in anger but then saw the funny side of what he'd been saying. Next minute we were both laughing, great snorts that rumbled up from our bellies, at the wonderful human comedy of our lives. We were older and wiser and it was so good to sit in the sun and to affirm our shared history.

I patted my old friend on his shoulders. 'Let's not leave too many more years before we see each other again, eh?'

Michael nodded. We shook hands and then Michael pulled me into a fierce hug; the strength of feeling behind the hug surprised me. Quickly, as if to hide the feeling, Michael looked at his watch. 'Ker-rist, we'd better be getting back to the hospital,' he said. As we were going to his car, however, he turned to me.

'One more thing,' he began. 'I need to apologise.'

'What for?' I asked, surprised.

'That fourteenth birthday party of mine.'

Michael had invited me but, came the day, his mother rang up and said he was sick. I'd already bought him a present so I went to his house to give it to him. I knocked on the door. His mother answered. Behind her, I could see Michael and other friends sitting down to the birthday feast. His mother at least had the decency to appear embarrassed. 'Would you like to come in?' she asked. 'Thank you, but no,' I answered. Michael came to the door to see me. 'I told Mum I wanted you to be here,' he said. 'I've never ever thought of you as being a Maori, Tama. You're just my mate, eh.'

'There's no need to apologise, Michael,' I answered. 'All that stuff, it's all in the past. It never affected our friendship. I've always thought of you as being my best friend from those days.'

I saw a huge weight lifting off Michael's shoulders. 'I just want to tell you, Tama, that my mother never forgave herself. It wasn't her fault. In her day, New Zealand was a nasty, racist, homophobic, sexist, miserable bloody society. Now, of course, we have a burgeoning of Maori identity, women are running the bloody country, gay people don't have to live secret and miserable lives, and this new generation has everything to look forward to.' His lips trembled. 'In a strange kind of way, looking after your mum has given me the chance to make some recompense for what my mother did. It's been an honour.'

We stepped into Michael's car. 'In the end,' he asked, 'Gisborne was kind to us, wasn't it, mate?'

I pondered the question. In those days Gisborne had been like a frontier town. Its population was half Maori and half Pakeha. Now it was blended, laminated. The lives of two peoples had become inextricably entangled and it was predicted that within a generation every New Zealander would have some Maori blood or at least have a Maori relative within the new New Zealand family.

And what of our dreams? Had they also become blended, laminated? I remembered Mr Grundy reciting a poem written by Denis Glover in the 1960s: 'I do not dream of Sussex downs or quaint old England's quaint old towns; I think of what may yet be seen in Johnsonville or Geraldine.'

The times of puzzling dichotomies were gradually receding. Maori and Pakeha were trying to work out the crucial issues of Waitangi, notably possession and contested spaces, as we tried to redefine the ways of living together.

And yes, so many of our people had been born and had died on this soil.

'Yes,' I answered Michael. 'We got on with life.'

6

My mother was waiting on the kerbside of the hospital, sitting on her suitcase. She was wearing a silver-sheened dress and, with her silver hair, looked like a beautiful moth whose wings had stilled around her. Ripeka was fussing over Mum, scolding her for something or other. She had been joined by Mere and Wiki, and all of them were dressed in severe black.

Michael stopped his car next to Ripeka's ute. As soon as Mum saw me get out she stood up, smoothed her dress and gave me a quick kiss and a hug. 'Hello, son,' she said. 'I'm glad you were able to come so quickly.'

'Don't worry, Mum,' I answered. 'Things will work out.'

'What things?' Ripeka asked. She could always hear conversations outside the normal decibel range of human hearing.

Mum waited, rather impatiently, as I greeted Mere and Wiki. My sisters were looking as finely weathered as Ripeka, but Mere had sure put on the poundage. All the butter she put on her toast was going straight to her hips. Wiki wasn't looking her usual slim and sylph-like self either. When she was a schoolgirl she was always referred to by her older sisters as 'the pretty one'; she still had a lovely face but from the neck down she looked like her sisters. 'Don't say it,' Wiki wailed, because she was still figure-conscious, 'and anyhow Darren likes me this way.' Darren was her Pakeha husband, owner of a secondhand car sales yard, whom she'd met twelve years ago on the Gisborne golf course while teeing off at the fifth hole. Boy oh boy, did Ripeka and Mere give him the going over when he came courting.

I pulled Wiki into a big hug. Of all my sisters she was the one who had been most affected when Dad died. She lost confidence. In a group, she was happy to go along with what everyone else wanted to do. Where you found Ripeka and Mere you could be sure that Wiki wouldn't be too far behind.

As if we had just seen each other yesterday, Mum picked up her suitcase. 'You're finished greeting each other then? Good. Let's go.'

Mere glared at her. 'Mum couldn't get out of the hospital fast enough,' she said to me. 'She's been keeping us waiting here outside where she could catch her death of cold.' Mum was already walking towards Ripeka's ute. The rest of us ran to catch up. When Mum said, 'Let's go,' she really meant it.

'I'll take Mum, Wiki and Tama with me,' Ripeka yelled to Mere. 'You go and collect Marama and Hone from the Wellington flight. As soon as they arrive bring them out to Waituhi.'

Mere was on the run to her car. 'Put the kettle on, eh? What with mother dear playing up this morning, I'm a wreck already and I'll need a cup of tea.'

'Okay, sis,' Wiki answered. 'I got a lovely surprise to go with your cuppa. A pavlova with raspberries on the top.'

'Yummy,' Mere said. 'In that case, I'll stop off at the blue shop and buy some whipped cream.'

My sisters had grown into a formidable threesome who liked to organise everyone and everything in their lives. They also loved eating. When Dad died, both Marama and Hone had been brought up by their three older sisters, whom Hone somewhat irreverently called 'The Sisterhood'. Ripeka was Mother Superior, Mere was Sister of the Holy Watercress (she made him eat his greens) and Wiki was Our Lady of the Jailhouse Door (when he was a teenager, Hone was always on a short leash). When he grew into adolescence, Hone would often phone me and yell, 'Please, bro, get me outta this nunnery!' I would send him a plane ticket so he could join me wherever I was in the world, where he could devour steaks and not have to sneak out the window.

I caught up with Mum and took her suitcase. 'Who are your friends?' I asked her, kidding.

'When I woke up they frightened the living daylights out of me,' she said. 'Standing around the bed, all dressed in black like that. They tell me they're your sisters.' She opened the driver's door. Ripeka had just enough time to stop her from clambering into the driver's seat.

'Oh, no you don't,' Ripeka said.

Mum glared at her. 'Just because I'm sick doesn't mean that I can't drive.' She turned to me and whispered, 'Ripeka's really irritating right now but we have to forgive her. She's on her moon.'

Ripeka compressed her lips. 'Back seat for you, Mummy darling,' she said, giving Mum a very forceful push. 'You too, brother dear. Wiki, you sit up front with me.'

'Oh, happy day,' I smiled at the sun. 'Oh lovely day. What a perfect joy to be home again.'

Te Whanau a Kai panapana maro.
Te Whanau a Kai never retreat.

'There she blows,' Wiki said.

Ahead was Pukepoto, the powerful-looking ancient hill fortress which was the entrance to Waituhi.

Ripeka, in her usual racing-driver fashion, had got us along the eighteen kilometres from Gisborne in twenty minutes. She had roared past lorries on the concrete bridge at Matawhero, squeezed around semi-trailers at Patutahi, and any sheep or cattle that strayed into her path, tough. Still in fourth gear, she zoomed through the village, past Rongopai meeting house and Tawhiti Kaahu, the billowing dust of her wake ruining every piece of washing put out to dry that day. On the right was the entrance to the farm, now sporting a new sign saying *Mahana Wines Limited* and, in smaller letters, *R & S Mahana, Vintners.* Like everybody else involved with my sisters, poor Sam Walker had been absorbed into the family and had disappeared like the helpless victim of an alien blob in a science fiction film. In the distance I saw some workers irrigating the vines; one of them, Sam, waved his hat.

'Hey, Tama,' Sam yelled. 'That boy of yours has sure grown taller.'

'Nathan?' I turned to Ripeka. 'Has Nathan been to Waituhi?'

'Don't you ever keep up with your own kids?' Ripeka answered. 'He stopped over to see Mum on his way down to Antarctica. He's a good boy, always loved his grandmother and his aunties.' She braked the ute outside the homestead. Once upon a time the homestead had been a cottage, but the prosperity of the vineyard had brought add-ons in the form of two bedroom wings to the original house. 'Well, you must be jetlagged,' Ripeka said solicitously as we got out of the ute. 'Why don't you and Mum go and have a nice sleep.' In other words, *Wiki and I will be busy cooking up a storm and, when Mere arrives, we won't want you and Mum under our feet.*

'If it's all right with you,' I answered, ignoring Mum's semaphoric signals to take her with me, 'I think I'll go for a walk and stretch my legs.' In situations like this it was every man for himself. 'Don't worry, Mum, you have your sleep. When Mere gets here with Hone and Marama, we'll all have our talk.'

'Good idea,' Ripeka and Wiki said as they shepherded Mum inside. 'Don't worry about your bags. Sam can bring them in later.'

I struck out for Lavenham Road, the main road through Waituhi. The sun was hot, its rays bringing out the heightened colour of the landscape. Once a producer of sheep and cattle for the lamb and beef market, the valley had been transformed first into a kiwifruit growing region and, now, wine production. Gone were the rolling vistas of hillside grasslands and river plains growing subsistence crops of maize, marrows, kumara and kamokamo. Waituhi had always been my Eden but now it was a *new* Eden, glowing like greenstone and stretching to heaven. Watered by the Waipaoa River, the vines flaunted a rich, dark green studded with the translucent grapes for chardonnay and chablis production.

I crossed over Lavenham Road and started to walk up Tawhiti Kaahu. By the time I reached the ridge above Takitimu Hall I was perspiring but exhilarated. From here I could look across the landscape to the sea. Right at the intersection of sky and earth, Rongopai, the painted meeting house, still held up both so that I could stand upright in the bright strand between. Here was the place of the heart, the centre of my universe. This was the place of the Te Whanau a Kai. They were the tangata whenua and, although much of their land had been confiscated, they had fought tooth and nail to hold on to this piece of it. They were still contesting the government for the adjoining Patutahi block, taken as reparation for the Poverty Bay wars. How fortunate I was to have such a valley running through my heart and a people who were still fighting for it. How privileged that I had such wonderful grandparents and whanau in my life. I was a prince only because I came from such royal stock.

I raised my arms and voice and gave my usual salute to all the marae of the valley:

'Pakowhai, Rongopai, Takitimu e!'

Then I walked through the gate of the graveyard and gave my greetings to my village dead. I acknowledged them with both tears and gratefulness.

'E nga tupuna ma, kui ma, koro ma, tamariki ma, kua haere koutou ki Te Po, tena koutou.'

They were all gone now, the old people of my boyhood who structured my life and gave it meaning. Dad was gone, and most of his brothers and sisters — Uncle Te Ariki, Uncle Alexis and Aunt Hiraina among them — were gone. The Matua was gone, and all those wonderful grandparents and aunts and uncles, cousins and kin who gave me grace and dignity: Bulibasha, Ramona, Aunt Ruth, Aunt Sarah, my strange Aunt Tiana whom we called 'The Dream Swimmer', my beloved cousin Haromi, all gone. The great Tamati Kota, he, finally and gladly, went to God at the fine old age of one hundred and eleven years; there, Riripeti had indeed kept him a place at the table of the Lord.

After the Matua died, Nani Tama married Mattie Jones. 'That old woman had planned it from the start,' Uncle Pita told me, on one of my visits home. 'When she died, she gave Mattie a biblical deathbed instruction, "You are to go in unto my husband and lie with him." Although Tama was twenty years older than Mattie, had not the Matua been twenty years older than Tama? Once the commandment had been given, the Matua said to her mate, Maka tiko bum, "Maka, how about a last game of cards?"'

The Matua had hoped that Mattie would take over the role as Matua of the village; she would have been pleased to see the renascence of that leadership, not through one charismatic person, as she and Riripeti had been, but through a new runanga, a tribal-based committee system for the iwi. The irony was that Mattie had had a relationship of some kind with Sam Walker but, when Mattie and Nani Tama married, that left Sam as loose change in Waituhi's pocket. Ripeka spied him like a silver coin, picked him up and put him in her purse before he knew it had happened.

Aue, Nani Tama has also left this earth. After his death, Mattie returned to the South Island where she has become a formidable presence in the thrilling ascension of the Kai Tahu as one of the great power brokers in New Zealand fisheries, Maori economic development and South Island politics. Also gone were Charlie Whatu, Hepa Walker and all those Mahana shearing-gang uncles like Uncle Joshua, Uncle Hone and Uncle Pani, who had defined my masculinity and sense of what a man was supposed to be: a good provider, a strong father, brother, son or husband, a bringer of fish or fowl to the table. The younger generation confused them — my cousins Simeon, Andrew Whatu, my gay cousin Michael Mahana — because we turned to Pakeha professions in law, literature, gender politics and journalism. They tried to keep us to traditional relationships and, when Dad died, Uncle Pita always opened his house to me.

Uncle Pita died after a harsh winter four years ago. Of all my uncles, he was the one I loved most. He took me out pig-hunting and diving for paua. Even he was unsure of how to handle this new young warrior who came into his midst looking Maori but with Pakeha skills and manners. After Dad's death, when I began to achieve some reputation as a journalist in Wellington, Uncle Pita always asked that I stay one night with him whenever I came back to Gisborne; it was his way of keeping an eye on me and making sure I was not becoming too proud in my new ways. His wife, Aunt Miriama, had died of breast cancer some years before and he was living with a lovely, cuddly lady, Missy, in a new house in Mangapapa suburb. I went to see him and he showed me where I was to sleep — in a huge double bed, all to myself. During the night I got up. I wanted a drink of water. I walked toward the kitchen and in the sitting room found Uncle and Missy sleeping on a mattress on the floor. I woke them up.

'Uncle, have I changed that much? Look at me. It's me, still Tama, your nephew.'

My generation was the first to start crossing over. The old people didn't know where we were heading and, because they had a natural instinct to protect, they either didn't want us to leave or else found it difficult to let us go. Departing the tribal hearth meant our generation was walking away from the tribal world. Indeed, the great rural to urban migration was as huge a disruption to that Taura Tangata — that Rope of Man — as the Land Wars had been. Not only were we leaving our many marae depleted, we were also displacing ourselves outside our cultural frameworks. It took us a long time to learn our lesson: we had to take those frameworks where we were going so that our cultures could cross over with us.

Even so, some of us went further than most. My gay cousin Michael probably had the hardest journey; Uncle Monty, his dad, banned him from coming back to Waituhi and he's still out there somewhere trying to create a new gay tribe for New Zealand. As for me, I probably went the longest journey. I panicked my parents and grandparents, and all those who loved me, by crossing to the outer, far-flung edges of space. It must have been frightening for them to see me go into Te Po, the Darkness, where nobody could reach, even beyond Te Po and into Te Kore, the Void, where only dream swimmers could go.

I walked toward a familiar gravestone. One of my sisters must have been up recently because Dad's plot was looking lovely. The lawn above him was trimmed, and around his headstone were flowers and toy windmills turning in the wind.

I stood, head bowed, remembering the loving man who had been at the centre of my life.

'Hello, Dad.'

What do you know? You're just a freezing worker who's so busy slitting sheep's throats you wouldn't recognise what's happening around you until it shat in your face.

I was nineteen when my relationship with Mum and Dad hit rock bottom. I was torn between my loyalty to my parents and my need to find my own way in the world. I flailed around like a drowning man and, in desperation, began to look for ways of getting out, going away, finding some place else where I could just *be*. Like all the friends of my generation I had already begun the process of leaving home, even before I actually left. I had a girlfriend named Janice, a nurse, and although our relationship wasn't going anywhere, it had its own unsettling effect. My generation had puzzling and inexplicable reasons for wanting to escape the nest; mainly, we wanted to live our own dreams and they were not the dreams of our parents.

It was Morag who saw the vacancy advertised for a reporter at *The Evening Post* in Wellington. 'Don't you like me?' I kidded her.

'That I do, lad,' Morag answered. 'But there's no place for your advancement herrr-e. Not only that, but you're getting too guid, lad, and some of the others are getting worrr-ied.'

I knew what Morag meant. Although Jock Burns had been interested in supporting me, the office was staffed by married men, with wives and children. As was the case with most rural newspapers, people who worked in them were there for life. Indeed, when I asked Jock if I could apply, he said, 'Go for it, young Mahana. There's nothing more I can do for you.' He gave me a reference and I found myself on a shortlist. Without being interviewed, I was offered the job.

When I told Mum I was going to Wellington, she was angry. 'Don't your father and I have a say in your decision?' she asked.

Dad interrupted her. 'Let him go, dear, it's better this way.'

I said goodbye to Janice. When I left on the train, Dad and I had made a kind of peace with each other. He gave me a piece of four by two with a nail in it. 'Whenever you think that job's getting difficult, bang on this and take a reality check. I'm proud of you, son.'

I went to Wellington in 1972.

I stepped off the train and straight into one of the great celebratory events of the 1970s: the election of Norman Kirk as prime minister of New Zealand. I put my bag in left luggage and ran up to Parliament grounds to join the throng of well-wishers. Just as America had President Kennedy, New Zealand had Kirk. Like Kennedy, he was young, charismatic and captured the popular imagination. As I cheered myself hoarse I couldn't help feeling the tug and pull of national and international currents, swirling around me and taking me onward and ever outward into the world.

Dad had made arrangements for me to stay with his brother Alexis, but I decided from the very beginning to be independent of family. I checked into the YMCA and, next morning, started looking in the paper for a flat. I telephoned three places before finding something hopeful with the fourth: TWO GUYS SEEKING THIRD FOR ALL MALE FLAT. ANYBODY WHO CAN COOK REAL FOOD WOULD BE GREAT. The flat was in Newtown, and the two guys were Jasper and William. When Jasper answered the door he said to me, 'The last applicant cooked cordon bleu, the one before him brought his own wok, so you're going to have to be bloody awesome.' I blew the competition away. When it comes to kai, it's not style that counts but substance. With steak and eggs sizzling in the pan, and mashed spuds and peas coming up, all doused with tomato sauce, the third bedroom was mine. Afterwards, William said, 'Just one more thing. I'm gay. Do you have a problem with that?'

'No,' I said. 'I'm Maori, do you have a problem with *that*?'

The next day I presented myself to *The Evening Post*. The paper had just been acquired by Independent Newspapers Limited, then New Zealand's largest media company. At the height of its history, INL owned nine dailies and two Sunday newspapers, an extensive stable of free community papers, a range of magazines, an internet operation, and a magazine distribution business. It had strong links with the News Corporation, or NewsCorp, Rupert Murdoch's Australian-based global media company. This link was to have a profound impact, eventually providing the bridge to an international career.

My boss, Mr Ralston, explained why he hired me. 'First of all, yours was the only Maori application and, second, I've had enough of inexperienced graduates from schools of journalism. Yours wasn't the best application but, on the plus side, you came out of Jock Burns' paper and I knew I'd not have to put up with split infinitives. More importantly, I didn't want somebody who could do the same job as we are already doing. I wanted somebody with a point of difference. Are you that person? I'll give you some time to settle in. Then I want you to show me the stuff you're made of.'

I loved the buzz of arriving at the office. Throughout 1973, I gradually learnt the ropes, becoming involved in the teamwork necessary to bring out every daily edition. At the time, Wellington had two newspapers, *The Dominion*, a morning newspaper, and *The Evening Post*, which published in the afternoon. The urge to be the first to break the news in the capital created a sense of competition between them that brought out the very best in my work. If I thought I had been working hard and fast at *The Gisborne Herald*, it was nothing compared to the speed, fast thinking, and ability to think laterally and spontaneously — to click stories together in a second — that was later to serve me so well as a television anchorman.

I particularly loved arriving early and listening to the meetings of the news executives — the editor, editorial writers and department heads — as they talked about the news of the day. I made a nuisance of myself eavesdropping on the editors as they individually briefed the chief reporters about their assignments. Nothing gave me greater pleasure than to scan other newspapers to see if we had scooped anyone — *The Dominion* especially — or missed anything. When the newspaper was printed every day, I'd grab a copy to read the front-page stories.

And what stories they were! Our new prime minister was highly active in implementing new policies in housing, health, employment and education; he was seen by many as a champion for ordinary New Zealanders. Just as thrilling, his government took a similarly active approach to foreign relations. I envied our senior writers when they covered New Zealand's recognition of the People's Republic of China, the prime minister's cancellation of the South African

Springbok tour, and the government's protests against French nuclear testing at Mururoa.

Alas, other reporters were writing the stories. As for me, I was mainly researching and gofering for the senior reporters — and pleading with the deputy chief reporter, features editor, business editor, sports editor, hell, anybody who would listen, to give me a reporting job. Happily some of the editors saw my eagerness and began to offer assignments that would familiarise me with the capital and the people who lived in it. And, no doubt, to get me out from under everybody's feet. The thorn in my side was that the office was filled with somewhat controlling types, like Ted Smith, who seemed to regard any young newcomer as his personal property, existing only to do his research. On the plus side, I found a good mate in Ray Hargraves, who was older than I was, and was our newspaper's representative in the parliamentary press gallery.

I also met Sandra. Let's face it, living in Wellington wasn't all hard work. I finally bought a motorbike and went out to the pub and partying, and I had a couple of great girlfriends before that fateful night when William invited me to go with him to a party. It was hosted by a bunch of American students who were celebrating the two hundredth anniversary of American independence. There were banners along the front of the house: HAPPY BIRTHDAY, UNCLE SAM. Most of the partygoers were, well, boys, and when I zoomed up with William on my pillion, it was an entrance made in gay heaven. 'Bette Davis,' William sighed, 'eat your heart out.' Somewhat gloomily I allowed myself to be groped, fondled and petted. In the half gloom I saw a figure that looked female, had bumps in the right places and, yay, wasn't a boy in drag. But when I tried to pick her up, Sandra gave me the cold shoulder. 'I don't go out with gay boys,' she said. She was very cross with me — and so were some of the boys. I took her for a ride on my bike and, at the top of Mt Victoria, made it plain just what side of the bed I slept on. In those days I liked to hit and run, but Sandra ambushed me and we soon started to date seriously. I liked to tease her by telling our friends whenever they asked the inevitable question, 'How did you two meet?' that she had been the prettiest boy of the bunch.

Shortly afterwards, Sandra and I began to date seriously. A kindergarten teacher, she was the kind of girl who was petite and pretty and fitted under my shoulder when we walked along the beach. She was just the right size to make me feel strong, manly and protective. Although our son Nathan has taken after me in terms of height, build and dark complexion, our daughter Holly is very like her mother when we were dating: curly blonde hair, full-breasted in an old-fashioned way, small hips and what I told her were 'the best ankles in the animal kingdom'.

Our relationship deepened. Apart from seeing each other during the week, Sandra came to watch me play club rugby on Saturdays; William had inveigled me into playing for a very hopeless amateur Scots team. After the game, we would commiserate with each other on yet another loss by drinking lots of beer. Sandra would stay over with me for the rest of the weekend.

Meanwhile, back at the office, Mr Ralston was watching me. Biding his time. Waiting for me to break from cover.

And what of Mum, Dad and the family at Waituhi?

I tried to go home as often as I could, and Dad sometimes came down to Wellington to see me. On one visit, he and Ray went to the pub and came back reeking with booze — and my father *never* drank. On another visit, Dad saw me on the way back from the West Coast where he had been on business that he would not disclose. But I knew the visit had been to do with a family matter and, when he confessed it, we resolved what we should do about it.

Dad's secretive ways also coincided with his strange behaviour back in Gisborne. Mum began to phone me, worried. 'On your father's days off from the works he hops in his truck and goes somewhere. I never know where he is these days.' Mum discovered from Uncle Pita and the Matua that Dad was going out to Waituhi regularly. 'Something's up,' she told me when she phoned me again.

Sure enough, one night Dad told her that the Matua had given him a cottage on farmland in Waituhi; he wanted to return to the valley. Only Mum, Dad, Wiki, Marama and Hone were moving — I was in Wellington and Ripeka and Mere, by that time, were married and had their own lives.

I was so happy at the news. Returning to Waituhi, in my opinion, was a better reality for Mum and Dad than living in Gisborne city. Although the farm was rundown, it would provide Dad with a new challenge of building life back into it and of breaking in the land. And Mum had had enough of their urban experiment: after seeing Dad go day after day to the freezing works, and how his spirit was dying, she had realised that, at heart, she and Dad were rural people who lived simple lives. Living in Gisborne had been a detour. They relished the idea that they had been given a second chance.

'Who would have thought that we'd go over the rainbow only to land back here,' Mum said. Yes indeed, Waituhi was their Kansas.

I went back to Gisborne for three days to help them shift. It was good to see Dad's spirits reviving. After all, Waituhi was papakainga. It wasn't just a few houses strung along a country road; it was home and they had finally come home to stay. Life would always mean hard work. Fences would have to be put up, scrub cut, cattleyards erected, sheep and cattle shifted from one part of the farm to another, mustering during winter, dosing, docking, lambing, shearing, haymaking, planting potatoes and maize, hoeing. What others might think of as monotony, they accepted as being what life was about. There was always a sense of contentment in feeling a rhythm beneath their feet. That season would follow season and that the rhythm would never alter — this brought them peace. Waituhi was their inescapable reality.

'There's another reason for returning, son,' Dad confessed. 'Not only you but also your sisters — your entire generation — are going too wide out. I want to make sure that you find your way home. I have to be your lifeline back to us.'

When Dad said that, I was reminded of a scene in *2001: A Space Odyssey*. A crewman on a spaceship had gone tumbling into space and it was only because he was attached by a line to the captain of the spaceship that he was able to be pulled back to safety.

On the day I was due to catch the train back to Wellington, Dad drove me to the station at Gisborne. He wanted to come alone, and my mother understood. No matter the tensions that had existed between us, it was not easy for me to leave him. He must have been sick then; I didn't realise it. When it was time for me to board the train he whispered to me, 'Thanks, son, for coming back to help us move. I'm glad that you still remember your obligations and duties.'

A soft wind came curling across Tawhiti Kaahu. The toy windmills began to spin and spin. I heard, from far away, the sound of a car horn and saw that Mere had returned from the airport with Hone and Marama. Whirring and whirring, the windmills cut into my consciousness with their accusations.

'Obligations? Duties? Tell them now, Tama Mahana. Tell them about this dutiful son, who sits on top of a hill remembering his father. Oh yes, you've always been so good at showing yourself in the best light, haven't you? But, after all, you've had practice, smiling your lopsided smile before the world. If you don't tell them, we will. We will say, 'Don't be misled by the romantic view of a boy talking to his dead father in a family graveyard. Never trust this son, do not believe what he says about himself and his relationships because this dutiful son is unreliable as a narrator. Trust only in what really happened, in the truth.'

I never went back.

In 1973 Dad died and, after his tangi, I returned to Wellington, supposedly to pack up, resign from *The Evening Post* and say goodbye to Sandra and my friends. I promised Mum, my sisters and brother that I would be back. But I broke that promise.

When I returned to work, Mr Ralston was waiting with an offer. 'Okay, Tama,' he began, 'it's time for you to step up to the plate. Do you remember when I hired you? I said I didn't want you to do the same job as the rest of my reporters are doing. Have you heard of Harry Dansey?'

Harry Dansey was the man I most wanted to emulate, a reporter on the *Auckland Star* and the only Maori journalist I had heard of in the country.

'National Maori politics are reaching a new phase,' Mr Ralston confirmed. 'You may be the right person at the right time. This paper needs an insider. I'm making you our Maori news reporter. Let's give Dansey a run for his money.' He called Ray Hargraves in. 'Mr Hargraves, take Tama under your wing, will you? And sub his stories before they are published. He's to have his own byline on big stories.'

I hyperventilated on the spot. I knew I should go home to Mum but, if I was to look into my heart, I saw that I had never really intended to return to Waituhi. All those promises to go back had been made to console my family, to get them over Dad's dying and make them feel safe — but I had never meant them. I asked Sandra for her advice. She was relieved I was thinking of staying in Wellington.

'Tama, you must follow your own destiny,' she said. 'You can't live other people's lives for them. I'm sure your family wouldn't want to stand in your way. This is such a good opportunity for you. It's what you've been working for. And, if your family don't understand, well, whatever happens to them is their karma.'

Sandra wasn't being cruel — and her words would come back eventually to haunt her. Life is filled with shifting alliances and alternatives and Sandra had become as important in my life as my family. But when I turned to her for advice

I should have known that because she loved me she would say what she thought I wanted to hear. And I needed her to say those words because, by that stage, neither of us wanted to leave the other.

I called Mum on the phone. 'Hello Mum,' I said. 'Look, some urgent work has come up at the paper and I can't make it home right away. Can you cope without me for a while?"

I was trying to be kind. Holding to Mum's expectation that I would return. Delaying the inevitable.

'Okay, son,' she answered. 'Just as well I've learnt how to plough straight.'

She was trying to make the best of it. I felt ashamed that I was not being straight with her. What I should have done was bloodied my hands and come out with the truth — 'I'm not coming back, I'm never coming back' — but I was too much of a coward.

In 1974 *The Evening Post* reached a circulation high of 99,704 readers. For the third time in ten years, we were named the country's top newspaper — and I was thrilled that I was playing a part in that success.

Mr Ralston had been right in surmising that Maori activism was rising in New Zealand and that, despite a benign government, rapid urbanisation and a new radical Maori generation were placing increasing pressure on the nation to listen to Maori in a new, often frightening, way. For Maori, these were the heady days when Maori sovereignty burst, putting them on a collision course with unresolved and long buried grievances against Pakeha. For Pakeha, they were times of increasing bewilderment and resistance to what they considered were calls for separate racial development.

I grasped the nettle. I began the year with a bang. I discovered an opportunistic streak in myself. The queen was coming to New Zealand for the Commonwealth Games and, as part of her visit, was attending the Treaty of Waitangi celebrations. I convinced Mr Ralston that I should take a cameraman and do an eyewitness report. That report of Maori protests on the Treaty grounds, complete with photographs of banners reading THE TREATY IS A FRAUD and NEW ZEALAND, LAND OF THE LONG WHITE SHROUD, was mixed in with pictures of a smiling, benevolent monarch waving to the crowd. It was my first front-page feature, and it shocked readers who, until that moment, had thought our relationship was a model for the rest of the world.

Ours was a country with a deeply ingrained conservatism. It was also a country that truly thought it had done well by 'our Maoris'. The problem was that New Zealand had a traditional view of its relationship with Maori and, up to the 'in your face' 1970s, believed that it should be conducted with a sense of decency, decorum and diplomacy.

Given my head, I couldn't be stopped. Mr Ralston was impressed by the passion and perspective I brought to the piece — and nobody at the paper objected to my being given a byline. Ted Smith even congratulated me on it. Very soon I was reporting on the rise and radical activities of Nga Tamatoa (the Young Warriors) and the Polynesian Panthers. WE SHALL FIGHT ON FOREVER AND EVER. I was covering every Maori event of the moment. NOT ONE MORE ACRE OF MAORI LAND and MAORI LANGUAGE, TE REO RANGATIRA and WE ARE UNDERREPRESENTED IN PARLIAMENT. Throughout the year I interviewed every major Maori player in New Zealand politics. I honed my skills talking to giants like Whina Cooper, the Mother of the Nation, at a Maori Women's Welfare League conference; Joe Hawke, on the grounds of Bastion Point; the luminescent Hana Jackson and Syd Jackson during the presentation of yet another of their petitions on Maori language and the establishment of Maori broadcasting in Aotearoa; Eva Rickard on the golf course at Raglan; Matiu Rata, John Rangihau and Ranginui Walker. On a visit to Auckland to talk to Pita Awatere in his cell at Mt Eden prison, I ran into Harry Dansey. 'So you're the young blighter who's showing me up,' he grinned as he shook my hand.

My star was rising. My sap was rising. In a visit to the Beehive I realised that I wanted to begin writing stories about how government was responding to or resisting Maori calls for a greater say in our own destiny. With Ray's support, I began to write from within Parliament, watching the House in action from the press gallery and evaluating the government's Maori policies as they were being enacted.

The gallery consisted of media representatives accredited to cover parliamentary business from a 'gallery' above the chamber. I was in awe of them all — and Ray was regarded as one of the best. By reporting on what was said and done in Parliament, they were an important part of democracy in ensuring the general public knew what was happening.

'But what you see is not always what you *see*,' Ray taught me, echoing Mr Grundy, 'and making sure that we get the real story rather than smoke screen or the mirror reflection is the difference between doing our job or becoming the stooge, the lackey that people accuse us of being. Don't let this happen to you, Tama, mate. Don't end up in any politician's pocket.'

I found it exhilarating to charge around Parliament under Ray's wing. His modus operandi was never to ask permission from politicians, always to go on the offensive in interviews with them, and to take no prisoners when seeking the truth. He was responsible for some of the great political stories of the 1970s; I inherited his style and put it to use in my Maori-interest stories. After a while, Ray realised what I was doing — but he gave me his blessing.

'Go, Tama, you're not my bumboy. You canny bugger, you'll be able to get inside the stories in a way I can't. Keep on covering the Maori revolution in our country. After all, you're the same colour. Go after the politicians — but watch your back. Go, Tama, go.'

Watch your back. Although I admired the prime minister, I could not help showing more and more undisguised passion at New Zealand's slow response to Maori sovereignty. I could have mediated my stories, but Mr Ralston encouraged me to go for the jugular. 'Although Mr Kirk is benign, interrogate not just his government but the opposition also on Maori issues. Get people to think harder about New Zealand's policies as they relate to Maori and Polynesians. Get them to see. Get them involved.'

However, even Mr Ralston thought twice about a piece I wrote near the middle of the year, accompanied by a cartoon of the Maori situation in Aotearoa. So did Sandra, who said, 'Tama, do you really have to do this? Why can't somebody else do it?' At the time I took her comments as expressions of concern for me, and I loved her all the more for it.

The story was a departure for me. With it, I crossed the line from just reporting the news to creating the news, to becoming an activist myself. It was a satirical piece, making an analogy between the Maori predicament and the film *Planet of the Apes*. At the last moment, the printing presses were delayed from running that day's edition until our lawyers had considered the legal possibilities that the paper might be sued for defamation. In the end, Mr Ralston bit the bullet. 'Print it,' he said.

That afternoon, the story and a cartoon — showing the Beehive as a cage with Maori as humans in a cage and parliamentarians on both sides of the house as apes — created an outcry in Wellington's political circles. The reaction gave me my first taste of political condemnation.

Mr Ralston showed his mettle. He came back with an editorial. 'We live in a democracy,' he said. 'The subversive voice in New Zealand is not one that our country has ever liked to nurture. But a society that does not have such a voice, especially when that voice is Maori, is not a healthy one.'

I have kept Mr Ralston's editorial to this day.

Then, in August, Norman Kirk was admitted to hospital. He had been suffering heart problems but had kept up his intense work schedule. He died at the end of the month and, just as I had gone to welcome him when he had become prime minister, I went to farewell him. I took Sandra with me and we joined the Maori mourners — there had always been underground rumours that he had Maori ancestry. Karanga after karanga pealed out to him as his coffin was brought onto Parliament grounds for a state funeral.

Shortly after Kirk's death, Mr Ralston called me to his office. 'The Murdoch Group is expanding NewsCorp, its global media company. The growth is mainly in their television news reporting, and all of us in the Group have been asked to recommend young and talented men and women who might be interested. I've recommended you to Mr Murdoch — and he would like you to go over to Sydney to join them.'

I was both thrilled and afraid. Leave New Zealand? 'But I don't know anything about television reporting,' I said to Ray Hargraves. 'I'll have to stand up with a mike in my hands. I'll be so exposed. I don't know if I can do it.'

'Look, mate,' Ray said, 'ever since you came here, I've had a gut feeling about you. Most of us in the print business have to hide behind our words. You, however, you've become a frontrunner, and you can stand in front of the words. You have a personal style, you're quick on your feet, you're slippery behind the scrum and you sell the perfect dummy.'

'I presume that's a compliment,' I answered.

'Best of all,' Ray continued, 'you like to interrogate and to voice an opinion. In a job like television reporting, you'd be in your element. And let's face it, you're prettier than Ted Smith.'

I was in turmoil. I asked Sandra what I should do.

'What does this mean to us?' she asked. 'Are you planning to go alone? If you do, you'll meet an Aussie surfie chick and we'll never get married. And what about your mother and your family?'

It didn't dawn on me how ironic it was that Sandra should use Mum and the family as a reason for staying. And she should have known that of course I wanted her to come with me.

I decided to kill three birds with one stone. First, I accepted the job. Second I asked Sandra to marry me and come to Australia. Third, I rang Mum and told her that I was leaving New Zealand. Just like that. No ifs, no buts, no maybes — no asking Mum if she liked it or not. This was my life, my decision and I was going for it.

Almost a year had gone by since I had promised I would go home. By that point, I think Mum had become reconciled to the fact that it was never going to happen. In those two years, Ripeka and Victor had joined her on the farm. They were thinking of going into kiwifruit and grape production. Even so, Mum and I ended up weeping over the phone — me for not keeping my word and Mum because she couldn't bear the thought that I wasn't coming back.

'Oh Tama,' she cried. 'How will we survive? How will you survive? But don't worry about us, we'll be okay. Goodbye, son.'

On my last day at *The Evening Post*, Mr Ralston gave me some of the best advice I have ever had about a career in journalism.

'There will be people who will try to persuade you to write their way, and others who will try to convince you that they are telling you the truth. Even I have tried to do that with you, Tama, and I have been pleased to see you hold to your own truth. In the future, there will be others more devious than I, who will be only too pleased to see you agreeing to their opinions and their views. Interrogate them, young man. Maintain your critical faculties. Stand on the rock of yourself. Hold that rock against all who would want to wrest the top from you. Never be afraid of becoming the last man standing.'

They were stirring, generous words, and they came from a man who all his life had had ink in his veins. They blended with Morag's admonition to stand up for the weak, the underprivileged, the coloured. They became the main tenets on which the moral and ethical framework within which I lived and worked was based.

Yes, Mr Ralston, I did become the last man standing. But I had some damn good defenders, like you and Ray, watching my back.

The toy windmills whirring, whirring, whirring. I heard Ripeka shouting from far away. She always had the loudest voice in Waituhi. She was a tiny figure, like Mrs Rumpelstiltskin, jumping up and down in one spot, wanting me to come back to the house. Mere's car was in the driveway; she had returned from the airport with Marama and Hone. I saw Ripeka gesticulating to them to come up the hill to get me.

'Time to go, Dad,' I said to him. 'I'll be back again soon.' I washed my hands at the gate. 'Apiti hono, tatai hono, te hunga mate ki te hunga mate. Apiti hono tatai hono, te hunga ora ki te hunga ora.'

My pretty sister and carelessly handsome younger brother came laughing up Tawhiti Kaahu. 'The Sisterhood sent us,' Hone said.

Emotion overwhelmed me as I greeted them. They had been only very young children when Dad had died. Mum and my older sisters had raised them — and they'd done a good job. Marama worked in police headquarters in Wellington. She and Hone had always been close so we weren't surprised when he joined her in the capital, working as a chef in an upmarket bar.

I grabbed Marama in a fierce hug. *I'm so sorry, God, I'm so sorry.*

'What was that for?' she laughed. She made way for Hone, who lifted me off the ground. He liked to let me know that although I was the oldest, he was not only bigger and taller but also stronger.

Marama threaded an arm in mine. 'Your mother,' she said, excluding herself, 'has refused to go to bed. She's sitting in the front room like a very cross Queen of Sheba awaiting your immediate return. What's this about, brother? Why have you come back so quickly this time? It's not as if Mum's at death's door, is it?'

'No, it's something else,' I answered as we walked down the hill together.

The dead to the dead.

Time to deal with the living.

7

*t**his is my watch*

There was a day in my boyhood when Dad and I were taking fenceposts across a gully. The fenceposts were roped to two packhorses. Normally, we would have taken the packhorses across a swingbridge, but rain was falling and wind was gusting down the valley. Suspended in space, the bridge yawed and crackled in the wind currents. Whenever the strain threatened to snap the cables, sharp reports like rifle shots would ricochet, crack, crack, crack. Some of the boards looked slippery.

I didn't realise how dangerous it was. I wondered why Dad was hesitating and I thought he was waiting for me to go across first. He stopped me. 'I think we better go down to the river rather than use the bridge today,' he said.

'It will be faster if we use the bridge,' I answered.

'Yes,' he said, 'but you're with me.'

It's time to tell the family.

There were times when my father could not always keep the watch on our lives. My mother and I had a pact with each other about one of those times, and we had kept it a secret since I was twelve. Nobody knew it — not Dad, not my sisters or brothers — except us. Mum's sister, Auntie Maggie, who had lived on the West Coast, and the Matua had also shared the secret, but they were both dead now.

Over a year ago, however, just before Mum was diagnosed with leukaemia, the secret she and I had both thought was safely buried forty years ago had suddenly risen from the past. Now that Mum was dying, we felt we had no option but to tell the family. They deserved to know. They also needed to have a part, once they knew what the secret was, in resolving it.

Even so, over the past three months Mum had been oscillating about confessing what had happened to her. 'Can't it wait?' she pleaded with me whenever she phoned me in London. 'Can't you wait until I am dead before you tell your sisters and brother? Can't you sort this out in secret, without anybody knowing? Must we go through with this, son?'

I was firm with her. 'No, Mum. This has got to be resolved while you're still alive and while there's still a chance to fix it. The longer we leave it, the less chance there is to make a decision.' So we had made a bargain. Two weeks ago Mum had been admitted to the hospital for her latest check. I had been waiting for her acceptance that, now that she was actually dying, there was no turning back.

'Come home now, son. It's time to tell the family.'

Don't do that, Mum said. You might make Tangaroa angry.

My mother was seated in a tall chair looking out the window. When I entered the room with Hone and Marama she didn't turn to look my way. Mere and Wiki were having a cup of tea and pavlova, looking for all the world like they were attending an afternoon gathering of the Maori Women's Welfare League. Ripeka, of course, was in a temper.

'Well, mother dear,' she said, 'and brother dear, we're all present and correct. Just the immediate family. Nobody else is here, as requested, no husbands, no children, just us. So what's this all about?'

Only then did Mum look at me. My mother and I have always had a close relationship. The way she liked to tell it, it was because mine had been the most difficult birth of all her children. 'When Tama was born,' she began, on those evenings when we huddled in bed with her, 'oh, he just didn't want to come out! Finally, when he made up his own mind, did he cry and cry? Did he what. Not like you girls, you were such angels compared to him.' I never understood why being the most difficult birth would predispose my mother and me to closeness; I would have thought it was the other way round. So the way *I* liked to explain our close relationship was to point to my being the eldest — even if only by default due to my brother Rawiri's death — and also to my being the boy, the male successor. Naturally, my sisters disagreed with this argument. And Mum's response? 'Don't kid yourself, son.'

Whatever the reason, the close relationship between Mum and me was not to be doubted. Maybe it was because I was the one who left home, the child who always gave her the most to worry about, the son who lived overseas and therefore the one on whom all her parental anxieties were channelled. No matter where I was in the world, Mum and I would always talk on the phone. Our conversations across datelines and continents were to be treasured in a way that her exchanges with my sisters and brother over breakfast weren't. Then, of course, when I became 'almost famous' as Ripeka liked to scoff, and was making good money, I was the one who sent a cheque whenever it was needed.

And, most important, we'd been bound together by what happened that day when I was twelve years old.

'Well?' Ripeka asked, impatient, alarm showing in her voice. 'Mum? Tama? What is it you want to tell us?'

I wondered how Mum wanted to handle this disclosure. I wanted to ask her, 'Was what happened my fault, Mum? When I was twelve and we arrived at that place by the ocean, and I did a boyish haka filled with bravado to the waves, did I really make Tangaroa angry?'

We were living up the Coast. Dad was on a scrubcutting contract. Our home was an isolated worker's whare in a valley near the sea. When we first arrived there, Dad rode in to the property every day but, because he was spending too much time travelling backwards and forwards, he had taken to staying on the block every second night. He left Mum to look after us in the whare. Ripeka, Mere, Wiki and I caught the schoolbus to school in Ruatoria while Mum stayed at home to wait for our return. The schoolbus would pass a road gang constructing a new culvert; winter was coming and the old culvert had a habit of flooding. There were seven men in the gang: the man who drove the grader, another two men on a truck, and four labourers who did the hard work. The man on the grader would smile and sometimes wave as the schoolbus passed. The four labourers would lean on their shovels and yarn with one another. One of them was a big beefy man with red hair. He wore a white singlet and he was the leader. Whenever he caught sight of any of the older teenage girls on the bus he held his crotch, bunched his fist and made a gesture — there was no doubting what it meant. His three mates would ogle and jeer.

The whare was right on the beach. My sisters and I first saw it on a bright summer's day and we couldn't believe how beautiful it was — a mix of sand and pebbles, with a reef stretching from a crumbling cliff out into the bay. As the winter approached, however, the days turned grey, so did the sea, and the surf came crashing over the reef. Mum became afraid of the beach. There were too many cross-tides and undercurrents. Even so, it was always a thrill for us to go down there swimming and shellfishing after school. On stormy days, the waves came rushing through the reef into a blowhole. I would laugh and laugh and, one day, as the spray spumed around me, I did a boyish haka, challenging the waves. 'You can't catch me,' I said, showing my bum to them as they tried to sweep me into the sea.

Mum may have been right. Perhaps I was indeed the one who invoked the events that occurred to us.

Must we go through with this, son?

'I suppose we should begin,' Mum said to me. I nodded. She turned to talk to my sisters and brother. 'By the grace of God, I am thankful that only Tama was old enough to remember what I am about to tell you. You, Ripeka, Mere and Wiki, were too young to remember that time your dad and I were up the Coast, eh. And I hadn't had you Hone and you Marama yet.'

Mum reflected on her life as if it was a dream. 'You know, when I married your father we took each other as partners for life. Not like today, when you're lucky if you are married for more than a year before you get traded in for another, newer model. I am proud that my three older daughters have followed our example. You, Ripeka, it was not your fault that death took your first husband, Victor; but you have found a fine second husband in Sam, and I know you are as faithful to him as you were to Victor. Mere, your marriage to Koro is to be treasured; I like watching you both telling each other everything that has happened during your day. Wiki, I did not approve of your marriage to Darren but over the years I have come to see how much you both trust in the other. Marama and Hone, I look forward to the time when you find good and loving partners. As for you, Tama' — Mum gave a confidential look to my sisters and Hone — 'we all know that your oldest brother is a law unto himself and conducts his relationships exactly as he wants to.' My sisters and brothers smiled at Mum's sly dig. *Yes, that's Tama all right.*

Mum waited for them to resettle. 'Your father and I had the same relationship as you, my three older daughters, have with your husbands,' she continued. 'But although we shared all our thoughts and there was nothing hidden between us, there was one thing that I could never tell your father. Never.'

'Do you want me to carry on, Mum?' I asked her. She was distressed, her lips quivering.

'No,' Mum answered, regaining control. 'The secret concerns what happened when we were living up the Coast. As I say, I never told your father about it. And all these years since — forty years, Tama? — I thought we were all safe from it. Indeed, when your father died, I was grateful to God that he had never discovered my secret. I thought I had got away with it and I never gave it another thought until a year ago.'

'A year ago?' Mere asked.

'Yes,' Mum answered. 'I had put the past behind me. But it is true, children: one can never escape the past. Never. There is always a reckoning, a payment due. I don't mind paying the past back, but I do mind that you are part of the payment. I always thought I could protect my family but I can't protect you from this.'

My mother began to weep. The tears spilled like glistening stones from her eyes. The sight of her tears made Ripeka, Mere and Wiki cry also; they began to hug each other, afraid. Hone put his arm around Marama. They looked at Mum and then at me, frightened, needing to know what beast was lurching out of the past towards them.

'It's all right, Mum,' I said. 'I'll tell them.' I went to her and stood behind her, my arms resting on her shoulders. 'A year ago, Mum was reading *The Gisborne Herald* and she happened to glance at the personal columns. She saw a notice —'

My mother had just put dinner on for Ripeka and Sam. She was checking the roast and reading the paper at the same time. When she saw the notice, she was so frightened that she dropped the roast and collapsed onto the kitchen floor. The notice read: 'I AM SEEKING THE MAORI MOTHER OF MY SON, BORN 7 FEBRUARY 1966, GREYMOUTH HOSPITAL. I WOULD HAVE RESPECTED YOUR WISHES FOR CONFIDENTIALITY BUT YOUR SON NEEDS YOUR URGENT HELP.'

'I remember that day,' Ripeka said to Mum. 'I came home with Sam and we found you unconscious on the floor. That was the day we took you to the hospital for a check-up and Dr Kavanagh diagnosed your leukaemia had spread.' Ripeka always had a sharp memory. You could never get away from her recall of money owed her or favours that were required to be paid back.

'Yes,' I told Ripeka. 'After her check-up, Mum phoned me in London, but I was doing a television story in Kandahar. However, Harriet managed to track me down and tell me that Mum had phoned, so I rang Mum from there —'

'I remember your phone calls, too,' Ripeka added. 'Weren't they to do with Mum's cancer?'

I could tell what Ripeka was thinking. Clever Mum and Tama, leading us all up the garden path by pretending that what they were talking about was Mum's cancer and the options for treatment — and instead it was about something else, something worse than cancer, if that was possible, that they would not share with us.

Mum was hysterical over the phone. 'Son, son, what are we to do?'

As Mum cried, I started to shiver. I was the one who had washed her and cleaned her up after it was over. It was to me that she had whispered her instructions: 'Never tell your father about this. It's just between us. Promise me.' It was a blood pact. A family oath, Sicilian in its ferocity, and that intensity had welded us closely together.

My mother and I had kept that vow over all these years. Nobody knew what had happened except us. But with that newspaper advertisement the door to the past had opened again and those four men from the road gang had come walking back through it.

They had been stalking Mum. They had kept an eye on Dad's movements. They watched as Dad saddled his horse, kissed her, and left to go to his work. They saw Mum farewell Ripeka, Mere, Wiki and me when the schoolbus came. They went to work at the culvert but, after lunch, the man with the red hair said to the man in the grader, 'We're stopping for the day, boss.' The man in the grader thought the four men were going back to Ruatoria. Instead, they got on their truck and headed for the whare. The red-haired man knocked on the door.

When school finished, my sisters and I left Ruatoria on the schoolbus. When the bus stopped at the corner where our whare was, I saw a truck outside the door. I sensed something wrong but Ripeka, Mere and Wiki got off the bus before I could stop them. They were in a hurry to show Mum some drawings they had done at school. They opened the front door and ran into the bedroom. 'Mummy! Mummy!'

My mother was being held down on the bed by three men; one of them had his hands over her mouth so that she could not yell out to us. Another had a knife to her throat. A third was holding Mum's legs. The fourth man, the man with the red hair, was on top of her.

'Hello, little girlies,' the man with the red hair said. 'Your Mum invited us over for a couple of drinks and a bit of fun, didn't you, darling.'

'*No*, Mum,' Ripeka said. 'Please say it's not true.'

My mother looked at her, as if for mercy. 'You will never know, children, how terrified I was when I heard the schoolbus stopping at the corner. I tried to shout to you, "Don't come in, don't." But one of the men clamped his hands over my mouth and another put his hands around my throat so that I couldn't scream. They were afraid if I caused a commotion the bus driver would hear and come to investigate. I heard the door to the whare as it opened and you, Mere, were calling to me, "Mummy, Mummy!" You girls burst into the bedroom. And then Tama came in.'

I pressed my mother on the shoulders. 'It was too late to call to the bus driver,' I said. 'The bus was already halfway down the road. Inside the whare, I heard Mere asking, "What are you doing to our mother?" I saw the four men. One of the men laughed, looked at my sisters and said, "Hey, boys, we've got some more girlies to play with." He grabbed Wiki. But, at his words, Mum struggled, bit the man who had his hands over her mouth and began screaming.'

Mum resumed the story again. 'I bargained with them. I said to the man with the red hair, "Let my children go." He answered, "If I do that, will Mummy behave herself?" What else could I say but yes? He nodded and told the one who was holding Wiki to give her to Tama. When he had Wiki safely in his arms I yelled to him, "Tama, get away. Take the girls! Run." I submitted to them. All I could think of was that this was the only way to save my family. What those men were doing to me was as nothing compared to what I feared they might do to you. I have always put my family first — and your father.'

Suddenly, Mere looked at Ripeka. She began to make plaintive little noises.

'Was that the time the Bad Men came?' Mere asked. 'You told us it was just a bad dream. We ran down to the rocks and we stayed there a long time —'

Grief overwhelmed me. 'But it happened so long ago,' I said. 'Please, Mere, tell me that you were too young to remember? Wiki? Oh no.'

Ripeka, Mere and Wiki were holding each other, frightened and wailing, as if they had suddenly been enfolded in a nightmare that was real after all. Ripeka was seething.

'You and Mum always lived in your own dream land,' she said. 'Of course Mere and Wiki are old enough to remember. So what did I do? Turn it into a fairy story so that they could pretend it didn't happen. But you went back, brother,' Ripeka yelled. 'You returned to help Mum against those men. Why couldn't you stop them? You should have battled those men. You should have fought until either you or they were killed. How could you let them do that to Mum?'

Yes, I went back.

I said to Ripeka, 'Run, sister. Take Wiki and Mere and go to the far end of the beach and wait.' I raced back to the whare. My heart was pounding with fear. As I approached, I picked up a piece of wood. I charged into Mum's bedroom. When she saw me coming through the door she yelled out, 'Tama, no, get away.'

The men were raping Mum again. This time the man with the red hair was smoking a cigarette and watching. I threw the wood at him. Surprised, he deflected it with an elbow, 'What the hell?', and it rebounded onto the man who was on top of Mum. 'Get off her, get out, get out,' I yelled. Unbalanced, he lost concentration and Mum was able to push him off. She saw the man with the red hair punching me; I thought he was going to kill me, he was so angry. 'Leave my son alone, you bastard,' Mum screamed. She picked up the wood and launched herself at him. But the other three men trapped her in a hold, one slapped her and I heard her groan as she went down. Next moment, the man with the red hair picked me up and threw me against the wall. I lost consciousness. When I came to, somebody was beating me with a belt and another person was kicking me in the head. I blacked out again.

'That's what happened,' Mum said. 'When I recovered, Tama was tending to me, washing my face and body. The men had gone.'

Silence fell. Then, one by one, my sisters and brother hugged Mum.

'It's okay, Mum,' Wiki said. 'You couldn't help it. It wasn't your fault.'

Then Ripeka's voice came across the room. 'You were a weakling, brother,' she said.

I flinched. 'Do you know,' I answered bitterly, 'how many times I've blamed myself for not saving Mum?'

'Stop that talk,' Mum commanded. But now that Ripeka had her dagger in the wound she twisted it. 'If I'd been a boy I would have fought to the death to save her,' she said. 'Why didn't you?'

My mother walked swiftly to Ripeka, raised her hand and slapped her hard. Ripeka's eyes widened with anger. The welt crimsoned immediately. 'Your brother did all he could,' Mum said. 'There was nothing more that he could do. He is not to blame for what happened to me. None of you are to blame.'

Ripeka folded her arms, grim, unrepentant.

'What more can I tell you?' Mum continued. 'Tama came down to the beach to find you, my daughters. All of you were so frightened and I had to get you over your fears. I made you a hot bath. I attended to my brave son. The next day, you all went to school again. Your father arrived home that evening. I couldn't tell him I had been raped. He would have taken a gun and shot those men right between the eyes; or, maybe, they would have shot him. What use would it have been to tell him or to go to the police? I would have only exposed myself and your father to shame and ridicule. So I decided to carry on as if nothing had happened. But the first time he touched me and wanted to make love to me, oh, I was so ashamed. I hid my face in the shadows and, although he whispered words of love into my ears, all I could do was weep that I had become so defiled, so dishonoured.'

Gradually we all calmed down. Mum kissed Ripeka on the forehead. 'I'm sorry, daughter,' she said, relenting. 'I shouldn't have raised my hand against you and slapped you like that.'

'Count yourself lucky,' Ripeka answered, 'that you're a helpless little old lady with cancer, otherwise I would have slapped you back.'

'What about the advertisement?' Mere asked. 'The advertisement a year ago, in the newspaper?'

'My womb betrayed me,' Mum answered. 'It has always been fertile and, from the time I gladly gave my virginity to your father, it has blessed me with my children. This time, I cursed its fertility. The seed that one of those men planted in me grew. I went to see the Matua to ask her to give me something that would get rid of it. I had no attachment to the seed. But no matter what the Matua gave me, the child fought to live. The Matua remarked on it, "It will not be flushed from your womb. It holds on to the lining and will not let go." When she told me that I would have to bear the child to term, I tried to kill it myself. Oh, I could have told Rongo that it was his. But I would know it wasn't.

'Your father never knew I was pregnant. I went to stay with my sister, your Auntie Maggie, on the West Coast in the South Island. Women always do this: they turn to other women so that the menfolk and the family are protected. I stayed with Maggie, watching my belly expanding, and hating every minute of my confinement. Whatever maternal feelings I may have had for a wanted child I did not spend on this unwanted foetus. I was so glad to go into labour. I told the doctor, "Be quick. Rip this child from me." I hoped his knife would slip. I prayed the child would be strangled with its own birthcord as it came out of my birth channel. I felt it push eagerly out into the world. I heard the slap the doctor administered to it to make it breathe. I prayed, "Don't. Don't breathe." But it wailed its welcome to the world.

'The doctor told me that the child was a boy. Why should I care? I didn't want to see him. I turned my head away. All I saw was white skin, so white it was almost like chalk, and a shock of red hair. Nor did I wish to take the child, even once, into my arms. As soon as I could, I got up from my bed, signed some papers giving him up to his own destiny, and walked away from him. All I wanted to do was to get back to Gisborne. The most difficult part was seeing you all waiting for me at the bus terminal —'

My mother saw us in sunlight. She was suddenly afraid. Would we be able to tell that she had had a baby? Would Dad see her sin?

Fear was still in her eyes as the bus came to a stop. She hesitated at the steps but, when she saw her children, love overflowed for them. Dad had made us all dress in our Sunday best for the occasion; I was in my school uniform, Ripeka, Mere and Wiki in identical pale yellow frocks and Dad had on an open-necked white shirt and a sports jacket. My sisters ran into her arms. 'Mummy, Mummy, we've missed you.'

Mum hugged them and gave a deep, hoarse moan. For a moment, Dad and I watched the reunion. Mum looked up and saw me, astonished, and cried, 'This can't be my Tama. This handsome young man?'

Then Dad came forward, hesitant, unsure, and said to her, 'It's so good to have you back, dear.'

Until that time, Mum had not looked Dad in the face and, when she did, something like a plea for forgiveness flashed through her eyes. Dad embraced her, holding her so tight that I thought she would break in two.

'There, there, husband,' she said as she stroked his back. Her face stilled, became calm, as whatever apprehensions she may have been harbouring drained from her. That evening, when he made love to her, she stared at the moon. Some day, all this would heal. Some day.

'Mum and I should have known,' I told my sisters and brother, 'that this day would come to pass. The boy was born after Wiki and before Hone. He is now a man of thirty-nine. The mother who adopted the boy has spent a very long time searching for us.

'He's our brother.'

part three

8

i was having breakfast with Ripeka and Sam the next morning when Harriet phoned me on her arrival in Auckland from London.

'You can take the call in Sam's study,' Ripeka said, without asking Sam. Her eyes were red, as if she'd been crying all night. Still angry, she'd hardly spoken a civil word or looked me in the eye all morning.

'Be my guest,' Sam gestured, good-humouredly. He was looking with concern at Ripeka. Who would have thought that beneath his bad boy exterior lurked a man of sympathy and generosity, someone who truly loved his wife, could roll with her punches, and was genuinely worried for her?

I excused myself from the table. Last night's confession had exhausted Mum and she couldn't go on. We had decided to postpone any further talks until tonight, but I agreed that Sam, Koro and Darren should be included if they wanted to be. Mere had left in tears with Koro. Wiki and Darren had taken Marama and Hone to stay with them.

'Oh Lord and Master, thank you, thank you, *thank* you,' Harriet breathed over the connection. 'Your every wish is my command.' I had whispered in Paul's ear that it was time Harriet got a trip away for all the sterling work she was doing for WWN and that, if there was room in the budget, she should be part of the crew coming down to New Zealand. She'd decided to ask her boyfriend, Zeb, to join her and, what do you know, they'd decided to get married and stay on after the broadcast for their honeymoon. They were planning to go down to Queenstown and celebrate by bungy-jumping off a bridge together.

Honeymoon regardless, *Spaceship Earth* had a show to put on. Harriet had arranged a conference call with Paul, Kim, John and Otis, and a couple of locally contracted researchers in Television Three's offices in Auckland. Paul's first, somewhat cool, words to me were, 'Hello Tama, I hear we're having a live audience.'

Oops. 'I meant to tell you about that,' I answered lamely. 'My arm got twisted by John Campbell when he interviewed me a couple of days ago. He wants free tickets.'

'Yes, I've heard,' Paul said. 'When are you going to stop being such a buccaneer, Tom? It's difficult enough as it is to come all the way around the world to do the show from New Zealand without you bloody increasing the budget and complicating the logistics.' Did I hear Paul swearing? Paul *never* swore. Time to be contrite, meek and mild.

'Sorry, Paul,' I answered. 'I'll be a good boy from now on.'

'I'll believe that when I see it,' Paul said. I heard a general murmur of sceptical agreement in the background, so decided I had better expand my apology to include everybody and prostrate myself before Harriet in particular. 'Sorry John, Kim, Otis — and you too, Harriet.' She had a habit of resigning on me after every live show and, now that she was getting married, she just might mean it. I made a mental note to buy her a really expensive wedding prezzie and give her a good bonus at Christmas.

Paul proceeded to go through his production notes. He, Kim and John had arrived that very morning. Kim was jetlagged after the long flight and was crossly sitting in on the conference call with a coffee in her hands. John was already at work with a New Zealand crew replicating our London studio set. Paul had developed the ideas we had earlier discussed about our special interview segments.

'The world has a new pope,' he began, 'Pope Benedict XVI. At seventy-eight he is the oldest pope to be elected since 1730. Do you want to talk to him?'

'Definitely,' I answered. I looked around Sam's study for paper and a pencil, and started to jot down some notes. 'Kim should anchor the interview. Aren't there 1.1 billion Catholics worldwide? Wasn't he an outsider? Hasn't he got a Nazi past? I've met him once. I thought he was a hardliner.'

'Harriet is already onto the research,' Paul said, 'and, yes, I think Kim would be ideal for the slot. The new pope is an opponent of same-sex marriage, contraception and an expanded role for women in the church. The Nazi connection is interesting. In his memoirs the pope wrote that he was enrolled against his will in the Hitler Jugend. I'll get Jurgen, our stringer in Berlin, to go to his old hometown in Traunstein to follow up on that.' I heard Paul rustling his papers. 'We also talked about having the Dalai Lama on the programme now that India and China may be reaching a historic agreement —'

'Let's leave that for next week. Two heads of churches on the programme is one too many.'

'That's a relief,' Otis said. 'Do any of you guys know how hard it is to organise a live link with Lhasa?'

'Excellent point,' Paul said to him. 'Let's talk about the other segments we were looking at covering: the second anniversary of the fall of Saddam's regime and the demise of the National Party in South Africa. Do you want Nelson Mandela for the South African story?'

I hesitated, and Paul picked up on the hesitation. 'Uh oh,' he said to the others, 'Tom sounds as if he's going cold on the other segments.'

Kim mumbled a few choice expletives but Paul overrode her. 'Tom, what's on your mind?'

'Let's cancel the story about the fall of Saddam's era. However, it's a go on the South African story. What I'd like to do with it is, indeed, to have Nelson in the segment. But I'd also like to bring a local orientation and get together a small group of people who protested against apartheid in New Zealand into the studio. We had a civil war down here over the issue of No Blacks No Tour.'

'And what about the third segment?' Harriet interrupted. Her tone was somewhat steely, and with reason. Poor Harriet often had to do the research at the last minute and, after all, she now had to buy a wedding dress, and I was being, well, an absolute pest.

'I'm still mulling that one over,' I answered. But I had been greatly intrigued by Michael Kavanagh's comment about the matriarchy ruling New Zealand. I made a decision to go for it. 'You know, I've never done a programme on what has been happening in the good old home country. New Zealand was the first country in the world to give women the vote. Well, here we are in 2005 and not only do we have a woman prime minister, governor-general, speaker of the house, chief justice and heading the largest corporation in the country, but in opposition we also have Tariana Turia leading the Maori Party, and Jeanette Fitzsimons leading the Green Party. Not to mention the first transsexual parliamentarian. There's no other country in the world with this kind of stunning record. I'd like you to get them all into the studio.'

'Oh, jolly good,' Harriet said, lightening up a bit. No problem with research on that one.

'Consider it done,' Paul agreed. 'Now, one last thing. We all agreed that the finale should be something celebratory to coincide with *Spaceship Earth*'s tenth anniversary. Originally, we had planned on Tony Blair coming on, or maybe Kofi Annan or Bob Geldof, to give a birthday greeting. Elton John would love to sing "Happy Birthday". Mr Blair has an election coming up and is not doing well in the polls, so he's keen to make an appearance.'

'I'll get back to you,' I said. 'I need to do some more thinking on it.' *Spaceship Earth* had always taken a non-partisan political approach to presenting the news. The idea of a politician affirming our status, even one whose views we might support, somehow went against the grain.

'Okay,' Paul said. 'But we've only got a couple of days to get this done, Tom.' His voice had risen to a sharp crescendo.

'Not to mention,' Otis muttered, 'my organising any extra live relays you might wish me to make to godforsaken locations. Don't, under pain of death, ask me to link with Timbuktu, Mogadoodoo or anywhere in the Gobi Desert, okay?'

'Okay,' I said somewhat unconvincingly. I put the phone down. I noticed in the bookcase a copy of my autobiography, *Only the Highest Mountain*. The book had been successful in the UK and New Zealand, making the bestseller lists in both countries — but for different reasons. New Zealanders loved the first half about my growing up in Aotearoa. British readers preferred the second half about my life as an international television correspondent and anchorman. It was flattering to see the book in Sam's study.

Could I have included in it the story of what happened to Mum when we were living up the Coast? No. Some things were better left unsaid but, in all other respects, the book was honest enough.

I walked to the window. The study had a wide view of the Waituhi valley. I hoped I had done the valley justice in my book, and I prayed for forgiveness if I had erred. At that time of the morning, the valley sparkled and glistened with beauty.

For most of the people who called the valley their turangawaewae, this was the centre of their world. This was the place of their marae, their sacred mountain, their river, their ancestors. Once upon a time it had been the centre of mine.

Absent-mindedly, I began to doodle with my pencil. When I was finished, I was surprised to see that I had inscribed a spiral, in the shape of a double helix. 'Te torino haere whakamua, whakamuri,' I mused. 'At the same time as the spiral is going out, it is returning. At the same time as it is going back, it is going forward.'

I heard a chuckle behind me. Sam was looking over my shoulder. 'Your sister,' he began, 'has sent me to tell you that Sandra phoned yesterday. Like everybody else in New Zealand, she must have been watching television and saw your arrival in Auckland. Anyhow, she asked if you would call her back. She wants to talk to you about Nathan.'

'Okay,' I answered. 'I'll do it soon.' Poor Sandra. She was always worrying over the children, what they were doing and where they were in the world. She blamed me for their wanderlust and their refusal to come home to New Zealand and settle down where she could keep a maternal eye on them.

Sam took a closer look at my drawing. He took the pencil from my hand and began to add more spirals to it, wider and wider.

'When your dad was alive,' Sam said, 'we often talked about you. I was helping him out on the farm before it became a winery. The farm raised sheep and cattle then. I loved helping your dad — and I haven't told you this before, but I really appreciated it when you let me take your place carrying him to the graveyard. In many ways I was closer to your dad than to my own father, though he probably would not have liked the idea of my marrying Ripeka! Anyhow, about you: Rongo used to get so frustrated about you and your disobedient ways. He really wanted you to come home. Sometimes, instead of calling to Good Boy, he would yell, "Get in behind, Tama!" But you always kept on going out further, eh.'

With a laugh, Sam extended the pencil line away from the spiral I had drawn. Pretending that the pencil was a spaceship — and still drawing a line in the air — he threw the pencil out the window. He turned to leave, but then hesitated. 'I may as well get this off my chest,' he began. 'I have no problem with you for leaving the family, Tama, and following your own career. I'm the last person who should criticise — it'd be like the pot calling the kettle black. But Mum shouldn't have slapped Ripeka last night, and you should know, Tama, that if your sister hadn't taken over the reins after your dad died, this family would have been in shit street. She was only in her early twenties when she and Victor came out to help Mum run the farm, and although I won't speak ill of the dead, Victor never had the brains for it. She bullied Mere and Koro into joining her as partners. She was the one who decided to go into growing grapes, and she put herself through correspondence courses on agriculture to figure out how to do it.'

Sam looked out the window at the winery and the grapevines beyond. His eyes were shining with pride at his wife's achievements.

'Last night, Ripeka was really upset,' he continued. 'I know that you and Mum had your reasons for keeping her secret all these years, but Ripeka loves Mum as much as you do. And you know what hurt her the most? It was that after all these years of looking after Mum, neither of you confided in her. Don't do it to her again.'

9

V ietnam, 30 April 1975. That was when it started, this going wider out.

After a blissful honeymoon in Queensland, where we went snorkelling on the Great Barrier Reef every day, Sandra and I arrived bronzed and happy in Sydney. We were very much in love and, to be truthful, both relieved that we'd managed to escape our families. In my case, Mum and my sisters didn't object to the wedding, considering that I'd already been 'going Pakeha' for years, so what was new? In Sandra's case, I hadn't realised until I went to Picton and met her elderly parents, or 'the olds' as she called them, how controlling their relationship with her had been. When we married — a small ceremony in a registry office — they turned their backs on us. 'You're all I've got now,' she said.

I wasn't due to report to NewsCorp for a couple of weeks. Sandra and I searched for a flat and, meantime, stayed in a hotel just off King's Cross. We were like two kids having fun in a big bad world. Sandra played teasing little games with the prostitutes and junkies soliciting on the pavement, but always clutched my arm whenever somebody propositioned us or the junkies saw through her games and swore at her to fuck off.

One evening, as we were passing some sex shops, I heard a voice roar, 'Don't you go past with your nose in the air.' When I looked back, a tall and enormous transvestite, perched on the highest stilettos I had ever seen, was wiggling his way towards me. It was my uncle, Chantelle, aka Alfred Tuhata until he had headed to Sydney where he now appeared as one of 'Les Girls' at the most notorious cabaret in the city. It was he who told us about an apartment in Bondi

Beach. Although any recommendation from a transvestite was dubious, we went to look at it. Sandra thought it was ideal for us and, when we had paid a month in advance, suggested we celebrate.

While making love, Sandra said, 'I want to crawl into your skin. Will you let me?' Not under; *into*. She made me shiver when she said it. Part of me thrilled to the whole idea that somebody would want to be so close, so intimately involved with me as to be absorbed into my being. Another part of me realised that there was something disturbing about the notion. But people say lots of strange things to each other in the first months of marriage, and make silly promises to each other that cannot possibly be kept, like 'It will be just you and me, back to back against the rest of the world', or 'I'll never leave you', or 'We'll grow old together' — and this was just another of them. At the time, I was simply thankful that I had found a girl who was on my side, prepared to support me no matter what, to stand by me and, crucially, to validate my decisions.

Yes, sometimes when you're in love you say silly things. A few nights later, while lying in bed, I said something like, 'One day, I want us to have children, a whole rugby team.'

Sandra reacted spontaneously to the comment. She hopped out of bed, skipped to the bathroom and came back with her packet of contraceptive pills. 'Out they go!' she said, throwing the packet out the window. 'Let's start making babies. First five-eight or fullback?'

The following week I reported for work at NewsCorp. My boss was Ken 'Dingo' McCracken. 'Glad to meet ya, Kiwi,' he said as he shook my hand, 'but don't sit down, mate. You ever been to television school?' Dingo had that Aussie accent that flattens vowels to smithereens so that 'school' came out as *skuul*. 'In my opinion it's better to learn on the job but, there ya go, Kiwi. It's the brand new way of teaching rookies and turning them out like sausages — and you're starting with the new intake tomorra.'

For the next three weeks I didn't even put my foot in the door of NewsCorp's television news division. Instead, every day I took a train across the Sydney harbour bridge to North Sydney where, with fifty other young hopefuls, I learnt about news anchoring, reporting, interviewing, writing and editing news stories and recording newscasts. I first met Bob Blakeney, who was to become my rival in more ways than one, at television school. I enjoyed the courses so much that

I couldn't wait to get home to Sandra and tell her what had happened during my day. 'Darling,' Sandra would say, 'I'm so proud of you.'

We often had friends from television school to our apartment for dinner. Sometimes we'd go over to a pub in Glebe and hang out at parties with our new Aussie mates. Sandra liked nothing more than for us to be regarded as the happy young couple — and there were quite a few guys who would hit on her. 'You're lucky to have me,' she'd say to me when we returned home after a party.

Was I ambitious? My bloody oath. I studied hard, did my homework and, as a consequence, got top marks in most of my classes. One of them, on speech and television acting, was crucial. All of us were sat in a studio and assessed on our appearance, voice production, articulation, breathing, volume and advocacy. At the end of it, Bob said to me, 'You bugger, you're showing us Aussies up. Even a deaf and dumb dingo would know what you're saying if the sound was switched off.' I said a silent prayer of thanks to Fiona and Morag, and for all those hours of 'making faces' at *The Gisborne Herald*. My ability to control a news team out on the job — cameraman, soundman and myself as interviewer — was also commented on. 'Oh no,' Bob sighed again as our tutor praised my skills of communication. 'Do us all a favour and go back across the ditch, won't ya?' I loved the role-playing of real situations and problem solving when technical, location or interviewee glitches jeopardised the filming of a story. I particularly enjoyed being in simulated studio on-air environments.

Nothing I learnt, however, could have fully prepared me for the day when Dingo called me at home to interrupt my homework. 'How y'doin' my Kiwi sausage?' he asked. 'Feel about playing hookey from skuul for a coupla days? A trip's come up to tropical climes. It's about time you got some work experience, whaddya reckon? Our reporter up there, Frank Kinsella, has phoned for some backup so you may as well go in as an understudy. It's an easy gig. There's a ticket waiting for you at Sydney airport to join him sipping maitais beside a hotel pool.'

'But you can't go,' Sandra wailed when I told her. 'We've only just got here, we haven't finished furnishing the apartment, I didn't think you'd be going out on an assignment this soon — and I'm pregnant and I want you to stay with me and celebrate.'

Wow, quite a list. 'You're having a baby?' I asked. I thought of that old saying about Mahana boys being able to make a girl pregnant just by looking at her. I was happy but, even so, next time I would wear a mask. 'When you threw your pills out the window I thought it was just a joke.'

'I thought you'd be pleased,' Sandra answered. 'I did it for you. Aren't you happy?'

'Yes,' I said. 'Of course I am.' At the time, I wasn't so sure whether I was ready to be a dad. 'I'll only be away a few days. When I get back, I'll be all yours.'

Maitais? Yeah, right.

Eighteen hours later, I found myself dumped unceremoniously from a helicopter outside the American mission in Saigon. Sweat started to pop immediately I hit the ground. The place was going insane. The North Vietnamese army was approaching Saigon and the Americans were withdrawing. A thousand people, American civilian evacuees as well as loyal Vietnamese, were trying to get through the gates of the embassy. What with the dust, the noise and the heat, I had trouble finding Frank Kinsella and the NewsCorp television crew. When I did, they were already on the job, filming the withdrawal.

'Are you Tom?' Frank yelled over the noise. 'Gidday, no time to brief you, mate. Just stay close, operate this —' he shoved a clapper board in my hands '— and try not to get run over by the traffic. Now let's do it.'

With that, Frank yelled to his cameraman, Arnold, 'Okay, roll it.' His soundman, Vince, operating the Nagra recorder, shouted, 'Speed.' Arnold affirmed, 'Rolling . . . and mark it!' He panned to where I was holding the clapperboard. 'Slate 512, take 1,' I yelled.

Frank started his piece to camera. Helicopters were taking off, one after another, whirring overhead, taking terror-stricken civilians to safety. They created duststorms that only increased the havoc.

'It's absolute chaos here.' Frank began talking into his handheld mike. 'Behind me you can see the American embassy. Tonight, that flag that you see flying will be replaced by one from North Vietnam. Overhead, you can see the helicopters, carrying those lucky enough to get aboard to safety. Over there,' he pointed to the gates of the mission 'sixty-five US marines stand between the crowd outside, trying to get in, and the route to freedom. On this day —'

All of a sudden, something came out of the duststorm. It looked like a small piece of tile roofing dislodged by a departing helicopter, and it clipped Frank over the head. He went down. 'Fuck, fuck, *fuck*,' he swore. When Arnold, Vince and I reached him, blood was streaming from his skull.

'Go and get help,' I yelled at Vince. Quickly he went to show his pass to the US commander and secure a stretcher team from the compound.

'That's it, we're buggered,' Arnold said. He started to take the barney off the Arriflex and pack up.

'No,' Frank answered. He looked at me, 'Looks like you're on, Tom.' He thrust the microphone in my hands.

'Are you serious?' I asked.

Vince returned. 'The marines have agreed to put Frank on the next chopper out,' he yelled.

'You can do it,' Frank said to me. 'And it doesn't get much bigger than this, mate.'

At his words, a light went on in my head. What was it Mr Ralston had once said to me? *Show me the stuff you're made of.* I saw Frank and Arnold watching and waiting to see whether I would shit my pants — or do it. Then, from the direction of the embassy compound I saw the stretcher team approaching. I took a deep breath and went for it.

'Arnold,' I ordered, 'stop packing your camera and get it operational. Vince, there's no time for slating.'

'You're taking over?' Vince asked, astonished. 'But you're just a rookie.'

I got on with the job. I put the microphone to my lips. 'Okay, I'm ready, turnover.' Arnold yelled, 'Roll,' and Vince, who was still too surprised to object, squealed, 'I'm rolling . . . tail slate!'

I looked down the barrel of the Arriflex. With as much drama as I could muster, I began — with a new name, one inadvertently given me by my downed colleague. 'This is Tom Mahana, reporting from outside the American embassy at Saigon. Just a few seconds ago, our correspondent, Frank Kinsella, was injured. As I speak, his blood is on the microphone, but he's okay. We've got a stretcher team taking him to one of the helicopters.' I nodded at the stretcher-bearers. 'Let's get going, boys —'

So began my first on-camera eyewitness account for television news. I based my approach on the fact that the best TV reporting I had ever seen was when the reporter took you through the screen and made you believe you were *there*, an actual eyewitness. If I could tell a story at the same time as reporting the news, I could make the news into a dramatic event. The drama was supplied by our run through the milling crowd as we got Frank to the safety of one of the departing helicopters. I reported the scene as I saw it, in short, sharp, controlled observations, pausing every now and then to interview evacuees as they crowded aboard. When Frank was safely strapped down he whispered in my ear admiringly, the cameras still rolling, 'Oh, you opportunistic son of a bitch.'

Arnold filmed the flight of the helicopter as it lifted overhead, panning to take in the departure . . . and then returned to me for my closing piece to camera. 'This is Tom Mahana, reporting to you from Saigon for NewsCorp news.' I paused a moment and then yelled to Arnold, 'And cut!'

Arnold gave me the thumbs up. 'Cut.'

I couldn't believe I had done it. The adrenalin was still pumping.

'Great job, Tom,' Arnold said. 'Now it's time for us to get out of here.'

But something had taken hold of me. Something in my brain kept hammering and hammering away as insistently as the chopper blades. Perhaps it was the call of destiny, that voice that tells you you're in the right place at the right time and this is *it*.

I took a deep breath. 'No,' I answered. 'What we've done, it's not enough.'

'What do you mean, it's not enough?' Vince echoed, his voice going up a couple of notches. 'Of course it's enough. We've done our job. Arnold, you're senior here. Give the order.'

Even then I knew that replacing Frank Kinsella would not cut the mustard with Dingo McCracken and the team back in Sydney. This had been Frank's story, not mine; this frightening drama, this desperate evacuation and Alamo-like defence of the embassy walls. I had to show them that the new boy wasn't just a replacement. I had to create *my* story and show that Tom Mahana was capable of going for broke. I knew exactly what I had to do:

The wild, free-for-all ride wasn't over. I had to make myself a hero.

An incoming message on Vince's radio gave me the chance — and I took it. 'We've got to leave,' Vince said. 'There's been a lightning advance, in front of the main North Vietnamese army, and it's making for the presidential palace.'

I nodded, but instead of making for the helicopters, I walked in the other direction. 'We're going to film the entry of the army into the city,' I said. Just be good, boys, and follow the rookie into the line of fire. Would they follow? Would Arnold abdicate his senior status and give it to me? *Yes*.

'You're bloody insane, mate,' Arnold said as he ran after me. Cursing, Vince caught us up.

We made our way to the presidential palace. Don't think I wasn't jackrabbit scared. Before we began filming I told Arnold and Vince, 'No matter what happens, just keep the film rolling and keep the sound going. Don't you bastards chicken out on me. Okay, roll it!'

The first Soviet-made T-54 tanks were driving up to the gates. The crowd went insane, some cheering like mad, others covering their faces with their hands as if the world was coming to an end. The press of people ebbed and swelled like a huge ecstatic sea. And there was I, with Arnold and Vince, right in the middle of it. Again I tried to get across the dramatic atmosphere of the event.

Suddenly, one of the leaders of the lightning strike saw us filming and pointed us out to his troops. He began to shout and gesture: Get them, stop them. Next moment, a squad detached itself, coming after us.

'This time we really have to go,' Arnold yelled.

Amid the noise, tumult and danger, and with the North Vietnamese squad closing in, my nerves held long enough for me to sign off.

'This is Tom Mahana, Presidential Palace, Saigon, reporting to you on the day that Saigon fell.' A couple of seconds later, I nodded to Arnold to wind the film down. 'Check the gate,' I said — the squad was so close I could hear them shouting — 'and if it's clear, that's a wrap for this location.'

Then the three of us were on a heart-thumping run. Drenched with fear and panic we pushed through the crowd, helping each other away to safety. Five streets on, we took a breather. All I could think of was, 'Did you get all that on film and sound? Are you sure you got it all?' I was gulping the air down.

'Yeah, you maniac,' Arnold answered.

My nerves held long enough.

'You little beauty.' On my return to Sydney, Dingo McCracken slapped me on the shoulders. 'We send you out to understudy and you come back a bloody star. Good on you, mate.'

I was on my way. The report on Saigon catapulted me to the front ranks of NewsCorp's reporting team — but not to the top. There was a problem. 'Australia isn't ready to have a Kiwi, let alone a May-ori, reporting on our politics or reading our news,' Dingo told me, 'so we're gunna put you on our team reporting regional news from Southeast Asia — you look as if you could be one of them, anyhow. What do you know about Singapore, Malaysia, Indonesia and Thailand?'

Zip, actually. Once I had finished television school, back I went, this time to day classes at university, studying Asian history, politics and cultures and, at nights, to language classes where I'd get the basic phrases, like 'How are you?', 'Where am I?' and 'Help!' It didn't assuage my ego that Bob Blakeney kangaroo-jumped over me into our bureau office in Canberra — but, after all, he was the right colour and he said 'yes' instead of 'yis' and 'sex' instead of 'six'.

Meanwhile, Sandra was growing as big as a house. 'You don't have to produce the entire football team all at once,' I kidded her as she fretted about whether she'd get her body back after the birth. Uncle Chantelle and his girlfriends from Les Girls clucked and preened over her while she was pregnant. He tied a gold ring on a string and twirled it over Sandra's huge stomach. We watched with bated breath to see which way it would revolve. 'Definitely a boy,' he pronounced, disappointed. He'd hoped for a girl.

'I could have told you that,' Sandra said as Nathan gave her an almighty kick. 'Stop treating me like a football, you little bugger.'

Nathan was born in the middle of an afternoon when I was trying to wrestle with Cambodian history. He was a bright-eyed child with a faraway look that spelt trouble. Sandra was delighted with him. 'He looks just like a miniature you,' she told me as she hugged him close. As for Uncle Chantelle, well, he and his girlfriends weren't about to give up on Nathan. Even though he was a boy they showered him with sweet little pink dresses — and Uncle Chantelle gave him the latest Barbie.

Just after Nathan's birth, Dingo casually sidled up to me and asked, 'Do you reckon the little wife will let you go out on assignment again?'

'No,' I answered. 'But this is my job — and I'm sick of skuul.'

'It'll be for two months,' Dingo continued. 'Had any weapons training?'

My senses were immediately alert. 'If I need to defend myself, point me to the shooting range and get me some target practice.' This assignment sounded serious.

Sandra hit the roof — and I hadn't even told her about the weapons training. 'Can't somebody else go? And for two months? That's like a lifetime.'

'You'll be all right,' I answered. 'You've got good friends now, and Uncle Chantelle and his girlfriends will look after you. I'll be back soon.' I didn't want to worry Sandra, so I told her I was being sent to do a job on the amazing transformation of Singapore into a world financial capital. Instead, I headed for Dili to cover the Indonesian invasion of East Timor.

Going direct from the comfort of Sydney to the shocking revelations of wholesale human butchery in Timor brutalised me. After just two days I felt that I had left heaven, bypassed purgatory entirely and gone straight to hell. Arnold, the cameraman who had been in Saigon, came with me. Vince said, 'No *way*,' and he was replaced with Manila 'Manny' Jones, a young Filipino who had some local experience. The assignment oscillated between sheer boredom and blood-pumping terror as we secretly filmed the occupation. Sometimes we were only minutes ahead of pursuing Indonesian troops, shepherded through the tropical terrain by our guerrilla minders and hiding out in friendly villages. At other times, the only way to escape was to head for safety into Papua New Guinea. After every shoot, we entrusted our precious film to guerrilla couriers to get it out of the country.

The occupation sickened me: it was riddled with massacres, programmes of forced sterilisation, hunger, and other attempts at cultural annihilation. At that time, over 200,000 people were killed by the Indonesian military.

As if East Timor wasn't tough enough, I went straight from there to Cambodia, and that was even more hellish. I told Arnold he wasn't coming on with me and Manny. Even though he was relieved, he nevertheless asked, 'Why not?'

'You'll stick out like a sore thumb,' I told him. 'I need somebody more like Manny and myself, somebody who can blend into the countryside; a tall blue-eyed whitey just doesn't pass muster.' The office sent me a replacement cameraman, a young Australian-born Indian named Ashok.

I flew with Manny and Ashok to cover the 'Killing Fields' — the brutal Pol Pot rule of Kampuchea. We filmed ordinary Cambodian citizens being rounded up and executed just for speaking a foreign language, wearing glasses or even being able to read. Former bureaucrats and businessmen were ruthlessly hunted down and killed, along with their entire families. We were smuggled into Kampuchea by CIA operatives and made contact with one of the bravest men I have ever met. His name was Dith Yathay and his wisdom reminded me of my old Maori elder, John Rangihau. He was putting himself in great danger by helping us.

One day, when we were hiding out in one of the larger villages in the mountains, Pol Pot forces swept through on one of their regular purges. Soldiers were going from house to house and there appeared to be no way out other than to show my press credentials and surrender.

'Don't,' Dith said. 'Do you think the Pol Pot regime would want your pictures shown to the world?' Instead, he created a diversion by running out of the house and into the fields. As Ashok, Manny and I made our escape, I saw Dith in the sunlight, his hands behind his head, being bludgeoned to death. I like to think that some compensation for his execution came when we screened our footage to the world. Estimates of the dead ranged from one to three million, out of a population estimated at 7.3 million.

East Timor and Cambodia blooded me. When I returned to Sydney, it took me a while to adjust to normal living. I kept seeing Dith, murdered by military thugs so that I could live. Why did he make such a choice? Why didn't he save himself?

I had leave owing and, when that was over, refused any further overseas assignments. Dingo didn't put any pressure on me to take on any jobs. Instead, Sandra and I spent as much time together as we could, and waited for me to heal. Motherhood had come naturally to her and she enjoyed her role. She gave Nathan lots of love and attention. A special family outing was to take the ferry from the city to Taronga Zoo. One day, I watched Sandra pointing out the lions to Nathan. Every time the lions would approach the cage, she would pull him away. Every time, that same movement of mother protecting her child. I burst into tears. I kept seeing Dith, in sunlight, dying so that I could live.

'What's the matter, honey?' she asked, alarmed.

'I'm just wondering,' I answered. 'If something happened to me, would you be able to go on with your life, you and Nathan?'

I expected her to say, 'Of course we will.' Instead she said, 'But nothing's going to happen to you, silly.' Her reply put me into a spin. I realised that she would always expect me to be *there*, no matter what. She had put her life, her expectations, everything entirely in my hands.

It was make or break time for me at the office. Matters weren't made any better when Dingo confessed, 'Actually, Kiwi, I didn't think you'd take the last assignment. I expected you to scream and run back to your shaky isles with your tail between your legs.'

I was so pissed off with him that I took a poke at his ugly Aussie mug. 'You bloody Aussie bastard,' I said. I was quivering with rage that he could be so blasé about an experience that had taken me to hell and back.

He wiped the blood from his bottom lip. 'I guess I deserved that. The question is — so where do you want to go from here? Have you got the guts to stay? Things could get a whole lot worse.'

I could have chucked it in, but I didn't. There's a moment in your life when you know you've passed the point of no return. I thought of Dith again and the sacrifice of his life, and I knew I couldn't give up now. I decided to stay with NewsCorp.

My next major assignment was in 1977 during the time of the 'boat people' when thousands of displaced people were streaming out of the East Asian archipelago — anything to get away from the Asian version of the holocaust. Arnold was my loyal cameraman, and I had Vince as my soundman. I had the bright idea that we should take TV viewers on board a Vietnamese boat, *Sea Serpent*, to get a close-up view of the terrors faced by boat refugees as they poured out of Vietnam.

There were eighty desperate men, women and children on that floating coffin. I had expected that the assignment of filming them in all their filth, fear and cramped conditions would only take a week, ten days at the most, and I had arranged for us to be taken off the boat wherever we were at sea. The problem was that our communications went down and we couldn't radio for the pick-up. A week later, we were still on board the *Sea Serpent*; we were starving, along with everyone else on the boat, and our water supplies ran out.

'You bastard, Tom Mahana,' Vince swore. 'All this for a story? Fuck you.'

Luckily for us, Dingo McCracken was on our case. From home base in Sydney, he radioed the Australian airforce to sweep every inch of the Indian Ocean until we were found. One of their planes pinpointed us and we were all picked up by a British freighter, *Minstrel*, just as the boat was about to sink.

We watched impassively as the *Sea Serpent* disappeared beneath the waves. Arnold was white as a sheet but, at my command, he filmed the sinking. What a dramatic ending to our story!

I said my closing piece to camera. 'We were the lucky ones,' I said, as Arnold panned across the refugees. 'But others have not been so lucky in their perilous attempts to reach freedom. This is Tom Mahana, somewhere in the Indian Ocean.' I paused, then nodded to Arnold. 'That's a wrap.'

His response was to put his camera down and sock me in the jaw. 'We could have drowned, you bastard,' he said.

This time, I had told Sandra I was reporting on the royal family of Japan.

However, when I went missing, Dingo was forced to tell her where I really was and what I was doing. When I returned to Sydney, she ran into my arms. 'I thought you were dead,' she sobbed. She clung to me as if she would never let me go.

I was twenty-five when our second child, Holly, was born in 1979. This pregnancy was difficult and Sandra took a long time to recover from it. Matters were not made any easier by Nathan who, at three, was a hyperactive little boy. He was into everything and he exhausted his mother. Luckily Uncle Chantelle and his girlfriends loved to take him out with them; God knows what sights he saw as they trailed him through their colourful cabaret lives. But they had given up on bringing dresses and dolls. Uncle Chantelle knew he was going to be a red-blooded boy when, on presenting him with the latest Barbie, Nathan placed the doll on the rim of his cot, went 'Brrrrm, Brrrrm, Brrrrm,' and treated her as if she was a toy car.

Surprisingly, Sandra now seemed to take my career absences in her stride. As spirited as ever, however, she wasn't about to lie down and let me trample all over her. Every assignment had to be negotiated, and every time she would remind me, 'What about your family? What about me? Don't forget, you said we would love each other forever.' Often, we would have heated arguments about my lack of responsibility to her and our children as we went off on our usual trip to Taronga Zoo — this time with Nathan on a harness and Holly in a frontpack, dribbling horrible things down my shirt.

But there's no doubt that we still loved each other, although I had begun to be unfaithful while I was away. I'm not making any excuses, but frontline reporting hardened me, took away some of my innocence and made me seek for comfort, skin on skin, when I needed it. Casual sex just seemed to come with the territory. When I was on assignment and drinking in a bar in Hong Kong or Thailand, sex was as easy to buy as a drink; and it was often the best way to get over the stress of high-pressure reporting on war and death. Sandra herself had a few near misses — she told me that Bob Blakeney had done a line with her on one trip while I was away in the Philippines. As far as I know, she was always faithful to me; the thought made me feel more ashamed about breaking my commitment to her.

At the zoo, I loved Nathan's curiosity and the way he reached out to grab at everything. He drove Sandra to distraction as he rushed off to every cage in sight and tried to unlock it. 'Nathan, don't do that,' she would scold him. 'The animals are happy in there, sweetie. They've got lots to eat and they're safe.' The look Nathan gave me said everything. His mother might like to visit the zoo and look at the animals under controlled circumstances but he had already made up his mind. No wonder, when he became an adult, he joined Greenpeace and wanted to save the planet.

In 1980, Ted Turner launched CNN. Today we take for granted that, if we want to, we can switch to news-only channels broadcasting breaking news and updating the news twenty-four hours a day — but back in the 1980s, the concept was revolutionary. However, maintaining such a service also took news gathering to a higher level. Huge infrastructures involving correspondents, anchors and staff were required to enable the around-the-clock harvesting of news wherever it was happening.

To do the harvesting, CNN International established seven regional networks. One of those networks was the Asia–Pacific region. Turner was on a visit to Australia, and he asked me to have a drink with him at the Sydney Hilton. 'Can I call you Tom?' he drawled as he shook my hand. 'Tom, there's a whole new media world out there. When I established twenty-four-hour news the critics said nobody would want to watch it — but they were wrong. People from around the world, wherever they can tap into the CNN signal, are tuning in. They're hungry to know what's happening. We're just a global village after all.' He paused. 'I'd like you to think of joining us. Are you interested?'

Was I what. 'The idea of being in the elevator as it's leaving the lobby is attractive,' I answered. 'What's the deal?'

'I've established the Asia–Pacific bureau in Hong Kong,' Turner grinned. 'That's where the regional headquarters with production facilities will be set up. From there, we want to develop coverage using correspondents throughout the region, in Japan, Thailand, Singapore, Indonesia, Australia, New Zealand, wherever news is made. I'm hoping you'll be interested in joining the Hong Kong office and being one of our anchormen, specialising in political reporting. I can't understand why NewsCorp have never used you in this role.'

'I'm not Australian, I'm the wrong colour and I've got the wrong accent,' I answered.

Turner frowned. 'Frankly, ethnicity and gender are outdated notions in international news,' he said. People reporting and fronting for us will have to come from all races and backgrounds if we are to truly appeal to world audiences. But Tom, the job is bigger than that. You're also going to have to go out, as you are doing now, and bring home the news. Our audiences don't want anonymous reporters. They want somebody who they can get to know and welcome into their lounge. American and European viewers will particularly need somebody who can interpret Asia and the Pacific to them. Frankly, Tom, Americans are afraid of Asia. They're afraid because our relationships, especially during the Second World War and Vietnam, have been violent. Asia's a bogeyman with slit eyes. Tom, I want somebody who can show the region in a way they can understand — the history that drives its peoples and the issues that it faces. Will you do it?'

When I raised the job with Sandra, she started to shiver. 'Why do you want to take this job? Aren't you happy here?'

'Yes,' I answered, angry at the question. 'But it's not enough. Honey, this is what I *do*.'

'But who are you doing it for? What are you trying to prove? Why are you always putting yourself on the line?'

Her questions got under my skin. I deflected them. Living in the safety of Sydney, Sandra would never be able to understand my growing commitment to Asia and the debt I felt I had to repay its people. 'Hong Kong's a great city,' I answered. 'You and the children will enjoy it there.'

'Oh, I see,' Sandra said. 'So now you're making decisions about what we'll enjoy and what we won't. Do you really want to know what I think? Hong Kong will just be another city to be lonely in.' She took a deep breath. 'You've already said yes, haven't you.'

'It's what I've always wanted,' I answered.

'And what about me?' Sandra asked. When I didn't respond she looked at me, angry. 'All I've ever wanted is to have a husband and children who loved me and placed me at the centre of their lives. I thought we had that understanding, but now I realise that, with you, there are no guarantees. Okay, Tama, you may have forgotten that when we married, we vowed we'd be back to back together against the rest of the world; but I haven't. I'll come with you and I'll bring Nathan and Holly with me; but I don't know how much longer I can take this kind of life. I'm sick of worrying when you go away on a job that you mightn't come back. I'm tired of bringing up the children by myself. And when I sleep alone in our bed, I keep wondering what whores you're spending the night with — I'm not a fool, Tama. Who knows, one of these nights I might get so angry with you that I'll go out and find myself some comfort too. I'm not a woman who likes to be alone. If that happens, Tama, I'll have to leave you. You might not be embarrassed to come back from your assignments smelling of other women and making love to me. But if I did what you've been doing to me, I'd never be able to look you in the eyes again, honey, ever.'

I resigned from NewsCorp and joined the CNN Asia–Pacific team. I was sad to say goodbye to Dingo McCracken, Arnold, Vince and Chico. Uncle Chantelle and his girlfriends were bereft at the thought that Sandra, Nathan and Holly were leaving them. I packed up the family and we all shipped out to Hong Kong.

We settled into a house with servants and household staff on The Peak, one of the city's most exclusive suburbs. There, I tried to balance the competing obligations to career and family. I didn't blame Sandra for maintaining such a rigid focus on family. Indeed, I found huge comfort in knowing she was still supporting me and taking the responsibility of bringing up the children. However, it was clear that a lot of trust and love had gone out of our relationship and that we were settling for less.

For the next eleven years, Asia remained my beat. I covered the Asian waterfront, further consolidating my position as a talented (and stupid) buccaneer who would take on any of the difficult frontline political events, not just in Southeast Asia but throughout the entire region.

I flew to the Philippines to do an exposé of the Marcos regime and, in 1983, covered the assassination of opposition leader Benigno 'Ninoy' Aquino. It was this act that coalesced popular dissatisfaction with Marcos and his wife Imelda. I interviewed Madame Marcos at the royal palace, and we filmed her singing 'Melancholy Baby' and accompanying herself on a white grand piano that Liberace would have killed for. I even persuaded her to let us film her shoe closet; she was a vain woman, self-delusional like her husband, living in a world propped up by fetishes and dreams. I did not weep when she and Marcos were forced to flee the Philippines. In fact, I was there to film their air convoy when it left and, again, their arrival in Honolulu on a clear Hawaiian day. I wanted to make sure they had truly gone.

The next year, Indira Gandhi was assassinated, 31 October 1984, and her son Rajiv took her place. I interviewed him when he took over; and I was grieved to cover *his* assassination, apparently by Sri Lankan Tamil extremists, on 27 May 1991.

In 1989, I was in Tibet when the Panchen Lama died. I covered the dilemma that occurred when the Dalai Lama and the Chinese authorities recognised different reincarnations. I was on a plane following the Dalai Lama when he fled into exile in India. Even today, I still continue to harbour hopes that the Dalai Lama's government will once again rule in the holy city of Lhasa.

All those years, my greatest thrill as a political correspondent was to see the Asian autocracies throughout the region being shaken by people power movements. In 1986, in Taiwan, I covered the formation of the Democratic Progressive Party, the first opposition party to counter the Kuomintang administration. I was in China between April and May 1989 when tens of thousands of demonstrators, led by students, assembled around the Monument to the People's Heroes in Tiananmen Square, Beijing. There, they staged pro-democracy rallies against the 'Gang of Four' who governed the People's Republic of China. I can still remember, with tears in my eyes, the sight of the unknown rebel who simply walked out in front of the column of tanks, halting the progress of the military in their eventual and brutal quelling of the revolt. He looked for all the world as if he had just been shopping — he was still holding his shopping bags in both hands. Whenever the tanks moved to go past him, he moved to prevent them. Could I have done that? I don't think so.

And I returned to East Timor in 1999 when the people voted overwhelmingly for independence in a UN-conducted popular consultation. However, the Indonesian military reaction was swift. They murdered 2000 East Timorese, displaced two thirds of the population, raped hundreds of women and girls, and destroyed much of the country's infrastructure. Again, I was forced to flee to escape the reprisals. It was no comfort to me that as an international reporter I could get out; such salvation was not available for all the peoples of Cambodia, East Timor, Vietnam and elsewhere.

Why did I do it? Why did I keep on going out there into Asia?

If Sandra was to ask me that question today, I would know how to answer: Somebody had to bear witness against man's inhumanity to man. Someone had to track the beast as he slouched into people's lives, most often in the guise of a man with a gun and with an army of thugs to support his cowardice. Someone had to film him at his work and expose him for the murderer he was and turn over every stone where he lay hiding.

More important, somebody had to document the heroism with which ordinary people fought their oppressors. It was not enough for them just to live; they had to stand up for liberties that many others throughout the world took for granted. And when they died, like my Cambodian friend Dith Yathay, somebody had to speak up for them. Somebody had to justify the deaths and tell the dead, 'You did not die in vain.'

The great honour of those years was to realise the spark of divinity that was *there*, in the souls of itinerant villagers in East Timor or patriots facing firing squads in Cambodia.

No, they did not go into the darkness of death unnoticed.

There were another couple of reasons.

Maybe I did have something to prove to myself. When I left Waituhi, perhaps I needed to make sure that if I was called to account I would have on record that the choice had been worth it — I had made a difference to the world.

And I had also had personal experience of the beast when he came visiting. Perhaps I was trying to atone for what happened when I was a twelve-year-old boy and unable to stop four men from slouching into my family's lives and violating my mother.

10

te torino haere whakamua, whakamuri.

I sat in Sam's study completing my phone calls. It was six in the evening and I had been working hard, mainly on the continuity script for the forthcoming tenth anniversary broadcast of *Spaceship Earth*.

Earlier in the day, I'd also decided on the nature of our celebratory finale. For our birthday bash, we needed something big to end with. Our international audience would be looking forward to celebrating our anniversary with us; we couldn't disappoint them. Before coming to New Zealand, Paul and I had been brainstorming on ending with something spectacular — a big fireworks display across the Thames where our studios were, or a televised concert with Mr Blair cutting a cake — but, somehow, those kinds of ideas seemed more appropriate to a musical variety programme than a current affairs show. What we needed was something that reflected *Spaceship Earth*'s philosophy and our wishes for all the peoples of the earth. Something that looked forward to the future, brought hope and made the spirit soar.

I thought I had found it. When I outlined the finale over the phone to Paul, he was ecstatic. He passed the idea by Lord Sanderson — after all, he would have to foot the bill. In subsequent phone calls we sorted through the logistics. Finally, Paul called back to confirm we had the green light.

'Lord Sanderson has approved the budget,' he said. 'He thinks the finale will be brilliant. Those guests that you want for it are a perfect match for what our show represents. Obviously they won't be appearing in person, so they'll be coming to us via live links or as videotaped pre-shot items. Is that okay with you?'

'That's fine by me,' I answered. 'The question is whether Otis can handle all the communications traffic? We'll be beaming our guests in pretty fast via our satellite — and over a ten-minute period. If we drop any of the catches, it'll show.'

A loud explosion of anger sounded behind Paul's voice. Why didn't he tell me that I was on a speakerphone and that Otis was with him?

Oops. 'Sorry, Otis,' I said meekly. 'I'm sure you have everything under control.'

'Yes I have, captain,' Otis answered gruffly. 'I'm already in the process of booking the relays with London, Paris, New York, Rome and Sydney. Of course,' he added sarcastically, 'we'll be in danger of losing some of the other links, particularly the one to Nairobi — and it will take longer to set up communications to Mount Tanganyika and Irian Jaya, let alone some godforsaken village in the middle of the Amazon jungle, but I'm working on that.'

'Perhaps those guests can be brought in as pre-shot VT items?' I suggested, trying to keep the peace.

I heard Otis give a long, irritated intake of breath. 'Captain, you concentrate on flying the ship. Leave the engine room to me. When you want warp speed power you'll have it.'

That was telling me. 'Thank you, Otis,' I answered.

Paul cut in quickly. 'On other matters,' he said, 'why didn't you tell me your local New Zealand technicians are so good? With their help John has the studio up to speed in record time. It's looking like our usual set: Vidiwall, your and Kim's consoles, and the audience will be seated to the right of the studio. We'll have you both radio-miked so that you can walk across and say hello to them. Elton John is working on some suitable music for the finale. He can't compose anything original, given the timeframe, but he's come up with a terrifically inventive idea — I think you'll like it. John Campbell keeps coming by the set. Yesterday I caught him sitting at your console. I've put him right in the front row of the audience with Carol Hirschfeld, but he really wants your captain's seat! Tom, the whole team up here in Auckland sends you their congratulations. Oh yes, and I've got Harriet standing by and she wants to talk to you.'

'Hello Mr Mahana,' Harriet said. She never called me by my surname unless I was in deep doggy-doo-doo trouble. 'So you've finished the continuity script? Perfect!'

Harriet's voice came down the phone in a huge loud blast. 'Just make sure you get it to me pronto as an attachment so that I can do *my* job? The local camera director is already agitating about translating your continuity script into camera moves and shots — and you're holding us up. Each camera needs its own marks and cues otherwise they'll be in the wrong place and you'll be talking to the wrong one — and I still have to load the teleprompt. And have you forgotten you have a co-presenter? Kim would be ever so grateful to know what she's supposed to be saying and doing! Do you comprende, Mr Mahana? If you want to save your life, send the continuity script *now*. How do you expect me to coordinate the live links and VT items into our overall running time? I also have to sort out the segment times, VT times, continuity script times and ad lib times. And would it be too much to ask that you get here early for our rehearsal? We're presuming you will be here for that, if you would be so kind. Otherwise, do you know that tiny bald spot you are developing at the back of your head? I will instruct the lighting man to highlight it during the show so that all the world can see it. Got that?'

I put down the phone, started up the computer and sent my continuity script immediately. The family was due at eight to resume our discussion on the matter of our half-brother. I had tried to call Sandra earlier in the day. There was just enough time to try her again — and then have a bite to eat and a glass of Mahana wine before the meeting. I dialled her Wellington number. Her husband, Stewart, answered. 'I'll just get Sandra for you,' he said.

As I waited, I thought of our last year together in Hong Kong. My nerves had held, but hers hadn't. Hong Kong had indeed turned into yet another city for her to be lonely in; that is, whenever she wasn't worrying over Nathan and Holly. Nathan in particular treated Hong Kong like one huge playground. Even going to an international school didn't slow him down. Quite the reverse, it gave him lots of other schoolfriends to tempt into explorations and adventures around the city. He thought it was huge fun to escape The Peak and play truant in Kowloon. There, he would create havoc with the stallkeepers in the teeming markets or the fishermen on the busy harbour: letting chickens out of bamboo cages and fish out of nets. When Holly started walking, she was an obliging follower in his escapades — and Sandra often worried that they'd be taken by slavers across the border into mainland China. She had every right to be anxious, but Hong Kong was actually a city of a million eyes and most of them got to know the children well. While scolding them in their high-pitched Chinese voices, they also protected them.

'Tama?' Sandra picked up the phone. 'Thank you for calling me back. Stewart saw you on television yesterday so we knew you'd come home. When Nathan was here a few weeks ago from Antarctica, he told us that Mum had cancer. Is that why you're here? Is Mum dying?'

'No,' I answered. 'But she's just come out of hospital, and there was some family business to be settled before too much longer.'

'Oh, thank God,' Sandra said. 'I was expecting the worst. Nathan was very upset when he saw Mum. He's always called her his very special girlfriend. You know, don't you, that ever since he joined Greenpeace he's been promising to take her to the Galapagos Islands? He said to me, "Mum, I don't think Grandma's going to be able to make the trip."'

'Where is that son of ours, anyway?' I asked.

'Who knows!' she laughed. 'I think he said Tierra del Fuego in his last email. I could never tie him down. I could never tie you down, either! How are you?'

'I'm fine,' I answered. 'And you and Stewart?'

'We're spending more and more weekends going up to the bach at Taupo. Once he retires from the legal firm we'll probably sell the house and move up there. Tama, you will promise to let me know if there's any change in Mum's condition, won't you?'

We chatted on. My thoughts went back to Hong Kong. There came a day when Sandra finally had enough. What kind of life was it to have a husband who was always on assignment and never there to help her bring up the children? Her decision to leave, however, was not precipitated by my continuing infidelities or her meeting somebody herself. What happened was that we found ourselves expectant parents again — but I wasn't keen to have a third child.

'What about our football team?' Sandra joked. 'This time we could have a winger!' The light went out of her eyes when she saw that I was so adamantly opposed to the baby. I never suggested that she should terminate the pregnancy but, as it happened, she lost the child in her second trimester. The child would have been another boy, and his death put her into a spin. When she came out of it, she had made up her mind about us. 'I'm going back to New Zealand,' she said, 'and I'm taking the children.'

Of course it wasn't as simple as that. I was your usual male — it's not until you're taken to the wall that you realise what you're losing. The thought of not having the children in my life was awful but, after all, what ground did I have to stand on when Sandra pointed out I wasn't *there* half the time? Although I made promises to do better, they sounded hollow to her — and she had heard them all before.

For Nathan and Holly's sake, we pretended that the separation was only going to be temporary. We told our friends that we'd decided it was time for Nathan and Holly to grow up in Aotearoa; if they were going to swear, we preferred that they swore in Maori and not Chinese. Of course the children put up a fight — and I don't blame them. Hong Kong was home for them and, at the airport, I was totally amazed at the number of people who turned up to say goodbye, not to Sandra, but to them: old Chinese ladies who had fed Holly when she was hungry and fishermen who had rescued Nathan when irate stallkeepers had threatened to throw him into the harbour. I was somewhat ashamed that these strangers seemed to have a more intimate connection to the children than their father.

The goodbyes were tearful. The boarding calls, which at first had been neutral, soon turned sharp. 'Would Mrs Sandra Mahana, Nathan Mahana and Holly Mahana please report to gate seven for immediate departure.' Nathan gave me an angry look. 'This is all your fault, Daddy,' he said.

Sandra had the last word. She was stormy, and she wasn't going to let me go without telling me exactly what she thought of me. 'I'm really furious with you, Tama,' she began. 'You said you wouldn't let the wind come between us, but you did. You said we'd go on and on and end up together as two old folks sharing the same bed and still kissing each other before we went to sleep — you lied.' Then, as suddenly as it began, her tirade was over. 'Come on, children. Say goodbye to Daddy. It's time to go.'

Now, here I was, years later, talking to her on the phone, and I couldn't help myself. 'Sandra, can I tell you how sorry I am about what happened to us?'

There was a pause in Sandra's chatter. 'Please don't,' she answered.

'Are you happy?' I asked, insistent. I needed to know that no matter what I had done to her she had found what she deserved: peace, happiness, a safe haven.

'Yes, of course I am,' she said. 'Tama, we tried out best. We have two gorgeous children to show for it — and I'm very proud of you. We were just two people who had different ideas of what we wanted out of life. Do you know that silly saying, "If you love somebody let them go and if they love you, they will return to you?" When things started to go bad with us, I had to take the risk. The trouble was that you didn't come back.'

I tried to make a joke. 'There's an extra sentence to that saying. "And if they don't return, get a gun and hunt them down."'

'Don't worry,' Sandra laughed, 'that thought did cross my mind. But, Tama, the children and I got on with our lives. It was our karma.'

At the same time as the spiral is going forward, it is returning.

Eight o'clock, and the family was assembled again in the sitting room. Mum was in her usual chair, holding Hone's hand. Marama sat at her feet. Ripeka, Mere and Wiki bustled around making sure everybody had a cup of tea and some of Mere's lovely scones with lashings of whipped cream and strawberries on top. Sam and Koro were standing in the doorway; Darren had asked Wiki to give his apologies, due to a committee meeting at his golf club.

I looked at my sisters, Hone and brothers-in-law, and I thought of all the various spirals that we had all brought to the making of the Mahana family. Here I was, back in Waituhi to resolve a new tension, a new spiral that had arisen out of nowhere and was threatening to explode our family apart.

The double helix pattern that I had drawn on a piece of paper earlier that day popped into my head. I remembered that in one of *Spaceship Earth*'s recent programmes I had interviewed Stephen Jay Gould, the renowned professor of zoology and geology at Harvard University, on precisely that same pattern.

'The shape of the double helix,' he began, 'is the same shape of the universe as it expands and contracts; it's the shape of infinity, with a unique curve into three-dimensional space. The ratio of the curvature is a constant, a result known as Lancret's theorem.

'The double helix is also the shape of the chromosome, the geometric shape of that compact spool of DNA, which holds our genetic inheritance from our parents. Two helices spiral around each other, connected by molecular bonds, resembling a rope ladder that has been repeatedly twisted along its length. There are twenty-three pairs of chromosomes, one set from our mother and one set from our father, and they carry the hereditary code which locates us within the human race and a particular family, identity and nation. The genetic information binds us one generation after the next in a connection that spells out our personal genealogies, and the strength — and nobody should underestimate just how strong it is — of the double helix is exactly in that capacity to *bind*.'

In my family's case, a brother none of our family had ever known about had appeared at our genetic gateway. He had twenty-three pairs of chromosomes from our mother, but none from our father. Those chromosomes were from an alien father who had interpolated his genetic makeup. The question was whether or not we could accept this binding — a binding which had not been given with our mother's or our consent — and lock it into our own blood relationship as a family, our history and genealogy.

Before we even started to talk about the dilemma, Ripeka laid down the law.

'I don't want anybody to refer to that man who is supposed to be Mum's son as our brother or even half-brother. I know who my brothers are. They are Tama and Hone. Who is this person and what does he want?'

Ripeka had been working herself up about this all day and she was already breaking apart. A quick glance at everyone else told me that they, also, were frightened and resistant.

'You tell them, son,' Mum said with a sigh. 'You tell them what happened.'

When my mother rang me in Kandahar to tell me about the notice in the personal columns of *The Gisborne Herald*, it was as if a hole had opened in the air and something that had been dead, flyblown and rotting for almost forty years had been thrown out of it. The man with the red hair punched me in the throat and threw me against the wall. I had taken the call on my carphone and I stopped the car, opened the door and gasped for breath.

I AM SEEKING THE MAORI MOTHER. 'What shall I do?' Mum cried. OF MY SON, BORN 7 FEBRUARY 1966. 'I know it's me, I'm the person they're looking for. GREYMOUTH HOSPITAL. 'That's where I had him.' I WOULD HAVE RESPECTED YOUR WISHES FOR CONFIDENTIALITY. 'When I adopted him out, I made it clear to the doctors that I was not to be named on any documents. I did not want to be located. I thought I was safe.' YOUR SON NEEDS YOUR URGENT HELP. 'But what can I do now, Tama? Whoever is looking for me, it must be his parents, must have a good reason for seeking me. Do you think it's something medical? Has he had an accident and is he on life support? Do you think it's serious? Is it life-threatening? Does he need a blood transfusion? Oh, son, what shall I do?'

The dilemma, the choice my mother was being forced to consider was extremely distressing for her. She was a woman who, in both Maori and Pakeha society, had been brought up with traditional values to do with upholding her personal reputation and not bringing shame to her family. She maintained high moral and ethical standards for herself. My father was the only person she had ever loved and, apart from the rape, the only man she had ever had physical relations with. No rumour or gossip ever attached to her reputation. She was strict about the way in which people should conduct themselves and was, herself, a woman of great modesty. All these years she had been able to close herself up against the memory of what had happened to her; she knew that because it was an act of violence, she was not accountable and could not be held at fault.

'Don't worry about this, Mum,' I told her over the phone. 'Let's just sit on it for now. We don't have to do anything if you don't want to. Why don't I call you when I get back to Britain?'

I thought, in the interim, that she might let go of the issue. Put it behind her. Walk away from it. But two days later, when I returned to London, I knew she hadn't. As soon as I walked into the apartment I saw the red light blinking on my phone. There were three messages from Mum, and it was clear that she was hurting, really hurting. 'Son, are you back yet? What are we going to do? Ring me as soon as you can? BEEP. Son, I'm trying to get you. Please call me. What kind of person refuses help when asked? What should I do? BEEP. Son, please call. It's your mother here. I never wanted to bring shame on my family and your father. I love you.'

I phoned her immediately. It was the middle of the night in Waituhi. Ripeka answered the phone and I asked her to put Mum on. 'What's wrong with her?' Ripeka asked. 'She thinks we can't hear her crying, but we can. I wish she would stop worrying about her cancer.'

As soon as Mum heard my voice, she started to weep. 'Oh, son, I keep on hearing a voice calling across a dark sea. I know it's him.'

'I know this is difficult for you, Mum,' I said, trying to ease her pain, 'and that you only want to do what's best.'

She was in deep distress. She said so many things, all jumbled up and confused, about her love for Dad and for us — but that this cry for help from a de facto son was no ordinary plea. It was addressed to *her*. Whether she liked it or not, she was this man's mother. Even though her love for us was greater, how much obligation did she have to him?

We kept on going round and round in circles. Exhausted, I offered her a way out. 'Okay, Mum,' I said. 'I'll make some enquiries. Try to get some sleep now. Go to sleep, Mum. Please.'

I made a call to *The Gisborne Herald*. Jock Burns had long retired but, over the years, I had kept contact with some of the newspaper staff. The paper always liked to boast that 'Tama Mahana was once a cadet reporter with the *Herald* before achieving international renown as Tom Mahana, television anchorman'. I asked to be put through to Alice, Morag's daughter, who now worked for the paper. Sadly, Morag had died two years ago, living out her life as a grande dame in an old people's home, where she had been the reigning champion in Scrabble and the cryptic crossword.

'Yes,' Alice told me, 'all of us are intrigued by the advertisement. It first began to appear in the *New Zealand Herald* three months ago. According to our information, it was lodged by a lawyer in Dunedin. The lawyer rang us in Gisborne last month. Apparently his client had information that the mother who is being looked for is from this area. We've published it four times. Obviously, no takers yet, because we've not had any instructions from the lawyer to withdraw it. Are you following the story for *Spaceship Earth*? It's a bit off your track, isn't it? Do you want the lawyer's address and phone number? Here they are.' She rattled them off.

I put the phone down. I picked it up again, intending to call the lawyer in Dunedin, and was suddenly frozen with the realisation that my enquiries had already gone too far. If I kept going, Mum and I might only be drawn more and more into a situation that, in the end, would force her into an inevitable position.

I phoned Mum again. 'I'm not sure if we should go any further,' I said to her. 'Let me suggest something to you. If you hadn't read the newspaper item, you wouldn't have known about this man, would you?'

Mum, however, had passed the point of no return. 'But I did read it,' she answered. 'Although I have made up my mind that, in this matter, my family comes first, I am honour bound to help this man. If I can, I'll do it; after all he was born of my womb.' Mum was, at least, committed to find out more about the help he required. 'And who knows,' she continued, 'the request might be a small thing rather than a large thing — but we won't know until we find out what it is.' Softly she began to weep. 'I am only glad that your father never knew. It would have killed him if he had known.'

I duly made the call to the lawyer. His name was James Leighton. 'I just about fell off my chair,' he said, 'when my secretary told me who was phoning me, from where, and what about. This isn't a joke, is it?'

'No,' I assured him. I had concocted a story that would get me through our conversation. 'I'm ringing on behalf of a relative of mine, who saw your advertisement in the *New Zealand Herald* a few months ago,' I lied. 'It's taken her some time to consider what to do. She thinks she may know the Maori woman you are looking for. She has asked me to deputise for her. Can you give me some further information?'

'I'd rather not handle this over the phone,' James Leighton answered, 'but in this case, it's not as if you could have a cup of coffee with me in the Octagon tomorrow, is it? So let me give you some of the details my client has allowed me to advise enquirers to separate the genuine enquiries from the crackpots. My client and her husband, who is deceased, adopted the boy as a baby. He is now thirty-nine years old. They were told that he was half-Maori, half-Pakeha. They were also told that the mother was a Maori woman, not a young girl, but somebody of mature age, probably in her thirties. My client knows nothing about the reasons for the adoption, but she and her late husband were told that the mother did not wish, under any circumstances, to be contacted or have her identity divulged in any way whatsoever. Is this enough for you to go back to your relative to ascertain any congruence?'

'Yes,' I answered. Then, 'Could you tell me what the urgency is? This will make all the difference with respect to whether or not my relative continues to respond to your client's enquiry.'

'I understand the son concerned is institutionalised with extreme psychological problems. I am not at liberty to tell you any more than that.'

I phoned Mum again. She had calmed down. She sounded defeated. Lost.

'It *is* him,' she said, her voice drained of hope. 'It *must* be. We'll have to go on with it.'

'So he was suffering,' Ripeka burst out. 'So what?'

'And what has this got to do with us?' Mere continued. 'What about the suffering that our mother went through? Someone has got to pay. Let him rot in the dark hole he's in.'

All this happened three weeks after the fist of God slammed Southeast Asia, Indonesia and Thailand. At 6.58 am local time, 26 December 2004, a point nine magnitude earthquake hit the coast of Sumatra. The epicentre was located 155 miles southwest of the provincial capital of Banda Aceh, and it unleashed a series of tsunami that crashed into coastal towns, fishing villages and tourist resorts in at least eleven countries from Sri Lanka to India, Thailand and Malaysia. I went to Banda Aceh with Paul and Harriet to make a special report for *Spaceship Earth* on the recovery and relief effort. The programme showed satellite images of the devastation along Thailand's Khao Lak and Phuket coastline and Indonesia's Aceh and Medan regions: in some places, forty-foot waves had moved inland over a mile and, when they receded, they destroyed everything and everybody in their path. In Aceh alone, 220,000 died or were missing and 800,000 were displaced. Whole villages were wiped out. I filmed the situation in the temporary camps. The stench of rotting bodies was so bad that I didn't want to breathe the air.

To make matters worse, the situation was compounded by ongoing military tension between the Indonesian government and the Free Aceh Movement, who had been fighting for an independent homeland since 1976.

I wrapped up the programme and told Paul that I was taking a few days to go to New Zealand to visit my mother before returning to London. Then I phoned Mum.

'Hello, Mum,' I said. 'I'm on my way. I'm coming home to sort this business out. I love you.'

I made a second call to James Leighton. 'The opportunity has come up for me to take a short visit to New Zealand,' I told him. 'I'd therefore like to make an appointment for the woman I am representing to meet with your client. I'll come clean: the woman is my mother. She may be able to help your client. She might not. I can give no assurances. Can you make the appointment? My mother does not want your client to come to Gisborne. We will come to her.'

James Leighton said he would talk to his client. That evening, he phoned me back in Banda Aceh. 'My client is keen to discuss this with your mother,' he said. 'Her name is Mrs Birgit Amundsen and she lives in Timaru. There is an old, historic hotel in town, and Mrs Amundsen suggests you meet there. Perhaps for afternoon tea, in the lounge, on Thursday?'

Two days away. I asked Harriet to make the bookings, and she arranged for me to stop over in Singapore and arrive in New Zealand on Thursday morning. I rang Mum again. 'Can you fly from Gisborne to Auckland to meet my international flight?' I asked her. 'Once I clear immigration we'll catch a domestic flight from Auckland to Christchurch and then another flight to Timaru.'

At that point my mother had begun radiation treatment for her leukaemia. Even so, when I came out of customs and saw her, she was looking radiant. Perhaps it was a case of less oil in the lamp making, as they say, a stronger flame. The sight of my mother brought tears to my eyes. I could not bear the thought of her illness and that she might die soon. I tried to hide my grief and Mum pretended not to notice it.

'Thank you for coming,' Mum said. 'You've always been a good son.'

We made our way from the international terminal to the domestic terminal. I could see that she was nervous about the trip; but she made light of the excursion. 'Your sister, Ripeka,' she whispered conspiratorially, 'is getting suspicious. I told her you were taking me shopping in Auckland, so we better get me a nice dress before you send me back to Gisborne.'

On the plane to Christchurch, however, all Mum's playfulness dropped away. Her nervousness increased on the connecting flight to Timaru and she clung to my arm so tight that her fingers left deep marks.

The weather turned nasty as we dropped below the clouds. Timaru appeared, a city of old architectural magnificence, emerging out of the storm. When we landed, a cold wind was blowing from the sea. The waves were white-tipped, the spray cascading shoreward.

We had two hours before our appointment with Mrs Amundsen, so I checked us into a motel. Mum had not brought an overcoat, and this provided me with the excuse to take her shopping. We hired a car and drove into the city where we bought her a beautiful wine-coloured suede number, and that 'nice dress', which looked stunning with her silver hair. A quarter of an hour before our appointment, we arrived at the meeting place — the old historic hotel. Mum excused herself to check on her appearance in the ladies room.

While Mum was away I ordered tea and scones. No sooner had she returned, than I noticed a woman driving up to the hotel. She was younger than Mum, about ten or fifteen years younger, blonde, slim, wearing a scarf, and she ran with little steps into the hotel foyer. Once inside she shivered, took off her scarf and started to primp at her hair in a hotel mirror. She saw us in the reflection of the mirror. Her eyes widened. She smiled and composed herself. As she came towards us, I stood up.

'You must be Mrs Amundsen,' I said, shaking her hand. 'My name is Tom Mahana. This is my mother, Huia. Won't you sit down?'

'I'm pleased to meet you, Mrs Mahana,' Mrs Amundsen said to Mum. 'And of course I know your son from television. Yes, I'd be pleased to sit.' Her voice had a pleasant, foreign lilt. There was a slight awkwardness between all of us.

The tea arrived and I asked Mrs Amundsen if she would like a cup. She nodded, Mum poured, and we sat there, sipping, trying to think of how to begin our conversation. Finally, I put my cup down.

'Perhaps, Mrs Amundsen,' I began, 'you can tell us about the advertisement.'

'Yes,' Mrs Amundsen answered. 'If I say from the beginning that my lawyer has advised me that you may not be the people I am looking for, that will break the ice? Even if you are, I understand also that you, Mrs Mahana, cannot make any assurances that you can help. Is that correct? Yes? In that case, let me tell you about Eric, and how my husband and I came to adopt him. To begin with, my husband and I were both from Sweden and had been living in New Zealand for five years. Lars was a marine engineer with Port Timaru and, well, we were childless. We had our name with the adoption authorities and, one day, in February 1966, I received a phone call to say that a Maori baby, a boy, was available for adoption. Forgive me for saying this but, in those days, Maori babies were not as wanted as European babies — but I rang Lars and together we rushed down to the hospital to see him.' Mrs Amundsen's eyes lit up at the memory, 'Well, when we saw Eric, I had this huge attack of giggles. I couldn't stop! I thought, there must be some mistake. And Lars, he started to bellow with laughter too. You see, it was Eric's red hair. And Lars, well, he had red hair too. We just couldn't believe it. It was if this adoption was meant to be — Eric was meant just for us. Would you like to see a photograph of my husband, Mrs Mahana?'

My mother hesitated. 'I'd be pleased to see it, Mrs Amundsen,' she nodded. Mrs Amundsen took a photograph from her purse. 'A strong-looking man,' Mum said.

Mum and Mrs Amundsen began to chat. I looked at her and she gave me a sign that she would be okay talking alone with Mrs Amundsen. 'I'll be in the bar if you need me,' I said. 'I've got some phone calls to make and some work to do to keep me busy.' From the bar, I watched them talking. Later, Mum told me what Mrs Amundsen said to her.

'It's clear that Birgit and Lars Amundsen loved that boy,' she said. 'Eric wanted for nothing as he was growing up. Nobody could have loved him more. He did well at school, became a prefect at Timaru Boys High School, and was a lock in the school's first fifteen — so he must have been a big boy. He was accredited with University Entrance and went to Otago. He did a degree in architecture and overseas studies at York University, Toronto. He married a Canadian girl, came back to New Zealand and set up his own architectural firm. His family life was happy, and he had three children. Then, a year ago he became severely depressed —'

From that point on, the conversation between my mother and Mrs Amundsen became difficult. In telling about Eric Amundsen's depression, Mrs Amundsen began to make some uncalled-for assumptions about my mother, our family and our Maori background.

'When Eric had his depression,' she said, 'Coral, his wife, and I thought it was due to the death of his father, my husband Lars. Lars and Eric had such a close relationship — sailing, canoeing, going out hunting — and Eric idolised his father. The doctor prescribed tranquillisers and they worked for a time. Then Coral and Eric lost their oldest child, Lars Junior, in a car accident, and that only seemed to exacerbate Eric's condition. His depression deepened and his local GP gave him a referral to Dr Stephens, a psychiatrist with his own private practice here in Timaru. We hoped that Dr Stephens would be able to treat his depression, but Eric's life and health continued to suffer and, with it, his business.' Mrs Amundsen paused, looking at my mother. 'Do you understand what it's like to watch a child suffering, Mrs Mahana? Can you understand how Coral and I felt, watching Eric descending into deeper and deeper depression? Then, eight months ago he took a turn for the worse. Despite his medication, he had the first of a series of psychotic episodes. He began to exhibit strange behaviour and, when we tried to prevent it, he became violent. He assaulted me and tried to kill Coral. That was bad enough, but when he turned on his two children, we had to call the police. He is now in a psychiatric institution, still under Dr Stephens' care, undergoing treatment. Most days he is heavily sedated. We are still no nearer to knowing what's wrong with him.'

Mrs Amundsen took a deep breath. 'That is why I placed the advertisement in the newspapers in the North Island. One of the orderlies at the hospital thought that the problem might be genetic. You might know him, Mrs Mahana, his name is Wiremu Gray? No? Mr Gray had taken a special interest in Eric and asked if he had Maori ancestry. When I said yes, he told me that Eric should be taken back to his tribe. They would know what to do, he said.'

My mother put her cup down. She frowned, and then realised what Mrs Amundsen was suggesting. 'What are you trying to imply, Mrs Amundsen?' she asked. 'Are you saying your son has inherited some mental condition from his Maori ancestry?'

Mrs Amundsen began to talk fast. 'Please forgive me for speaking plainly. Eric has now gone into a world inside his head and nobody can get him to come back. I believe we are running out of time. If we don't diagnose what's wrong with him, he will be institutionalised forever.'

But Mum was deeply offended. 'There is no madness or insanity in my family,' she said.

I saw my mother's distress and came running. 'Are you all right, Mum?' I turned to Mrs Amundsen. 'Be warned,' I said to her, 'my mother is not well. If you step out of line again, this is the last you'll see of us. We have come here out of sympathy. Don't abuse it.'

Mrs Amundsen gave me a pleading look. 'I'm sorry to hear about your mother's health,' she answered. 'I want nothing from your family except your help — if you are the right people to give it. Once Eric is well, we'll go on with our lives and your family can go on with yours. I have already lost my husband, Mr Mahana, and my first grandchild. I do not think I could bear losing my son. To be a widow is one thing but to lose a child, even if he is adopted, is another.'

Before I could stop her, Mrs Amundsen turned back to Mum. Her question went straight as an arrow. 'Are you Eric's biological mother, Mrs Mahana? Is there anything you can tell me which might give us a clue as to how to help him?'

If my mother had walked out of that hotel and away from Mrs Amundsen, I would not have blamed her. But Mum has always had a generous and forgiving nature. When people sought her assistance, her natural inclination was to say yes. I watched her face as she tussled with Mrs Amundsen's question. No sentimentality should be ascribed to her answer. She recognised the maternal instinct in Mrs Amundsen and was compelled by aroha.

'Take us to your son, Mrs Amundsen,' she said.

'You should have brought Mum home,' Ripeka seethed.

'Yes, brother,' Hone added. 'Why should Mum have taken on the burden of someone else's problem? Mum owed that woman and her son nothing. Nothing.'

The psychiatric institution where Eric Amundsen had been committed was some ten kilometres out of Timaru. Before leaving the hotel, Mrs Amundsen phoned Dr Stephens.

'He's approved our visit,' Mrs Amundsen told us, looking relieved. 'I told him that you only wanted to see Eric but not talk to him. He's in a secure wing and there's an observation room where we will be able to do this. Dr Stephens and the orderly I spoke of, Wiremu Gray, will meet us at reception. Will you come in my car or follow in your own?'

I elected to follow Mrs Amundsen. As we were travelling fast through the rain out of Timaru, Mum told me what Mrs Amundsen had insinuated. 'We have always been a Christian family,' Mum said. 'That's what offended me most, son, that a woman like her would think we would be so ungodly as to be punished with a history of insanity.' I had a good mind to turn the car around there and then and head back to town but Mum would not let me. 'There may be some other purpose at work,' she said.

Once in the country, the storm worsened. The road streamed with brown silt. At one corner, a tree had been brought down by the rain. Mum was silent all the way, watching the windscreen wipers sweep back and forth, back and forth.

Half an hour later, as we climbed up a steep hill, we saw the hospital. It appeared on the skyline, large, two-storeyed, against a backdrop of grey turbulent sky.

As agreed, Dr Stephens and Wiremu Gray met us at the door. Wiremu Gray's open and smiling face soon fell as Mum whipped into him with a scathing attack, in Maori, about Mrs Amundsen. 'How dare you,' she said to him. 'My family are followers of the Old Testament beliefs of Te Kooti. You had no right to suggest to this Pakeha woman that there may be mental illness in our whakapapa.'

Tempers were fraying as Wiremu Gray apologised to both of us. 'I have been misrepresented,' he said. 'All I suggested was that if Eric Amundsen had Maori ancestry, perhaps his own people had ways of healing him that we didn't. That is all.'

We followed Dr Stephens down the hallway and up a wide staircase to an upstairs wing. The interior was white, clinical, but not unpleasant. Apparently, the house dated from 1906 and had once belonged to a rich Timaru merchant who imported Italian stone, marble, ceramics and decorative interior and garden sculptures to New Zealand. Some of the merchant's design taste was evident in the fluted ceilings and small embellishments set into the marble floor. When we reached the upstairs wing, we came to a large door with a sign on it: RESTRICTED. DOCTORS AND MEDICAL STAFF ONLY.

Dr Stephens took us through a side door to a small observation room. A male nurse was on duty. From the room was a large window looking into the wing; there was also a television monitor showing it from different angles. It was large with tall, padded walls and a glass skylight in the ceiling. Around a dozen patients roamed the perimeter or stood or sat on the floor. Some looked as if they were play-acting. Others were talking to imaginary friends. A few were frozen, absolutely still, as if they hoped no one would notice they were there. Every now and then, somebody would make an uncoordinated run from one side of the room to the other.

But, oh, it was so easy to recognise which patient was Eric Amundsen.

Standing on a chair in the middle of the room, staring up at the skylight, was a big beefy man with a shock of red hair. His father must have been around his age when he raped my mother and threw me against the wall. As I was watching him, he turned his attention from the skyline to look at the window and *through* it to where we were standing. *Is this the man of the house? the red-haired man mocked. Hello little man. Your mum invited us over for a couple of drinks and a bit of fun, didn't you, darling.* One look. Then he went back to watching the skylight.

That one look was enough to make me remember what the man with the red hair and his mates had done that day — and I recoiled. Beads of sweat and fear popped on my forehead. I had never told Mum that while she was lying unconscious those men turned on me. What they did — rape is one form of molestation and it has many other obscene and sickening variations — had haunted me throughout my boyhood. I had at least the small comfort of knowing that while they were having their fun with me they weren't ripping like a pack of rottweilers into Mum.

If I was having such a reaction to Eric Amundsen's appearance, my mother's was even more pitiful. She hid her face in my arms and shivered.

'Why does he have to look so like his father?'

I watched Eric Amundsen, repelled by him and angered at myself for bringing Mum to see him. All of a sudden he saw something in the light streaming from the skylight and, with a huge effort, accompanied by a loud yell, he jumped at it from the chair.

'Eric keeps on seeing a huge glowing river,' Dr Stephens explained. 'It's a river that comes out of nowhere and recedes into some darkness way beyond the room he is in. In our sessions with him, Eric has been able to tell us about the river. It's the most beautiful thing he's ever seen. It's threaded with many colours, like a glorious rainbow. There are voices in the river and they are calling him.'

Eric Amundsen was making desperate swimming motions, his face a rictus of pain. As the river flowed through the room, he tried to join it. Unsuccessful, he gave a cry of frustration and, panting, climbed back on the chair.

'He won't give up,' Wiremu Gray said. 'Whenever he swims towards it, the river bends away from him like refracted light. It's as if it doesn't recognise him. He's been trying for four months now. Every day he does the same repetitive action. Gets on the chair. Jumps. Fails. Gets back on the chair. Jumps again. If anybody tries to stop him, he attacks them.'

Sure enough, Eric Amundsen looked up at the skylight and resumed his wait. I knew exactly what was happening.

'It isn't a river,' I said.

'What did you say?' Dr Stephens asked. But before I could answer, Mum turned to Mrs Amundsen. The cumulative tension and stress, culminating in seeing Eric Amundsen, spilled over.

'You asked me back at the hotel,' she began, 'whether I had ever had to watch any of my children suffering. Of course I have. But what about my suffering, Mrs Amundsen?' Mum's eyes were blazing with anger. 'Not once have you asked me about *my* pain, my suffering. Not once have you asked why I gave that man in there away when he was born.' She turned to Wiremu Gray, 'And you, taurekareka, you set this Pakeha woman on my trail and now she thinks I'm the salvation of her son, and you don't even know anything about the circumstances of my suffering and why I gave him up. Well, I will tell you both, Mrs Amundsen and Mr Gray. I was taken against my will by his father and his friends. They raped me repeatedly. They did it in front of my children. Again and again.'

Mrs Amundsen blanched. 'Raped? I'm so sorry —'

My mother was shaking apart. 'Sorry doesn't cut it, Mrs Amundsen. Why should I have mercy for the son of a man who raped me? Seeing Eric Amundsen again is like being confronted by the father. You ask me to help him? I will not.'

With that, my mother turned to me. 'Son, please, take me away from here.'

Pale and distressed, my mother clung to me as we left the observation room. Together, we walked away from the first-floor wing. However, as we were descending the stairway, I heard rapid steps coming behind us. When we looked up, Mrs Amundsen was looking down the stairwell.

I had to admire her tenacity as she unloosed her last arrow at Mum.

'Mrs Mahana,' she called. 'Must the sins of the father be visited on the son?'

We were all gathered in the sitting room of Ripeka and Sam's homestead at Waituhi. My mother sighed and looked at us. 'Up until that time,' she said, 'I had made up my mind that I owed Eric Amundsen nothing. But that arrow of Mrs Amundsen's lodged in my heart and no matter how hard I have tried, I have been unable to dislodge it. That was two months ago, and I have still not been able to resolve the dilemma of whether to help Eric Amundsen or not.'

'So I told Mum,' I interrupted, 'that perhaps this was something she should not take responsibility for by herself. She agreed with me that I could bring it to you, the family, and we would discuss it among ourselves and come to a family decision. This is why I have come home from London.'

'I wasn't dying then,' Mum said with a rueful smile. 'Now that I am, it makes a difference.' She stood up, firm and resolute. 'I cannot have this matter on my conscience,' she said. She moved among us, kissing us on our foreheads. 'Must the sins of the father be visited on the son? Beloved children, I beg you to take the burden of the decision.'

By that time, it was ten o'clock in the evening. Mum was tired and said she wanted to go to bed and, anyway, she didn't want to influence our family decision about what to do. We were more concerned about her, however, and one by one we knocked on her bedroom door and went in. She was in bed, brushing her hair. We told her to move over and make room.

'Don't you think you kids are too old to come and sleep with your mother?' she asked. 'Ripeka, Mere and Wiki, go back to your husbands. You, Tama, and you, Marama and Hone, you're all adults and should know better.'

Nobody was budging. Ripeka made us all a cup of tea and, very soon, we were all eating homemade scones and reminiscing about the old days. Hone and Marama tried to get under the quilts but Mum said, 'No, your feet are cold.' Even so, it was soon like all those nights when Dad was snoring and Mum was still awake and we would crawl into bed with them. Of course sentimental Mere just had to get the family photograph album, and that was always the way we got around Mum — and inveigled stories about Dad out of her.

'Oh, your *father*,' Mum sighed. 'You know, don't you, that he was seven years older than I was? When he started courting me I told him that he should find someone his own age and that he should date my older sister. But he was persistent and, well, after a while, he turned my opinions around on the matter of May marrying December. In the end I thought it was —'

'. . . better to be an old man's darling,' we chorused, 'than a young man's slave.'

So there we were, my sisters, brother and I, all grown-up and still sitting on our mother's bed as if we were children: me in my fifties, my sisters Ripeka, Mere and Wiki, in their formidable forties with their grey hair and extra poundage, and the two 'babies' now in their thirties and almost like our own children. Wiki kept the memories going by asking, 'Remember how Mum used to call us home at nights? "Tama! Ripeka! Mere! Wiki! Where are you kids? Come home before the kehua get you!"'

'That was when we were living in Gisborne,' Mere remembered. 'Oh, the pain of having a mother who had the loudest voice in Kaiti. And it was never ever dark.'

'You children are making this all up,' Mum said.

'No matter what we were doing,' Wiki continued, 'we'd hurry home as quickly as we could because otherwise Mum would keep on calling all night. She didn't care about the neighbours, did you, mother dear? When we moved and I met them in Gisborne they told me they missed the sound of Mum calling us.'

'Oh, but the worst part,' Ripeka butted in, 'was figuring out what to tell Mum when we finally got home. We couldn't tell her about our going into Poho o Rawiri meeting house because if she found out she'd give us a good clip over the ears —'

'Did you kids go into the meeting house? That meeting house was tapu. I hope none of you did anything naughty in there.'

'It wasn't what Mere did in the meeting house that we couldn't tell Mum,' Ripeka said, dobbing in her sister. 'It's the naughty things she was doing in the bushes with Johnnie Chambers, eh, Mere. Instead, we'd tell Mum we had stayed late at school *swotting*.' My sisters all roared with laughter at our mother's gullibility. Koro, who was standing in the door, glared at Mere, 'I didn't know you had been in the bushes with Johnnie Chambers.'

Mere protested her innocence. 'It's all lies, honey.'

'Ripeka, I don't know how you get your stories so wrong,' Mum interrupted in a rather droll manner. 'It wasn't Johnnie Chambers, it was that freckly-faced boy Andy Harrigan. When I saw him in the street, I snuck up on him and gave him a good boot up the behind and he knew what it was for.'

We all laughed. Wiki started Mum up again. 'Of course, we weren't the only ones that Mum had to call home. Can you remember when Dad used to disappear on Saturday mornings?'

'Oh,' Mum smiled, batting her eyelids. 'You're talking about the only other competition I had for his affections, the floozies. Always spending his money on them.'

'None of them were any good, eh, Mum,' Mere said. We were actually referring to the horses that Dad would take twenty dollars each way on.

'Nope,' Mum answered. 'It was only when I started to bet on the horses that we ever made any money at all. The secret was that my dreams were better than his and I could interpret my dreams accurately. Can you remember when I won six hundred dollars?'

Did we what? Mum bought us all rollerskates and laughed out loud at the skating rink as we fell over. Afterwards, we went to the movies, a double feature with a western called *The Last Outpost* starring Ronald Reagan and Rhonda Fleming and then *Salome*, in which Rita Hayworth as Salome danced to save John the Baptist from being beheaded. Man oh man, the Hollywood version of history and the world.

After a while, I decided I needed a breath of fresh air. I walked out onto the verandah and looked up at the stars. I suspected that the family would say enough is enough insofar as this half-brother of ours was concerned. Part of me agreed with them. The other part? Well, I had my reasons for pushing the issue as far as it could go. Nevertheless, I would abide by the consensus.

I looked through the window at my sisters and brother as they talked with Mum on her bed, remembering her and Dad and our lives. We were all so much in love with each other.

Then Ripeka gave a squeal of outrage, no doubt because the story being told targeted her, and soon somebody picked up a pillow and a pillow fight was all on. Mum was laughing so hard the tears were falling down her cheeks. Ripeka got up in a huff and walked to the door, oblivious of the pillows that were thrown at her.

'What was all that about?' I asked Ripeka.

'Oh your sisters and brother,' she said to me, as usual excluding herself from any family connection. 'They're all arguing about who will be buried next to Mum, when they know that I'm the one.' Take it or leave it and if you don't like it, tough, suck on it.

Ripeka saw me looking at the night sky. 'Your head was always in the stars,' she said.

'Yes,' I answered, 'but you, everybody, made sure that my feet were firmly on the ground, eh.'

She laughed. 'Not firmly enough.' She threaded an arm in mine. She always did this when she wanted to make some accounting of something that had happened in the past. It was her way of making sure I couldn't get away from her. Sure enough, 'And by the way,' she began, 'I want to tell you how that day ended, when those bastards came to our house.'

My heart gave a lurch. Ripeka was shaking, watching me accusingly.

'They came after us too,' she said. 'I took Mere and Wiki way down the end of the beach like you told me to do — but it wasn't far enough. After they left you and Mum, they terrorised us, calling, "Here chick, chick, chick." I put my hands over Wiki's mouth to make sure she wouldn't cry, but they got closer and closer to where we were hiding. So I left Mere and Wiki there and ran off, hoping they would follow me. I ran and ran and ran and luckily it was dark. But what would they have done if they caught me, or if they had gone back and found Mere and Wiki —'

Here chick, chick, chick. Ripeka began to shudder, huge sobs convulsing her body. I hugged her tight; no wonder she was so against Eric Amundsen. Suddenly she pushed me away — and went off on a tangent. 'When Dad died, you never intended to come back, did you.'

The question hit an exposed nerve. 'It wasn't to be. When I returned to Wellington and *The Evening Post* I was promoted. Then I was asked to go to Australia, you know that. I couldn't turn it down. I rang Mum about it. I sent money regularly, whenever you needed it.'

'Yeah,' Ripeka mocked, 'cash by telegram, your answer to everything.'

'Don't be so quick to scorn my money,' I said angrily. 'It put Hone and Marama through school. It paid the bills on the farm. You wouldn't have this wine-making business if it hadn't been for my money.'

Ripeka wasn't giving any ground. 'And was Mum supposed to say, "No, don't go," to you?' Ripeka shook her head. 'From what I remember, you never really gave her the chance anyway. It was, "I'm going," and, next moment, you were off and away into the wild blue yonder. Mum would never have said no. Don't make her your excuse for following your own selfish ambitions and desires. You know you should have come back.'

How much longer would I have to atone? 'Waituhi has always been where you were meant to be,' I answered, 'and you are what you are supposed to be. As for me, I was meant to be somewhere else, someone else.'

'Don't kid yourself,' Ripeka yelled. 'Don't you think I had my own dreams too? I would have given anything to go to Wellington or Auckland and make my own life.'

We stared angrily at each other. After all these years and still so much hurt and pain between us. Then Ripeka sighed and made a helpless gesture. 'It's been a long time since we had a good shouting match,' she said. After a while, she kissed my cheek. The kiss was not without tenderness. 'We managed without you.'

At that moment, Mere bustled out and interrupted us. 'Mum has started to cry,' she said. 'You'd better come in quick.'

Ripeka restrained me for a second. 'I better tell you now that Mere, Wiki,

Marama and I will not help Eric Amundsen. Our feeling is that if we do this we condone his father's sin. It will pass to our mother and this family. We won't have it, this passing of the sin to us by giving of our forgiveness.'

As it happened, Mum had already reached her own decision and she wished to enforce it.

She told us what it was.

11

The following day I was supposed to be in Auckland for our rehearsal. I never made it.

When I told Harriet I wasn't coming she screamed bloody murder. 'I knew this would happen,' she seethed over the phone, 'I just knew you would do this to me.'

'Please don't take this personally,' I answered. 'It's just that I'm in the middle of a family crisis. Be a dear and carry on?'

'Carry *on*?' Harriet exploded. 'What do you mean carry bloody on! This is for your benefit, Mr Mahana, as well as ours. John can work out the scripting so that all our cameras know when they're on and when they aren't, and Otis can get his live links and videotape inserts sorted out — but you still need to practise your own continuity links. Apart from which, I was hoping to run a rough draft of the script through the teleprompt to get us all stopwatch-perfect and avoid blind cuts. You're making my life very difficult, Mr Mahana — and I've got my own problems. I'm getting married to Zeb tomorrow and, oh, why did I ever agree that after the wedding we would bungy-jump off a bridge?'

Harriet began to shout imprecations to whichever gods of television were listening and, coward that I am, I decided the best thing to do was to put the phone down, tiptoe away, and wait until she got over it. Sure enough, five minutes later, the phone rang again.

'Is that you, Tom?' It was Paul. 'Harriet has explained you won't be here today.' There was a meaningful pause — I knew Paul must be popping tranquillisers by the handful to keep himself from losing his temper. 'As it happens, John Campbell has taken a distinct liking for your captain's chair. He's only too happy to sit in and rehearse your lines for you — your intros and outros, turns and throws to Kim, her throws back to you, so that the inserts can be brought in at the right place and right time. Just make sure you get here in plenty of time tomorrow for the taping so that at least Harriet, John and I can quickly brief you before you go on set? Jolly good.'

The next morning, I made sure I got to Gisborne airport for the 8.30 flight. Just before I left, Gabriella phoned from her cottage in Surrey to wish me luck. I needed it.

'It must be lovely down there in New Zealand,' she said. 'But mornings like we had today redeem England somewhat. Palpably warm sunshine at dawn, dew heavy on the grass, an orchestra of birds outside. I do hope your trip is going well and that you are not being pulled in too many directions. You have such huge horizons these days. Say hello to the soul of your country for me? And come back soon.'

No sooner was I on board the Metroliner, however, than all the passengers had to disembark and go back to the terminal. The plane had developed some problem in its circuitry. 'Not to worry, folks,' the pilot told us. 'A replacement plane is on its way to us from Wellington and we'll have you back up in the air and on your way in a jiffy.'

A jiffy? That wasn't going to cut any ice with Harriet; I was for the high jump now. The scheduled flight would at least have got me to the studio to have that conversation with the production team and, if time allowed, with Otis and the technical crew — and also to quickly run through the final continuity script. You think that a television show just happens? Think again. *Spaceship Earth* was on countdown to launch. Paul and Harriet would be busy in the control room with the vision switcher, VT operator and director's assistant, ticking off their checklist hour by hour, then quarter hour by quarter hour, then minute by minute, until we reached zero, CHECK. John would be on his own countdown with the floor technicians, lighting operators, cameramen and teleprompt operator to make sure the studio was efficiently firing up, CHECK. Meanwhile, Otis would be establishing the live links to our London studio — and to all our correspondents around the world — and, thirty minutes before we went to air, running them on standby so that they would be available at call, CHECK. As for Kim, she would be prepping her own segments and pissing everybody off by making mad dashes out of the studio to have a smoke, CHECK.

The trouble was — where was the captain? I phoned the studio to tell them the bad news about the plane's delay. I didn't dare speak to Harriet or Paul in person, so I told the phone operator at Television Three to pass on my message. Then I ordered up a cup of tea and biscuits and waited for the replacement aircraft.

A comment Gabriella had made during her phone call flashed through my mind. Huge horizons? Yes, indeed. In 1987, the year after Sandra and the children left Hong Kong, I was asked if I'd like to transfer as an anchorman to CNN's Washington bureau. Ironically, among the others who were considered for the job was Bob Blakeney, my colleague from NewsCorp days. I got the job; he didn't. From that time on, we became competitors.

While on a quick trip to New York for a celebrity function, I met a Black American model, Victoria. After a whirlwind romance, we married. You can call it the consequence of a rush of blood to the head. I mistook beauty for love, flattery for commitment, passion for politics. Apart from which, Victoria was decorative and made me look good. Otherwise, the marriage was a mistake and mercifully short. I was better off single and able to commit myself wholly to my job.

From Washington, I travelled the world for CNN. Whenever the news was breaking, I was on a plane to report on it wherever it was: Iran, Kosovo, Israel, Guatemala, Iraq, you name it. I covered every international story that hit the headlines and, often, reported on the stories that then made the headlines.

Sandra met Stewart, a lawyer and widower with two children of his own, at some solo parents' potluck or other. They blended their two families together and managed to retain their sanity through all the squabbles and uproar of bringing up teenagers. Brave souls, they even had the courage to have their own child, Nathan and Holly's half-sister, Anna.

Of course it wasn't as easy as all that. Although Holly forgave a fantasy father who was always travelling around the world and whom she only saw now and then, Nathan didn't. He hated leaving Hong Kong and he rebelled against his stepfather. Just after he completed his sixth form year at school, Sandra shipped him off to stay with me in Washington for six months where we embarked on a series of stormy father–son encounters filled with bitter recriminations and accusations.

'You abandoned me, Dad,' he cried. 'I waited for you to come and get me in New Zealand and you didn't, you selfish bastard.'

'Don't you use that language with me, young man,' I answered. 'Okay, I'll apologise for not being there when you might have wanted me to be — but look at you now. You're grown up, your mother tells me you're doing well at school, and I'm proud of you. And don't we have fun together?' Whenever he and Holly came on holidays I would always take them somewhere adventurous like whale-watching off the coast of Hawaii, climbing ancient Aztec pyramids in Mexico or swimming with stingrays in Tahiti or skiing in Switzerland.

'Yeah,' Nathan said. 'Well thanks, but no thanks. Did you ever stop to think what it was like for Holly and me when we got back to New Zealand after visiting you? No, you didn't, did you.' Tears were streaming down his face. 'Holly cried herself to sleep at nights. As for me, I soon realised you weren't worth crying over. I can get along without you just fine.'

'Nathan,' I answered, as I tried to embrace him, 'a manual doesn't come with the job of being a father. I did the best I could. I'm the only dad you have and you're the only son that I have — and we've got to get through all this stuff between us.'

In 1995, I had another job offer. This time it was from my current boss, Lord Sanderson, a Richard Branson-type but without the showbiz style. He was setting up World Wide News in London. 'Name your price,' he said.

To be frank, I had reached an impasse in America — and I was itching to go to the next level. I was really attracted to Lord Sanderson's vision of setting up a service which would be an alternative to the way in which CNN, TBC, MSNBC and Fox News, with their overriding American imperatives, were broadcasting and distributing international news to the world. I named my price. Lord Sanderson didn't even blanch — which made me wish I had gone higher. I moved to London. All this, including my rivalry with Bob Blakeney, who became anchorman for the BBC's own weekly news show at the same time as I started helming *Spaceship Earth*, is written in my autobiography, *Only the Highest Mountain.*

As for Nathan and Holly, they grew into an independent pair of adults that any parent could be proud of. Nathan twigged to the fact that, actually, the whole world was a playground. He joined the Ministry of Foreign Affairs and then, while on a posting to Geneva, jumped ship and began a career in international environmental law — it was only a short dive from there to the more adventurous and activist approach to saving the world offered by Greenpeace. Holly had always been the sensible one; she went into banking, where at least she was able to make good money.

Somehow, although Nathan and I continued to have intense arguments that exhausted us both, we all survived.

Finally, the replacement aircraft arrived and, two hours behind schedule, we took off for Auckland.

'Sorry folks,' the pilot said breezily from the cockpit, 'but this looks like it's going to be one of those days. Auckland airport is closed by fog.' *Fog*? 'We're hoping it will have dispersed enough by the time we arrive for us to land.'

Although we wouldn't begin taping until 2 pm, I began to feel anxious. Nevertheless, there was nothing I could do about it so I sat back and, instead, tried to enjoy the company of an energetic brunette woman named Liz who was connecting in Auckland to a flight to Los Angeles. A young entrepreneur in the plastics industry, she showed me the design boards of a product she was taking onto the international market. People were always doing this to me: showing me their wares and telling me their stories and dreams.

'We must reinvent ourselves,' Liz said. 'And as for New Zealand conquering the world? It's already a done deal.'

We were interrupted by the pilot. 'Hello again, folks,' he said, as relaxed and casual as ever. 'It looks like Auckland airport remains closed, so we're going to make a teeny weeny detour to Hamilton. We have a message for Mr Mahana from a very cross PA of yours named Harriet. A car will be waiting for you at Hamilton with strict instructions to get you to the Auckland studio pronto double pronto.'

At Hamilton, a young chauffeur was waiting at the gate and, after I had given him my autograph, he sat me in the back of his limousine. Very soon we were speeding to Auckland. I picked up the carphone and dialled Harriet.

She completely lost her cool. 'It's going to take you at least an hour and a half to get from Hamilton to the studio,' she said, 'and you've already missed most of the windows in our schedule today. Oh, well, so what else is new.' Harriet was referring to other fly-by-Tom's-pants tapings which had occurred over the years when I had either missed scheduled flights to London from New York or Paris — or been held up by bad connections from, say, Marseilles to Paris to London.

The consequence was that sometimes I arrived just as the show was going on air. On one occasion, the cameras had started showing the credits and there I was, behind them, with a makeup girl dusting my face with powder and Harriet berating me and threatening to hit me over the head with her clipboard.

'So where are we at with the countdown?' I asked.

'Well, John Campbell has heard you've been delayed and, right now, he's on bended knees begging Paul like you wouldn't believe to fly the big bird. The guests for your second and third segments will be arriving in the Green Room in an hour and doors will open to the audience in ninety minutes. The stopwatch is ticking.'

I heard the telephone being snatched from Harriet's hands. Paul came on the line, and his breathing was erratic. 'So you're on your way then? Good-oh.' Of all the production staff, Paul's job was to maintain an imperturbable calm even in the worst possible circumstances. 'Despite your late arrival, I am not expecting any problems with the first three quarters of an hour of news and the three interview segments that follow. However, we are all extremely anxious about the continuity for the finale, Tom. This is a big technical exercise for us, the biggest we've ever tackled. It's going to be nerve-wracking enough to get all our live links coming in on time. There's a hell of a lot of cutting and mixing to do with the studio and the VT links as well, and a huge potential for disaster.'

'Okay,' I answered. 'As long as all our people are ready to beam aboard *Spaceship Earth* we'll be fine. Are they?'

'Yes,' Paul answered. 'Our African reporter, Umbelo, is broadcasting from Kilimanjaro. Sylvia, over in France, will be on her mark at the bottom of the Eiffel Tower. Pedro, in South America, plans to join us from somewhere in the middle of the Amazon. Rachel in our New York office is having trouble with the city officials about our use of the Statue of Liberty for our show but, if it's impossible, she'll be in a tugboat as close to old Lady Liberty as she can get. I've got Jurgen coming to us from the Holocaust Museum in Berlin and Bob is beaming in from Uluru in Australia. In Iraq, Peter is coming to us somewhere on the border — that's a difficult one, but we'll pinpoint him via our satellite and beam him aboard. Where else? Oh, you mentioned East Timor. Sakiri is already on her way to the rendezvous with the cameraman in Dili. As for Lord Sanderson, he's hoping to come to us from Princess Diana's fountain memorial; otherwise, he plans to be aboard a hot-air balloon.'

The usually imperturbable Paul was betraying unusual tremors in his voice.

'But, Tom, I know your penchant for ad libbing. Would you mind keeping it to a minimum, there's a good chap? Otis tells me that the live links to Kilimanjaro, the Amazon and East Timor are fragile and, if the show runs overtime, there's a danger of losing them. And Sakiri's link is via laptop.'

'Just tell Otis to follow my lead,' I said. One way or another, the grand finale was going to end with a bang. What kind of bang was the question.

'I was afraid you'd say that,' Paul answered.

I reached Auckland's Television Three studio with half an hour before cameras started rolling. The live audience, waiting to get in, clapped as I arrived at the stage door. Not so Harriet, who was waiting with her letter of resignation.

'This looks familiar,' I told her. 'Didn't you last give it to me in 2004? You could at least have retyped it on a fresh piece of paper. Submit it again after the next show.'

Harriet stormed after me with her clipboard as I headed to talk with Paul in the production room.

'Thank God,' he said. 'I was just about to tell John Campbell to suit up.' Now that I was there in person, he let fly. 'Why do you always have to be such a damn buccaneer? We've been stretched to the max here and, had you joined the countdown when you were supposed to do, life would have been a whole lot easier. Now we're into the final, oh no, thirty minutes, Jesus Ker-rist.' He turned away from me towards the rows of monitor screens and began speaking into his headphones to John on the studio floor and Otis in the communications suite. 'You'll be pleased to know that the captain has arrived,' he said.

I took a quick look at the monitors. Each screen showed different pictures: either the shots of the set from cameras 1, 2 or 3, or pictures of the VT items or live links that were being cued for eventual showing on portals 1 to 6 of the Vidiwall. On the first of the screens I saw Kim, already at her console and furiously chewing gum. The second screen showed John Campbell holding on tight to my chair, not wishing to relinquish it. On the third was Robin, beaming in to us from our London studio; he was our co-anchor whenever Kim and I did outside broadcasts. The fourth screen showed a VT item, giving the quick history of apartheid, which would run during our segment on the demise of the National Party in South Africa. On the fifth was a shot of a studio in Johannesburg where Nelson Mandela was being miked in preparation for his live interview to go with the South Africa story; he gave a cheery wave to the camera. The sixth screen showed the studio audience, seating themselves for tonight's show.

As for me, Harriet yanked me after her to makeup. 'You've been stressing me out big time,' she muttered. I was getting very nervous. They were stretched to the max? What about *me*? I had to appear in front of the camera and keep our hour-long show on track. If they messed up, no problem. But if I did, the whole world would be my audience. While I was in the makeup chair, Harriet took out her stopwatch and started my own countdown.

'Ten minutes to lift off, Mr Mahana.' Harriet had reverted to formality because she was so cross.

I sat in the chair being dusted, powdered and styled and tried to calm my own nerves. Basically, as Paul had noted, the first three quarters of an hour would look after itself. In the first fifteen minutes we would have the news of the world. My various correspondents would call in, file their reports, and I would then get into a short conversation with them about the issues arising from their reports. The second half hour involved the three segments on South Africa, the new pope, and the interview with some very special New Zealand women — they would require closer attention. Paul, Harriet, John and Kim preferred to have a script that was nailed down and word-perfect. I had always taken a looser approach; I believed in bringing a certain amount of stress to every broadcast. I liked to leave gaps for spontaneity. The secret was to leave enough unscripted for the possibility of the illuminating moment, the surprising insight. That meant that sometimes the show scaled the heights to the sublime. Sometimes, however, I ended up with egg on my face. I hoped that this afternoon was not going to be one of those times. Anyhow, hadn't Paul told me to go easy on the ad libbing?

The ten-minute finale was the one to be really worried about.

'Five minutes,' Harriet announced. 'Time for Mr Mahana to take his seat in *Spaceship Earth*.' She yanked me unceremoniously out from the makeup chair and pushed me toward wardrobe where she shoved me into my high-collared black jacket.

'Ouch,' I said. Harriet was fastening the buttons so fast she clipped my chin with a sharp fingernail.

'I'll give you ouch,' she muttered. 'And,' she continued sotto voce, ruffling the back of my head, 'that will make sure your bald spot really shows. Three minutes —'

As meek as a lamb I followed Harriet into the studio. My arrival was greeted with whistles and cheers except from John Campbell, who yelled out, 'You made it, you bugger!' Then a boy with blond hair, sitting to one side, called, 'Hey, Dude!' It was Henrik Kruger, the young Gisborne Boys High student, with his parents. I'd asked them to appear on the show during the segment on South Africa.

'Two minutes,' Harriet said, waiting as I kissed Kim on her somewhat frigid cheek. I smiled to the audience and took my chair. 'Mr Mahana is in the captain's seat.' The sound man clipped on my microphone and inserted my earpiece. Just before Harriet went to join Paul in the control room I turned to her. 'Thank you, Harriet,' I said. 'You know I couldn't fly this thing without you.'

'Oh, you, you —' she spluttered before she rushed off.

'Are you in position, Tom?' Paul's voice sounded in my earphone. 'Can we have a sound check on Tom, please? That's excellent. Can we have a sound check on Kim, please? Thank you very much. Studio standing by. Audio standing by. Opening on titles in thirty seconds. Going in ten seconds, and —'

'Ten.' The lights went down on the audience. 'Silence in the studio, please.' The lights came up on the set. It was stunning. Kim and I sat at our separate consoles, opposite each other.

'Nine, and cue music.' The sound engineer brought the theme from *Star Trek* slowly up, increasing the volume. Camera 3 tracked past me and Kim. I felt the usual adrenalin rush. My thoughts went back ten years ago, to 1995. On my first day with WWN, Lord Sanderson said to me, 'You may be wondering why I wanted you to work for me? I want you to be the anchorman of a weekly news digest show. I need a popular concept and I want a show that will be the flagship for WWN's news fleet.' I came up with the concept of *Spaceship Earth*, put myself in the captain's seat, and the rest was history.

'Eight, and open all portals please.' I loved this moment. The set was curved and, one by one, windows began to slide open showing the universe. Against the backdrop of the Milky Way were stars twinkling and dazzling until all the windows were open — and the stars were singing and moving, and we were a spaceship flying through space.

'Seven.' There were whistles and cheers from the audience as the music reached a crescendo. I heard Paul call for a better match between Camera 1 and Camera 3. God, what a journey *Spaceship Earth* had given me. Over ten years I had been witness to all the world's great events. I had seen the births and deaths of many nations. I had been privy to the momentous political upheavals which had shaken the world in Kosovo, Saudi Arabia, Iraq, Korea and the African continent. I had covered the US presidential elections, the British elections, all the major elections of the EC, the Middle East and Africa.

'Six, and roll VT, cue Earth.' The floor of the set shimmered, disappeared and suddenly, there was the globe of our planet below, and Kim and I appeared to be suspended above it. This time, the applause from our live audience was louder. Energised, I grinned at Kim.

'Five.' Wherever there had been a major international event, *Spaceship Earth* had been there to cover it. I'd reported the world's tragedies like 9/11 or the Bali bombings. I had covered the pain of those events and witnessed the rebirth of the human spirit. I had interviewed everybody from Kofi Annan to President Chirac, from Madonna to Jonah Lomu, from Katherine Hepburn to Sting.

'Four, and cue credits.' And now, *Spaceship Earth* was circling the globe. Below, the world revolved. The credits began to roll. WWN. SPACESHIP EARTH. WITH TOM MAHANA AND KIM PRENTICE.

'Three.' I heard Paul's voice in my earphone. He gave the habitual phrase. 'Houston, we have reached park altitude. All yours, Tom.'

'Two, and Cam 1, tight on Tom please. Standby live link, London Newsroom.'

'One. You're looking good, Tom. Autocue rolling on Cam 1.'

I lifted my face to the light, smiled my lopsided grin, and began my piece to camera. 'Good evening, all of you who love our planet. My name is Tom Mahana and you are watching *Spaceship Earth*. Thank you for joining me and my co-host, Kim Prentice.' I made an eyeline throw to Kim. She picked up on it.

'This is a special night for us, isn't it, Tom,' she said. 'Tonight we celebrate the tenth anniversary of *Spaceship Earth*.'

I saw Camera 2 crab to the left and looked into it. I couldn't stop myself. 'And you don't look a day older than when you joined us,' I answered. The reply was unscripted, and Paul admonished me through the earphones, naughty, naughty. But it got Kim out of her mood. Laughing, she volleyed with, 'Neither do you, Tom.'

'Get back on track, boys and girls,' Paul said.

I turned to Camera 4. 'Tonight,' I continued, 'we're coming to you live from New Zealand.' As I said the words, the Southern Cross appeared on portal 3. The entire studio erupted into cheers and wolf-whistles. 'And tonight we'll be celebrating our tenth anniversary with some special guests from New Zealand

and around the world, so stay with us. Okay, Kim, what's been happening on our planet this week?'

Portal 2 opened. Robin, in London, appeared and began to read the news. 'In Britain today, Prime Minister Mr Tony Blair announced —'

We were on our way.

By the halfway mark, the broadcast was going to plan. Not only that, but the live audience was racking up the amps, a sure sign that the energy was coming off the studio floor and zapping, spontaneous and uncontaminated, through the ether into every home that was watching us around the world.

Stopwatch in hand, Paul patiently kept up his running instructions to Kim and me, John's studio crew and Otis's technical team, directing us all with focus, patience and kindliness — even when we made the occasional errors. His calm repetition of the words 'thank you' kept us all up and buoyant. John was particularly pleased with the camera crew working the floor. Under Otis's supervision, the New Zealand technicians were doing a fantastic job catching the incoming signals that bounced into our studio in Auckland: from Washington DC, where President Bush was giving a briefing on his forthcoming trip to Europe to attend celebrations marking fifty years since the end of World War II; from Iran, where three days of rioting had broken out in the oil-producing Khuzestan province; from Russia where President Putin was making moves towards another term in office. The technicians hadn't dropped a catch and it was just beautiful to see the way they dissolved and cut the pictures onto the portals.

The first interview of the evening went extremely well. I was anchoring the segment. 'Standby portal 3,' Paul instructed Otis, 'for VT insert on Tom's last words, "Split the world with its policy of apartheid." Roll first image forward.'

On set, I did my piece to camera. 'The world has seen governments come and go,' I began. 'Today, we record the passing of the organisation that was once one of the most powerful administrations on the African continent, an organisation which, in its time, split the world with its policy of apartheid.'

'Roll VT,' Paul said. The segment began with black and white images of African men and women living in a segregated nation. They were harsh, punitive, images of brutality and murder, and ending with a montage of poverty-stricken Soweto.

'But this is Soweto today,' I continued. I watched admiringly as Paul and Otis fluidly mixed and cut the videotaped documentary onto all the portals. Of course I knew what was coming next — but the live audience didn't. All of a sudden, through the studio doors rushed South African students living in New Zealand. They came dancing, they came singing in celebration of the end of a rule of tyranny, and some of them were in traditional African costume. The audience began to applaud. As Paul mixed their images onto the Vidiwall, the portals exploded with the vibrant colours of freedom and joy. Among the group were friends of mine who had protested against the Springbok tour of New Zealand in 1981. Joining them — this time not in a haka but a Zulu war dance — was Henrik Kruger. *A blond South African boy? Doing a Zulu dance?*

Then I heard Paul cueing me in. 'Tom, Nelson Mandela is coming in on live feed from Johannesburg. Remember that there is a two-second delay in responses between you both. Otis, please boost the signal. Thank you.'

The benign face of Nelson Mandela appeared in the studio. The audience cheered as I turned to that glorious man and asked, 'Any words, Nelson?' He grinned and raised his hand. 'Amandla! Amandla Soweto!'

Thirty minutes to go, and Paul was euphoric. Kim did a great job interrogating the pope's Hitler Jugend past in her conversation with Jurgen, our stringer in Berlin, reporting from the pope's old hometown in Traunstein.

'Jurgen,' she said, 'this is a man who has become one of the most powerful leaders in the world. Yet his election, matched against almost every index of what the cardinals were supposed to be looking for in a successor to John Paul II, is puzzling. What's the inside story? And what's the prognosis for the Catholic Church in the future?'

During a four-minute commercial break in the studio, Paul sprinted from the control room to shake my hand. 'We must do these live broadcasts more often. We've got *Spaceship Earth* on a good orbit. Keep it up there. Lord Sanderson has rung in person from London to say that the audience figures for tonight's show are coming in and it looks like we've gone through the roof. Well done, old chap, jolly good.' The buzz coming off the studio audience just kept on getting better and better.

I stood on the sidelines, having a glass of water. Half my face had slid off and my makeup was being repaired.

Then it was my turn again. 'Back to your chair, Tom,' Paul instructed. 'Autocue rolling on Cam 2.'

'Over a hundred and twenty years ago,' I began, 'it was the country that we are reporting from, New Zealand, that was the first in the world to give women the vote.' As I was speaking, the videotaped documentary of New Zealand suffragettes appeared on the screen. 'Now, in 2005, that same country has the distinction of having a woman prime minister, a woman governor-general, a woman as speaker of the House, a woman as chief justice, two women heading opposition parties, a woman heading New Zealand's largest corporation, and the first transsexual member of any parliament in the world. Ladies and gentlemen, please welcome the New Zealand matriarchy.'

To whistles and cheers, Helen Clark, Dame Silvia Cartwright, Margaret Wilson, Dame Sian Elias, Jeanette Fitzsimons, Tariana Turia, Theresa Gattung and Georgina Beyer strode onto the set. Georgina tried to take over the position at my console, which caused great hilarity. I hadn't even started the interview when the prime minister, Helen Clark, looked at the audience and the cameras and laughed, 'So what's the problem?'

After that, all I had to do was to signal to the matriarchy that the stage was theirs and to watch them, in admiration, as they let it *rip*.

Five minutes later, Paul began his briefing for the finale. 'I know we're all enjoying ourselves, ladies and gentlemen, but here comes the hard part. Otis, how are those links with Kilimanjaro, the Amazon and East Timor? Do they have audio contact? Harriet, please be prepared to mix VT links if we have problems. John, I am relying on you, also, to mix studio shots if necessary. Here we go. Standby, Otis. Standby, John. Standby, Tom and Kim. Fast windup, 5, 4, 3, 2 and 1. The captain has the con.'

I turned to the camera. The mood was electric. 'Well, we've had a great night, haven't we, Kim?' I asked.

'Yes,' Kim answered, ad libbing. 'We couldn't have had a better programme to celebrate our tenth anniversary, and a more beautiful country to celebrate it in than New Zealand.'

Cheers and whistles erupted from the audience. 'Surprise, Tom,' Paul said into my earpiece. 'Bring in the birthday cake.' I laughed out loud. The cake was five tiers tall.

'Is somebody jumping out of this?' I asked.

'Keep it tight,' Paul said into my earpiece. Harriet must have drawn Paul's attention to his stopwatch. 'Time to bring the show home.'

I smiled to camera. 'I want to thank our guests, our presenters, all the crews who have worked on *Spaceship Earth* over the last ten years. We've been committed to bringing you the news of all the men and women of this planet, their dreams, desires, successes, failures. But why do we do it? Why witness our failures and our triumphs? Who is it for? The wise people I am descended from have asked the same question but in a different way: "What is the most important treasure in the world?" Ladies and gentlemen, the answer is children. They are our future. Tonight we dedicate our finale to the children — because how can you have a birthday, or a future, without them? Ladies and gentlemen, introducing the children of the world.'

'Here we go,' Paul said. 'Good luck to all.'

And, oh, it was so fantastic to see Paul, Harriet, John and Otis doing their job. All the portals opened. The music swelled and shimmered.

Bring me my bow of burning gold. Elton John's orchestration filled the studio and, suddenly, all the screens began to fill with walking, running, laughing, joyful children. They were climbing Mt Kilimanjaro at dawn with Umbelo, our African reporter.

Bring me my arrows of desire. They were standing in front of the Eiffel Tower with Rachel, waving sparklers against the coming of night. They were splashing water with Pedro in the middle of the Amazon River while a huge rainbow arced into the sky. They were walking with Jurgen through the floodlit Holocaust Memorial in Berlin.

Bring me my spear. Oh clouds, unfold! Rachel in New York was laughing, 'Well, we couldn't get the Statue of Liberty but we got this,' and the shot widened to show six tugs with children on them, the tugs spouting water into the air. Bob was climbing Uluru in Australia.

Bring me my chariot of fire! They were children of all sizes, colour and gender. But as they flashed on the screen, their images began to change. Peter appeared with children on the border of Iraq, suddenly emerging out of a cloud of dust. 'We haven't got much time,' he said to the camera. 'Happy birthday, everybody. Remember us.' The children looked frail, fragile, like injured birds who might not be able to make the journey home. Then Sakiri came in from East Timor. The children she had with her were shepherded towards the camera. 'Happy birthday,' they called shyly.

Finally, Umbelo came back. In his arms was a dying African child.

Paul froze that image on the screen. Faded the music down into silence. Panned across that ravaged, bony body with its tiny heart beating within its skeletal frame. Did a close up on those huge, luminous eyes, looking out at the world, eyes that did not have enough moisture to be able to cry.

You could have heard a pin drop.

Yes indeed, somebody had to bear witness to man's inhumanity to man, especially when it was directed against the most innocent among us all. Someone had to track the beast as he slouched into people's lives, most often in the guise of a man with a gun and with an army of thugs to support his cowardice, especially if the victims were innocent children. Someone had to remind the world that a child died every three seconds, most often from poverty caused by adults and that, with them, we died too.

I stood up from my console and walked towards the Vidiwall. As I did so, the image of the dying child repeated itself on all the portals. My nerves were at stretch point.

'One child is everybody's child,' I said. 'Every child in the world is our child. It's too easy to give up, to despair, to say it's too hard. We've got to have more courage, more determination, try harder. The questions are very simple. What will we leave our children when we are gone? Will we leave them enough food? Enough water? Enough energy resources to keep them warm? How safe will their world be? Will we have left them a future which, if not free of wars, contains at least the hope that someday there will be peace on the planet?

'Daunting and complex though the challenges are, let's put poverty on notice. Let's tell those governments whose repressive acts kill children or violate their rights that they will not be tolerated. Let's not leave our children political, economic, cultural debt that they have no capacity to repay. Death should not be their legacy. They deserve life and the chance to grow into the fullness of their years.'

In the studio, the audience was standing up and cheering. John Campbell had tears in his eyes.

My nerves *held*.

'It's up to us.'

And Paul brought the music to crescendo. Back on the portals were the live links from around the world, with all the world's beautiful children in their joyous innocence. But when Paul spoke to me on the earpiece his voice had an urgent tone. 'Tom,' he said, 'we lose our links in thirty seconds.'

I shall not cease from mental fight. The screens showed them all: Aboriginal children, African children, First Nations Indian children running across dispossessed plains.

'Tom,' Paul said, 'our relay is breaking up with the Amazon. It's also fading with Tanganyika. We can't hold it much longer.'

Nor shall my sword sleep in my hand. They were American children outside the Lincoln Memorial.

'Sorry, Tom,' Paul said, his normal calm fragmenting, 'we've lost the link to Dili. Don't go over. Get out of there, quick.'

Till we have built Jerusalem in all our green and pleasant lands. Finally, an avuncular presence, Lord Sanderson, walked with children of all races in Kensington Palace Park.

'Ten seconds to credits, Tom,' Paul said. 'Fast windup.'

I turned to the camera and smiled my lopsided grin. 'This is Tom Mahana, and this has been our report on the human race from *Spaceship Earth* this week.'

The theme music from *Star Trek* filled the studio. The tumult in the audience was deafening. People were whistling and roaring with excitement. I didn't even hear the cue that Tom sent to Harriet. 'He's all yours, Harriet, dear.' I didn't even see Harriet until the last moment when she grabbed the top layer of the birthday cake, a really nice, creamy, soggy segment and, giggling with merriment, took aim.

'You wouldn't,' I said. She did.

'Mmmm, strawberry flavoured,' I deadpanned. I hoped that somewhere in the world, children laughed.

'Roll credits, standby to fade to black, fade music, stop recording.' Paul gave a deep sigh. 'Well, ladies and gentlemen,' he continued, 'we made it by the skin of our teeth.' Behind him, I could hear shouts of jubilation. 'Thank you all. Thank you, Kim. Good job, Otis and your crew. John, please say thanks to our New Zealand floor staff. Well done, Captain Mahana.'

'It's a wrap.'

12

'**h**aere mai, e te manuhiri tuarangi e, haere mai, haere mai, haere mai.'

Two days after the broadcast, I stood with the people of Te Whanau a Kai on the marae at Rongopai. My mother sat on a chair on the porch, looking across the sunlit courtyard to the gateway. She had made her decision about Eric Amundsen and, on this day, closure of some kind would occur for him, for her and for our family.

My mother always took particular care over her appearance. There was something about her that was timeless. Her face was eternal. She could have been sitting there for a thousand years. On either side, my sisters Ripeka, Mere and Wiki were standing guard like an Amazon sisterhood around their queen.

'Karanga mai, karanga mai, karanga mai e te tipuna whare e.'

The answering call came from the gateway. Standing there, preparing to approach, was a small group of strangers. They had come from the South Island. Wiremu Gray was their elder and he had brought his mother to perform the visitor's karanga as they came on to our marae. They were escorting Mrs Amundsen, Eric and Coral Amundsen and their two children to Rongopai. With them was Dr Stephens. They had come because Rongopai was a place of healing. My mother had agreed to acknowledge Eric's blood relationship.

I looked at my own whanau group: Mum, Ripeka, Mere, Wiki, Marama, Hone, Sam, Koro and Darren. I had sought out my cousins, Andrew, Michael and Simeon, and their families to support us. No sentimentality should be attached to the way we were feeling about this outcome. My mother's face had etched upon it the inevitability of acceptance, but Ripeka was as angry and resistant as ever. In all our arguments, one theme had been constant with her: 'Why should we forgive and forget? Why should we accommodate? Why should we offer reconciliation? Will this always be our burden?' Ripeka blamed me for what was happening. She said I should have overruled our mother; but I had a reason not to. Ah well, so what else was new between Ripeka and myself? It wasn't the first time Ripeka had been angry with me and it sure as eggs wouldn't be the last. As for my other sisters and my brother Hone, they, like the spiral, oscillated between acceptance and rejection. The brothers-in-law were staying well clear. In time, a further weighing of past with present would occur. Perhaps at some point, somewhere, we would find the balance. Meantime, even though a decision had been made, it had not yet settled.

Wiremu Gray led the group onto the marae. The karanga echoed back and forth between Mrs Gray and Hine Ropiho, who was our kuia. I watched Eric Amundsen as he approached. He was making swimming movements with his arms, his eyes were glowing with gladness. What did he see as he swam towards the river that wasn't a river? Did he see the destination on the other side? The meeting house with a roof sloping upward to the painted koruru at the apex, affirming that Rongopai was still holding up the sky? The maihi, the boards, extending like arms from the koruru to welcome him and his family? Inside the porch, swirling kowhaiwhai designs, did he see the richness of tribal history? Did he see that the meeting house was, itself, a tupuna?

If he did, all its millennial dreams would be his legacy too.

And how would he feel when he walked into Rongopai? Would he have the same emotions as I always experience when I walk into this house? Would he see his own destiny within that illuminated forest? How would he react to the glistening creatures as they slithered amid the stars of that woven sky, the people who stood or climbed among the branches and the glittering creatures of another world soaring upward to the rafters?

'The past is not behind you, Eric Amundsen, it is in front of you. It is a long line of ancestors to whom you are accountable and with whom you have an implicit contract.'

Would he, in the fullness of time, commit to his ancestors?

Only time would tell. Only time.

Wiremu Gray, Mrs Amundsen, Eric Amundsen and the rest of their ope stood before Rongopai. Heads bowed, they paid their respects. After a while, I signalled that they should take their seats so that the mihimihi between tangata whenua and waewae tapu could begin.

But Eric Amundsen would not move. He stood there, looking at the space between himself and Rongopai. For two years he had been dreaming of a river and had tried to join its stream, but it wasn't a river. Spiralling out of nowhere was a rope stretching from the beginning to the end of time, from the beginning of the universe to the universe's end. The rope was as breathtaking as it was immense. It was the Rope of Man, Te Taura Tangata, singing its eternal songs.

Eric Amundsen blinked. He looked at Mum. 'Are you my mother?' he asked.

Tears of despair were streaming down my mother's eyes. 'Yes,' she said.

This time as he swam towards the river, the rope recognised him. A strand of the rope, like a plant's tendril, reached out to wrap itself around him and caught him as he fell.

In the evening, I stood on the verandah and looked up at the stars. Somehow or other, the night over Waituhi was always so bright with stars, as if all the eyes of heaven were clustering above the valley. I had never known such clarity except over deserts, ice wastelands or veldt where Man had not obscured the night with his own artificial light. The stars poured into the valley.

Earlier that day Nathan and Holly had phoned. Nathan had completed his work in Tierra del Fuego and was in New York with Holly on his way up to the Arctic Circle to protest about the Canadian government's culling of the seals. 'Have you seen the pictures in the newspapers, Daddy?' Holly asked. 'And those awful hunters shooting them?'

'It's really good to hear from you,' I said. 'I wish you and your brother were both here with me in Waituhi.' I was feeling sentimental and emotional.

Nathan came on the phone. 'Hi, Dad,' he began. 'We saw *Spaceship Earth* this week. Congratulations, you really nailed it.' Then he laughed. 'Missing us, huh?'

His words made me realise how difficult our relationship still was, and I wanted to say to him, 'Nathan, enough already.' Instead, 'Of course I miss you,' I answered. I still had a lot of work to do with him and his sister before they gave me the unconditional love they had for Sandra. The kind of relationship we were trying to forge was that of adults treating each other in a grown-up fashion; we were working on it. And even though I had not been there for them in the past,

I was now, goddammit.

'How's Grandma?' Nathan asked. 'Tell her I'll be coming down her way to take her on a date to see some turtles in the Galapagos.'

'Make it soon, son,' I said. 'Make it soon.' Thoughts of my mother's mortality made me think of my own and, although I was not insisting that Nathan feel any obligation to his father, he did to others in his life. 'If anything happens to me, look after your mother and sister.'

I put down the phone. My words to Nathan sounded familiar and I began to smile as I realised the irony in them; my own dad had said something similar to me, those many years ago. I wondered if Dad had been as frustrated with me as I sometimes was with Nathan as he pushed his wilful way through the world. What was it that Stephen Hawking had once told me on *Spaceship Earth*? He had talked about the chaos theory and the butterfly effect, something about the fact that a butterfly flapping its wings on one side of the world could cause a cyclone on the other. All I had ever done, many years ago, was leave Waituhi as a young man. Now I lived on the other side of the world, and all around was the turbulence of my passage on arrogant wings.

I heard laughter from inside the homestead. My mother, sisters and brother were all in the sitting room. Love for them spilled over the rim of my heart. I thought of Dad and how proud he would have been to see us in our adulthood. He had loved this family, and we loved being a family.

But what kind of shape was the family now being forced to take? Indeed, what shape was the New Zealand family taking, as new pressures, new challenges, new blood took us all beyond traditional kinships? All I knew was that the absorption of Eric Amundsen into our family was leading to transformations which we were struggling with. When Mum had called us to hear her decision two nights ago she had said, 'This is not a decision for me to make — or you. Let the meeting house decide.'

Whether we liked it or not, Rongopai had made the decision. Eric Amundsen's blood and, therefore, his heritage could not be denied him. As a consequence, an ungainly shape was lurching out at us. Bits were sticking out. Odd angles. Difficult compulsions. We had tried to grapple with issues of legitimacy, illegitimacy, legal and human rights. We had learnt a lot about life's surprises. Things came at you when you weren't looking and, before you knew it, the future was changed. Although accepting Eric Amundsen was a redemptive act, an act of reconciliation, this wasn't the end of it. This was just the beginning. There were lots of big issues and intimate ones ahead which would challenge our sense of humanity. We'd just have to make the best of it.

I heard the door twang and saw Mum coming to join me. She threaded an arm in mine and, for a moment, we didn't speak. Instead, we kept on looking at the stars as if they would give us some answers to what was happening around us.

'Son,' she began, 'you are not to blame for what happened to me. It was not your fault that you were a twelve-year-old boy who could not defend his mother.'

Her words broke me apart and I began to weep. I guess she was right. There was a certain part of me which had always recognised that one of the reasons I never came back to Waituhi was because sometimes it was hard to look Mum in the face. It had always been easier not to confront my own feelings of guilt. 'I tried my best, Mum,' I sobbed. 'I really tried —'

'I know you did,' she answered.

I wiped my tears away, blew my nose and tried to control myself. 'I have to go back to London, Mum,' I said after a while. 'I have to go tomorrow, but I don't want to. What if something happens to you when I'm gone?'

This time, it was my mother's turn to weep. 'Go, son,' she said. 'Don't stay here waiting for me to die. Let us say our goodbyes now, and touch our cheeks together, warmth to warmth, and then go, please, go. Your sisters will tell you when I no longer breathe. Come back and support them because they have been fine daughters and they love me too much. They will dress and prepare me well; that is their task. You know what yours is. On the third day, let it be your hands, and your hands alone, that place the lid lovingly on my coffin. Close me away, and let me go to your father.'

The stars in the sky went crazy for a moment, tipped off their axis by our sorrow and falling from heaven. They kept showering around us while we tried to regain our equilibrium. 'And your father loved you, son,' Mum said. 'He and I always suspected you would never come back. We knew from the very beginning that although you might have belonged to the iwi, your destiny was out in the world.'

But sometimes I can become maudlin. Her words set me off again and, when she saw I was still sorrowing, she got cross.

'Oh, get over yourself,' she said.

I've never liked long goodbyes. I packed my bags that night and, next afternoon, took the flight from Gisborne to Auckland. My flight to London was leaving Auckland in the evening.

The family came to say farewell. Ripeka brushed my cheek with her lips and then, relenting, hugged me close. 'We'll tell you if Mum has a bad turn,' she said. 'We'll give you plenty of time to get home.'

I kissed her, Mere, Wiki and Marama and shook Hone's hand. Then, one last farewell to my mother.

I had never told Mum that Dad had known about Eric Amundsen. I wondered if I should tell her, now, that when I was twenty Dad visited me in Wellington. He had been on his way back from the West Coast. I met him at the airport and when he wouldn't tell me why he'd been in the South Island, I said to him, 'Dad, don't treat me like a child, I know why you've been.'

'Really?' he asked, piercing me with a look. 'You know what happened to your mother? Then I won't have to tell you what to do if I can't do it, will I?'

'No,' I said. Impossible though it was to contemplate, my father in all his humanity and generosity would have brought Eric Amundsen — if he had found him — back to Waituhi to be raised with us. I was so angry at Dad for even thinking this, and for the way he was putting the responsibility on me to fix things if he couldn't. As he walked to the plane, something vicious came out of me, something that had been hurting me for a long time. I yelled out to him, 'Why did you have to be away from home that day, Dad? Why didn't you know what would happen to us while you were gone?'

Dad looked at me in despair. 'I wish I had, son,' he answered. 'Believe me, if I had known I would never have left your mother and you children that day.'

No, I could not tell Mum. What good would it have served to tell her that Dad had known about Eric Amundsen? She would be upset and would grieve again over a husband whom she had loved forever.

I took her into my arms and breathed her in. As I felt how thin she was, I started to grieve. How would I be able to survive when she was gone?

'I love you, Mum,' I said.

There's a moment I've always loved on the journey from New Zealand back to the top of the world. It comes at the beginning of the flight when passengers, excited about their journeys ahead, do not think of the mind-numbing, body-tiring, twenty-six-hour trip from Auckland to London via Los Angeles. Behind me, I could see New Zealand as a dark shape retreating southward.

'Island fortress, e noho ra.'

The plane banked steeply and then began to ascend through the clear night. I was lucky. Tonight the moon was full. Just before we rose into the clouds, that moment came when I always felt suspended between heaven and earth — in freefall, with the great South Pacific Ocean glowing below.

As I whispered my farewells to my country, to my iwi and family, 'E Aotearoa, e tu, e tu, e tu, stand forever and ever,' a sudden question flashed through my mind. If I was drowning on a midnight sea and there was only one person I could call to come and rescue me, who would it be? I imagined myself alone in that vast sea, floating on the dark surface. All around were vertiginous, mountainous waves. Above, a wide empty sky. The waves cascaded around me. I felt myself go under. My chest heaved with exhaustion. I struggled upward to the surface.

After all these years, I now knew the right answer to the question. Although the first instincts were to cry out a name, once your heart had steadied and you had lost the feeling of terror, the best response was to realise your own resources and not wait to be rescued.

Instead, no matter how ungainly, strike out for safety yourself.

I looked at my reflection in the window.

'Even if you don't make it to that distant shore, wherever it might be,' I said to my reflection, 'the salvation that you are looking for is within yourself. And you've always been a good swimmer.'

The stars came out. I was floating on a luminescent skein of silver dreams. A shooting star blazed a glorious beauty across the night. The universe was singing.

I struck out across a sea of stars.

epilogue

London, April 2005.

And so I wait for news about my mother, dying, in New Zealand.

Meantime, life goes on, and here I am, sitting in a chair in the BBC studio being interviewed by my arch rival, Bob Blakeney, for *Face to Face*. Bob is spitting tacks about the ratings *Spaceship Earth* achieved for our tenth anniversary show. His questions are probing and persistent.

To make matters worse, I am jetlagged and I have a cold that I caught from a whole planeload of coughing and spluttering passengers. So much for travelling first class. Obviously the cold does not recognise any difference in a passenger's status or how much I paid for my ticket.

Gabriella was waiting for me at Heathrow, but did I get any sympathy from her? Nope. She saw my condition, streaming eyes, red nose, rattling breath, and said she'd bring me to the BBC but would wait until I got better before coming to the apartment. I know this is sensible, but it isn't very romantic. The only consolation I had was a message on my answerphone from my darling daughter, Holly.

'Hi, Dad. Nathan's gone off to Canada and I'm on my way with friends to Gallipoli. It's a spur of the moment thing. If I've got time, I'll call in and see you in London on my way back. Bye-ee, Daddy! Love youuuuu.'

So Bob Blakeney is asking his questions and I honestly don't know what answers I am giving. He's questioned me about my view on Iraq, the Palestinian problem, and whether or not the American president and the British prime minister will be able to maintain the moral high ground with respect to US and British policies in the Middle East. God, what else is he going to ask me? How long is this interview? How am I going to get through the next twenty minutes without sneezing all over his nice pinstripe suit? I feel in limbo, and now the painkillers I collected from a pharmacy on the way here are kicking in.

My mind wanders off on a tangent. So my darling daughter is off to Gallipoli. In 1915, just under 3000 New Zealand soldiers died there. This year is the ninetieth anniversary. I reflect on the extraordinary pulling power of Gallipoli on young Kiwis. They wear T-shirts that say, proudly, *New* New Zealand. Will Holly really call on me on her way back? I hope so. What's the use of having children if they can't come and see daddy dearest when they're in the neighbourhood?

Suddenly, Bob pounces. He is trying to find some way of undercutting my authority as an anchorman.

'Can you tell me how you came to call your programme *Spaceship Earth*?'

'When I was a boy I loved *Star Trek* and always wanted to be the captain of the Starship Enterprise,' I answer. That should be good for a laugh. 'No, it actually comes from something my father once said to me about my village, Waituhi, and why he wanted to return there. He said it was so that I would always know where home was. From there, he could keep a lifeline out to me. As I was growing up, I liked the idea that if ever I got lost in space, Dad would pull me back home across the universe to Spaceship Waituhi.'

'Is that what you do in your programme? Remind people of where they are?'

'Yes, we're all on planet earth, hurtling through space. I like to think that my programme reminds viewers of their humanity. As human beings on our planet, I like to encourage all of us to find the divinity in ourselves, and to nurture and protect it in all our nations so that it can survive any adversity.'

'You're Maori, aren't you. Many people don't realise this.'

I look at Bob, puzzled. He's trying to get under my skin and lift it to see if there is anything he can critique underneath. 'Yes, I am,' I answer. 'My heritage has made me who I am.'

'Does it make you better?' Bob's needles are coming quick and fast.

'It makes me different,' I answer. 'It makes me see things in a different way. But although I am from a Maori valley, I also belong to the world. The test for me has always been to find the balance. At the same time as the spiral is going out, it is returning. At the same time as we go forward we are going back. Somewhere in the tensions is the answer.'

Then Bob takes me between his teeth and gives a quick, violent shake. 'So what, Tom Mahana, can Maori bring to the world?'

Ah well, shit happens. All my usual skills of charm and sidestepping are not going to get me out of this one. My mind is whirling as I search for an answer. I stall for time.

'That's a question to stop a charging rhinoceros in its tracks.'

My whole life flashes before me.

I think of Dad who, after my interview with the headmaster at Gisborne Boys High School, said to me, 'We are of the Maori race, a race who had the indomitable courage of the undefeated.' I think of my mother, who told me, just before I left New Zealand to come back to London, 'We always knew you would never come back to Waituhi, son. You may belong to the iwi, but your destiny has always been out in the world.'

Crowding into my head come all those young New Zealanders whose paths I have crossed during the past two weeks. I remember David Carruthers and his friends whom I met in the pub off Charing Cross just before I left London. Gabriella had made the observation, 'No matter what you New Zealanders start talking about, you all end up conversing about your own country. The longing is so palpable. But it's more than homesickness, it's mal du pays — love of country.'

I think of Henrik Kruger and that beautiful group of young New Zealand boys I met on my arrival at Auckland International Airport. 'Hey, boys, it's Tom Mahana, one of the old boys of our school,' Henrik said. Spontaneously, he gave the command, 'Kia mau.' *Kia mau? From a blond South African boy?* Next minute, the crowd cleared as the boys hunkered down into a raucous, ringing haka.

'Ka mate, ka mate! Ka ora, ka ora! Ka mate, ka mate! Ka ora, ka ora! Tenei te tangata puhuruhuru nana nei i tiki mai, whakawhiti te ra.' The ground shook, the earth roared.

I think of my old school mate, Michael Kavanagh, who showed me his great-great-great-great-grandmother's bill of passage from Tilbury Docks to Port Nicholson. When we were growing up, Gisborne was like a frontier town. The population was half-Maori, half-Pakeha. Now it was blended, laminated. The lives of two peoples had become inextricably entangled so that it was predicted that within two generations every New Zealander would have some Maori blood or at least a Maori relative within the new New Zealand family.

I remember my old schoolteacher, Mr Grundy, reciting Allen Curnow: 'Not I, some child, born in a marvellous year, will learn the trick of standing upright here.'

Had we done that? Learnt the trick of standing upright at long last? Yes, oh, *yes*. And no matter how wide out we went, an invisible umbilical cord would always connect us to Aotearoa. We would never be lost.

And I realise — with a terrible certainty — that Bob Blakeney's question is limited. I think of that Rope of Man, te taura tangata. Not only Maori but also Pakeha are now entwined in the rope, bringing hopefully new strengths, not weaknesses, new possibilities.

What can I say to Bob Blakeney's question?

'So what, Tom Mahana, can Maori bring to the world?' he asks again.

The moment is getting longer and longer. Later, I find out that it is the longest pause in the history of the BBC.

Dad, where are you?

Suddenly, I feel giddy, disoriented by my cold, the painkillers, the lights. I feel as if I am on a swingbridge strung above a raging, swollen river. I am standing in the middle, and Dad is at one end. The swingbridge is suspended in space, swaying in the wind gusting down the valley. The rain dripping from the wire frame transforms the bridge into a shivering, jewelled cobweb spun in the air. Dad waves his hand, farewell.

No, son, this is your watch.

Yes, this is my watch.

New Zealanders are taking their place in their own land and throughout the world. Wherever we meet, we cry, sing and chant our songs through a hostile universe and, when we gather together, it is like a tribe around a campfire telling our stories of the iwi to each other. We are a great diaspora of brilliant innovative young minds whom New Zealand has educated and raised. To what purpose, if not for us to go back out into the world with all our entrepreneurial skills, the same skills that brought all our forebears to New Zealand in the first place? Go, Kiwi.

I realise I have become an emissary of Aotearoa. I must speak for all of us from our fortress far to the south. What do young Kiwis dream about? What dreams are there ahead?

When they come, the words of my reply to Bob Blakeney are oracular, filled with inner meaning and power.

'All Maori and all New Zealanders jointly bring an example of what can be achieved in terms of excellence, equity and justice to all mankind. In our own country we are showing that it is possible to resolve issues of blood, race, ancestry and identity. Internationally, we bring a certain grit, determination, moral compass and integrity to the world's future.'

Yes, that's it. But more is required of me. In my ears, my father's voice rings across the years.

Yes, son, yes. Whaia te iti kahurangi. Me te tuohu koe, me tuohu ki te maunga teitei. Tell them. Tell them all. Give them their blessing.

My nerves hold. New Zealanders are still in the process of becoming. The next great transformation is about to begin. Dreamers, awake.

I smile at Bob Blakeney and say to him:

'We bow only to the highest mountain.'

acknowledgements

*t*angi, the original novel which begins *The Rope of Man*, was one of three books I wrote while I was on honeymoon and subsequent working holiday with Jane Cleghorn in London in 1970: *Pounamu Pounamu* (short stories) was published in 1972, *Tangi* (novel) in 1973 and *Whanau* (novel) in 1974. With *The Rope of Man* I have completed new versions of the three books, which all now appear in modern editions in the Ihimaera 30th Anniversary Collection. As in the first edition of *Tangi*, I wish to express my gratitude to Rarawa Kerehoma for the use of excerpts from *Waiata Tangi*, translated by Barry Mitcalfe.

When *Tangi* was published in 1973, it was the first novel written by a Maori. It won the Wattie Book of the Year Award in 1974 and has since sold over 50,000 copies in New Zealand. It was translated into French by Professor Jean-Pierre Durix, who later became a colleague and close friend. At the time of writing it, I felt I needed to obtain permission from my parents Tom and Julia Ihimaera Smiler Jnr; Dad said it was okay but Mum said, 'If you write about the tangihanga and about a boy and his father, people will think it's about you and your dad. You should therefore write it before he dies so that we and other people will be able to regard it as fiction.' So I did; I wrote a letter to my then publisher David Heap setting out the situation and then, on acceptance, had a terrible year of worrying and telling Dad that under no circumstances was he to even think of abandoning me to life. What he and I did not realise was that, on publication, readers would think that the fiction was based on reality. 'I'm getting sick and tired,' he grumbled to me one day, 'of people looking at me as if I'm not supposed to still be here.' And

I can remember one particular occasion when I introduced him to some people at a literary function and one of them screamed with shock, 'Oh, but I thought you had died.' Thirty-five years later, Dad — and Mum — are still here to illuminate the lives of all their children, grandchildren and great-grandchildren.

The Rope of Man was begun in October 2004 and the first draft was completed on 12 May 2005. In my creative writing class at the University of Auckland, I try to teach my students how to write *through* life, but I must admit I wouldn't want to write a book again in quite the circumstances that prevailed during this period. Apart from professorial duties and teaching I also enthusiastically embraced literary and indigenous commitments in Hawaii (Distinguished Lecture Series, University of Hawaii), the USA (Indigenous Literature in Translation at the University of California at Irvine; the Second International Indigenous Council Roundtable, Arizona; Senior Fulbright Fellow, George Washington University, Washington DC), Great Britain (the London Book Fair and the UK launch of three of my titles by Robson Books), Canada (The Northrop Frye Festival), and New Zealand (Auckland Writers Festival). One positive outcome is that I have now perfected the art of writing on planes.

The television interview which ends Book Two, *The Return*, is based on a twenty-four-minute interview I personally had with Gavin Esler on the BBC talkshow, *HARDtalk*, during the London Book Fair in March 2005. I muffed the final question, 'What can Maori bring to the world?' and was really cross with myself. The answer that Tama gives in the novel is the answer I should have given in the interview and I am pleased to have had this opportunity of putting the matter right — and of expanding the answer to make it inclusive of not just Maori but all New Zealanders. What was my original answer to the question? Well, if you watch the interview you will see me going into a lame riff, which doesn't seem to make any sense, about a visit I once made to the British Museum and the evaluative comparisons that went through my mind between ancient civilisations and a small tribe of Maori at the bottom of the world. In the end I *think* I say something like, 'If you don't watch out, a Maori will be sitting in your chair and we will rule the world.'

As always, my thanks to Jessica and Olivia, my constant inspiration. Thanks also to Jane, who made it possible for me to begin a career in writing, and to David Heap, my first publisher, who took a chance on a young Maori boy who wanted to be a novelist. My abiding aroha to my sisters and brothers and the great Smiler and Keelan families who have nurtured me. Jenny Gibbs has supported me with so much love over the last few years. Jenny Te Paa, Terry and Tammi have been my Maori family in Auckland. My deep and abiding aroha to my agent, Ray Richards, who has always been the wind beneath my wings. Gillian Kootstra edited, with much patience, the manuscript of this novel.

To my new friends around the world: David, Sharon, Shinichi, Karen, Tim, Marcus, Eleanor, John, Joyce, Jeremy, Gil, Rachel, Winton, Madhavi, Yong, Kateri, Brad, Anita, Frances, Ed, Kavita, Glenn, Lyndon, Winton, Vikram, Bill and those many others whom I met during the time I was writing *The Rope of Man*, please know that your strength and spirit went into winding the fibres so that they were strong, flexible and resilient. My thanks to Fulbright New Zealand for the fellowship to Washington, DC where I began writing this novel. Sue Carty read the Wellington chapters of the book relating to the history of *The Evening Post;* all my literary papers, including the drafts of *The Rope of Man*, are stored in the Victoria University of Wellington Library, under the auspices of an archive project first established by the late Mike Robson, Independent Newspapers Limited (INL). I gained a huge appreciation from Margaret Henley, Film, Television and Media Studies, University of Auckland, of the complex technical and logistical support that would have been required to broadcast *Spaceship Earth*; my thanks to her 201 class of Congs and Wetas who sat me in an interviewer's chair in a television studio and gave me practical experience. Finally, thanks also to Brian Shennan for his advice on the operation of a television crew during the Vietnam War. If there are any errors of chronology and newspaper and television practice, they are my own.

I pay tribute to the great *new* tribe of New Zealanders, Maori and Pakeha, from whom I have sprung, the seeds of a modern Raiatea. May you all achieve your destinies. The voyaging spirit of all our ancestors is in all of you and will not rest until you reach the stars.

Apiti hono, tatai hono, te hunga mate o te wa, haere, haere, haere.

Apiti hono, tatai hono, te hunga ora katoa,

Tena koutou, tena koutou,

Tena koutou katoa.

Auckland, New Zealand

May 2005